a time of omens

By Katharine Kerr

DAGGERSPELL
DARKSPELL
THE BRISTLING WOOD
THE DRAGON REVENANT
A TIME OF EXILE
A TIME OF OMENS

POLAR CITY BLUES
RESURRECTION

a time of omens

A Novel of the Westlands

katharine kerr

BANTAM BOOKS
New York · Toronto · London · Sydney · Auckland

A TIME OF OMENS
A Bantam Spectra Book / August 1992

Library of Congress Cataloging-in-Publication Data
Kerr, Katharine.
    *A time of omens : a novel of the Westlands / Katharine
Kerr.*
        p.   cm.
    ISBN 0-553-08913-7 (hc)
    ISBN 0-553-35235-0 (pbk)
    I. Title.
PS3561.E642T57   1992
813'.54—dc20   92-1267
                    CIP

Published simultaneously in the United States and Canada

---

*Bantam Books are published by Bantam Books, a division of
Bantam Doubleday Dell Publishing Group, Inc. Its
trademark, consisting of the words "Bantam Books" and the
portrayal of a rooster, is Registered in U.S. Patent and
Trademark Office and in other countries. Marca Registrada.
Bantam Books, 666 Fifth Avenue, New York,
New York 10103.*

PRINTED IN THE UNITED STATES OF AMERICA

FFG   0 9 8 7 6 5 4 3 2 1

Dedication

For Nance Jordan Ashton
My Grandmother

Acknowledgments

As usual, I owe a lot of friends a lot of thanks. Some are:
Brian Carnright, who keyboarded above and beyond the
call of duty,
Elizabeth Pomada, who once again performed
wonders of agenting,
Alis Rasmussen, who understands what
plot problems mean,
Mark Kreighbaum, who helped me
fine-tune the manuscript,
and as always, my husband, Howard Kerr,
who is Himself.

A Note on the Pronunciation of Deverry Words

The language spoken in Deverry is a member of the P-Celtic family. Although closely related to Welsh, Cornish, and Breton, it is by no means identical to any of these actual languages and should never be taken as such.

Vowels are divided by Deverry scribes into two classes: noble and common. Nobles have two pronunciations; commons, one.

A as in *father* when long; a shorter version of the same sound, as in *far,* when short.

O as in *bone* when long; as in *pot* when short.

W as the *oo* in *spook* when long; as in *roof* when short.

Y as the *i* in *machine* when long; as the *e* in *butter* when short.

E as in *pen.*

I as in *pin.*

U as in *pun.*

Vowels are generally long in stressed syllables; short in unstressed. Y is the primary exception to this rule. When it appears as the last letter of a word, it is always long whether that syllable is stressed or not.

Diphthongs generally have one consistent pronunciation.

AE as the *a* in *mane.*

AI as in *aisle.*

AU as the *ow* in *how.*

EO as a combination of *eh* and *oh.*

EW as in Welsh, a combination of *eh* and *oo.*

IE as in *pier.*

OE as the *oy* in *boy.*

UI as the North Welsh *wy,* a combination of *oo* and *ee.* Note that OI is never a diphthong, but is two distinct sounds, as in *carnoic* (KAR-noh-ik).

.   .   .

Consonants are mostly the same as in English, with these exceptions:

C is always hard as in *cat.*

G is always hard as in *get.*

DD is the voiced *th* as in *thin* or *breathe,* but the voicing is more pronounced than in English. It is opposed to TH, the unvoiced sound as in *th* or *breath.* (This is the sound that the Greeks called the Celtic tau.)

R is heavily rolled.

RH is a voiceless R, approximately pronounced as if it were spelled *hr* in Deverry proper. In Eldidd, the sound is fast becoming indistinguishable from R.

DW, GW, and TW are single sounds, as in *Gwendolen* or *twit.*

Y is never a consonant.

I before a vowel at the beginning of a word is consonantal, as it is in the plural ending *-ion,* pronounced *yawn.*

Doubled consonants are both sounded clearly, unlike in English. Note, however, that DD is a *single letter,* not a doubled consonant.

Accent is generally on the penultimate syllable, but compound words and place names are often an exception to this rule.

I have used this system of transcription for the Bardekian and Elvish alphabets as well as the Deverrian, which is, of course, based upon the Greek rather than the Roman model. In spite of the ridiculous controversy still continuing in certain university circles, I see no reason to confuse the ordinary reader with the technical method of Elvish transcription in common use among linguists and scholars. Anyone who wishes to learn this system may of course refer to the standard works upon the subject available from the University of Aberwyn Press; the average reader of popular fiction would no doubt rather forgo such a formidable experience. I am surprised at the stubbornness of certain professors of Elvish, to say nothing of a certain Elvish professor, which has forced me to append such a self-evident remark to these notes. One can only assume that these persons are underemployed by their academic institutions if they have the leisure to write scurrilous articles about contemporary novelists rather than devoting themselves to their proper areas of expertise.

Prologue

Wmmglaeðð,
1096

On the Inner Planes, Time as we know it no longer exists.
This is why an omen may refer to things which we perceive
as long over and done with as well as to things in process at
the moment in which the omen is cast and to things which
we have yet to perceive at all. Past, Present, Future—these
states do not exist in the world from which an omen pro-
ceeds, yet there is no denying, of course, that they do exist
in ours. . . .

The Pseudo-Iamblichus Scroll

In those days the eastern border of the elven lands lay in the middle of a forest. A traveler leaving the high plains and heading east came down a long gentle decline into the oaks to find several rivers that might mark a border—if only anyone at all had lived on either side of them. In that vast tangle of tree and shrub, bracken and thorn, finding the lands of men (that is, the three western provinces —Eldidd, Pyrdon, Arcodd—of the kingdom of Deverry) was no easy job. If you wanted to go from west to east, the sandy coast of the Southern Sea made a much more reliable road, if, of course, you could fight your way south to reach it. The ancient forest had a way of tricking travelers unless they or their companions knew the route well.

The woman who rode out of the forest late on a summer day traveled with a horde of such companions—not that most human beings would have seen them. Sylphs and sprites hovered round her in the air; gnomes clung to her saddle or perched on the back of the spare horse she was leading; undines rose out of every stream and pool she passed to wave a friendly greeting. Her friends weren't the only odd thing about Jill. If you looked carefully at her silver hair, cropped short like a lad's, and the fine lines that webbed her eyes round and latticed her cheeks, you realized that she had to be at least fifty years old if not somewhat more, but she radiated so much vitality, the way a fire gives off heat, that it was impossible to think of her as anything but young. She was, you see, the most powerful sorcerer in all of Deverry.

The first human settlement that any traveler coming from the west reached on the coast was the holy precinct of Wmmglaedd, although in those days, before the silting of the river and the meddling of humans had extended the shore, the temple lay a little ways out to sea on a low-lying cluster of islands. Jill rode along the sea cliffs through meadows of tall grass to a rocky beach, where the waves washed over gravel with a mutter, as if the sea were endlessly regretting some poor decision. A fair mile offshore, she could see the rise of the main island against the glitter of the Southern Sea.

She led her pair of horses down to the two stone pillars that marked the entrance to a stone causeway, still underwater at the moment, though when she looked at the water lapping at the carved notches along the edge of one pillar, she found each wave falling a little lower than the one before. Crying and mewling, seabirds swooped overhead, graceful gulls and the ungainly pelicans that were sacred to the god Wmm, all come to feed as the dropping tide exposed the rocky shallows. At last the causeway emerged, streaming water like a silver sea snake, to let her lead her horses across the uncertain footing. At the far end of the causeway stood a stone arch inlaid with colored marble in panels of interlace and roundels decorated with pelicans; it sported an inscription, too, "water covers and reveals all things."

About ten miles long and seven wide, with a central hill standing in the midst of meadows of coarse sea grass, the island sheltered four different temple complexes at that time, brochs as tall as a lord's dun, clusters of wooden guest houses, cattle barns and riding stables as well as a series of holy shrines placed at picturesque locations. Although the temple had been founded in the year 690 as a modest refuge for scholars and mystics, during the long civil wars of the ninth century its priests had the shrewdness and the good fortune to play a crucial role in placing the true king on his throne. When the wars were over, their fame drew an occasional desperate soul seeking an oracle, and as the long years went by, the rare case became a swarm of pilgrims, all laden with gifts to earn the favor of the god.

Now Wmm was rich. Still leading her horses rather than riding, Jill left the causeway and followed a fine road, paved with limestone blocks, through the smallish town that had sprung up near the temples. In among the round, thatched houses townsfolk and visitors strolled around or sat in the windows of one of the many inns, and peddlers kept accosting her with trays of sweetmeats or baskets of little silver medals and pottery souvenirs. She brushed them all off and strode on her way, skirting the main complex, too, bustling with visitors and priests here in the summer season, and took a little-used path that ran southeast through pine trees, all twisted and bowed down from the constant wind. In a little bay of rocky shore a jetty stood with a ferry bobbing at anchor beside it. Beyond, a scant mile away, she could see the rise of East Island, a long sliver of land that most visitors knew or cared nothing about.

"Jill, halloo!" The ferryman, a stout priest draped in an orange cloak, waved both hands at her as she led her horses gingerly down the steep path. "Back so soon?"

"I am, at that. How have things been? Quiet?"

"They always are, out our way." He grinned, revealing brown and broken teeth. "His holiness has pains in his joints again."

"I'm surprised you aren't all as bent and stiff as village crones, frankly, out here in the fog."

"True, true. But well, we've got a bit of sun today at least. Enjoy it while we can, say I."

Since the tide was running out, the journey was quick and easy, though the ferryman was bound to have a harder trip rowing back by himself. Jill coaxed her horses off, left him sighing at the job ahead, and headed across a wind-scoured meadow to a complex much smaller and plainer than those of the main island. At the base of a low hill stood a clutter of roundhouses and a stables, shaded by a few stunted oaks. Dust drifted and swirled over the threadbare lawns and sickly vegetable gardens. She turned her horses over to a groom, carried her saddlebags and bedroll to a hut that did for a guest house, dumped her gear onto the narrow cot, and decided that she'd unpacked. With a deferential bob of his head, a servant came in, bringing her a washbasin and a pitcher of water.

"His holiness is in the library."

"I'll join him there."

After she washed up, she lingered in the silence for a moment to get her questions clear in her mind. Like all the other pilgrims, she'd come to Wmm's temple for help in making a decision, in her case about a voyage to the far-lying islands of the Bardekian archipelago, a very major undertaking indeed in those days. It was likely that she'd be gone for years and almost as likely that she wouldn't even find what she was looking for, the translation of a single word that she'd found inscribed inside a ring. The word, written in Elvish characters though it made no sense at all in any language, might have been a name or sheer nonsense for all that she knew. What she did know, in the mysterious way that dweomermasters have, was that the inscription would make the difference between life and death to thousands of people, men and elves alike. When, she didn't exactly know. Someday, perhaps even soon.

She suspected—but only suspected—that the answer lay in Bardek. She was hoping that the priests of Wmm could either confirm her suspicion or lay it to rest.

The library of Wmm was at that time an oblong building in the Bardek style of whitewashed stucco, roofed in clay tiles to cut down the fire danger. Inside, in a row of hearths peat fires constantly smoldered to keep the chill and damp off the collection of over five hundred books and scrolls—a vast wealth of learning for the time. Jill found the chief librarian, Suryn, standing at his lectern by a window with a view of the oak trees beyond. Unrolled in front of him was a Bardekian scroll. He looked up and smiled at her; as always, his weak eyes were watering from the effort of reading.

"Oh, there you are, Jill! I've been looking for that reference you wanted."

"The history scroll? You've found it?"

"I have indeed, and just now, so it's a good thing you wandered in like this. Must be an omen."

Although he was joking, Jill felt a line of cold run down her back.

"In fact, I've found both of the sources you were talking about." He tapped the papyrus in front of him with a bone stylus. "Here's the scroll, and it does indeed have a reference to elves living in the islands. Well, maybe they're elves, anyway. Take a look at it, and I'll just fetch the codex."

The scroll was an ancient chronicle of the city-state of Arbarat, lying far south in the Bardekian islands. Since Jill had learned to read Bardekian only recently, it took her some minutes to puzzle out the brief entry.

"A shipwrecked man was washed up on shore near the harbor. His name was Terrso, a merchant of Mangorat. . . ." There was a long bit here about the archon's attempt to repatriate the man, which Jill skipped through. "Before he left us, Terrso told of his adventures. He claimed to have traveled far, far south, beyond even Anmurdio, and to have discovered a strange people who dwelt in the jungles. These people, he claimed, were more akin to animals than men, because they lived in trees and had long pointed ears. Because he was so ravaged by fever, none took his words seriously."

"Curse them all!" Jill snapped.

"They don't truly go into detail, do they?" Suryn came up at her elbow. "Here's the Lughcarn codex. Do be careful with it, won't you? It's very old."

"Of course I will, Your Holiness. Don't trouble your heart about that. May I take it back to the guest house to read? I need to rest from my journey."

Suryn blinked at her for a moment.

"Oh, you've been gone. Of course—silly of me. By all means, keep it with you if you'd like. There's a lectern in the hut?"

"A good one, and a candle-spike, too."

Jill bathed and ate a sparse dinner before she got around to looking at the codex. By then, early in the evening, the fog was coming in thick, darkening the hut and turning it chilly, too. She laid a fire in the hearth, lit it by the simple means of invoking the Wildfolk of Fire with a snap of her fingers, then stuck a reading candle, as long and thick as a child's arm, onto the cast-iron spike built into the lectern. Before she lit the candle, though, she sat down on the floor by the fire to watch the salamanders playing in the flames and to think for a while about the work she had in hand, gathering every scrap of available information about the mysterious inscription. Although it was a pretty thing, made of dwarven silver and graved with roses, the ring itself carried no particular magic. It might, however, be important as a clue.

She already knew much of its history. Once it had belonged to a human bard named Maddyn, who had traveled to the western lands and given it to an elven dweomermaster as a gift. That master had in turn given it to a mysterious race of not-truly-corporeal beings called the Guardians. She was assuming that the Guardians had added the unintelligible inscription for the simple reason that the ring hadn't been inscribed before they'd got hold of it, but when one of their kind returned it to the physical world by giving it to another bard, elven this time and named Devaberiel, it carried its little riddle. As far as dweomermasters could tell, the Guardians perceived important omens about future possibilities as easily as most men see the sun. Since they insisted that the inscription had some important Wyrd to fulfill, Jill saw no reason to doubt them. Abstract terms like "why," however, seemed to have no meaning for them, and there was much in the way of explanation that they'd left out of their tale.

As she always did toward evening, she found herself thinking about her old master in the dweomer and missing him. Although Nevyn had been dead for months now, at times her grief stabbed so sharply that it seemed he'd died just the day before. If only he were here, she would think, he'd unravel this wretched puzzle fast enough! A gray gnome, a creature she'd known for years, materialized next to her and climbed into her lap. All spindly arms and legs and long warty nose, he looked up at her with his pinched little face twisted into a creditable imitation of human sadness.

"You miss Nevyn, too, don't you?" Jill said. "Well, he's gone on now like he had to. All of us do in our time."

Although the gnome nodded, she doubted if he understood. In a moment he jumped off her lap, found a copper coin wedged into a crack in the floor, and became engrossed with pulling it out. Jill wondered if she would ever meet Nevyn again in the long cycles of death and rebirth. Only if she needed to, she supposed, and she knew that it would be years and years before he would be reborn again, long after her own death, no doubt, though well before her next birth. Although all souls rest in the Inner Lands between lives, Nevyn's life had been so unnaturally prolonged by dweomer—he'd lived well over four hundred years, all told—that his corresponding interval of rest would doubtless be unusually long as well, or so she could speculate. It was for the Lords of Wyrd to decide, not her. She told herself that often, even as her heart ached to see him again.

Finally, in a fit of annoyance over her mood, she got up and went to the lectern to read, but the chronicle only made her melancholy worse. She'd been trying to recall an event that had happened in one of her own previous lives, but she could remember it only dimly, because even a great dweomermaster like her could call to mind only the most general outlines and the occasional tiny memory picture of former lives. She was sure, though, from that dim memory, that she—or rather her previous incarnation, because she'd been born into a male body in that cycle—had been present at the forging of the rose ring. During that life, as the warrior known as Branoic, she'd ridden with a very important band of soldiers, the true king's personal guard in the civil wars— that much, she could remember.

What she'd forgotten was that Nevyn had been not only present but very much an important actor in those events, perhaps the most important figure of all. There was his name, written on practically every page. As she read the composed speeches the chronicler had put into his mouth, she found herself shaking her head in irritation: he never would have sounded so stiff, so formal! All at once, she realized that she was crying. The flood of long-buried grief, not only for Nevyn but for other friends her soul had forgotten this two hundred years and more, seemed to work a dweomer of its own. Rather than merely reading the chronicler's dry account, she found herself remembering the isolated lake fort of Dun Drwloc, where Nevyn had tutored the young prince who was destined to become king, and the long ride that the silver daggers had taken to bring the prince to Cerrmor and his destiny. All night she stood there, reading some parts of the tale, remembering others, until the sheer fascination of the puzzle buried her grief again.

past

*Pyrdon and Deverry
843*

Nothing is ever lost.

The Pseudo-Iamblichus Scroll

1.

The year 843. In Cerrmor that winter, near the shortest day, there were double rings round the moon for two nights running. On the third night King Glyn died in agony after drinking a goblet of mead. . . .

The Holy Chronicles of Lughcarn

The morning dawned clear if cold, with a snap of winter left in the wind, but toward noon the wind died and the day turned warm. As he led his horse and the prince's out of the stables, Branoic was whistling at the prospect of getting free of the fortress for a few hours. After a long winter shut up in Dun Drwloc, he felt as if the high stone walls had marched in and made everything smaller.

"Going out for a ride, lad?"

Branoic swirled round to see the prince's councillor, Nevyn, standing in the cobbled ward next to a broken wagon. Although the silver dagger couldn't say why, Nevyn always startled him. For one thing, for all that he had a shock of snow-white hair and a face as wrinkled as burlap, the old man strode around as vigorously as a young warrior. For another, his ice-blue eyes seemed to bore into a man's soul.

"We are, sir," Branoic said, with a bob of his head that would just pass for a humble gesture.

"I'm just bringing out the prince's horse, too, you see. We've all been stable-bound too long this winter."

"True enough. But ride carefully, will you? Guard the prince well."

"Of course, sir. We always do."

"Do it doubly, this morning. I've received an omen."

Branoic turned even colder than the brisk morning wind would explain. As he led the horses away, he was glad that he was going to be riding out with the prince rather than stuck home with his tame sorcerer.

All winter Nevyn had been wondering when the king in Cerrmor would die, but he didn't get the news until that very day, just before the spring equinox. The night before, it had rained over Dun Drwloc, dissolving the last pockets of snow in the shade of the walls and leaving pools of brown mud in their stead. About two hours before noon, when the sky started clearing in earnest, the old man climbed to the ramparts and looked out over the slate-gray lake, choppy in the chill wind. He was troubled, wondering why he'd received no news from Cerrmor in five months. With those who followed the dark dweomer keeping a watch on the dun, he'd been afraid to contact other dweomermasters through the fire in case they were overheard, but now he was considering taking the risk. All the omens indicated that the time was ripe for King Glyn's Wyrd to come upon him.

Yet, as he stood there debating, he got his news in a way that he had never expected. Down below in the ward there was a whooping and a clatter that broke his concentration. In extreme annoyance he turned on the rampart and looked down to see Maryn galloping through the gates at the head of his squad of ten men. The prince was holding something shiny in his right hand and waving it about as he pulled his horse to a halt.

"Page! Go find Nevyn right now!"

"I'm up here, lad!" Nevyn called back. "I'll come down."

"Don't! I'll come up. It'll be private that way."

Maryn dismounted, tossed his reins to a page, and raced for the ladder. Over the winter he had grown another two inches, and his voice had deepened as well, so that more and more he looked the perfect figure of the king to be, blond and handsome with a far-seeing look in his gray eyes. Yet he was still lad enough to shove whatever it was he was holding into his shirt and scramble up the ladder to the ramparts. Nevyn could tell from the haunted look in his eyes that something had disturbed him.

"What's all this, my liege?"

"We found somewhat, Nevyn, the silver daggers and me, I mean. After you saw us leave, we went down the east-running road. It was about three miles from here that we found them."

"Found who?"

"The corpses. They'd all been slain by the sword. There were three dead horses but only two men in the road, but we found the third man out in a field, like he'd tried to run away before they killed him."

With a grunt of near-physical pain, Nevyn leaned back against the cold stone wall.

"How long ago were they killed?"

"Oh, a ghastly long time." Maryn looked half-sick at the memory. "Maddyn says it was probably a couple of months. They froze first, he said, and then thawed probably just last week. The ravens have been working on them. It was truly grim. And all their gear was pulled apart and strewn around, like someone had been searching through it."

"Oh, no doubt they were. Could you tell anything about these poor wretches?"

"They were Cerrmor men. Here." Maryn reached into his shirt and pulled out a much-tarnished message tube. "This was empty when we found it, but look at the device. I rubbed part of it clean on the ride home."

Nevyn turned the tube and found the polished strip, graved with three tiny ships.

"You could still see the paint on one shield, too," Maryn went on. "It was the ship blazon. I wish we had the messages that were in that tube."

"So do I, Your Highness, but I think me I know what they said. We'd best go down and collect the entire troop. No doubt we're months too late, but I won't rest easy until we have a look round for the murderers."

As they hurried back to the broch, it occurred to Nevyn that he no longer had to worry about communicating with his allies by dweomer. It was obvious that their enemies already knew everything they needed to know.

Even though Maddyn considered hunting the murderers a waste of time, and he knew that every other man in the troop was dreading camping out in the chilly damp, no one so much as suggested arguing with Nevyn's scheme. If anyone had, Maddyn himself would have been the one to do it, because he was a bard of sorts, with a bard's freedom to speak on any matter at all, as well as being second in command of this troop of mercenaries newly become the prince's guard. The true commander, Caradoc, was too afraid of Nevyn to say one wrong word to the old man, while Maddyn was, in some ways, the only real friend Nevyn had. Carrying what provisions the dun could spare them at the end of winter's lean times, the silver daggers, with the prince and old Nevyn riding at the head of the line, clattered out the gates just at noon. With them was a wagon and a couple of servants with shovels to give the bodies a decent burial.

"At least the blasted clouds have all blown away," Caradoc said with a sigh. "I had a chance for a word with the king's chief huntsman, by the by. He says that there's an old hunting lodge about ten, twelve miles to the northeast, right on the river. If we can find it, it might still have a roof of sorts."

"If we're riding that way to begin with."

They found the murdered men and their horses where they'd left them, and it ached Maddyn's heart to think how close they'd been to safety when their Wyrd fell upon them. While the servants looked for a place where the thawing ground was good and soft, Nevyn coursed back and forth like a hunting dog and examined everything—the dead men, the horses, the soggy ground around them.

"You and the men certainly trampled all over everything, Maddo," he grumbled.

"Well, we looked for footprints and tracks and suchlike. If they'd left a trail we would have found it, but you've got to remember that the ground was frozen hard when this happened."

"True enough. Where's the third lad, the one who almost got away?"

Maddyn took him across the field to the sprawled and puffing corpse. In the warming day the smell was loathsome enough to make the bard keep his distance, but Nevyn knelt right down next to the thing and began to examine the ground as carefully as if he were looking for a precious jewel. Finally he stood up and walked away with one last disgusted shake of his head.

"Find anything?"

"Naught. I'm not even sure what I was hoping to get, to tell you the truth. It just seems that . . ." Nevyn let his words trail away and stood there slack-mouthed for a moment. "I want to wash my hands off, and I see a stream over there."

Maddyn went with him while he knelt down and, swearing at the coldness of the water, scrubbed his hands in the rivulet. All at once the old man went tense, his eyes unfocused, his mouth slack again, his head tilted a little as if he listened to a distant voice. Only then did Maddyn notice that the streamlet brimmed with glassy-blue undines, rising up in crests and wavelets. In their midst, and yet somehow beyond them, like a man coming through a doorway from some other place, was a presence. Maddyn could barely see it, a vast silvery shimmer that seemed to partake of both water and air like some preternatural fog, forming itself into a shape that might not even have existed beyond his desire to see it as a shape. Then it was gone, and Maddyn shuddered once with a toss of his head.

"Geese walking on your grave?" Nevyn said mildly.

When Maddyn looked around he saw Owaen and the prince walking over to them and well within earshot.

"Must be, truly. Here, Owaen, did you and the lads find anything new?"

"Doubt me if there's aught to find. Young Branoic did come up with this, though. Insisted it might be important, but he couldn't say why." Owaen looked positively sour as he handed Nevyn a thin sliver of bone, about six inches long, barely a half inch wide, but pointed on both ends. "Sometimes I think that lad is daft, I truly do."

"Not at all." Nevyn was turning the sliver round and round in his thin, gnarled fingers. "It's human bone, to begin with. And look how someone's worked it—smoothed it, shaped it, and then polished it."

"What?" Owaen's sourness deepened to disgust. "What is it, some kind of knife handle?"

"It's not, but a stylus to rule lines on parchment."

"A stylus?" Maddyn broke in. "Who would make a thing like that out of human bone?"

"Who indeed, Maddo lad? That's the answer I'd very much like to have: who indeed?"

In his role as a learned man Nevyn recited a few suitable lines of Dawntime poetry over the corpses; then the silver daggers mounted up and left the servants to get on with the burying. When they rode out they headed for the river. Maddyn spurred his horse up next to the old man's and mentioned the decrepit hunting lodge.

"It'll be better shelter than none, truly," Nevyn said.

"You don't suppose our enemies camped there, do you?"

"They might have once, but they're long gone by now." He gave Maddyn a wink. "I have some rather reliable information to that effect. Tell the men we won't be out hunting wild geese long, Maddo. I just want one last look around, that's all."

Only then was Maddyn sure that he had indeed seen some exalted personage in the stream.

Just at sunset they reached the lodge, a wooden roundhouse, its thatch half-gone, standing along with a stables behind a palisade that was missing as many logs as a peasant his teeth. As soon as they rode within five hundred yards of the place the horses turned nervous, tossing their heads and blowing, dancing a little in the muddy road. Maddyn had the feeling that they would have bolted if they hadn't been tired from their long day's ride.

"Oho!" Nevyn said. "My liege, you wait here with Caradoc and most of the men. Maddyn, you, Owaen, and Branoic come with me."

"You'd better take more men than that, Councillor," Maryn said.

"I won't need a small army, my liege. Most like there's naught left here but bad memories, anyway."

"But the horses—"

"See things men don't see, but men know things that horses don't know. And with that riddle, you'll have to rest content."

Nevyn was right enough, in the event, although the 'bad memory' turned out to be bad indeed. The men dismounted and walked the last of the way to the lodge, and as soon as they stepped through the gap they saw and smelled what had been spooking the animals. Nailed to the inside of the palisade, like a shrike nailed to a farmer's barn, was the corpse of a man, half-eaten by ravens and well ripened by the spring weather. Yet the worst thing wasn't the stench. The corpse was hung upside down and mutilated—the head cut off and nailed between its legs with what seemed to be—from the fragment left—its private parts stuffed into its mouth. Branoic stared for a long moment, then turned and ran to the shelter of the palisade to vomit, heavily and noisily.

"Uh gods!" Owaen whispered. "What?!"

For all his aplomb earlier, Nevyn looked half sick now, his face dead white and looking with all its wrinkles more like old parchment than ever. He ran his tongue over dry lips and spoke at last.

"A would-be deserter, most like, or a traitor of some sort. They left him that way so he'd roam as a haunt forever. All right, lads, get back to the troop. I think they'll all agree that we don't truly want to camp here tonight, shelter or not."

"I should think not, by the asses of the gods!" Owaen turned to Maddyn. "I know the horses are tired, but we'd best put a couple of miles between ourselves and this place if there's a haunt about."

"You're going to, certainly," Nevyn broke in. "I'm going to stay here."

"Not alone you aren't," Maddyn snapped.

"I don't need guards with swords, lad. I'm not in danger. If I can't handle one haunt, what kind of sorcerer am I?"

"What about this poor bastard?" Owaen jerked his thumb at the corpse. "We should give him some kind of burial."

"Oh, I'll tend to that, too." Nevyn started walking for the gate. "I'll just get my horse, and then you all go on your way. Come fetch me first thing in the morning."

Somewhat later, when they were all making camp—in a meadow about a mile and a half downriver—it occurred to Maddyn that Nevyn seemed to know an awful lot about these mysterious people who had left that ugly bit of sacrilege on the palisade. Although he was normally a curious man, he decided that he could live without asking him to explain.

With the last of the sunset, Nevyn brought his horse inside the tumble-down lodge, tied him on a loose rope to the wall and tended him, then dumped his bedroll and saddlebags near the hearth, where there lay a sizable if dusty pile of firewood already cut, left by the hirelings of the dark dweomermaster behind this plot—or so he assumed anyway. As assumptions went, it was a solid one. After he confirmed that the chimney was clear by sticking his head up it for a look, he piled up some logs and lit them with a wave of his hand. Once the fire had blazed up enough to illumine the room, he searched it thoroughly, even poking at the rotting walls with the point of his table dagger. His patience paid off when under a pile of leaves that had drifted in through a window he found a pewter disk about the size of a thumbnail, of the kind sewn onto saddlebags and other horse gear as decorations. Stamped into it was the head of a boar.

"I wonder," he said aloud. "The Boar clan's territory lies a long way from here, but still, if they thought the journey worth it for some purpose . . . are they in league with the dark dweomer then?"

The idea made him shudder. He slipped the disk into his brigga pocket, then paced back and forth before the fire as he considered what he was going to do about the possible haunt. First, of course, he had to discover if indeed that poor soul whose body rotted outside was still hanging about the site of his death. He laid more wood on the fire, poked it around with a green stick until it burned nice and evenly, then gathered up a mucky little pile of the damp and mildewed thatch that had slid from the roof over the years. If he needed it, the stuff would produce dense smoke. Then he sat down in front of the hearth, let himself relax, and waited.

It was close to an hour later when he felt the presence. At first it seemed only that a cold draught had wafted in from the door behind him, but he saw the salamanders in the fire turn their heads and look up in the direction of something. The room turned thick with silence. Still he said nothing, nor did he move, not even when the hair on the back of his neck prickled at the etheric force oozing from the haunt. There was a sound, too, a wet snuffling as if a hound were searching for a scent all over the floor, and every now and then, a scrabbling, as if some animal scratched at the floor with its nails. As the air around him grew colder, he concentrated on keeping his breathing slow and steady and his mind at peace. With a burst of sparks the salamanders disappeared. The thing was standing right behind him.

"Have you left somewhat here that won't let you rest, lad?"

He could feel puzzlement; then it drifted away, snuffling and scrabbling round the joining of floor and wall.

"Somewhat's buried, is it?"

The coldness approached him, hesitated, hovering some five feet off to his left. He could feel its desperate panic as clearly as he could feel the cold. Casually, slowly, Nevyn reached out and picked up a handful of the grubby thatch.

"I wager you'd like to feel solid again, nice and solid and warm. Come over to the fire, lad."

As the presence drifted into the warm light Nevyn could feel its panic reaching out like tendrils to clutch at him. Slowly he rose to his knees and tossed the half-rotten hay onto the hottest part of the fire. For a moment it merely stank; then gray smoke began to billow and swirl. As if it were a nail rushing to a lodestone the presence threw itself into the fire. Since it "lived" as a pattern of etheric force, the matrix immediately sucked the smoke up and arranged the fine particles of ash to conform to that pattern. Hovering above the fire appeared the shape of a youngish man, naked but of course perfectly whole, since his killers' knives could do no harm to his etheric body. Nevyn tossed in another handful of thatch to keep the smoke coming, then sat back on his heels.

"You can't stay here. You have to travel forward, lad, and go on to a new life. There's no coming back to this one."

The smoke-shape shook its head in a furious no, then threw itself out of the fire, leaving the smoke swirling and spreading, but ordinary smoke. Yet enough of the particles clung to the matrix to make the haunt clearly visible as it drifted across the room and began scrabbling again at a loose board between floor and wall. Nevyn could see, too, that it was making the snuffling noise inadvertently, rustling and lifting dead leaves and other such trash as it passed by.

"What's under there? Let me help. You don't have the hands to dig anymore."

The presence drifted to one side and gave no sign of interfering as Nevyn came over and knelt down. When he drew his table dagger and began to pry up the board, the haunt knelt, too, as if to watch. Although that particular board was somewhat newer than those around it, still the rotted wood broke away from its nails and came up in shreds and splinters. Underneath, in a shallow hole in the ground, was an oblong box, about two feet long but only some ten inches wide.

"Your treasure?"

Although it was faint now, a bare wisp of smoke in the firelight, the thing shook its head no and lifted both hands—imploring him, Nevyn thought, to forgive it or do something or perhaps both. When he reached in and lifted the box, some weight inside lurched and slid with a waft of unpleasant smell from the crack around the lid. Since he considered himself hardened to all forms of death, Nevyn threw open the lid and nearly gagged—not from the smell, this time, but from the sight. Crammed inside lay the corpse of an infant boy, preserved with some mixture of spices and liquids. Only a few days old when it died, it had been mutilated in the exact same way as the corpse nailed to the palisade.

Since the box brought a lot of dust up with it, the haunt kneeling nearby looked briefly solid, or at least its face and hands were visible as it tossed its head back and threw up its arms in a silent keen.

"Your child?"

It shook its head no, then slumped, doubling over to lay its head on the ground in front of him like a criminal begging a great lord for mercy.

"You helped kill it? Or—I see—your friends were going to kill it. You protested, and they made you share its Wyrd."

The dust scattered to the floor. The haunt was gone.

For some minutes Nevyn merely stared at the pitiful corpse in its tiny coffin. Although he'd never had the misfortune to see such mutilations before, he'd heard something about their significance —some half-forgotten lore that nagged at the edges of his memory and insisted that he examine the corpse more carefully. Finally he summoned up all his will and took the box over to the fire where there was light to work in, but he got bits of rag from his saddle-bags to wrap his hands before he reached in and took the muti-lated pieces of the tiny mummy out. Underneath he found a thin lead plate, about two inches by four, much like the curse-talismans that ignorant peasants still bury in hopes of doing an enemy harm. Graved on it were words in the ancient tongue of the Dawntime, known only to scholars and priests—and some words that not even Nevyn could translate.

"As this so that. Maryn king Maryn king Maryn. Death never dying. Aranrhodda ricca ricca ricca Bubo lubo."

His face and hands seemed to turn to ice, cold and numb and stiff. He looked up to find the room filled with Wildfolk, staring at him solemnly, some wide-eyed, some sucking an anxious finger, some gape-mouthed with terror.

"Evil men did this, didn't they?"

They nodded a yes. In the fire a towering golden flame leapt up, then died down to a vaguely human face burning within the blaze.

"Help me," Nevyn said to the Lord of Fire. "I want to get that corpse outside in here, and then burn it and this pitiful thing both. Then both souls can go to their rest."

Sparks showered in agreement.

Nevyn slipped the lead plate into his pocket, lest melting it cause Maryn some harm. He gathered his gear and loaded up his mount, then untied the horse and led it about a quarter mile down the river, where he tethered it out in safety. When he got back to the lodge, he found that the fire had already leapt from the hearth to smolder in the woodpile. With the Wildfolk pulling as he pushed, Nevyn got the rotting log that bore the corpse free of the ground and hauled it inside. He positioned the corpse and log as close to the fire as possible, then laid the mutilated baby on the desecrated breast of the man who'd tried to save it. Although he felt more like vomiting than ever, he forced himself calm and raised his hands over his head to invoke the Great Ones.

"Take them to their rest. Come to meet them when they go free."

From the sky outside, booming around the lodge, came three great knocks like the claps of godly hands. Nevyn began to shudder, and in the fire, the flames fell low in worship.

Even though Nevyn had asserted, and quite calmly, too, that there was no danger, none of the silver daggers were inclined to believe him. After the men had tethered out the horses and eaten dinner, Caradoc gave orders to scrounge all the dry wood they could find and build a couple of campfires. Maddyn suspected that the captain was as troubled as any man there by this talk of a haunt and wanted the light as badly, too.

"Full watches tonight, lads," Maddyn said. "Shall we draw straws?"

Instead, so many men volunteered that his only problem was sorting out who was going to stand when. Once the first ring of guards was posted, some of the men rolled up in their blankets and went to sleep—or at least pretended to in a fine show of bravado— but most sat near one fire or another, keeping them going with sticks and bits of bark as devotedly as any priest ever tended a sacral flame. After about an hour, Maddyn left the prince to Caradoc's and Owaen's care at one of the fires and went for a turn round the guards. Most were calm enough, joking with him about ghosts and even making light of their own nerves, but when he came up to Branoic, who was posted out near the herd of horses, he found the younger man as tense as a harp string.

"Oh, now here, lad! Look at the horses, standing there all peaceful like. If there was some fell thing about, they'd warn us."

"You heard what Nevyn said, and he's right. There are some things horses can't know. Maddyn, you can mock me all you like, but some evil thing walks this stretch of country. I can practically smell it."

Maddyn was about to make a joke when the knocks sounded, three distant rolls booming out like thunder from a clear sky. Branoic yelped like a kicked dog and spun round to point as a tower of pale silver flame shot up through the night. As far as Maddyn could tell, it was coming from the old hunting lodge. Even though they were over a mile away, Maddyn saw the river flash with reflected light as it seemed that the flames would lick at the sky itself. Then they fell back, leaving both men blind and blinking in the darkness. In the camp, yells and curses broke like a rainstorm. Around them horses neighed and reared, pulling at their tethers.

"Come on!" Maddyn grabbed Branoic's arm. "Somewhat's happened to Nevyn."

Stumbling and swearing, they took off upriver, running because it would take too long to calm and saddle horses. Just as Maddyn's sight was finally clear someone hailed them: Nevyn himself, leading his horse along as calmly as you please.

"Ye gods, my lord! We thought you slain."

"Naught of the sort. I did get a little carried away with that fire, didn't I? I've never tried anything quite like that before, and I think me I need to refine my hand."

Nevyn refused to say anything more until they reached the camp. Shouting for answers the men surrounded him until Maryn yelled at them to shut up and let the councillor through. It was a good measure of the prince's authority that they all fell back and did so. Once Nevyn reached the pool of firelight, he mugged a look of mild surprise.

"I told you I'd lay the haunt to rest, lads, and I did. There's naught more to worry about." He glanced around with a deliberate vagueness. "If someone would take my horse, I'd be grateful."

Owaen grabbed the reins and led the trembling beast away to join its fellows.

"Oh, come now, good councillor." With all the flexible courage of youth Maryn was grinning at him. "You can't expect to put us off so easily."

"Well, perhaps not." The old man thought for a moment, but Maddyn was sure that he had his little speech all prepared and was only pretending to hesitate. "To lay a haunt you've got to burn its corpse. So I made a huge fire and shoved the ghastly thing in. But I stupidly forgot about the corpse-gas, and up went the whole lodge. I hópe your father won't be vexed, my liege. I've destroyed one of his holdings, old and decrepit though it was."

Much to Maddyn's surprise, everyone believed this, to him, less-than-satisfying tale. They wanted to believe it, he supposed, so they could stop thinking about these dark and troubling things. Later, when most of the men, including the prince and the captain, were asleep in their blankets, Maddyn heard a bit more of the truth as he and Aethan sat up with the old man at a dying fire.

"You're just the man I want," Nevyn said to Aethan. "You rode for the Boar up in Cantrae, didn't you? Take a look at this pewter roundel. Is that pig the same heraldic device or some other version of a boar?"

"It's the gwerbret's, sure enough." Aethan angled the bit of metal close to the last blazing log. "The curve of those long tusks gives it away, and I've been told that pointed mark on the back is the first letter of the word *apred*."

"So it is. That settles it, then. There was at least one Boarsman in that lodge this winter—although, truly, he could have been someone who was ousted from the warband, I suppose, and brought his old gear with him."

"I can't imagine any of the lads I used to ride with treating a dead man that way."

"Ah. Well, the man this belonged to might well have been the man who was killed. He was murdered for trying to do an honorable thing. I did find out that much."

"You talked with the haunt?" Maddyn found it hard to speak, and Aethan was staring horrified.

"Not to say talked, but I asked questions, and he could nod yes or no." The old man gave him a sly grin. "Don't look so shocked, lad. You were mistaken for a ghost yourself once, if I remember rightly."

"True enough, but I wasn't exactly dead."

"Well, while this poor fellow was a good bit less alive than you, he wasn't exactly dead either. He is now, and gone to the gods for a reward, or so I hope." Nevyn considered for a moment, frowning at the roundel. "Tell me somewhat, Aethan. When you rode for Cantrae, did you ever hear any rumors of witchcraft and dark wizardry? Did anyone ever say that so-and-so had strange powers or the second sight or suchlike?"

Aethan started to shrug indifferently, then stiffened and winced, like a man who shifts his weight in the saddle only to pinch an old bruise.

"An odd thing happened once, years back. I rode as a guard over the gwerbret's widowed sister, you see, and once we went out into the countryside. It was late in the fall, but she insisted on taking a hawk with her. There's naught to set it on, say I, but she laughed and said that she'd find the game she wanted. And she did, because cursed if she didn't fly the thing at a common crow, and of course the hawk brought it right down. She took feathers from its wings and its tail and threw the rest away." He was silent for a long moment. "And what do you want those for, say I, and she laughed again and said she was going to ensorcel my heart. And she did, truly, but whether she used the wretched feathers or not, I wouldn't know. She didn't need them." Abruptly Aethan rose to his feet. "Is there aught else you want from me, my lord?"

"Naught, and forgive me for opening an old wound."

With a toss of his head Aethan strode off into the darkness. Maddyn hesitated, then decided it would be best to leave him alone with his ancient grief.

"I *am* sorry," Nevyn said. "Did Aethan get thrown out of the warband for courting the gwerbret's sister?"

"He did, but things came to a bit more than fine words and flowers, or so I understand."

"Ah. I saw the Lady Merodda once. She was the most poisonous woman I've ever laid eyes on. I wonder, lad. I truly wonder about all of this. Here, keep what you just heard to yourself, will you? The men have got enough to worry about as it is."

"And I don't, I suppose."

"Oh, here." Nevyn chuckled to himself. "As if you weren't burning with curiosity."

"My heart was ice, sure enough. Well, my lord, I'm about snoring where I stand, and I'd best get some sleep."

Once he lay down in his blankets, Maddyn drifted straight off, but he did wake once, not long before dawn, to see Nevyn still sitting up and staring into the last embers of the fire.

On the morrow a subdued troop of silver daggers rode straight home to Dun Drwloc. That night Nevyn summoned Maddyn and Caradoc to the king's private chambers for a conference. Casyl had a map of the three kingdoms, drawn in great detail by the priests of Wmm, and, as he remarked, it had cost him far more than the weight of its thin parchment in gold. While Nevyn and the king chewed over the problems involved in getting Maryn to Cerrmor, Maddyn stared fascinated at the map in the flaring candlelight. Although he couldn't read, he could pick out the rivers and the mountains, the Canaver and the Cantrae hills where he'd lived his early life, the long rivers of central Deverry running down from the northern mountains, and, finally, the Aver El, the river with the foreign name whose source lay in the lake just outside the window of the conference room.

All the borders of the kingdoms and their provinces were there, too, marked in red. Even without letters Maddyn could see that it was going to be a long ride and a dangerous one from Loc Drw down to Cerrmor. As long as the prince was in Pyrdon, he was safe, but the Pyrdon border lay a good hundred miles from the border of the Cerrmor holdings. Part of his journey, therefore, would have to lie through hostile Cantrae lands.

"It aches my heart that some enemy knows of Maryn's Wyrd." Casyl's voice brought Maddyn back to the present meeting. "What matters the most, of course, is where their lands are, and whether or not the prince is going to have to pass through them, though I can't help wondering just who they are, and where their loyalties lie."

"I strongly suspect, my liege," Nevyn said, "that their loyalties lie only to themselves, but I'll wager they're not above selling information to whomever can buy it."

Caradoc nodded in a grim agreement.

"There's mercenary troops, and then there's mercenary spies," the captain pronounced. "I've come across a few of the latter. Fit for raven food and naught else, they were. All the honor of stoats."

"If that's the case," Casyl went on, "then I'll wager the chief buyer for their foul goods is the king in Cantrae."

"Don't forget, my liege, that Cerrmor is doubtless boiling over with intrigue at the moment," Nevyn said. "For a long while now there have been omens of the coming of the true king as well as much speculation as to his name. I'm sure that by now Maryn's bloodlines are well known there. And then we'll have a good many ambitious men who won't see why the omens couldn't apply to them or their sons—with the right trimming and fitting, that is."

"Just so." The king traced out the Pyrdon border with his fingertip. "There could be several different enemies laying for our prince. Here, Nevyn, do you know who's regent down in Cerrmor? Or has the fighting over the throne already begun?"

"I fear the latter, my liege, but I don't truly know. If you'll excuse me, I intend to find out."

The king nodded a dismissal, taking this hint of dweomer with a casual indifference. It was odd, Maddyn thought to himself, just how easily one did get used to dweomer, as if it were the natural order of things and a world without magic the aberration. Maryn was practically jigging where he stood in sheer excitement. Although Maddyn could sympathize—after all, the lad's Wyrd lay close at hand—he was also worried, just because he could remember being fifteen and sure that he would never die, no matter what happened to other men. He knew better now, and he had no desire to see his prince learn as he had: the hard way. It seemed that the captain agreed with him.

"If the Cantrae king comes out in force, my liege," Caradoc said, "there aren't enough men in Pyrdon to keep our prince safe."

Casyl winced.

"Forgive my bluntness, Your Highness, but—"

"No apologies needed, Captain. The point is both true and well taken. What do you suggest? I can see that there's somewhat on your mind."

"Well, my liege, maybe our enemies, whoever they are, know that the prince will be trying to reach Cerrmor, but they still have to find him on the road. I suggest that you send a troop of picked men, the sort you'd choose to guard the prince, down the east-running road. Then, a while later, we leave, heading toward

Eldidd, say. The prince goes with us—as a silver dagger. Who looks in a dung heap for a jewel?"

"Just so." Casyl nodded in slow admiration. "Just so, Captain."

"Oh, splendid!" Maryn broke in. "I've always wanted to carry one of those daggers. Have you looked at one close up, Father? They're truly beautiful."

"So they are." Casyl suppressed a smile. "One thing, though, Captain. I understand that you left Cerrmor in some disgrace. Will you be endangering yourself by returning?"

"If I live that long, my liege, I suppose I will. Haven't thought about all that in twelve, thirteen years, truly." He glanced at Maryn. "I suppose I could petition the true king for a pardon, if things came to that."

"You have my pardon already, Captain." Maryn drew himself up to full height, and all at once they could see the man he'd be someday. "No doubt you'll redeem yourself thrice over by the time I ride into Dun Deverry as king."

Abruptly Casyl turned away and paced over to the window. Maddyn was the only one who noticed that his liege's eyes were full of tears.

The next morning Nevyn came out to the barracks and fetched Caradoc and Maddyn for what he called a "little stroll." They went down to the lakeshore just outside the walls of the dun and sat down on the rocks right next to the water. For a moment Nevyn merely looked around him, but his eyes were so heavy-lidded and strange that Maddyn assumed the councillor was working some dweomer.

"I think we should be safe here," Nevyn remarked, confirming his suspicions. "The presence of the water will act as a sort of shield, you see, from the wrong sort of prying eyes. Now, then. Captain, I've received news from Cerrmor of a sort. The capital's in an uproar, but it's being torn apart by despair, not politicking. The only thing that's keeping the Cerrmor side together is the regent, a certain Tieryn Elyc, an honorable man and a shrewd one, apparently, but even he hasn't been able to stop a great many lords from switching their loyalties to Cantrae."

"Elyc? That's not Elyc of Dai Aver, is it?"

"The very one. You know him?"

"Did once, a cursed long time ago now. If he hasn't changed, he's a decent sort, truly."

"Well and good, then. In theory he's charged with running the kingdom until Glyn's eldest daughter marries and has an heir, but I doubt me if he'll be able to impose order for that many years."

"How old is the lass?" Maddyn said.

"Thirteen, just old enough to wed this year. Our prince will have to marry her, of course, and as soon as ever he can. I've no doubt that her mother will see reason if only we can get Maryn there. I'm told that everyone in the city lives in terror of anarchy."

"Then no doubt they'll welcome him with shouting and flowers in their hair," Caradoc said. "Good."

"Perhaps, but first we have to get him there. I suggest we leave on the morrow."

Since Caradoc wanted to keep the plan as secret as possible, he and Maddyn told the other silver daggers that they were going to ride a raid on the Eldidd border to provide a distraction when the Marked Prince left for Cerrmor with his escort. No one thought to question the plan, which was a decent one in its way. In a chilly dawn Maryn and Nevyn made a great show of riding out with a hundred members of the king's own guard and a wagon train filled with supplies and gifts for the Cerrmor lords. Ahead of them rode a herald holding the banner of Pyrdon. With them on the road went the king with an honor guard of his own—to escort them to the border, or so it was said. The queen wept openly; silver horns blared; the assembled populace cheered the young prince and his splendid Wyrd. Only Maddyn and Caradoc knew that hidden among the silver daggers' supplies were shabby clothes and armor for Maryn, and that those coffers of gifts were empty.

When the silver daggers assembled in the ward later that morning, only their own women came to watch. As he kissed Clwna good-bye Maddyn felt a pang of guilt; she was expecting them all home in a week or two, while he knew that it would be months before they could send for the women, if indeed they even lived long enough to do so. From his manner she seemed to pick up that something was wrong, because she kissed him repeatedly and clung to him.

"Here, here, my sweet, what's so wrong?"

"I worry, that's all. I do every time you ride to war, or haven't you even noticed?" Her eyes filled with tears. "Oh, Maddo, it's worse this time. Somewhat's going to happen. I just know it."

"Whist, whist, little one. If it does, then it'll be my Wyrd, and what can either of us do about that?"

Although she tried to force out a smile, her lips were trembling. She gave his hand one last squeeze, then ran for the barracks. She would be crying her heart out, he knew, and the guilt stabbed again, worse than a sword.

"Ah come on, Maddo!" It was Aethan, striding over with his horse in tow. "We'll be back soon enough. Those Eldidd dogs can't fight worth a pig's fart."

"So they can't, true enough." He forced out a smile of his own. The captain had insisted that he keep the truth to himself until they were miles from the dun. "Where's young Branoic?"

"Here, sir." Branoic came up, leading his horse into line. The lad was grinning as broadly as if they were going to some royal entertainment. "Let's hope our enemies can fight well enough to give us some sport, huh? Ye gods, I thought I'd go mad this winter, shut up in the dun with naught to do but loll around and dice."

"Listen to him!" Aethan rolled his eyes heavenward. "I'll wager we get our fill of blood soon enough."

The words stabbed Maddyn like an omen, but he kept smiling.

"Aethan, do me somewhat of a favor, will you? Ride with our young Branno here, and keep an eye on him."

Although the lad bristled, as if to say he didn't need such help, Aethan forestalled him with a friendly punch on the arm.

"I will, at that, at least until the fighting starts. Then he can keep an eye on me."

They laughed, both as excited as young horses turned into pasture after a winter in the stables. The sight of them together wrung Maddyn's heart for reasons that he hated to put into words, the one dark and grizzled, his oldest friend, the other blond and young, so new to his life that winter, and yet it seemed that he'd known Branoic for a hundred years. When the captain started yelling orders, the moment passed, but still, as they rode south, laying their false trail, Maddyn found himself brooding over it. It was a dangerous thing for a fighting man to care so deeply for his friends, especially when they were starting out on the bloodiest road they'd ever ridden.

"What's so wrong with you?" Caradoc said abruptly. "Your bowels stopped or suchlike?"

"Oh, hold your tongue!"

"Listen to him! Feisty today, aren't we?"

"My apologies, Carro. I hate lying at the best of times, and these are the worst. Saying farewell to Clwna, and her and the other women thinking we'll be back in an eightnight or so—it ached my heart."

"They'll have to live with the truth just like the lads will. Listen to me, Maddo. Today we start a ride ordained by the gods themselves. Our petty little troubles are of no moment. None. Do you understand me?"

"I do, at that." He shivered suddenly, just from the quiet way that Caradoc spoke of such grave things. "Well and good, then. A man's Wyrd comes when it comes."

"So it does, and ours is upon us now."

Maddyn turned in the saddle to look at him and wonder all over again just who Caradoc had been, back in his other life before dishonor sent him down the long road. It occurred to him that at last he was going to find out—if, of course, they all lived long enough to ride through the gates of Dun Cerrmor.

Branoic was surprised at how little ground the silver daggers covered that afternoon. Even though the spring days were short, they could have made some twelve miles before sunset, but instead they stopped for their night's camp on the banks of the Elaver just some five miles from the dun. Branoic tethered out his horse and Aethan's while the elder man carried their gear to a campsite and drew them provisions from the pack train. As glad as he was to be out of the dun and riding, Branoic's mood was dark that evening, and he swore at the horses for ducking their heads and grabbing grass while he was trying to change bridle for halter. He was disappointed, that was all, heartsick that he was stuck in Pyrdon instead of riding behind the true king on his journey to Cerrmor—or so he told himself. Since he'd never been an introspective man, the excuse rang true enough.

When he went back to the camp he found the troop settling in. Some men were spreading out their bedrolls; others were cursing flint and tinder as they struggled to light a fire. He found Maddyn and Aethan by a fire that was already blazing; although no one was sure why, it was common knowledge that fires always lit easily for the bard. As he walked up he felt his heart pounding in the strange way it did lately, a fearful sort of wondering as he looked over the campsite until he saw that Aethan had indeed dumped his gear there along with his own and Maddyn's. That he would be allowed to camp with them was so welcome, such a relief, really, from his fear that he'd be put somewhere else, that he briefly thought of going elsewhere just to pretend that he didn't care. Maddyn looked up with an easy smile, and he broke into a jog, drawn by that smile like a thirsty man to water.

"Does your horse need tethering, Maddo? I'll do it for you."

"Oh, I've already got him out. Are you lads hungry? We'd best eat now, because there might be a bit of a surprise later."

"A what?" Aethan looked vaguely annoyed. "Talking in riddles again, are you?"

"It's good for you, makes you exercise your wits. Well, what few wits you have, anyway."

Aethan threw a fake punch his way and grinned. They had known each other so long that at moments like these Branoic's heart ached from feeling that he was an outsider, some foreigner who would never know their private language.

"But I'm hungry, sure enough," Aethan went on. "What about you, Branno? Care to gnaw on some of the king's stale hardtack?"

"It'll do, truly. Maybe when we're raiding we can snag us a barrel of ale to wash this foul stuff down with."

At that perfectly ordinary remark Maddyn looked sly, but

Branoic let it pass. The bard would tell him his secret when he wanted to and not a minute before.

As it turned out, they didn't have long to wait. Just as the sun was setting, they heard a guard shout from the outer limits of the camp and rose to see what the trouble was. Two men came riding toward them from the east, and as the setting sun washed them with gold, Branoic realized that it was the Marked Prince and the councillor. Beside him Aethan laughed, a crow of triumph.

"So we're going to Cerrmor after all, are we? Well played, Maddo! They took us in good and proper with that fanfare and pomp in the ward this morning."

Cheering, laughing, the entire troop left the camp and jogged down the road to meet their liege. Since he was acutely aware of his place as the newest man in the troop, Branoic lingered off to one side rather than shove his way forward to get near to the prince. Muttering under his breath, Nevyn made his way free of the mob and came over, leading his horse.

"Ye gods!" the old man snapped. "They'll be able to hear all this shouting back in Dun Drwloc if it keeps up."

"Well, sir, we were all cursed disappointed when we thought we wouldn't be riding with the prince."

"Were you now? An honorable sentiment, that. Now listen, lad. From now on Maryn is a silver dagger and naught else. No doubt Caradoc will impress that upon you all, but it won't hurt to say it more than once."

"Of course, good sir. I take it he'll have a new name and suchlike?"

"He won't." Nevyn gave him a sly smile. "I decided that if our enemies saw through this ruse at all, they'd be expecting a false name, so he'll just be Maryn. It's a very common name in this part of the world."

"Well, so it is, but—"

"Trust me, lad. There are times when the safest place to hide something is out in plain sight." The smile faded, and he looked suddenly very weary. "I'll pray that this is one of those times."

"Well and good, then, sir. So will I."

"My thanks. Oh, by the way, lad, I have a favor to ask of you and Maddo—and Aethan, too, of course. Can Maryn share your fire and generally camp with you?"

"Of course! Ye gods, we'll all be honored beyond dreaming, good councillor."

"No doubt, but please, do your best to treat him the way you'd treat any other man. He won't take offense—he knows that his life depends on it."

Branoic nodded his agreement, but mentally he was half-giddy with pride—not because the true king of all Deverry would be dining with him that night, but because Nevyn had somehow assumed that Maddyn and he formed a unit, a pair you could take for granted. Me and Maddyn, he thought, it sounds right. Then he blushed, wondering why his heart was pounding so hard, the same way it did when he saw some pretty lass he fancied.

Although he of course never explained them to Branoic or indeed any of the silver daggers, Nevyn had several tricks at his disposal to hide the prince. For one thing, he simply withdrew all the glamours that the elemental spirits had been casting over the boy, so that when he changed into the scruffy brigga and much-mended shirt that Caradoc had ready for him, all his supernatural air of power and magnetism vanished along with the fine clothes. For another, with Maryn's complete cooperation he ensorcelled the prince and suggested to his subconscious mind that he had difficulty in speaking—though in nothing else. He also suggested that on a simple cue, the difficulty would vanish. Once he removed the ensorcellment, the suggestion took effect, and the prince who'd always held forth like the hero of an ancient epic now stammered as he struggled to find the right words to express a simple, routine thought. All of the silver daggers swore in amazement and said that they wouldn't recognize him themselves if they didn't know better, but they, of course, thought that the prince was merely acting a part.

Which in a way he always was, or, what was perhaps worse, the prince always lived his part in the strange epic that they were composing not with their words, but with their lives. At times, when he remembered the happy, charming little lad that Maryn once had been, Nevyn felt like a murderer. Over the years he had trained the prince so well that he'd stripped away all trace of the lad's individuality, pruned and sheared him as ruthlessly as a gardener in the king's palace shapes an ornamental hedge or splays a climbing rose over its trellis in order to torture it into an unnatural form. It was hard to tell at times whether Maryn was larger than life or smaller, a grand hero out of the Dawntime or a picture of a hero such as a Bardek illuminator would draw, all ink lines and thin colors. Either way, the kingdom needed him, not some all-too-human and complex man who would use the kingship rather than the kingship using him. Nevyn could only hope that in some future life either he himself or the Lords of Wyrd would make it up to Prince Maryn for slicing his personality away like the peel of an apple.

First, of course, they had to get the lad and his councillor safely to Cerrmor before he could be any kind of king. Nevyn figured out a way to hide himself, too. Since there had to be some reason for an old man to be traveling with a mercenary troop, he decided to pass himself off as a jewel merchant who'd paid the troop a fee for allowing him to ride in the safety of their numbers. He knew enough about precious stones to bring this ruse off, and since Casyl had given him what few royal jewels there were to take to the Cerrmor princess, he could use them as his stock-in-trade. The real danger now lay in their desperate need to keep up these ruses. Since working dweomer leaves obvious tracks on the etheric and astral planes for those who know how to look for them, Nevyn could use no dweomer at all until the prince was safely in Cerrmor territory—not one single spell, not even lighting a fire or scrying someone out. He'd also asked the kings of the elements to keep their people away from him and the prince, which meant that he was deprived of any danger warning that the Wildfolk might give him, too. After two hundred years of living wrapped round by dweomer, he felt naked, just as in one of those hideous dreams where you find yourself being presented to the High King only to realize that your skirts or brigga have somehow been left behind at home.

In the morning they had a more mundane problem to worry

about, or at least, Nevyn profoundly hoped that it was mundane. They woke to a slate-gray sky and a western wind that smelt of spring rain, and just after noon the storm broke. Although the rain held steady, the wind dropped in a few hours. Nevyn agreed with the captain that they'd better keep riding as long as the roads were passable. What troubled him was wondering if the storm was a natural phenomenon or if some dark dweomerman had called it up. There was nothing he could do to find out without giving their ruse away, and much less could he fight back with dweomer.

That evening, when he shared a cold dinner with Caradoc, he had to force his eyes away from the campfire lest he start seeing the Wildfolk in it. Since the captain was wrapped in a black hiraedd of his own, they had an unpleasant meal of it until Nevyn decided to ease Caradoc's mood.

"What troubles your heart, Captain? It must be a grave thing indeed."

"Do I look as glum as that?"

"You do, truly."

Caradoc sighed, hesitated, then shrugged.

"Well, good councillor—I mean, good merchant—I've just been wondering what kind of welcome I'm in for down in Cerrmor."

"Well, the king's pardoned you already—for all and sundry and in advance."

"But I'd never hold him to it if it was going to cause him trouble, and it might. There's a powerful lord who just might take umbrage at that kind of pardon, and I don't want him stirring things up behind the prince's back, like."

"Oh."

They sat in silence for a moment more.

"Ah horseshit!" Caradoc said abruptly. "What happened was this. I wasn't welcome at home for a number of reasons that I'll keep to myself, if you don't mind and all, and my father found me a place in the warband of a man named Lord Tidvulc. Ever hear of him?"

"I haven't, truly."

"Well, he was decent enough in his way, but his eldest son

was a slimy little tub of eel snot, not that you could tell his lordship that, of course. And so our young lordling—gods, I've almost forgotten his name—let me see, I think it was Gwaryn or Gwarc or suchlike—anyway, this little pusboil went and got a bondwoman with child. I guess he was enough of a hound to not mind the fleas. And then he had the stinking gall to try to kill her to keep the news from getting out! I happened to be passing by her hut, and luckily there were a couple of the lads with me for witnesses, because we heard the poor bitch screaming and sobbing as his noble lordling tried to strangle her. So I grabbed him and broke both his arms." Caradoc looked shame-struck rueful. "Don't know what came over me all of a sudden. She was only a bondwoman, but it rubbed me wrong, like."

"I wouldn't let myself feel shamed if I were you, Captain. Rather the opposite."

Caradoc shrugged away the implied praise.

"So of course Lord Tidvulc had to kick me out of the warband. I got the feeling he didn't want to, but it was his first-born son and all. The trouble is, his lordship was no young man when I left, all those years ago, and I'll wager anything you please that his son's the lord now."

"And no doubt he'll be less than pleased to see you? Hum, I see your point, but you know, he may be dead himself by now. There's been plenty of fighting down Cerrmor way."

"True spoken." The captain looked a good bit more cheerful. "Let's pray so, huh? Naught I can do about it now, anyway."

For five days the silver daggers rode wet and slept that way, too, as they picked their way across Pyrdon, keeping to the country lanes and wild trails and avoiding the main-traveled roads. Although the mercenaries grumbled in the steady stream of foul oaths typical of men at arms, they stayed healthy enough, but Nevyn began to feel the damp badly. At times he needed help to stand in the mornings, and he could hear his joints pop and complain every time he mounted his horse. Even his dweomer-induced vitality had its natural limits. Just when he was thinking of dosing himself with some of his own herbs, the storm blew itself out, only to have the weather turn hot and muggy. The midges and flies came out in force and hovered above the line of march as thick as smoke. Finally, though, just on the next day, they reached the river that marked the Pyrdon border, and, at its joining with the Aver Trebyc, the only truly large town in the west.

At that time Dun Trebyc was a far different place from the center of learning and bookcraft that it is today. Although it was nominally in Cantrae-held territory, and its lord sent some small tribute to reinforce the fiction, in truth it was a free city and scrupulously neutral, a town where spies from both sides mingled to the profit of both or neither, depending on how many were lying at any given time. Since it was also a place where everyone went armed, and mercenaries were common, no one remarked on the silver daggers when they rode through the gates late on a steamy-hot afternoon. After the slop-muddy road, the streets were welcome, even though they were paved only with logs instead of cobbles, and the prospect of a night in an inn more welcome still.

"I only hope we can find a place to ourselves," Caradoc remarked to Nevyn. "Last thing we need is a brawl on our hands, and when you mix two free troops in the same tavern, brawls are about what you get."

Much to Nevyn's relief, and doubtless the captain's, too, they were indeed lucky enough to find an inn over by the east gate that had just been vacated by another pack of mercenaries. Although the men had to sleep four and five to each small room, everyone had a place to spread their blankets and a roof over their heads. As befitted his supposed station as a wealthy merchant, Nevyn had a tiny chamber with a proper bed all to himself. Branoic carried his gear up for him, and Maryn insisted on coming along with a bucket of charcoal for the brazier.

"Nobody's going to believe a pr-prince would c-carry c-coals," the lad said. "Ye gods, I'll be g-glad when we reach the harbor town! Its rotten name is too hard for me to say. I'll never make f-f-fun of anyone who st-st-st-st who has trouble talking again, I sw-sw-swear it."

"Coming down for dinner, my lord?" Branoic said.

"I don't think so, truly. I've already told the serving wench to bring me up a tankard of dark and some cold meat. These old bones are tired, lads."

They were indeed tired enough to make him take a nap for a couple of hours after the girl had brought his scant supper. Since Nevyn usually only slept about four hours a night, he was quite surprised when he woke to a dark room and a charcoal fire that was burning itself out in the brazier. He added more sticks, blew on them like an ordinary man, then wiped his hands on his brigga and sat down to think.

More than ever he wished he could simply scry through the fire and talk with the other dweomermasters who were part of this scheme. He badly wanted to know whether the situation in Cerrmor had changed since his last talk with the priests of Bel there, and he would have liked some opinions on the character of this Tieryn Elyc, too. There remained as well the problem of their enemies, who might well have seen through their ruse.

"Nevyn?" It was Maddyn, hesitating in the doorway. "Have you seen Maryn?"

"Not since you two brought up my things." Nevyn leapt to his feet like a bounding hare. "Have you?"

"I haven't. I've looked all over this cursed inn, even out in the privies."

Swearing under his breath Nevyn followed the bard down to the tavern room, where a handful of silver daggers were drinking and dicing in the uncertain lantern light. From the way they fell silent and froze at the sight of their lieutenant, Nevyn felt trouble brewing. Maddyn apparently agreed.

"I want answers!" he snarled. "Where's Maryn?"

The men looked back and forth between one another for a good minute before a slender lad named Albyn finally spoke, and he stared fixedly at the far wall rather than at Maddyn.

"Out and about with a couple of the lads."

"That's not good enough. Out where and with whom?"

"Er, well, Branoic and Aethan, so he's in good hands."

"Where are they?"

"Ah, well, we were all talking, like, during the evening meal, and it turned out the lad had never"—he glanced Nevyn's way with a nervous tic of the cheek—"never been with a lass, like. So we were all thinking what a pity that was, and . . ."

"By every god in the sky!" Maddyn's voice was a growl. "Are you saying those two piss-poor excuses for dolts took Maryn to a brothel?"

"Just that. Er, it was just a prank, Maddo."

"You lackwit dog! Which brothel?"

"How would we know, Maddo? None of us have ever been in Dun Trebyc before. They went out to ask around, like."

When Maddyn's cheeks flushed a dangerous shade of purple, Albyn shrank back, half ducking a blow that never came. With a deep exhalation of breath, Maddyn got himself under control.

"We're all going to go out and ask around. All right, you six —hunt up the other lads and go out in squads, four men to a squad, say, and scour this wretched town down. Find him. Do you hear me? Find him fast."

As the men scrambled up and hurried off to follow orders, Nevyn barely saw them leave. He could feel the blood pounding in his temples, partly from rage, but mostly fear. Maryn was off in one of the most lawless towns in the kingdom, and he didn't dare use a trace of dweomer to find him.

"We'd best go look ourselves," Maddyn said.

"Just so. And when I get my hands on Aethan and young Branno . . ."

"Whatever it is you're going to do, I'll hold them down so you can do it."

Since Dun Trebyc was the kind of town it was, finding a brothel turned out to be easy enough. Down near the river the two silver daggers with their prince in tow came across the Tupping Ram, a surprisingly big two-story roundhouse with its own stableyard out in back and a palisade made of split logs all round. Over the gate, right next to the painted wooden sign, hung a well-worn broom smelling of sour ale.

"I'll wager they sell more than beer, judging from the look of that sign," Branoic said with a grin. "In we go, lads."

The stable turned out to be a big open barn without stalls. As they hitched their horses to a rail near the far side, Branoic noticed Aethan looking over the various other horses, as well as he could in the dim lantern light, anyway.

"There's a lot of devices and suchlike on this gear. Looks like the marks belong to some free troops. Listen, young ones: watch what you say in there. We've got rivals, and I don't want a brawl. Understand?"

"Just so," Branoic said. "I didn't come here with fistfights on my mind, anyway."

The ale room was stinking-hot from the fire in the hearth and the press of men packed into it—merchants, riders for the local lord, a couple of other silver daggers, and a good-sized mob of men from a mercenary troop that wore a black sword embroidered on one sleeve for a device. Strolling around or perching suggestively on the tables were a variety of young women in varying states of undress while three older women with hard eyes rushed round serving ale. Even though they'd had plenty to drink back at the inn, Aethan insisted on collaring one of the women and ordering three tankards of dark. Once they had their beer they found a free spot to stand in the curve of the wall and eyed the merchandise. Maryn's face was flushed scarlet, whether from the heat or embarrassment, Branoic couldn't tell. A little of both, he supposed.

"I rather fancy that redhead over there," Aethan said. "Either of you want her?"

Maryn merely shrugged and buried his nose in his tankard.

"Not me," Branoic said. "Go to, lad!"

As Aethan strolled off, a pale blonde who reminded Branoic a bit of Clwna came bobbing over, wearing nothing but a drape of red Bardek silk around her hips. Although she gave Branoic a smile it was Maryn that she sidled up to.

"And what's your name, lad?" she said, batting eyelashes pitch-black with Bardek kohl.

"M-m-maryn." He could hardly keep his eyes off her breasts and their nipples, which gleamed an unnatural red. "W-wh-wha— ah c-c-curse it!"

"Oh, now here, don't let a bit of a stammer bother you! A well-favored lad like you doesn't have to worry about fine words

when it comes to winning a lass's heart." She gave Branoic a sly
sidelong wink. "As for you, my handsome friend, it looks like our
Avra's sitting all lonely over there."

By the fire a tousle-headed blonde in a gauzy shift was lounging on a cushioned bench and eyeing him with some interest. Branoic left the prince to the practiced attentions of the young whore
and made his way across the room in a hurry, before someone else
could claim her. As he approached she sat up and gave him a slow,
sleepy smile. The shift was stuck to her back and breasts with
sweat. For some reason, that night, he found the sight utterly
arousing, and he sat down next to her and kissed her without
saying a word. From the sweet taste of her mouth she'd been chewing cinnamon.

"Oh, I do like that," she said, giving him another smile. "A
man who's got his mind made up. Can I have a sip of that ale?"

Grinning, he handed her the tankard, which she took in both
hands so she could gulp like a thirsty child.

"Hot in here tonight."

"Too hot." She handed him back the nearly empty tankard.
"It might be cooler upstairs. Want to go see?"

For an answer he set the tankard down on the floor and got
up, holding out his hand to catch hers and haul her to her feet.
Moving carefully through the packed crowd they made their way
to the back door and out, where a wooden staircase listed against
the outside wall and led up to a doorway and a spill of light from
lanterns hanging from the ceiling. At the top, just inside the open
door, a toothless old woman, her hair dyed sunset-orange with
henna and her gnarled fingers covered with cheap rings, sat on a
high-backed chair and made a desultory pretense of spinning wool.

"Take him down to the end, Avra love. The one with the
window's free," she said, yawning. "Gods, things are busy tonight,
eh?"

Soot-stained wickerwork partitions cut the top story of the
building up into a warren of tiny cubicles that reeked of spilled
ale and sweat and other humidities, but somehow the squalor
matched the whore's sweaty breasts and tousled hair, as if they
were all ingredients in some strange but potent sexual spell. When

she pulled aside a dirty blanket to reveal a tiny cubicle with nothing but a straw mattress on the floor, he ducked in after her, caught her round the waist, and kissed her hard, his hands digging into her back.

"Oh, this could be nice," she murmured. "I like a man who's a little bit rough, if you take my meaning, like."

When he slapped her across the buttocks, she giggled and reached up to kiss him in turn.

"Avra!" It was the crone's voice, as harsh as a crow. "Avra, you come out here right now, you little wench! There's Caer the blacksmith here, and he swears you stole a silver out of his pockets!"

"May a demon shit in his eye!" Avra yelled. "Did naught of the sort, you old harpy!"

"He's threatening to bust up the place, he is! You get your ugly ass out here now!"

"You'd best go." Branoic was wishing he could strangle the old hag and be done with her. "I'll wait. You look worth waiting for."

"My thanks, and I'll say the same for you. Open the shutters for a bit of air, will you, love?" This last as she was leaving: "I'm on my way, sow-tits!"

Shrieking at each other they moved off down the hall, where their voices were met by an angry masculine bellow. With some care for the rotting leather hinges, Branoic opened the shutters and stuck his head out to breathe the night's cool. Down below in the stableyard, in pockets of lantern light men were standing around, drinking, singing, or merely laughing together at some jest or another. When a woman giggled behind him he pulled his head in, hoping for Avra back again, but the sound was coming from the other side of the rickety partition to his right. Although he could hear a woman plain enough, the man with her was talking in a rumbling dark voice, and he couldn't understand a word.

"I learned it from a Bardek sailor," she went on, giggling. "And you've never felt anything like this before, I swear it. Oh, come along, five extra coppers can't be much to a man like you."

The rumble sounded skeptical.

"Because it's not so easy on a lass's back, that's why! First you've got to . . ." Here her words were drowned by mutual giggling. "And then I squeeze a bit, like. They call it coring apples. What do you say?"

Judging from his snigger of laughter, he was agreeing to the extra expense. Branoic paced over to the doorway and pulled back the blanket to look out, but there was no sign of Avra. As he was considering leaving to find her, the couple next door began giggling and grunting in turn, as if whatever exotic trick she was showing him took a great deal of coordinated effort to bring off properly. Branoic did make an effort to do the honorable thing and ignore them, but he was, after all, only human, with the stock of curiosity normal for that breed. He went back to the window, hesitated, then bent down to peer through the tiny holes in the partition, which proved to be clogged with old filth.

"Ooooh, ye gods," the wench next door snickered. "Well, let's try again, shall we?"

Her piece of work agreed with a long bellow of laughter. Cursing his own curiosity, Branoic looked around and discovered that the wickerwork stopped somewhat short of the ceiling about two feet above his head, and that the windowsill stood about three feet off the floor. After one last attempt to ignore this perfect confluence of circumstance, he gave in and hauled himself up to totter on the sill and look over the top of the partition. Unfortunately he'd forgotten that he'd been drinking ale for hours on a hot night, and the effort made his head lurch and swim. Without thinking he grabbed at the flimsy wickerwork to steady himself. It buckled, he grabbed harder, the couple beyond yelped and swore, and his foot slipped on the mucky sill. With a yell of his own that was half a warning Branoic pitched forward, all fifteen stone of him, and crashed into the partition. In a tangle of broken wicker he swooped down and landed on the half-naked pair.

Shrieking and screaming, the woman writhed around and got free just as the next partition over went down from the impact, and knocked the one beyond it, too, into the one beyond—and so on all along the round room. Stammering out a stream of apologies of some sort—he never could remember exactly what he said

—Branoic rolled over and staggered to his feet just as the fellow jumped up, pulling up his brigga and struggling to belt them, a big burly man and too furious to swear. The blazons on his shirt showed him to be a member of the Black Sword troop.

"Who are you—a cursed silver dagger! I'll have your ugly head for this, you young cub!"

"I didn't mean—my apologies—" Branoic was gulping for air out of shame, not fear.

Although the fellow started to draw his sword, his brigga slid down to his knees and forced a brief moment of peace as he swore and fumbled round for his belt. Just to be on the safe side, Branoic reached for his own hilt and was rewarded with another bellow of rage. The lass started screaming just as Aethan came plowing into what was left of the doorway.

"Put that sword away, Branoic you asshole, and come with me!"

The fellow was so stunned that he merely stood there, hiking his brigga, as Aethan shoved Branoic bodily ahead of him, down the collapsed corridor. Judging by the shrieking and writhing under the pile of broken wickerwork the brothel had indeed been busy that night. They shoved their way out the doorway and clattered down the stairs fast to the stableyard, where a curious crowd was beginning to form.

"I was just going downstairs again with the red-haired slut when I saw your stupid ugly mug poking up over the wall." Aethan's voice was so choked that Branoic thought him still furious until all at once the older man broke out into a howl of laughter. "Oh, ye gods, the look on everyone's face! Wait till we tell Maddo about this!"

"Ah shit! Do we have to?"

"I do," Aethan gasped out. "Don't know about you. I—oh, ye gods! Where's Maryn?"

In a wave of ice-cold shame Branoic spun around and headed, all unthinking, back toward the stairway with Aethan right behind. By then, though, men and women both were rushing down, clutching pieces of clothing or struggling to get clothing on, cursing and snarling and swearing they'd find the lout of a silver dagger who was responsible and slice his heart out. Aethan grabbed Branoic by the arm and pulled him back into a patch of shadow.

"Go get the horses and take them round to the street," he hissed. "I'll find the lad and try to warn the rest of our men, too."

Keeping to the dark places Branoic scuttled to the stable and found their three mounts. His heart was pounding in terror—what if something had happened to the one true king of all Deverry and it was all his fault? All at once he realized that their little prank was a dangerous one all round, taking Maryn into the heart of a strange town with only a couple of guards—who had then let him go off with a whore on his own. What if the lass had been in someone's pay? He gathered the horses' reins in one hand, threw open the stable door with the other, and started out only to run straight into Maddyn and Nevyn.

"Where's the prince?" Maddyn snarled.

"I don't know. Aethan's looking for him."

With a foul oath Maddyn slugged him backhanded across the face.

"I shouldn't be surprised you'd do such a stupid thing, but I expected better from Aethan. And why by the name of every god is this wretched crowd milling round out here?"

Branoic tried to speak, but his voice clogged and tears filled his eyes, no matter how hard he tried to choke them back. Nevyn grabbed his arm and shook it.

"Think, lad! Save the cursed shame for later."

"I—I—I . . ."

The horses began to stamp and toss their heads. By then Branoic's hands were so sweaty that he could barely hang on to the reins.

"Nevyn!" The whisper came from directly above them. "Is th-th-that you?"

"It is!" The old man sounded as if he'd weep, too, but from relief. "Maryn, where are you?"

"In the hayloft. We c-c-came up here to be private, like."

"Then come down! Give the lass some coins—I imagine she's more than earned them—and get down here right now!"

"I will, sir. S-s-straightaway."

There was a chink of silver, a giggle, and a rustle of hay; then Maryn clambered down the rope ladder and dropped lightly to the floor nearby. Nevyn threw both arms around him and hugged him.

"My apologies," Maryn stammered out. "But I—"

"I don't want to hear a word more about it, but if you ever do such a stupid thing again . . ." All at once Nevyn broke off with a warning glance up at the hayloft, where the lass was lingering, prudently out of the way. "Well, no harm done, I suppose." He turned to Branoic. "Here, lad, you don't need to grovel and look like cold death. The prank ended well enough."

Branoic only shrugged for an answer. He could never explain that what was eating his heart was Maddyn's scorn. The bard himself had run over to the stable doors and was peering out the crack between them; with an oath he came trotting back.

"Nevyn, take two of these horses and get Maryn out of here. When we rode in I saw a back gate over near those trees. Branoic, you come with me. We've got to find Aethan. I don't like the look of that crowd."

Much later it occurred to Branoic that he should have told Maddyn the truth right there and then, but at the time he was quite simply so miserable, wallowing in shame and the bard's disgust, that he was sure that Maddyn would think him a coward if he didn't go back. Outside, they found about thirty people of both sexes milling around and talking at the top of their lungs. Quite a few people were laughing, actually—one could guess that they'd all been elsewhere when the walls started going down—and promising to spread this magnificent jest around town, much to the rage of those caught in Branoic's unintentional trap.

"I think that's Aethan over by the tavern-room door," Maddyn whispered. "You're taller—can you see?"

Branoic raised himself up on the balls of his feet and shaded his eyes against the lantern light with one hand.

"It is." He started waving. "Good, he's seen me."

Unfortunately so had the burly fellow from the next cubicle. Fully dressed now and howling like a banshee he came shoving his way through the crowd.

"You! You're the little prick that started this whole cursed thing!"

His mouth half-open in surprise, Maddyn turned around to stare at Branoic, who felt as inarticulate as the ensorcelled prince.

"My apologies, I didn't mean—"

"You were trying to watch, you bloody little debaucher! I'll grind your head on the cobbles for this! I'll—"

Just at that moment Aethan and another two men from the Black Sword troop reached them. Behind them Branoic could see a gaggle of silver daggers and a bunch of black swords rushing forward, too, while all the other men round started taking sides. The experienced and politic women drew back to give them plenty of room as Branoic's victim threw a punch right at his head. Profoundly relieved that the matter wasn't going to swordplay, Branoic punched right back and connected with the fellow's jaw. Women screamed; the fellow went down, out cold; somewhere the old crone was shrieking for the town wardens. He could hear Maddyn shouting and Aethan howling as the rain-washed and slippery tavern yard exploded into a brawl.

In that kind of press it was hard to see who was enemy and who friend, especially as men kept slipping and falling into the mud and clambering back up to fight some more. Branoic squared off with a squint-eyed brown-haired fellow, slammed him once in the stomach and once on the jaw, nearly fell over him as he fell, dodged free and dodged a thrown tankard, paused to catch his breath on the edge of things only to have someone rush straight at him. He grabbed the fellow by one arm, swung him around, and flung him back into the heaving shouting mob, which reminded him at that moment of a bowl of yeast working and bubbling over. Just as he started back in, someone grabbed him from behind. He swung around only to pull his punch barely in time: Aethan.

"Come on, lad—they don't even remember why they're fighting. Hurry!"

"I was just starting to enjoy myself!"

"Come along and now! You won't be enjoying yourself if the captain decides to take the skin off your back, will you?"

Without another word Branoic followed him into the shadows by the open back gate, where Maddyn was riding one horse and holding the reins of two others. Out on the riverbank he could see the rest of the silver daggers, mounted and ready to ride.

"No one can beat a silver dagger when it comes to ducking the law," Aethan said, grinning. "Mount up, Branno. The town wardens are pounding on the front gate."

After he mounted, Branoic turned to the bard.

"Maddyn, I'm cursed sorry."

"Oh, hold your tongue! We'll sort it all out later, but I tell you, lad, I don't want to see your ugly face till I'm a good bit calmer, like."

As they rode back to the inn, at a nice stately trot to avoid suspicion, Branoic was thinking seriously of starving himself to death out of shame.

With all the trouble brewing out in the tavern yard, Nevyn and Maryn easily slipped out the back gate and rode off with barely a soul noticing. As soon as they were back at their own inn, Nevyn turned the horses over to another silver dagger and dragged the prince up to his private chamber. Although he tried to feign embarrassment, Maryn couldn't quite keep from grinning.

"Listen, lad," Nevyn said, and he felt defeated before he truly began his little lecture. "It's your safety I'm worried about. Slipping off into town with only those two bumbling idiots for guards was a very bad idea."

"Well, t-t-true enough, and I'm sorry."

"You don't look sorry in the least. After this, if you simply can't live without a lass, have your friends bring you one. For enough silver that sort of lass is always willing to take a little walk."

"No doubt my learned c-c-councillor would know."

Nevyn restrained the impulse to give the one true king of all Deverry a good slap across the chops. Very dimly he could remember being both that young and that smug about his first lass—some two hundred years earlier or about that, anyway. Such anniversaries had rather lost their importance for him. All at once Maryn let his grin fade and sat down in the one rickety chair to stare at the floor.

"Somewhat wrong?"

"Not tr-tr-truly. I was just thinking. Both you and Father were telling me that I'd have to marry Glyn's daughter."

"So we were, and so you do."

"How old is she?"

"Thirteen."

"Well, at least she's old enough." He looked up with a worried frown. "Is she pr-pr-pretty?"

"I have no idea."

"I suppose I'll have to m-m-marry her even if she's got twenty wens and a besom squint."

"Exactly right, Your Highness. She represents the sovereignty of the kingdom."

Maryn groaned and went back to studying the floor.

"Well, I hope she is pr-pr-pretty," the prince said at last. "Now that I know what . . ." And then he did blush, looking at that moment some ten years old. "I'd best get to b-b-bed."

"So you had. If I were you, I'd pretend to be asleep and snoring when Maddyn comes storming in. Our bard didn't seem to find the evening's sport amusing."

In the morning, over breakfast, Maddyn assembled the silver daggers who'd been at the Tupping Ram to piece out what had happened. He knew that it would be a good bit better for the miscreants if he settled this matter before Caradoc or Owaen took it in hand. As this less-than-pleasant meal progressed, he noticed that Branoic sat at the end of the table as far from him as possible, ate nothing, and spoke only when the others tormented him into doing so. Although Maddyn started out furious, by the time Branoic, stammering as much as the prince and twice as red, repeated the whore's remark about coring apples, he was laughing as hard as all the other men there.

"Oh, well and good, then," Maddyn said at last. "No one was killed, and so that's an end to it. Cheer up, Branno. I can't lie and say that I'd never have done such if I'd been you."

Everyone smirked and nodded agreement. Looking a bit less miserable, Branoic grabbed a slab of bread and busied himself in buttering it. Although everyone went on eating, Maddyn could tell that something was still bothering a couple of the men.

"Out with it, Stevyc."

"Well, by the hells, Maddo, I was just wondering." He glanced at Branoic. "Did you ever find out what they meant? About coring apples I mean?"

"I didn't. Everything happened too fast."

When Stevyc swore in honest regret, everyone howled and hooted. There was the true end to the matter, Maddyn assumed, and he pitched into his breakfast. Yet, as he was leaving the tavern room afterward, his little blue sprite appeared, and with her were two gray gnomes, dancing up and down with their normally slack mouths twisted into frowns. Her mindless blue eyes peered up at him in something like worry.

"What's all this?" Maddyn whispered. "You're not even supposed to be here. You'd best run away before Nevyn sees you. Whist!"

Yet they stayed with him, the sprite riding on his shoulder, the gnomes clinging to his brigga leg like frightened children. He considered for a moment, then went upstairs to Nevyn's chamber with the Wildfolk hurrying after. He found the old man sitting on the windowsill of his chamber and staring idly out across the spring countryside. Although Maddyn hesitated, wondering if he were interrupting some meditation, Nevyn turned to him and started to smile—until he saw the Wildfolk.

"What? You shouldn't be here!"

All three of them began to jump up and down and point up at the ceiling, their little faces twisted in an agony of concentration.

"Ye gods!" Nevyn sounded truly alarmed. "Someone's watching us?"

They shook their heads in a no, then frowned again and began pinching and shoving each other.

"Someone saw last night, when the men were fighting."

They all nodded, then disappeared. Even though Maddyn had no idea of what was happening, he went cold with fear just from the look on Nevyn's face—an icy kind of horror mingled with rage.

"This is serious, Maddo lad, truly serious. When did they come to you?"

"Just now. I came straight up here."

"Good, good. You did exactly the right thing." Nevyn began to pace back and forth across the chamber. "Ye gods, I don't know what to do!"

Maddyn's chill of unease deepened. For so long he had so blindly trusted Nevyn to solve every problem that hearing the old man admit helplessness was as bad as a death sentence.

"We've got to get out of Dun Trebyc," the dweomerman said finally. "But we've got to do so in the right way. We need to keep up our ruse of being a perfectly ordinary troop of mercenaries."

"Well, if we were, we wouldn't be leaving without a proper hire. No single jewel merchant's rich enough to engage a whole band of mercenaries. If he was, he'd have bodyguards."

"Just so. We'd best find a better excuse than me. I—who's that? Come in!"

The footsteps they'd heard turned out to belong to Caradoc, who came in with a bob of a bow for the old man.

"We've got to get out of here today, Nevyn. Been lucky so far, but I'll wager the town warden and his men are going to be coming around soon, asking questions about that brawl last night."

"I had the same thought myself. Hum. I think I know where I can find us a hire. Since I'm a merchant now, I'd best go pay my respects to my new god, hadn't I? I'll be down at the temple of Nwdd if you need me."

When the old man returned, not more than an hour later, he brought two merchants with him and prosperous ones from the look of the fine wool in their checked brigga and cloaks. Stout men in their thirties, the pair stood uncertainly near the door of the inn chamber as Nevyn introduced them round as Budyc and Wffyn.

"We might have a hire for you, Captain." Budyc stroked his dark mustaches with a nervous hand. "The jewel merchant here swears you're reliable."

"More than most, anyway," Caradoc said. "And every one of my lads can fight like a fiend from hell. I'll swear it on Gamyl's altar if you want."

The merchants exchanged speculative glances.

"They'll have to do," Wffyn said. "This time of year, it's a stroke of luck to find a free troop that isn't pledged to a lord already."

Budyc shrugged in nervous agreement.

"Very well, Captain. Name your price."

"A silver piece a man on contract, then one a week, two if we see fighting, and you pay full wages for every man killed."

Again the two looked back and forth, and again Budyc shrugged.

"Done. It's fair, and there's no time to haggle. Leave the city gates as soon as you can, Captain. I'll meet you on the south-running road."

"Where are we going?"

"I'll tell you after we're well clear of Dun Trebyc." Budyc allowed himself a scant smile. "This town is full of ears."

After a solemn handshake all round, the merchants left. Maddyn and Caradoc turned on Nevyn the moment the door swung shut.

"I can't tell you one blasted thing." Nevyn held up both hands flat in protest. "All I know is that they're Cerrmor men going south, and that they're both rich and reliable."

"Well, that should be enough, truly." Caradoc paused, thinking hard while he rubbed his chin with one hand. "Maddyn, make sure our young lad rides in the middle of the pack on the morrow, will you?"

"I will. I might detail Aethan and Branoic to keep an eye on him—personally, like. Give them a chance to redeem themselves."

"Good idea. Carry it out." The captain glanced Nevyn's way. "I was thinking of putting him between me and Owaen, but that'd look too suspicious."

"I agree. By the way, Captain, I heard all sorts of news down at the temple. I must say that the merchant guilds do themselves proud when it comes to hearing what there is to hear. The Cantrae king seems to be planning a major offensive on the eastern side of the border—round Buccbrael, the rumors say. He's been stripping the west of men for some big march, anyway."

"Splendid, if it's true. Let's pray it is."

"Provided he doesn't strike at Cerrmor before we get there. The extreme west has always been Cerrmor's weakest point, and it's doubtless worse now that the Wolf Clan's had to surrender their lands and go into exile."

"Uh, you know," Caradoc said. "The border's held a long time without the Wolves on it. They went into exile—oh, at least twenty years ago."

"Has it been that long? When you get to be my age, it's so easy to lose track of time."

Just before noon, the silver daggers left Dun Trebyc under a sky striped with scattered clouds that had everyone groaning at the thought of more rain, but it held off till they met their hire. About two miles down the road Budyc was waiting on a splendid roan gelding. When Caradoc slowed the troop, Maddyn fell back beside Nevyn, and the merchant trotted over and took the place beside the captain.

"We'll be continuing south till midafternoon," Budyc said. "Then heading west for a ways. Not far, though."

"How about telling us somewhat about this hire?"

"Not yet." Budyc rose in the stirrups and looked round the flat view as if scanning for enemies. "Still too soon. Tonight, Captain. Everything will come clear tonight."

When Maddyn shot Nevyn a nervous glance, the old man merely smiled and shrugged, as if telling him to rest easy in his mind. If it weren't for the prince, Maddyn might have, but as it was, he kept turning in the saddle and glancing back at Maryn. Since the road here was wide, the troop was riding four abreast, and Maryn was in the second file with Branoic on one side of him, Aethan the other, and Albyn just beyond Aethan—a formidable set of guards by anyone's standards. No doubt the young prince could swing a sword himself if he had to—he'd certainly had the best teachers that warlike Pyrdon could offer—but all that sunny afternoon Maddyn kept brooding on the painful difference between swordcraft on the practice ground and swordcraft in a scrap. Sooner or later Maryn would have to blood his blade, of course; Maddyn merely prayed with all his heart that it would be later.

A couple of hours before sunset the silver daggers came to a trail that led west off the main road, and Budyc pointed it out to Caradoc with a wave. Yelling orders, Owaen rode down the line and sorted the troop out into single file, with Maryn between Branoic and Aethan about halfway along. Although Maddyn was less than pleased with this vulnerable arrangement, the countryside around was certainly peaceful enough. As they jingled their way along, they saw two farmsteads, one herd of cows, and naught else but field after field of cabbages and turnips sprouting under the watchful eyes of crow-chasing small girls. At last, just when the sun was so low in the sky that everyone in the troop was squinting and cursing, they came to a deep-running stream, bordered by willows and hazels. Standing beside his black horse, Wffyn the merchant was waiting for them, and through a clearing in the trees Maddyn could see what seemed to be a canal barge tethered to the bank.

"There you are!" Wffyn sang out. "Good! First shipment just pulled in."

As Budyc trotted forward to meet him, it dawned on Maddyn that these men were smugglers of some sort, a suspicion that was confirmed later that evening, after the silver daggers had made camp. Along with Owaen, Maddyn followed Caradoc upstream to confer with the merchants on the morrow's route and found a line of four barges being loaded from a parade of wagons. Stripped to the waist and sweating in the torchlight, Budyc and Wffyn were bounding from barge to shore and back again as they gave orders to the crew or even leant a hand themselves to haul the cargo on board.

"Those look like ale barrels," Owaen remarked. "But I never heard of ale that heavy. Look at those poor bastards sweat!"

"Just so, and ale doesn't clank, either—it sloshes."

"What in the three hells is going on?" Caradoc muttered, somewhat waspishly. "And what?! Look at that lead barge!"

The cattle barge had slatted wooden sides, and just visible above was a row of cows' skulls stuck on poles and padded with wisps of straw. As the three silver daggers watched, openmouthed with amazement, a bargeman began wrapping the skulls with bits of leather, humming as he worked and stepping back now and again for a good look at his handicraft.

"At night and from a distance they look a good bit like cows,"

Budyc remarked as he joined them. "Enough to convince the passersby that we're a perfectly ordinary line of barges."

"All right, good sir," Caradoc snapped. "Just what is all this?"

"Know how the smelter masters weigh out raw iron up north? They say they have so many bulls' worth of weight—the measure's actually as much iron as you could trade a bull for back in the Dawntime, or so the guildmaster tells me. So that's what we've got —a load of bulls, and barrels of the darkest ale in the kingdom."

With a bark of laughter, Maddyn got the point of the joke and the journey both, but Owaen merely looked baffled.

"Iron, lad," Maddyn told him. "They're carrying smuggled iron down to Dun Cerrmor, and I'll wager they're getting a good bit more for it than a bull in trade."

"You could say that." Budyc preened a little. "But we're not making some splendid profit, mind. Think about it—we have to hire wagons for the dry parts of the journey, barges for the wet, and the country folk's silence, and then guards like you for the border crossing—it's worth our while, but only just, lads, only just. Then count in the danger. Why do you think we hired you? The Cantrae men'll stop us if they can, and they won't be making an honorable prisoner out of the likes of me. If it weren't helping to save Cerrmor, I doubt me if I'd make these runs."

"Tell me somewhat," Caradoc said. "Think there's going to be much left of Cerrmor to save by the end of the summer?"

"I don't know." Budyc's eyes turned dark. "We're living on hope alone now that the king's dead. Hope and omens—every cursed day you hear someone prattling about the true king coming to claim the throne, and the city still believes it, well, for the most part, anyway, but I ask you, Captain—how much longer can we hold out? The regent's a great man, and if it weren't for him, we'd have all surrendered to Cantrae by now, but even so, he's just a regent. Too bad he's so blasted honorable—if he'd marry the king's daughter and give her a son, we'd all cheer him as king soon enough."

"And he won't do it?"

"He won't, and he says he never will, unless someone brings

him irrefutable proof that the true king's dead and never coming to claim his own."

"Interesting, that kind of denial. Is he putting it about that he'd pay well for that kind of proof, like?"

For a moment Budyc stared; then he swore, glaring disgust at Caradoc.

"I take your ugly meaning, but never would Tieryn Elyc stoop so low, you—" He caught himself just in time. "My apologies, Captain. You're not a Cerrmor man, and you can think whatever you like."

"Oh, I was a Cerrmor man once, and I knew Elyc, you see, and thought well enough of him. I just wondered, like, what being elevated to a high place all of a sudden had done to him. One day he was just a lord with a smallish demesne; the next, practically a king. Some men can take that, some can't."

"True spoken, but Elyc's still got his feet on the ground. It's a good thing, too." Budyc's face turned wan. "Like I say, who knows how long the people can live on hope?"

It was well into the next morning before their strange caravan set out for the south. Although the stream was just deep enough to float heavy cargo, the current couldn't push it very fast, and so for the first stage of the journey the bargemen had their mules harnessed and pulling hard. Even so, the pace was dangerously slow. As the silver daggers let their horses amble along at their own pace, the line spread out into a ragged excuse for order along the streambank. Out of sheer impatience, Branoic thought he just might go mad before they reached Cerrmor.

"Ye gods, you look like you've bitten into a Bardek citron!" Aethan said. "What's making you so sour?"

"What's it to you? Go bugger a mule!"

"Br-bran, he's right," Maryn stammered. "Somewhat's aching your heart."

Since he couldn't bring himself to insult the young king, Branoic merely shrugged, wishing that he did indeed know what was bothering him so badly. Maryn thought for a minute, his eyebrows furrowing as he struggled to pick words.

"Leave it and him be, lad." Aethan forestalled him. "I don't take any offense. Branno, look—it's this cursed foul journey, never knowing if there's an ambuscade behind every bush or suchlike. I feel like I've got brigga full of burrs myself."

"Well, my apologies. You were right enough about me being sour. I wish we could travel faster."

"We will, we will. If I understand rightly, this stream widens into a proper river a few miles from here."

Although Aethan was right about the stream widening, it was nearly sunset before they reached water that was significantly faster-flowing. That night Caradoc posted a double ring of guards round the camp, and in the morning when they rode out, he sent point-men far ahead of them on both sides of the stream and rotating squads of ten men apiece on rear guard and in the van. Over the next three days, as they inched their way south, going from stream to stream and sheltering stand of trees to concealing thicket, caution became routine. With every prudent delay, even if it was only a brief wait to change point-men, Branoic's bad temper swelled like the black clouds of a summer storm.

That Owaen decided to harass him helped not at all. Maybe the lieutenant just needed something to pass the time, but it seemed to Branoic that every time he turned round Owaen was there to point out that his gear wasn't properly polished or his horse well enough groomed, that he slouched too much in the saddle or else sat too straight, that he looked sour as weasel piss or told too many stupid jokes. Since he was determined to win himself a silver dagger, Branoic gritted his teeth and said nothing to anyone. The last thing he wanted was to be known as a whiner. On the fourth night, when they were setting up camp in a bend of the river, Branoic went over to one of the barges to draw provisions and came across Owaen talking to Maddyn. Since Owaen's back was to him, and a lot of men were bustling around, the lieutenant never heard Branoic come up behind him.

"I'm not badgering him, curse you! He's just not measuring up," Owaen snapped. "What's our little Branno been doing, running sniveling to you and saying I've been persecuting him or suchlike?"

Branoic grabbed him by the shoulder, hauled him round, and punched him under the chin as hard as he could, all in one smooth motion. Owaen quite literally left his feet and flipped back to fall like a half-empty sack of grain into the grass. Swearing under his breath Maddyn ran over and knelt down beside him just as the captain came rushing up and half a dozen silver daggers crowded round to see the show. Branoic stood there rubbing his smarting knuckles and wanting to die or perhaps turn to air and drift away. He was sure that he was going to be flogged at best and turned out of the troop to starve at worst. When he felt someone's hand on his shoulder he spun round to find Nevyn, and much to his utter surprise, the old man was smiling—just a little, and in a wry sort of way, but smiling nonetheless.

"Arrogant little bastard, isn't he?" Nevyn remarked. "But you need to learn to control that temper, lad."

"Usually I can. There's just somewhat about Owaen . . ."

"I know. Oh, believe me, I know. Ah, here comes the captain. Let's see what he has to say about this."

Caradoc wasn't smiling in the least.

"Curse you, Bran! Haven't you got a lick of sense inside that ox's skull of yours? You could have killed him, slugging him like that! Broken his blasted neck! You had every right to challenge him, or come to me or suchlike, but to just—"

"Captain." Nevyn held a hand up flat for silence and arranged a portentous expression on his face. "Please, hold a moment! There are peculiar forces playing upon us, dark things beyond your understanding. I strongly suspect that our enemies have been trying to undermine us with strange magicks. Branoic is more susceptible to such evils than most men."

"By the Lord of Hell's crusted balls!" Caradoc went a little pale. "Can you do somewhat about that?"

"I can, if you'll turn the lad over to me."

"Of course. And I'll talk to Owaen—don't trouble your heart about that."

Nevyn tightened his grip on Branoic's shoulder and hurried him off before anyone could say a word more.

"My thanks, Nevyn, for getting me out of that. You know,

I've felt so odd and grim lately that I could almost believe I was ensorcelled, at that."

"You'd best believe it, because it's probably true."

Branoic swore, a brief bark of a vile oath.

"I'll admit that I was fancying things up a bit, like, for the captain's benefit," Nevyn went on. "But it's more than likely that our enemies are working on us with every foul sorcery at their command. If we start fighting among ourselves, their job will be much, much easier. Watch yourself very carefully, lad, from now on. If you find yourself getting into another black mood, come and tell me immediately."

"I will, sir. I promise with all my heart."

Yet, as he walked back to camp Branoic found that his spirits had lifted, just as if their enemies had stopped attacking now that their scheme had been discovered.

Since Caradoc was taking Owaen in hand, it fell to Maddyn to ride herd on Branoic, not that he minded the job, especially since the lad seemed to have put his sulk behind him. On the morrow morning Maddyn picked him, along with Aethan and six other men, to ride in his point squad. The country here was mostly flat, and some of the richest earth in all Deverry, thick black loam, well watered by the network of streams and small rivers that was currently carrying the royal iron down to Cerrmor. Before the civil wars, this area, the Yvro basin, as it's called now, had been covered with small freeholds, all marked out with hedges for want of stone to build fences; now they rode a long time between living farmsteads, and here and there they saw the black skeleton of a burnt-out house standing lonely on the horizon. Once the squad left the main body of the troop and Owaen with it, Branoic became his usual cheerful self, whistling and chattering as they rode along a shade-dappled lane.

"I hope the prince will be all right without us there, Maddo."

"Well, there's some seventy other silver daggers around him. I think he can spare the likes of us for a morning."

"I guess so." Branoic seemed utterly unaware of the sarcasm. "How much longer will it take to get into Cerrmor territory?"

"Two days, maybe?" Aethan joined in. "I heard the captain

and old Nevyn talking last night. Actually, we're probably on Cerrmor-held land right now, but we're still too close to the border to take life easy."

"Oh, we won't be taking life easy for years and years," Branoic said. "If ever again. The war's lasted for close to a hundred years already, hasn't it, and for all we know, it'll be another hundred before—"

"Hold your tongue!" Maddyn snapped. "Squad, halt! I hear somewhat."

Jingling and scuffling, the squad pulled up and eventually fell silent. At that point they stood in a twisty lane bordered with a hedge, tangled with grass and burdocks, but by rising in the stirrups Maddyn could see over it. Some hundred yards ahead the lane gave one last twist and debouched onto a wild meadow, where four dismounted riders were standing and holding their horses while they talked, heads together and urgent. Maddyn sat back down fast.

"Men ahead," he whispered. "Couldn't see their blazons clearly, but one of their shields had some kind of green, winged beast on it."

"Like a wyvern, maybe?" Aethan said.

"Maybe. Let's get back."

As the squad turned and retreated, Maddyn was cursing the inevitable noise, but if the men he'd spotted did indeed hear them, they never followed. It seemed to take longer than it should to reach the main troop and the barges; when they finally found them, Maddyn realized that the barges had been pulled nose into shore and tied up to hazels. Caradoc came trotting to meet him.

"Scout came in, Maddo. Looks like trouble ahead. Did you see anything?"

"We did, and that's why we're back. Looked like another point squad, and one of the men might have been carrying the green wyvern of the Holy City."

"The scout said he might have seen a Boar or two."

Aethan swore under his breath.

"Bodes ill, bodes ill," Caradoc went on. "Full arms, lads. We'll leave the barges here with a token guard."

"What about the prince?"

"He's safest coming with us. If this warband ahead's only on the track of the contraband iron, they'll try to outflank us and strike the barges, so there's no use in leaving him behind. If they're after him, as I somehow suspect they are, then they'll have to fight our whole ugly pack to get him."

"We'll want to circle around ourselves and try for a flank strike. There's a narrow lane ahead that could trap us good and proper."

"All right. Across the fields it is."

Heading south, they swung out to the east across plowed land that bore only nettles and dandelions. Since the fields sloped up from the riverbed, after a few minutes they were riding along a very low ridge of sorts and could see a reasonable distance ahead of them. To the south, on the same side of the river as they were, a warband was coming to meet them. Swearing under his breath, Caradoc flung up one hand for a halt, then rose in his stirrups to stare and count.

"About sixty, seventy?" he said to Maddyn and Owaen. "A good enough match, anyway. Well and good, lads. We'll make a stand and see if they come after us."

Just across a meadow was another thick hedgerow that would do to guard their rear, and in a shallow crescent they drew up their lines, two men deep, with Caradoc and Owaen in the center and the prince disposed anonymously in the second rank of the left horn, with Branoic on one side of him and Aethan the other. Even after all these years Maddyn felt faintly shamed as he followed their standard procedure and withdrew, taking shelter in some trees a couple of hundred yards away. For this battle, at least, he would have a crucial role to play as liaison between the troop and the fifteen or so men left behind to guard the barges. The orders were clear: if the scrap went against them, the survivors were to retreat back to the barges and die fighting around the prince.

Straight and purposeful the other warband came jogging along, pulling javelins from the sheaths under their right legs and loosening swords in their scabbards. There was not even going to be a pretense of a parley. The silver daggers sat slouched, from the look of them half-asleep in their saddles—a pose that had cost many a gullible warband dear in the past. As the enemies came closer, Maddyn could see that they were carrying a variety of blazons on their shields: the pale blue ground and golden ram of Hendyr to the north, the green wyvern of the Holy City sure enough, and scattered among them—indeed, in the majority as he counted—the red boar of Cantrae. Maddyn's stomach wrenched as he wondered how many old friends of his had survived the intervening years of warfare only to face up against his troop now.

As the warband drew up for the charge across the meadow, something else occurred to him with the force of a blow: this warband had been waiting for them, had indeed traveled hundreds of miles to catch them here, had somehow known exactly where to find them. He remembered, then, the rumors that the Dun Deverry king would be stripping the west of men—a ruse, a trap, to ensure that no loyal Cerrmor men would be within reach as the Boar lured the true king to this meeting of Wyrd. His heart thudding, Maddyn looked wildly around, wondering if he dared ride back to tell Nevyn. As if she felt his agitation, his blue sprite appeared on his saddle peak and grabbed one of his hands in both of hers.

"Go back to the barges. Get Nevyn. Get the guards. Hurry!"

Just as she vanished, the Boars howled out a war cry and led the charge. Sod flew shredded and dust plumed as they raced across the meadow, their captain pulling ahead to face off with Caradoc as the silver daggers threw their javelins in a flat arc, points winking as they whistled home, crossing paths with the enemy darts, flying just as straight and true. As the two captains met, both troops howled out a challenge and broke position: the mobs were joined. Cursing a steady stream of the foulest oaths he knew, Maddyn rose in the stirrups and tried to make out what was happening, desperately tried to find the prince in the swirl of rearing horses and shrieking men.

As he watched, he would just spot Branoic, whose height made him stand out above the mob of riders, when some squad or clot of fighting would swarm around him and lose Maddyn the view again, but he could never see the prince, who was one of the shortest men in the pack. He rode this way and that, on the edge of terror, wondering if Maryn had been killed in the first charge, while he struggled to see through the dust and chaos. Suddenly he realized that the fighting was coming to center on Branoic, that more and more enemies were struggling to cut their way toward him as more and more silver daggers peeled off to stop them. He could only assume that Branoic was desperately guarding Maryn—perhaps even a wounded Maryn—and without thinking he drew his sword.

He was just about to spur his horse down to join in the battle when he heard hoofbeats and shouting behind him. He turned to see the last squad of silver daggers, with Nevyn at their head like a captain, galloping straight for him.

"To the prince!" Maddyn yelled. "Behind Branno! To the prince!"

Howling a war cry, the men swept past him and down the rise to slam into the fighting from the flank. Nevyn pulled up beside him.

"Look, my lord," Maddyn gasped, half-hoarse from screaming. "Branoic must be trying to save him—that's where the fighting's thickest."

Dead-pale but as calm as death, Nevyn shaded his eyes with one hand and peered down at the screaming shoving mob.

"It's not Maryn they're after—it's Branoic! Ye gods, I should have thought of that! Ah by the hells—the ruse is torn anyway, and cursed if I'll sit here and not use the dweomer the gods gave me!"

With a snarl of rage the old man raised his arm to the sky as if he were saluting the sun with a sword, then slowly lowered his hand until he pointed straight at the battle below. Under his breath he muttered a few words in some strange language that Maddyn couldn't understand even though it sounded oddly familiar.

"Now!"

A thousand Wildfolk swept into manifestation and raced down the hill toward the enemy. When Nevyn shouted, blue and silver flames leapt from his hand and followed. Like bolts of lightning the illusory fire fell among the enemy horses just as the Wildfolk dove down from the air, pinching, clawing, biting beast and man alike. The terrified horses reared and pawed, screamed and danced, and the Boarsmen and their allies could do not one thing about it. Shrieking and bucking they broke. Those horses lucky enough to be on the edge of the mob plunged free and galloped away as if all the devils of hell were behind them; those caught in the middle began kicking and biting anything in their way. Owaen and Caradoc began screaming at the silver daggers to pull back and let them go. As the mob loosened its grip more and more Boarsmen pulled out of line and fled, the men screaming louder than their mounts as the Wildfolk streamed after, all claws and teeth.

Maddyn heard a strange noise. It was a moment before he realized that he and Nevyn both were laughing.

"I doubt me if they'll be re-forming for another charge," the old man said in the mildest possible tone of voice.

"True enough, and look, my lord, there's the prince, safe and sound and riding to meet you. Here, I'd best go fetch Caudyr and his wagon. We'll have wounded men down there."

Maddyn had only gone about a half mile when he met the chirurgeon trotting his team to meet him. They went to the battlefield together to find Nevyn already supervising as the silver daggers pulled the wounded free of dead and dying horses, while Caradoc, Owaen, and the prince held a hasty council of war off to one side. Since the battle had been so brief, the damage was small. A number of men were badly cut, but all in all, as Maddyn coursed the battlefield with a squad to look for prisoners, he found only three dead silver daggers, and a couple of horses so badly hurt that they'd have to be put out of their misery. Maddyn was just congratulating himself on their light losses when he found Aethan.

His legs trapped by his dead horse Aethan lay on his back near the riverbank. A chance thrust had split his mail and gone through his side to catch a lung. Although he was still alive, at every rasped breath he drew a bubble of blood broke on his lips and trickled down his chin. Maddyn dropped to his knees beside him and half kicked the horse away, half pulled him free, then slipped an arm around his shoulders to cradle his head against his chest. Aethan stared up at him with cloudy eyes.

"It's me—Maddo. Do you want some water?"

"Don't leave me."

"I won't. We've got to get Caudyr over here."

"Won't do any good."

Like a spear in his own heart Maddyn felt the truth of it.

"I'll make a song for you. Just like you were a lord."

Aethan smiled up at the sky with bloody lips. It was a long time before Maddyn realized that he was dead. He shut Aethan's eyes, laid him down, and sat back on his heels, simply sat there for a long time, staring at nothing, trying to put together a proper gorchan for Aethan and wondering why the words wouldn't come. Out of nowhere, it seemed, Caradoc materialized and knelt down beside him.

"He was a good lad. I'll miss him."

Maddyn nodded. When Caradoc laid a hand on his arm, he shook it off, and after a few minutes the captain went away again —Maddyn never noticed in what direction or why. All at once he was so tired that the world seemed distant and faint, stripped of all color and sound. He lay down next to Aethan on the blood-soaked earth, threw one arm around him, and rested his head on his shoulder. Dimly he heard his own voice in his head telling him that he was daft, that nothing in this world or under it was going to bring Aethan back, but at the time, reason no longer mattered. Daft or sane, he wanted to stay there with Aethan for a while, just a little while before they dumped him into a shallow grave on the battlefield. Although he was never conscious of falling asleep, all at once it was dark, and Caradoc was shaking him hard.

"Get up. Get up, or I'll slap you up. You've got to come away."

When Maddyn sat, Branoic grabbed him by one hand and the captain by the other, and between them they hauled him to his feet.

"Stay with him, Branno. I've got to get back to the prince. For the gods' sakes keep him from watching the burying."

Maddyn let Branoic lead him like a blind man to the camp upriver, where the barges were safely tucked into shore and already campfires bloomed in the meadow. Branoic sat him down by one of the fires, then rummaged in a saddlebag and brought out a clean shirt.

"You're all over gore. Change—you'll feel better."

Maddyn nodded like a half-wit and changed his shirt, tossing the filthy one onto the ground, then took the tankard of ale Branoic handed him.

"Those bastards on the barges had ale with them all along, but they were holding out on us. Old Nevyn made them hand it over. Said if we were going to risk our necks for them they could at least stand us a drink."

Maddyn nodded again and drank a few sips. When Branoic sat down next to him, he saw that the lad's calm was all a sham—tears were running down his face. Very carefully, very slowly, Maddyn set the tankard down next to his bloodstained shirt, then dropped his face into his hands and sobbed, howling like a child and rocking back and forth until Branoic grabbed him and pulled him into his arms to hold him still. Even as he wept, Maddyn heard his own voice rise to a keen, and for a long time that night he mourned, caught tight in the comfort of a friend's arms. Yet even in the depths of his grief, he felt that the most bitter thing was that Aethan had never lived to see Cerrmor and the true king come into his own.

"N-n-nevyn, I don't understand," Maryn said, picking each word carefully. "The enemy weren't after me. They wanted Branoic. I was p-p-protecting him—or trying to, anyway."

"Trying, indeed!" Caradoc broke in, and he was grinning like a proud father. "You did a splendid job of it, my prince. You can swing that blade like a silver dagger, sure enough."

Maryn blushed scarlet from the praise, but he kept looking at Nevyn, waiting for his answer. The three of them were sitting at Caradoc's fire, and talking softly to keep the rest of the men from hearing. Although he debated, Nevyn decided that after the spectacle he'd put on that afternoon, he might as well tell the whole truth of the tale.

"Well, my liege, it was an oversight on my part, though I'll admit it was a lucky one, all in all. I want both of you to keep this a secret." He glanced back and forth at prince and captain until they nodded their agreement. "Young Branoic has a natural talent for dweomer. Since it's totally untrained, he can't use it, mind—

he's not going to ensorcel anyone or suchlike. But consider our enemies, working in the dark, as it were, searching desperately for any trace they can find of the true king. Now, back in Pyrdon everyone knows what the prince looks like, but we're a long way from home, lads. And so, as our enemies here scry and work their spells, what do they find but a magical—oh, what shall I call it? Here, you know how a hearthstone will radiate heat after the fire's been burning for a good long time? You can see it glow red, and the air above it shimmers, like? Very good. Well, magical talent in a person puts out an emanation that's somewhat like that. So here's Branoic—tall and strong, a splendid fighter, a good-looking man—easy enough to mistake for a prince just on general principles, and on top of all that, he absolutely reeks of dweomer."

"They thought he was me!" Maryn burst out. "They might have k-k-killed him, thinking him me! I'd never forgive myself if they had."

"Better him than you, Your Highness," Caradoc said dryly. "And I know Branno would agree with me a thousand times over."

"Just so," Nevyn said. "You know, my liege, I'll wager they think you're the prince's page. Excellent. Let's let them go on wallowing in their error, shall we?"

"What shall I do? S-s-saddle and c-c-comb his horse on the morrow? I will and gladly if it'll help."

"Too obvious," Caradoc said. "We'll just go on like we were doing, Your Highness, if it's all the same to you. Seems to have worked splendidly so far."

"So it has." Nevyn thought for a moment. "Do you think I should go take a look at our Maddyn?"

"Leave him alone with his grief, my lord. There's naught any of us can do to heal that wound, much as it aches my heart. Ah, by the hells, he knew Aethan these twenty years at least, more maybe, ever since he was a young cub and fresh to a warband."

"That's a hard kind of friend to lose, then, and you're right. I'll leave him be."

For a few minutes they sat there silently, looking into the flames, which swarmed with salamanders—though of course, only

Nevyn could see them. Now that he'd rolled his dice in plain sight, he saw no reason to try to lie about his score, and Wildfolk wandered all over the camp, peering at every man and into every barge. Later, after the camp was asleep, he used the dying fire to contact the priests in Cerrmor. They needed to know that the one true king was only some three days ride away and that his enemies had tried to slay him upon the road.

2.

The year 843. We discovered that Bellyra, the eldest daughter of Glyn the Second, King in Cerrmor, was born upon the night of Samaen. The High Priest declared it an omen. Just as she was born on the night that lies between two worlds, and thus partook of the nature of both, so she was destined to be the mother of two kingdoms. Yet some within the temple grumbled and said that no good thing could come from such a birth that bridged the worlds of the living and of the dead, because she would belong to the Otherlands and only be a real woman on Samaen itself. She was, or so these impious traitors said, the lass who wasn't there. . . .

The Holy Chronicles of Lughcarn

In the very heart of Dun Cerrmor, at the center of all the earthworks and the rings of stone walls and the vast looming circles of joined brochs and towers, lay a garden. Although it was only about thirty yards across, it sported a tiny stream with an equally tiny bridge, a rolling stretch of lawn, some rosebushes, and an ancient willow tree, all gnarled and drooping, that, or so they said, was planted by the ancient sorcerer who once had served King Glyn the First, back at the very beginning of the civil wars. By hiking up her dresses and watching where she put her feet, Bellyra could climb a good way up into this tree and settle into a comfortable fork where the main trunk provided a backrest. In the spring and summer, when the leaves were draped down like the fringe on a Bardek shawl, no one could see her there, and she would often sit for hours, watching the sun glint on the stream and thinking about the history of Dun Cerrmor and her clan, and indeed, at times, about that legendary sorcerer himself.

Some years before she'd found a dusty old codex in a storage room up at the top of a tower. Since her father had insisted that all his children be taught letters, she'd been able to puzzle out the eccentric script and discover that her new treasure was a history of Dun Cerrmor, starting when it was built—some ninety years before the war—and proceeding, year by year, down to 822, when, much to her annoyance, the history broke off in midpage, indeed in midsentence. Over the past few years she'd used the old book as a guide to explore every room in every tower that she was allowed into and, by using a bit of cunning, most of the ones that she wasn't. With a stolen bottle of ink and reed pens that she made herself, she'd even continued the history, until almost all of the blank pages were full of scraps of information, gleaned from the scribes and the chamberlain, about the more recent additions and remodelings.

No one had ever noticed her poking around. For most of her life, no one had paid much attention to her at all, other than to make sure she was fed, clothed, and put to bed whenever someone remembered that it was growing late. Even her lessons, in reading, singing, needlework, and riding, came at irregular intervals, when some servant or other had time for her. When she was nine, her brother the heir died, and then, for a brief while, she became important—but only until her mother had another baby boy.

She could still remember the wonderful feasts and musical entertainments her father had given to mark the birth of a new heir. She could also remember the lies, the whispers behind his back, and the moaning coming from her mother's chambers when the truth became inescapable: his second son had been born stone-blind and could never rule as king. Just a year after his birth, the baby disappeared. Bellyra never did learn what had happened to him, and she was still afraid to ask. She had, however, recorded his disappearance in her book with a note speculating that the Wildfolk had taken him away. And now her father was dead, and her mother living on Bardek wine in a darkened bedchamber. There would be no more heirs unless she herself provided them to some man the regent and the court would pick out for her.

On that particular day she held the codex in her lap as she drowsed the afternoon away in the willow tree. She would read a few lines, almost at random, then daydream about how splendid the old days must have been, when her clan was strong and powerful, when its great kings had coffers filled with tribute and its mighty warriors had a chance of winning the civil wars. Now victory seemed profoundly unlikely, even though Cerrmor's loyal lords all told her that the gods would help them put her on a queen's throne in Dun Deverry. Every now and then Bellyra would look up through the leaves and consider the top of the tallest tower in the dun, just visible over the main broch. Once, or so her book told her, a hostage prince of Eldidd had languished in that tower for over twenty years. At times she had the awful feeling that she too would languish there, a prisoner for the rest of her life, until she died of old age and the Cerrmor line was dead.

"They might just strangle me, of course," she remarked to the tree. She often talked to the old willow, for want of anyone else to listen. "You hear about that every now and then, women being strangled or smothered to make sure they never have any babies. I don't know which would be worse, I truly don't, being dead or being shut up for ever and ever. The servants all say I belong in the Otherlands, anyway, so maybe it would be better to get smothered and be done with it. Or I could take poison. That would be more romantic somehow. I could write in my book, you see, as the poison was coming on. The noble Princess Bellyra raised the golden cup of sweet death to her lips and laughed a harsh mocking laugh of scorn for the beastly old Cantrae men pounding on her door. Hah hah, you dogs, soon I will be far beyond your ugly . . . ugly what? hands? schemes? Or here, how about, far beyond your murdering base-born hands. I like that better, truly. It has a ring to it."

The willow sighed in the breeze as if agreeing. Bellyra chewed on her lower lip and considered her plan. It would look splendid, once the Cantrae men broke down the door, if she were lying on her bed, her hair artistically draped across the pillow with a last sneer of defiance on her face. She would have to remember to put on her best dress, the one of purple Bardek silk that her nursemaid had cut from an old banqueting cloth they'd found in another storeroom. The Cantrae king might even shed a tear for her beauty and be sorry he'd been planning to smother her. On the whole, though, judging from what she'd heard about Cantrae lords, she doubted if they'd feel any remorse. Relief, more like, that she'd spared them the job.

Across the garden came a scrape of sound, the door into the broch opening on un-oiled hinges. She went still, her hands freezing on her book.

"Bellyra! Princess!"

The voice belonged to Tieryn Elyc, and through the leaves she could just see him, standing on the edge of the little bridge across the stream. To Bellyra the tieryn always seemed as ancient as the sorcerer of her daydreams, but in truth he was just forty that year, and still as lean and muscled as many a younger man, even though his blond hair was indeed going heavily gray, and fine lines webbed round his blue eyes.

"Bellyra! Come along, I know you're out here. The cook told me where you'd be."

With a sour thought for Nerra's treachery, Bellyra tucked her book into her kirtle and began to climb down. As the tree began to shake he crossed the bridge.

"There you are," he said with a low laugh. "You're getting a bit old to climb trees like a lad, aren't you?"

"Just the opposite, my lord. The older you get the easier it is, because your legs are longer."

"Ah. I see. Well, you know, you'd best take care, Your Highness, because you're the only heir Cerrmor has."

"Oh, come now. No one's going to let me rule in the female line."

"The point, Your Highness, is to keep you safe so you can marry the one true king when he reaches Cerrmor."

"And when, my lord, will that be? When the moon turns into a boat and sails down from the sky with him on it?"

Elyc let out his breath in a little puff and ran both hands through his hair. With something of a sense of shock, Bellyra realized that he was close to tears.

"My apologies, my lord. Oh, here, don't cry. I truly am sorry."

Elyc looked up, his eyes murderous—then he laughed.

"I feel as weepy as a wench, true enough, Your Highness. You have sharp eyes for one so young."

"It comes from living here, actually. You'd have them, too, if you had to grow up in the palace."

"No doubt. But listen, lass, for lass you are though a royal one, it doesn't do to tread on men's hopes when hope is all they have. Remember that."

"Indeed? Well, how do you think I feel, knowing I'll probably get smothered before I'm fifteen and even betrothed, much less married to anyone?"

Elyc winced, and for a moment she was afraid that he truly would cry this time.

"Your Highness," he said at last. "Cerrmor can still field an army of over three thousand loyal men. . . ."

"And Cantrae's got close to seven thousand. I heard you telling Lord Tammael that."

"You little sneak! What were you doing, creeping around the great hall when we thought you were in bed?"

"Just that. It's my hall, isn't it, since I'm the heir and all, and so I'll sneak around in it if I want to."

All at once he laughed in genuine good cheer.

"You know, Your Highness, at times you truly do have the royal spirit. But listen to me. Once the true king comes, a good thousand of those Cantrae men are ours again. Their lords have gone over to Dun Deverry out of fear and naught else, and they have a hundred years' worth of reasons to hate the Boars and their false king. Give them hope, and they'll flock to our banner."

"Well and good, my lord." She suddenly remembered that she was supposed to act regally at moments like these, not slang her cadvridoc like a fishwife. "Truly, we have great faith in your understanding of matters military."

Although it seemed to her that Elyc was suppressing a smile, he did make her a passable bow.

"Now, good regent, did you want me for some reason?"

"Not truly. I was just worried, wondering where you'd got to." He paused to glance round at the towering rise of stone. "You're probably safe enough out here."

"Unless an assassin comes creeping under the walls."

"Oh, indeed? Has the bard been amusing you with lurid tales?"

"He hasn't. Look, see where the stream comes out from under the wall over there? Well, that water comes from the dairy room, where they store the cheeses and suchlike. The running water keeps them cool in summer. But it gets into the dairy room through this underground tunnel that leads all the way outside the dun walls to that big stream that goes through the market district down to the river. The tunnel was built in 769 by Glyn the First when the sorcerer was here, the one who posed as a gardener to gain the king's confidence and . . ."

"Sorcerer? Don't prattle about some wretched sorcerer!" He was close to shouting. "I never knew about any cursed tunnel. Ye gods, Your Highness, this is a serious matter!"

"Well, so I thought. That's what I meant about assassins."

"We'll have to brick the tunnel up, or, wait, if things come to a siege, we'll need the water."

Muttering about portcullises and blacksmiths, Tieryn Elyc rushed off with barely a bow in her direction. Although Bellyra considered climbing back into her tree, her daydreaming mood was broken. It was also getting late; in a few moments the sun would drop below the circling walls, and the garden turn cold. She crossed the bridge and went inside a tower, climbed up a spiral staircase to a landing, crossed it to another set of stairs, which led down to still another door, which finally got her out to the ward. As she was going to the kitchen hut, she saw two of the scullery boys cleaning a butchered pig. Its liver lay steaming and bleeding on the cobbles.

"Modd, please, slice me off a bit of that liver, will you?"

"For that scraggly cat of yours, Your Highness?"

"She won't be scraggly when she's not half-starved. How's she going to have her kits if she can't make milk?"

When she gave him one of her most brilliant smiles, he relented, smiling in return, pushing back his forelock with a blood-crusted wrist and glancing round at the littered ward.

"Fetch me those cabbage leaves over there for a wrap," he said to the younger boy. "And we'll slice the royal puss up a bit of supper."

"She *is* the royal puss now. So there!"

The cat in question lived with her up in her chambers, the old nursery, which took up the floor above the women's hall. Half the round floor plan was filled by a single big room with a hearth, where she and her brother and younger sister had once had their baths and eaten their meals. Lying by the hearth were a pair of little wooden horses, left there by Caturyc on the night when he'd fallen ill. Somehow no one wanted to pick them up and put them away, even though he'd been dead for years. The other half was divided into small wedge-shaped chambers, one each for the children and one for their old nurse, who had accompanied Gwerna, Bellyra's eight-year-old sister, when she'd been sent off to an aunt's in a country dun—for her delicate health, everyone said, but Bellyra knew that they were keeping her safe, as the younger heir, in case Cerrmor was besieged at the end of the summer. As Princess of the Blood it was Bellyra's Wyrd to stay through the siege. She would have to be very brave, she supposed, and keep out of everyone's way.

Her own chamber held a single bed, a dower chest, one horribly faded tapestry on the wall, and the bottom of a cracked ale barrel that the carpenter had sawn down for her, ostensibly to make a bed for her dolls, but in reality for Melynna, a very pregnant ginger cat, whom Bellyra had found starving in the stables with a paw hurt badly enough to keep her from hunting. By now the paw was healing, and she was sleek again from being fed as many times a day as the princess could beg or steal food for her, but Bellyra hated to give her up, and Melynna certainly saw no reason to leave. As soon as Bellyra put the liver scraps down on the floor she lumbered out of her bed, lined with a torn-up linen shift that the princess had outgrown, and settled in for a good bloody munch.

"How's your basket of sand? Not too dirty? Good. When your kits are born, we're going to have trouble hiding them, aren't we? Well, I'll think of some clever plan then. I don't want anybody drowning any of them."

Melynna looked up, licked a whisker, and purred a throaty thanks.

Just outside the bedchamber, right by a window, was Bellyra's writing table, with her pot of ink, her stylus, and her pens laid out in a neat row. She laid the book down next to them, then sat on her stool and looked out the window at the main ward and the great iron-bound gates (built in 724 by Glyn the First's father, Gwerbret Ladoic), which were standing open to reveal the city street beyond. The iron hinges and reinforcements were rusty and pitted—iron did pit, in Cerrmor's salt air.

"It's all very well for Elyc to talk of putting in a portcullis," she said to the cat. "But where, pray tell, are the blacksmiths going to get the metal for it?"

At that precise moment, just like an omen sent by the gods, servants began running toward the gates and shouting in welcome. With an enormous rumble and clatter, ox cart after ox cart pulled into the ward, and from her high perch Bellyra could see that they were loaded to the brim with rough-smelted iron ingots. All round swarmed mounted riders, some mercenary troop, she supposed, hired to guard this precious cargo on its long, slow journey down from the north. She felt her heart pounding as she rose.

"O dear Goddess, do let it be an omen. It would be a splendid one, coming just like that. O dear Goddess, I do want to live to grow up."

She felt the tears pressing behind her eyes, hot and shameful. With a toss of her head she willed them away and ran for the door and the staircase. She should be in the great hall to welcome the merchants who'd brought her this treasure, she decided, be there and smile upon them and show them her favor, so they'd feel well rewarded beyond the coin her chamberlain would pay over.

By the time she reached the great hall, Tieryn Elyc, Lord Tammael the chamberlain, the seneschal, and the two stewards were already standing round the table of honor, up on the dais, with three merchants in checked brigga, two quite young, the other very old indeed, with a mop of thick white hair and a face as lined as an old burlap sack. Since everyone was arguing about paying for the iron no one noticed her make her entrance. Down on the floor of the hall servants rushed frantically round, trying to assemble enough ale tankards for the mercenary troop as the men strode in, laughing and talking, each with a dagger hilt made of silver gleaming at his belt. Bellyra hovered uncertainly behind Tieryn Elyc and waited for a chance to deliver her speech of thanks until, at last, the old merchant happened to look her way.

"Ah, the Princess of the Blood, no doubt," he said with an amazingly deep and agile bow. "I do have the honor of addressing Bellyra of Cerrmor, do I not?"

"You do, good sir." Bellyra drew herself up to full height and held out her hand for him to kiss. "You have our royal thanks for the risk you've run to bring us this black iron more precious than shining gold."

"Your Highness is welcome from the bottom of my heart."

Bellyra was annoyed to see Elyc smiling again, but the old man didn't seem to notice.

"And your name, good sir?"

"My name, Your Highness, contains a jest, but it's a name nonetheless. It's Nevyn."

"Just like the sorcerer!" She blushed, hating herself for blurting like a child. "I mean, I've read of a sorcerer with that name."

Elyc was downright laughing at her by then, and she decided she hated him, too, loyal regent or not.

"You'll forgive the princess, good sir." He stepped forward to take command of the situation. "She's a bit young for her position, truly, and—"

"Too young? Oh, she's not that, Your Grace, but unusually attentive to her lessons, I'd say. I've read the same book myself, I'll wager, because there was indeed a sorcerer named Nevyn who once lived in this very city—or so I heard." He gave Bellyra a conspiratorial wink. "Perhaps that's why my mother gave me that name, Your Highness, because it was famous in its own small way."

Elyc arranged a polite smile. Nevyn bowed and made room for the two young merchants to continue their earnest talk of due recompense. Bellyra could only hope that the treasury held enough silver to pay them; she rather doubted it. By then the royal warband was piling into the hall to see what all the excitement was about. Even though it was early in the spring, some of the lords faithful to Cerrmor had already brought their warbands to court, and they too appeared, the noble-born sitting down at tables on the dais, their men finding places on the lower level. Bellyra collared a couple of pages and told them to run tell Cook to get some sort of refreshments for the noble-born and to find the cellarer and fetch another barrel of ale for the warbands. As they trotted off she noticed that Elyc had left the discussion about payment to the chamberlain and wandered over to the edge of the dais. He seemed to be staring at one of the mercenaries sitting below. All at once he laughed and jumped down from the dais.

"Caradoc! It is you, by every god and his wife!"

Grinning in a stunned kind of delight, a man was working his way through the tables, a tall man with blond hair heavily laced with gray and hard blue eyes. Although he was filthy and unshaven from the road, he moved with such a natural dignity that Bellyra wasn't even surprised when Elyc threw his arms around him and hugged him like a brother. For the second time that day she saw the tieryn close to tears.

"You remember me, Your Grace?" Caradoc said.

"Don't talk like a blathering lackwit! Do I remember you? Would I ever forget you? O dear gods, you've given me one happy day at least in the midst of this cursed mess!" Elyc paused to look over the scruffy pack of mercenaries, who had fallen silent to watch all this with understandable interest. "These are your men, are they?"

"What makes you think I'd be the captain?"

"Knowing you so well, that's what. Come up on the dais with me. We'll have mead to celebrate this, we will." Then he turned and found Bellyra hovering nearby. "Well, if her highness would allow?"

"Of course, Lord Regent, provided you tell me who your friend is."

"A fair bargain, Your Highness. May I present my foster brother, Caradoc of Cerrmor, who was forced into exile by an act of honor and naught more."

"That's a fancy way of putting it, Elyc, but you always were a slick one with your words." The mercenary bowed to her. "Your Highness, I'm honored to be in your presence."

"My thanks, Captain. You and your men are more than welcome, but I don't know if we've got the coin to pay you what you usually get for fighting for someone."

"Bellyra! I mean, Your Highness!" Elyc snapped. "If you'd leave such things to me . . ."

"Ah, why should she?" Caradoc said with a grin. "It's her kingdom, isn't it? Your Highness, I'd be honored to fight in your cause for the maintaining of me and my men and naught more."

Bellyra decided that she liked him immensely.

"Done, then, Captain. No doubt you and your foster brother have much to confer about, and I shall leave matters of war to you."

Then she turned on her heel and marched off before Elyc could slight her again, only to run straight into the elderly merchant, who'd apparently been standing close by.

"My apologies!" she gasped. "Oh, I can't do anything properly today!"

"I think, Your Highness, that you're doing a great many things properly, and besides, you didn't knock me down or suchlike."

"My thanks, good sir. Everyone's always telling me I'm doing things wrong, but they never tell what I should do. Oh, it's so beastly, knowing everyone only wants you for your womb!"

She blushed, shocked that she could be so coarse in front of someone she'd just met, but Nevyn smiled and patted her on the shoulder.

"It must be, indeed, but your life does have a great deal more to offer. You've just got to learn how to find it. Come sit at the table of honor—not way down there! Take your rightful place at the regent's right hand." Nevyn pulled out a chair for her, then sat down at her left without waiting to be asked.

When Bellyra shot a nervous glance Elyc's way, she found him scowling at her, but with Nevyn for support she scowled right back and motioned him over with a wave of her hand.

"Your foster brother is welcome to sit at our table, at your left hand, even, if you so choose."

"My thanks, Your Highness." Somewhat unwillingly, Elyc obeyed her indirect order and came over to sit down with Caradoc following along. "May I order drink for me and my guest?"

Bellyra ignored the sarcasm, nodded her approval, then turned pointedly to speak to Nevyn. The noise in the great hall picked up in a buzz of whispers and speculation at the princess's rare appearance among important men.

"You said you read about this sorcerer in a book, Your Highness?" Nevyn said. "May I inquire as to which one?"

"It was just a record book of sorts that I found up in one of the towers. There's bales and bales of stuff crammed into the upper rooms, you see. Actually this was a codex, not a true book. The head scribe told me the difference, and he says it's very important. But anyway, someone—it never does give his name—wrote the history of Dun Cerrmor, when everything was built, and who lived here, and sometimes he even puts in what they spent on a feast or suchlike. And whenever he talks about the years from 760 to 790, he mentions the great sorcerer named Nevyn, who planted the old willow tree we've got in the inner garden and who ended up advising the king."

"Ah, I see. Well, by all accounts my grandfather was an amazing man, but I doubt me very much if he was a sorcerer. For a man to rise from gardener to councillor is very, very rare, Your Highness, and I imagine it must have looked like sorcery to some."

"Oh." Bellyra was bitterly disappointed. "No doubt you're right, good sir, but I had so hoped he was a real sorcerer! But still, it's rather splendid to get to meet his grandson after reading about him and all. I take it your family became merchants with the inheritance he left?"

"In a way, truly. I used to deal in herbals and medicinals, but the times are grave enough for me to lay aside my old trade and do what I can for the true king."

"Well, iron is the best medicinal for the army, sure enough. Do you really believe the true king will ever come?"

"I do, and with all my heart, Your Highness, I believe it will be very soon."

"I hope so. We can't go on like this much longer. I'm going to have to marry him, you know. I hope he won't be too ugly, or old like Tieryn Elyc, but it doesn't truly matter. Cook says that all cats are gray in the dark."

"I take it you and your mother will have no objections to such a match."

"My poor mother! The only thing she ever objects to anymore is her wine jug running empty. And as for me, well, if he really is the one true king of all Deverry, I'd be awfully stupid to turn him down, wouldn't I? I don't want to molder here the rest of my life."

"Your Highness has a very direct and refreshing way of expressing herself, and I think, if I may speak so boldly, that you're going to make an excellent queen."

"My thanks, good sir. You're the only one who seems to think so." With a sigh she rested her chin on one hand and looked away out to the floor of the hall, where the men were drinking and laughing over their perennial dice games. "But then, we've got a lot in common. You're named 'no one,' and I was never properly born."

"What, Your Highness?"

"I was born on Samaen—just after sunset, the worst time of all. The midwife sat on my mother's legs to try to stop me coming so soon, and when that didn't work she tried to shove me back in, but my mother hurt so bad that she made her stop shoving. So the midwife ran screaming out of the chamber and my mother's serving women had to deliver me. They had all sorts of priests in and everything to bless me straightaway so the Wildfolk or the dead spirits couldn't get me. I don't remember any of that, of course. They told me when I was older."

"That's an amazing tale! But you know, children are born on Samaen every now and then. Most of them are quite ordinary, too."

"I've always felt quite ordinary, actually." She pinched her wrist. "Rather solid, don't you think?"

"It looks that way to me, Your Highness."

By then the pages and serving lasses were bringing round baskets of bread and plates of cold meats and cheeses along with goblets of mead for the noble-born and ale for their men, including, of course, the mercenaries who belonged to Elyc's foster brother. Bellyra took a slice of ham and nibbled on it while she considered the regent and the captain, who were discussing old times with a deliberate intensity, as if they were trying to keep the present moment far away. Every now and then one of them would hit the other on the shoulder or arm, which she took as meaning they truly loved each other. Nevyn coughed politely to regain her attention.

"Have there been many omens of the coming of the true king, Your Highness?"

"There have indeed, good sir. Let's see, Elyc talks about them all the time, so I should be able to remember them. First of all, he's supposed to come before the last full moon before Beltane, which means he'd better get here soon, because that's tomorrow night. And then he's supposed to be from the west, but not from Eldidd. And then there's lots of stuff about stallions running before him or bearing him, which I think is truly odd, because no one rides a stallion as a battle horse. He's supposed to come in an army that's not an army, be a man but not a man—"

"Uh, excuse me?"

"Odd, isn't it? I mean, either you're a man or you're a woman, and there's not a lot in between, is there? But omens are that way sometimes. Let's see, what else? Some say he'll come as practically a beggar to his own gates, which I guess means Dun Cerrmor. . . ." She paused, struck all at once by a number of odd things. "Here! They say no one will be his herald."

"Do they indeed?"

"They do, at that. And a mercenary troop is an army that isn't an army, and that full moon is tomorrow night, isn't it?" She looked out over the hall, found herself staring at each mercenary in turn as her heart started to pound. She knew that Nevyn was smiling, but she was afraid to look at the old man for fear he'd break her hopes again. "A man that isn't a man? What about someone who's still a lad but who rides with the men and fights like one. He doesn't even have a beard yet, does he?"

"Who, Your Highness?"

"That blond lad over there at the last table, the one who's sitting next to that great big tall fellow with the scar on his face and not talking to anyone. Do you know his name?"

"The tall fellow's?"

"I don't mean him. Don't tease, Nevyn. Who's that lad?"

"His name is Maryn. It's a common name in Pyrdon, where he's from."

"The Pyrdon blazon's a stallion."

"It is, truly."

Her heart was pounding so badly that she felt it might thud into her mouth and keep her from speaking.

"What made you pick out that lad?" the old man said, and his voice had dropped to a whisper.

"I don't know. Or, you know, I think he's been looking at me."

"He has, truly. Her highness is a very beautiful lass."

"Oh, don't flatter! I know I'm plain."

"You're not plain in the least. I can see that until perhaps a year ago you were all long legs and stumbles, and your face must have been too thin and pinched—but that, Your Highness, was a year ago. We shall have to get you a proper mirror."

"I can't have one, but I'll make a wish that you're telling me the truth."

"Well, you know, there are times when wishes are granted." He paused impressively. "And times when they're not."

"Oh, you're only teasing me and naught more!"

"Wait, child. Wait and be patient for just a little while longer. I can't promise you that everything will be well and wonderful for ever and ever, but things *are* going to take a turn for the better and soon."

She hesitated, wondering why she trusted him so instinctively, but in truth, she'd simply never met anyone before who'd been kind to her.

"Well and good, then, Nevyn. And frankly, it'd be enough to know that things aren't going to get worse."

At a little cough at her shoulder she turned to find young Emryc, just twelve that summer and the head page. A copper-headed lad with squinty green eyes, he always looked down his nose at her as if he pitied her, and there were times when she daydreamed about having him beaten.

"Cook wants to know if we should start laying on the meal."

"Listen, lad." Nevyn leaned forward to intervene. "You should always add an honorific the first time you address royalty, and you should do it regularly after that, too."

"And just who are you, old man?"

Nevyn caught his glance and held it, stared at him and stared him down with his ice-blue eyes.

"My apologies, good sir," Emryc stammered. "My apologies, Your Highness."

"You're forgiven—well, for this time, anyway," Bellyra said. "And by all means, we've got a hall full of men so we'd best feed them. Oh, and tell Lord Tammael it's time to light the torches."

Emryc hurried off so fast that Bellyra found herself wondering if perhaps Nevyn's grandfather had been a sorcerer after all, and if the grandson had inherited a bit of his talent. The old man hardly looked magical at the moment; he was eating cheese and sipping ale, and yawning every now and then, too.

"It *is* getting dark in here, Your Highness," he remarked. "Must be nearly sunset outside."

"So I'd think, truly."

"Good."

"Is somewhat going to happen at sunset?"

"Wait, Your Highness. That's all I can say."

She had no choice but to do just that, wait and watch in an agony of impatience, as Lord Tammael made his slow round of the great hall, lighting the rush torches in their sconces and ordering the servants to push aside the chunks of sod in the hearth and mend up the fires that had been smoldering underneath all the warm day. When the light flared up, sending long shadows like spears across the hall, the warbands fell oddly silent, and Caradoc broke off his conversation with Tieryn Elyc to turn in his chair and look at Nevyn. The old man merely smiled, as bland as bland, and helped himself to more cheese.

"Do you bar the dun gates at sunset, Your Highness?"

"We don't, not till the midnight watch, because some of the townsfolk work in the dun and don't leave till late."

"Ah. Very good."

The torches suddenly seemed to burn brighter. Although there wasn't a trace of a breeze in the great hall, they flared up, and flames rose straight and steady with only the barest traces of smoke. Distantly, from somewhere out in the ward, she heard voices—no, it was chanting, and the sound of a soft drum. All at once bronze horns shrieked and blared.

"Priests!" Elyc whispered. "What by every demon in hell is happening out there?"

Before he could get up to see, the huge carved doors into the hall were flung open. The horns rasped out another shriek; the drums pounded; the chanting swelled. Walking four abreast the priests of Bel came marching into the hall, so many that Bellyra could only assume that every temple from miles around had assembled there in Cerrmor. They were shaven-headed and dressed in the long plain linen tunics of their calling, and round every neck was a solid gold torc, and at every waist glittered a golden sickle. In a long line they maneuvered their way through the crowded hall in time to the pounding drums and the long wailing chants from the Dawntime. At their head was Nicedd, the ancient leader of the temple, so old that he rarely walked abroad anymore, but that night he stepped as firmly as a young man up to the dais. Shaking a little, Tieryn Elyc rose to confront him.

"Your Holiness! Why are we honored this way?"

"Save your words, Regent! Where is the one true king?"

"What, Your Holiness? I don't know—I only wish I did—but I don't know."

"You lie! All the omens say that at this moment the one true king of all Deverry dwells within this dun. Where is he?"

The horns shrieked once; the drums fell silent. Every man in the great hall turned to stare at Elyc as if accusing him of the worst treason. The regent could only stare back, bewildered and terrified both.

"Bel has spoken this very day. Bel has given us omens. Bel has blessed us with true speaking."

"Blessed be the name of the Holy One," murmured the priests behind him. "Blessed be the Light of the Sky."

"When the Lawgiver speaks, all men and in truth all women too must listen. The one true king is within these walls, Regent."

Elyc tried to speak but failed miserably, and sweat was beading his forehead. Bellyra found herself considering her detailed knowledge of the dun; surely if the king was being held prisoner in some hidden chamber, she'd be the one to puzzle it out. Then she realized that during this mind-gripping ceremony Nevyn had slipped away from the table, and for the second time that evening, her heart started thudding in her throat. As Nicedd climbed up the three steps to the dais, the gold sickle swinging at his belt like a weapon, Elyc sank to his knees.

"Where is the one true king of all Deverry?" The priest turned on his heel to face the crowd. "He sits among you! Do you know him not?"

At the back of the hall Maryn stood up, a simple gesture, just a very young man standing up and tossing aside a dirty, torn cloak, but at that moment every person in the hall, noble lord and serving wench alike, caught their breath with an audible gasp. It seemed that the sun had returned to shine on him, just for a moment before it hurried about its business in the Otherlands; it seemed that a summer wind sprang up to breathe upon him, ruffling his golden hair and filling the smoky hall with the scent of roses; it seemed that the very air around him came alive, as if his simple presence were enough to fill the great hall with as much snap and power as a summer thunderstorm.

"Who calls for the king?" His voice rang out firm and clear.

"I do." Slowly and carefully Nicedd knelt beside Elyc. "Your Highness."

The crackling of the fires in the hearth seemed louder than thunder as the one true king of all Deverry strode the long way from the back of the hall and up the steps to the dais. Bellyra could neither cheer nor move nor even think clearly. Like a priestly chant words ran through her mind of their own accord: this is my husband, why didn't I comb my hair? When Maryn reached the dais, he stopped in front of Elyc and smiled at him with a boyish innocence that was like a flash of light.

"Am I welcome here, Regent?"

"My liege." Elyc tried to say more, but he was crying too hard. "O my holy liege."

Maryn bent down, caught the tieryn's hands in his, and raised him to his feet. At that the warbands could stand it no longer. They cheered and called his name and howled war cries; they stood and climbed on benches and tables; they began to stamp their feet while they cheered and screamed the more. Maryn smiled that same bewitching smile at them all, then flung up one hand for silence. As if they'd been rehearsed, every person in the hall stopped shouting. All at once Bellyra was afraid of him, this beautiful boy who seemed half a sorcerer himself, that he should ride in so suddenly and conquer them all without even unsheathing his sword.

"Men," Maryn was saying. "For this day I was born. For this day we were all born. This is the beginning. Some fine day there'll be a true king on the throne in Dun Deverry, and all the kingdom will be at peace. For the kingdom's sake far more than mine, let's every one of us pray that day will come soon."

When the cheers broke out again, a near-demented howling, Bellyra's fear turned to blind panic. No one noticed as she left the table and made her way through the shadows on the dais and slipped out the little door that led to a corridor. She stood in the darkness for a moment and felt the walls around her trembling from the cheers as if the very dun were in ecstasy at the coming of the king. Then she bolted, running down the corridor and up the stairs at the far end, round and round, up and up, until at last she could plunge panting into the safety of the nursery and her silence.

Out of habit some servant had lit the candles in the wall sconces and laid her childlike supper out on her writing desk: a bowl of bread and milk, another of dried apples soaked in watered wine and honey. Bellyra took the bread and milk to Melynna, then sat on the floor nearby and watched her eat. The cat's sides bulged, and she stood all spraddle-legged to lap her meal.

"You know what, Melynna? The king's here. His name's Maryn."

She actually looked up, licking her whiskers briefly, before she went back to work on the milk.

"Soon I'll be married, I suppose. And then one day I'll look like you do now. I'll only have one kit at a time, though. I'll bet men would like it if women could have litters like you do. They'd know straightaway how many heirs they'd have."

All at once she realized that she was crying. Even as she sobbed, she wondered at herself, that she would weep. Maryn was handsome, young, awe-inspiring, far more wonderful than she had any right to expect—she had never allowed herself to hope for so much, even to dream of so much in her husband. He'll never love someone like me, she thought, that's why I'm crying.

"Your Highness!" It was Nevyn's voice, soft and sympathetic, from the doorway. "What's so wrong?"

"He'll never love me, but he'll have to marry me anyway."

Although the room was all swimmy from her tears she could see the honest pity on the old man's face as he walked over, hesitated, then sat down next to her on the floor. Melynna looked up and went tense; normally she ran from everyone but Bellyra, but when Nevyn held out his hand, she sniffed his fingers, considered for a moment, then went back to slurping up the milk. Nevyn pulled an old rag out of his brigga pocket and handed it to Bellyra as solemnly as a courtier would hand over a square of fine linen. She blew her nose, wiped her face, and still felt completely miserable.

"Your Highness, Maryn is never going to love any woman, but he'll grow fond of you. I'm sorry from the bottom of my heart, but that's the way it will be. His one true love will always be the land and people of Deverry. I raised him, you see, so I know."

"You raised him?"

"I was his tutor from the time he was a child."

"Are you a sorcerer? Don't you put me off this time!"

"Well, as a matter of fact, I am."

"That's somewhat to the good, at least. I did so hope you were."

"I'll ask you, though, to keep the secret to yourself."

Much to her relief, Nevyn restrained himself from lecturing further. Unlike every other adult she'd ever known, he didn't wag his finger and tell her she should be grateful that the Goddess had chosen her for such a splendid Wyrd, or point out that most women would be glad to have any husband at all, much less a handsome one. He merely got up and stood looking round the nursery with a slight frown.

"Why don't you live down in the women's hall? You're certainly old enough."

"My poor mother is very ill. Or, well, to tell you the truth, she drinks Bardek wine all day, and then she weeps and throws herself from side to side and keens for my father, and then she starts in mourning my elder brother, and everyone says it's worse for her to have me there, because it bothers her that I lived when he didn't."

"Maybe I can cure her, once things settle down a bit. But I've brought jewels from Pyrdon to use as your dower-gift, and I think we'd best turn some into cold coin and outfit you a set of chambers of your own, splendid ones befitting your rank. Lyrra—may I call you Lyrra?"

"I'd be honored, Nevyn." She got up and curtsied, pleased when he bowed in return.

"Lyrra, your life will offer compensations, as I say, and there's no reason in the world that you shouldn't have them. For the first one, we'll get you out of this dismal nursery. Now, do you have any fancy clothes?"

"Lots, actually, but they're all on the shabby side."

"No doubt. Well, I know naught about such matters myself, but doubtless you'll know what you want once you've got the coin for fine cloth and all. Oh, and don't forget, now that you're going to be queen, you'll get to pick serving women of your own."

"Can I ask anyone I want?"

"Just that, and I'll wager they're all going to jump at the chance to live at court."

"Then Elyssa could come! That's Elyc's daughter from his first wife, you see, and she's my best and only friend. When it looked for a while like I'd have to marry him, the only good thing was she'd get to be my stepdaughter, which would have been truly odd, because she's fifteen. But anyway, after she's here, she can help me with clothes and furniture."

"It gladdens my heart that at least you won't be marrying Elyc, good man though he is in his way. Now, put on your best dress, and comb your hair down like a lady's. You can't wear it in a braid anymore. I've come to fetch you back to the great hall. Since the priests are here, Nicedd wants to solemnize your betrothal this very night."

"Are we to marry soon? I'll wager they all want me to get started on producing the beastly heirs."

"Considering your age, they may have to wait a bit, which will serve them right. But Maryn's going to have to go on campaign this summer. We've got to get you two married and him solemnized as king before Beltane."

While Bellyra changed into her purple dress and arranged her kirtle to hide the gravy stains from its previous incarnation as a banqueting cloth, Nevyn wandered off and found a serving lass to press into service as a lady's maid to do her hair. Since she had no mirror, Bellyra had to accept their word for it that she looked both lovely and years older with her hair combed down and clasped at the nape of her neck.

"Why don't you have a proper mirror, anyway?" Nevyn said.

"I'm not supposed to look into them. Since I was born on Samaen everyone's afraid that if I look into a mirror, I won't have any reflection at all, or maybe even I'll see a fiend looking back at me or some such thing."

"O ye gods! What utter nonsense!" He turned to the servant. "Here, lass, you run down to the dowager's hall and get a mirror. Now don't you argue with me! No doubt the dowager's fallen into a drunken sleep, and she'll never even know."

Even though she crossed her fingers to ward off witchcraft first, the lass did follow his orders, returning in a few minutes with a hand mirror of polished bronze glazed in Bardek silver. It took Bellyra a few minutes more, though, to overcome her fear and look. Although she knew she wasn't a fiend, she truly was afraid that she'd see nothing at all. Instead she found a remarkably pretty lass with wavy blond hair and big green eyes staring back with her delicate lips half-parted in surprise.

"Is that truly me?"

"It is." Nevyn got behind her and looked over her shoulder. "The reflection I see looks just like the princess I see."

Only then could she believe him.

As they came down the stairs she could hear a happy uproar, loud talk and louder laughter, from the great hall. At the little door she froze. If Nevyn hadn't been right behind her, she would have turned and bolted again.

"Come now, child, you know you've got the strength for this. When the priest asks you if you'll take him as your betrothed, all you have to do is say I will and let him kiss you—Maryn, I mean, not the priest. Kissing Nicedd would give me pause, too."

Bellyra managed a giggle, but only just.

When they walked out together onto the dais, men gasped and turned to stare. Everywhere she heard whispers: Is that the princess? Has to be, couldn't be, why here we never noticed how beautiful she is. She would never forget that moment; no matter what happened later in her life, she would always be able to pull it out of her mind like a jewel out of a treasure chest, the moment when she stepped through the little door into her womanhood, and the entire great hall fell silent to watch.

Maryn was sitting at the head of the table of honor, and some servant or other had found a cloak in the red, silver, and black plaid of Cerrmor to drape his chair, and a shirt embroidered with the ship blazon of Cerrmor for him to wear, so that when he rose to greet her he was already the king in the eyes of every man there. He bowed, caught her hand and kissed it, and smiled at her in a way that set her hand shaking in his.

"My lady," he whispered. "I'm lucky as well as honored that you're the Princess of the Blood." And then he winked at her, as cheeky as a page.

For an answer she could only smile, the blood hot in her face, and she felt as if she were falling from the highest tower in all of Dun Cerrmor, falling and falling, down and down into the little garden at its heart, falling toward yet never reaching the safety of the old willow and the tiny stream. He had conquered her, ridden in and captured her as well as the men without ever unsheathing his sword, and made her his prisoner for life. Although she was too young to see it at the time, only a few years later she realized that her Wyrd had given her an obsessive love that most women would have called a great treasure, but some, the wise ones, a cancer growing in her heart.

With the summer's battle season coming on, the priests lost no time in marrying the royal couple and investing Maryn as king. For a solid week both the dun and the entire city were given over to splendid festivities: mock combats, feasts, bardic competitions, guild parades, more feasts, regattas out on the harbor and dancing in the city squares. Wherever the new king went, the silver daggers went, too, as his personal guard of honor, all decked out in ship-blazoned shirts and red cloaks as a mark of their sudden status. Since the king had to attend every festivity, even if he could only stay for a little while, the troop sailed through those warm spring days on a drunken tide of laughter. Through the lot of them Maddyn wandered like a haunt, never smiling, talking only rarely, occasionally snarling at Branoic, who followed him everywhere, and then just as suddenly apologizing again. Yet even in his grief-shot rage he saw himself clearly, knew that part of his pain was the simple and certain knowledge that in time the pain would disappear, the mourning be over, and Aethan become only a memory kept alive by the death-song his friend the bard had made about him. In odd moments, when he could snatch a little peace from the celebrating, he would work on the gorchan and even at times get a word of advice or encouragement from one of the royal bards, who seemed to find his efforts at formal poetry touching in a child-like way.

Just after dawn one morning, before either the king or Branoic was up and around, he slipped off by himself to a hidden corner of the ward and sat down on a pile of old burlap sacks to tune his harp. He worked mechanically, humming out the intervals and tuning up the strings without consciously hearing himself, because he was thinking of all the times he'd done this job when Aethan was sitting nearby teasing him about how slow he was, or how sour the harp sounded, or other little jokes that somehow never rankled. All at once he was aware of being watched and looked up to find the queen herself standing nearby. She was barefoot, wearing a shabby pair of blue dresses, with her uncombed hair streaming over her shoulders, and she was carrying a bowl of milk.

"Your Highness! My apologies! I didn't see you."

"Don't get up and bow and all that. I just crept out to get a bit of milk for my cat. She had four kits in the last watch of the night."

"Well, my congratulations to her, then, but, Your Highness, you should have let a servant—"

"Oh, I suppose you're right, but truly, I'm not used to all this bowing and scraping, and having people swarm all around me all the time." She yawned, covering her mouth with her free hand. "Maryn was still asleep when I left. I'd best get back, I suppose. But how come you're sitting out here to play?"

"I just wanted a private spot, like."

"Well, come with me, and I'll show you a nicer one. It's supposed to be only for the royal family, but Maryn was telling me how much he honors you and Caradoc and Owaen, so you can use it, too."

Scooping up his harp, Maddyn followed her inside one of the towers, up half a flight of steps, down another, round a corner and through a maze of corridors, into another tower and out again, until at last he recognized that they were in a corridor that would eventually lead to the tower that housed the royal family. She ducked out one last little door, and they were in a garden, planted with roses and an enormous willow tree, all gnarled and drooping with age.

"There." Bellyra looked around in satisfaction. "If you climb up into that tree, no one can see you, although, of course, if you're playing, they'll hear you. I used to come here a lot, but I won't have time anymore." She looked briefly sad. "Anyway, you can sit on the bridge if you don't want to climb the tree, or just on the grass."

"My humble thanks, Your Highness. I wonder if I'll ever be able to find it again, though."

"Oh, ask one of the pages. Tell them I said you could come here. I'd best get this milk to Melynna."

She trotted off back inside, and Maddyn walked across the bridge and sat down cross-legged by the little stream. In the warm sun, sheltered by the rise of stone all round him, he felt a bit more of his grief ease. Aethan would be proud, he thought, if he knew I've gained the queen's favor. In a solemn crowd many-colored gnomes materialized around him, and his blue sprite appeared to hunker down near his harp and stare up at him.

"Oh, I'll heal, little one," he said to her. "But you ease my heart, you truly do, with your concern."

When she smiled, an honest soft smile instead of her usual malicious grin, for the briefest of moments he thought he saw true feeling in her empty eyes. Then she yawned, showing her needle-sharp teeth, and lay down on her stomach in the grass to listen while he finished tuning the harp and started practicing a few runs and trills. Since he was quiet and alone, Maddyn lost all track of time that morning; he stopped playing only when his stomach protested loudly enough to make itself heard over the music. By then he could see the sun over the high walls around him.

"Ye gods, it must be nearly noon!"

At the alarm in his voice the Wildfolk vanished. He gathered up the harp and went back inside, wondering if he could find his way to the great hall, but as he stood uncertainly at the foot of a staircase, Branoic came pounding down.

"There you are, you slimy little bastard! Where have you been? The whole cursed troop's hunting for you, and part of Tieryn Elyc's guard as well."

"What? What do they want me for? What have I done?"

"Naught, you stupid dolt! We were afraid you'd drowned yourself or suchlike out of grief."

"Oh, by the Lord of Hell's black balls! Have I been that bad off?"

"You have, at that."

Branoic was studying his face with a fierce intensity, as if he were trying to read every clue that might be there, no matter how small, to Maddyn's heart.

"Ah well," Maddyn said. "I wouldn't do anything that foolish, not when the king needs every man he can get. I'll swear it to you if you like."

"Your word'll be enough for me."

"Done then. You have it."

As they were walking out to the ward, Maddyn was wondering how much more grief lay ahead of him in the long wars. Branoic, Caradoc, even sullen Owaen in his own arrogant way—they all meant far too much to him for comfort's sake. A prudent man would have hardened his heart and sworn that he'd never let himself feel this kind of grief again, but then, Maddyn decided, he'd never been a prudent man, and he was too old to change his ways. Better to lose a friend than never find one, he told himself, truly, much better all round.

In the bright sun they paused for a moment while Branoic yelled at a Cerrmor man to tell everyone he'd found the wretched fool of a bard at last, and Maddyn happened to look up to one of the high towers. When he saw the young queen, leaning out the window and laughing and waving to him, his black hiraedd lifted a little more. At least she's happy, he told himself, and by every god, we'll all fight to keep her that way!

Some days after the wedding, Nevyn remembered the lead curse-talisman that he'd found back in Pyrdon and been carrying ever since. Although he hated keeping it, he was quite simply afraid to destroy it, just in case melting or shattering it should work some harm to Maryn by an induced sympathy. Logically, the act of magic that had created the curse should have had no true power, because it fell somewhere between outright superstition and the lowest rank of dark dweomer, yet whenever he held the lead tablet in his hands, he could sense a malevolent power oozing from it like a bad smell. Three times he tried to perform banishings and exorcisms; three times it stayed stubbornly the same. He tried meditating about it and scrying over it, all to no result. Whoever had charged it with evil had worked a spell beyond his powers to remove.

The question was, then, what to do with it. His first thought was simply to bury the thing deep in some out-of-the-way spot in the dun, but since it had been meant to be buried, he would possibly be increasing its power by doing so. If he left it hidden in his chambers, someone might stumble across it or even be actively seeking it. The enemy who had worked the spell was still at large, after all, as either an honest opponent in Cantrae's court or a traitor here in Cerrmor. Soon Nevyn would be accompanying the king on his ceremonial progress and his first campaign; if he carried the curse charm on his person, what would happen if he were captured and searched? It also occurred to him that if one of Maryn's friends and allies found him with it, he would have some hard explaining to do. He considered taking it to one of the great temples down in Cerrmor town proper, but priests had been corrupted or temples entered and robbed too many times before for him to consider it safe there. If he threw it in the ocean, its slow dissolution might perhaps work the king harm.

He wondered, too, if he should tell Maryn that the curse existed, but in the end he decided against it. For the rest of that summer, at least, Maryn absolutely had to project a supernatural air of confidence and calm if he were going to repair the shattered morale of his new kingdom. The slightest worry that might have tarnished his golden presence could well mean disaster later. Round and round Nevyn went on the problem until it occurred to him that there was indeed one person in the kingdom who could guarantee its safety, at least for as long as it mattered: the queen. She would never leave Dun Cerrmor until the war was over and Maryn crowned High King in Dun Deverry; if Cerrmor fell and she was captured, that disaster would mean Maryn was dead, all their hopes irrevocably crushed, and the lead tablet quite simply irrelevant.

That very morning he went to Otho the dwarf, the silver daggers' blacksmith, who had been given a big hut of his own for a forge and living quarters both. Even though he could trust one of the Mountain Folk to keep an oath of silence more than he could ever trust any human being, he told Otho only that he needed a strong casket of dwarven silver to contain something evil without ever mentioning what the vile thing might be. Otho worked night and day for the better part of a week and finally produced, on the evening before king and councillor were to ride out, an amazingly strong and heavy yet stunningly beautiful casket, with double walls, two locking lids, and a secret compartment in the bottom to hide the actual tablet.

"I'll solder up the compartment, and you put a few spells on it, my lord," Otho said cheerfully, "and the Lord of Hell himself couldn't get in or out of it."

"I believe you. Why, it must weigh close to two stones."

"Blasted near, blasted near. And I put all that fancy work round the top, just like you asked, so no one will wonder why it's in a lady's chamber. I rather fancy the way the roses came out, myself. The ladies do like a nice floral design."

"I like it myself, actually. Name your price, and I'll get it for you."

For a long moment Otho hesitated, shifting his weight from one foot to the other and back again, and from the agonized look on his face he was a man sorely torn and troubled. Finally he sighed as if his heart would break.

"Naught, my lord. Take it as a gift for the one true king and his grand little queen."

"Otho! My humble, humble thanks."

"Hah! I know what you're thinking. Never thought you'd see the day when I'd do a bit of work for free, did you?" All at once he grinned. "And no more did I."

That evening Maryn had one last council to hold with his warlords, and Nevyn took that opportunity to visit Bellyra up in the women's hall, which his great age would allow him to enter. He found her sitting in a high-backed carved chair, with her newly chosen serving women sitting round her and a ginger cat and four kits lying on a green silk cushion nearby, but even in her red silk dress with a queenly brooch pinned to her shoulder, she looked so young and lost that he had grave doubts about his plan. Yet he had no other choice, and when she greeted him, warmly and yet with the right degree of distance between their stations, he could see in her eyes the strong woman she would become.

"Your Highness, I beg a boon—a word alone with you."

"Of course." She turned to her women and dismissed them with a gracious wave of one hand. "You may rejoin us in a bit, and we can all have a nice goblet of wine or suchlike."

Smiling and curtsying, they all withdrew, and he could hear them chattering down the hall on their way to round up a servant to fetch the refreshments. Without waiting to be asked Nevyn sat down next to her and launched into his story, though he did omit telling her about the dismembered baby, just to spare her feelings. As she listened her wide eyes grew even wider, and she became all still attention.

"Will you take this thing and hide it, Your Highness?"

"I will, but I do wish you hadn't told me what it was. If this casket's got a secret compartment, you could just have shoved it in and sealed it up."

"You have to know what you're guarding, Your Majesty, and besides, never would I leave such an evil thing in someone's presence without their consent."

"Well, you're right, of course. Very well, I shall gush over the casket itself, and be very casual about what I put in it, as if it doesn't really matter much. And if ever anyone asks me for it, I'll refuse because to give it away would break poor stunted Otho's heart."

"Splendid, Your Highness! The exact right thing to say."

Yet even as he spoke, he felt a cold line of dread coil round his heart, wondering if he'd just given danger for a gift. Oh, don't be a dolt, he told himself irritably—the wretched thing can't have that much power, or you'd know! And sure enough, once it was bound inside the dwarven silver and sealed with his spells, he could no longer sense the slightest trace of evil leaking from either tablet or casket. On the morrow morning he and Otho together presented the casket to the queen, who in a fine show of being ever so surprised and pleased gave the dwarf a kiss, which made him blush and stammer and curse publicly—but from then on, Otho was the queen's man, heart and soul.

And together at the head of an army, Nevyn and Maryn set out on the long ride that later historians call the Rousing of the River Valley, the summer that would eventually bring lord after lord and warband after warband round to the new king's side and turn the hope of victory from an impotent dream to a sound gamble. Since he could foresee neither success nor failure that bright morning as they left the towering stone rings of Dun Cerrmor behind, Nevyn could only hope that he'd made the right decisions in more than the matter of the curse-tablet. Although the dweomer and the priesthoods had schemed and plotted and planned for many a long year, the matter was now far beyond their control. With the High King rode not their politicking, but his Wyrd.

The Wmmglaedd copy of the chronicle broke off in the middle of a page. Jill suddenly realized that gray morning light had overwhelmed her candle flame, and that her back was aching and stiff from her long night's trance. With a grunt of pain she turned from the lectern and found the fire dead in the hearth. Annoying though it was to lose the rest of the story, she didn't really need it, she supposed, because she could now remember the detail she needed. Otho the dwarf had made the rose ring for the queen to give to Maddyn the bard, years later, just as a token of thanks for some little favor he'd done her. In the closed and cloistered atmosphere of that court, where all the women were as confined and guarded as a treasury, there were those who had chosen to misunderstand the token, just—or so Jill suspected, looking back—to give themselves something to do. Whatever the reason, envy had come of it, and whispering rumor. What came of it she didn't know, though she could guess that the story had ended badly. In fact, as she thought about it, her ignorance was so complete that she could assume that Branoic had died shortly after the ring was made and given—in some battle, most like.

Those battles were long gone, their stories told by a thousand bards and chroniclers, but their repercussions still echoed, though it was two hundred years and more ago. And what of the other people involved? The young queen, for instance—would in time her soul reappear to add another knot to this puzzle piece? Jill felt that in its own way, the dweomer owed Bellyra a great deal to make up for that ancient tragedy. And what about those women who had helped move the tragedy along? They too had a debt to pay, perhaps, to the rose ring and its bearer. Otho the dwarf, of course, was still alive, though getting on in years even for one of the Mountain People. Did he still have some tie or bond with the ring he'd created so long ago? And then, of course, there was the soul once known as Maddyn—Rhodry of Aberwyn now—who'd been reunited with the rose ring and who wore it still . . . or again. With Nevyn gone, these problems were all hers to solve, these people hers to guard and guide. It was time she set about it.

Yawning and stretching, a servant came into the hut with a bowl of milk and bread and a fresh pitcher of wash water.

"Good morning, my lady. His holiness was wondering, by the bye, how long you were planning on staying with us? He's in no hurry for you to leave, mind. Just a-wondering."

"Tell him I'll be on my way this afternoon. I've a long journey ahead of me."

"Ah. Going to Aberwyn?"

"A bit farther than that. Bardek."

"Fancy that! A long, long journey indeed! Not going there alone, are you now?"

"I am. I suppose." She paused, considering. "Well, you know, there does happen to be someone I could ask to go with me, and it might be a good idea, at that. He knows the islands a fair bit better than I do. Hum. I'll have to think about this."

present

Consider the roots of a simple and mundane action, for instance, buying bread for your breakfast. A farmer has grown the grain in a field carved from wilderness by his ancestors; in the ancient city a miller has ground the flour and a baker prepared the loaf; the vendor has transported it to your house in a cart built by a cartwright and his apprentices. Even the donkey that draws the cart, what stories could she not tell if you could decipher her braying? And then you yourself hand over a coin of copper dug from the very heart of the earth, you who have risen from a bed of dreams and darkness to stand in the light of the vast and terrifying sun. Are there not a thousand strands woven together into this tapestry of a morning meal? How then can you expect that the omens of great events should be easy to unravel?

The Pseudo-Iamblichus Scroll

1.

The Knave of Flowers

*Bardek,
1098*

Down in the public square Luvilae's market spread
out, a lake of brightly colored sunshades and little
stalls. Acrobats performed on improvised platforms; minstrels sat in the shade of trees and
played for coppers. Wearing bronze helmets
topped with red plumes, the archon's men strolled
through in pairs to keep order. A warm breeze
carried the scents of incense and roast pork, flowered perfumes and spiced vegetables. Off to one
side, behind a line of stalls that sold blue and purple pottery, a fortune-teller was doing a reading
for a client. In the midst of striped and faded blue
sunshades and curtains, the two women haggled
over the price from either side of a low table.
Draped in black as befitted her trade in omens, the
elderly one sank onto her cushions with a moist
sigh. Dressed like a boy in a linen tunic and san-
dals, the young woman knelt on a pounded bark

mat and ran both hands through her mop of frizzy black hair before she settled back on her heels. Wheezing a little in the heat, Akantha took an ebony box from under the table and slid out the ninety-six tiles of polished bone. Most fell facedown, a good omen, but as Akantha turned the few wayward tiles over, one slid to the ground. With a frown she snatched it back.

"Help me mix them up, little one. Bring them over to the right side of the table—my right, that is."

Marka laid both hands flat on the layer of tiles and mixed with a sound like thunder.

"Enough," Akantha said at last. "Draw five to start with."

The old woman turned the chosen tiles faceup to form a square. The two of spears and the four of golds appeared, followed by three different tiles from the suit of flowers: the knave, the six, and finally the princess, which Akantha laid in the center of the square.

"Is that me?" Marka asked.

"It might be, it might be—or else, you will someday serve the princess. Not sure which yet. But I don't much like the look of this knave. Hum. A lover, maybe; he's the same suit, but he's no prince, is he? Watch out for him, girl. I do like the look of this six. Good fortune, girl, very good fortune indeed, though not without some trouble." She laid a long and bony forefinger on the two of spears. "But nothing your wits won't be able to get you out of, I'd say. Three flowers in the first draw is very lucky, very lucky. Now draw me four groups of three."

Each group formed a triangle. For a long time Akantha sucked her teeth in silence while she studied the layout; once or twice she started to speak, then merely shook her head. Marka knew just enough about the tiles to understand that the expanded reading simply wasn't coalescing into a whole. Omens of splendid good luck lay right next to signifiers of the grimmest bad fortune, while the minor, numbered tiles contradicted all the important trumps around them. The first was the three of flowers.

"Well, then, the reading should be a good one. Here's a flower coming up from the Earth. Now, we've got the nine of swords for Air, so you're in for a bit of rough sailing, sure enough. And now for Water we've got the queen of birds, which is not the kind of location I'd like to see for that tile. No, water and birds aren't a happy marriage, girl, not at all. But well, look at this! For Fire here's the ten of golds! Very good luck, the best there is. And finally, for the Ether, we have the . . . the prince of Swords? Oh, by the Star Goddesses themselves! This isn't making sense again. Listen, young Marka, sometimes the gods just don't want us to know the future. That's all there is to it. Don't you pay one bit of attention to anything I've said this morning, and as for your money, come back after dark and I'll try again for free. Sometimes letting the sun set on a reading changes things."

"Thank you, but I can't. We'll be putting on our show once it's dark."

"Ah. You're one of that bunch from Main Island, then?"

"Yes. I do the slack wire. I mean, I used to." She stopped herself just in time from venting all her bitterness on this sympathetic if hired ear. "I juggle now."

As she hurried away, Marka tried to leave the reading behind, but its bad aura hung round her like a wet cloak. Nothing, it seemed, was going right these days, not even a simple thing like getting her fortune told. Although Luvilae was the capital of Zama Mañae, the southernmost island in the Orystinnian archipelago, at a mere twenty thousand inhabitants it was not the sort of place where a wandering troupe of acrobats could make its fortune. Marka wondered why her father had brought them there, but then, these days her father did a lot of things that made no sense. She felt a constant dread, a line of ice down her back, a knowledge that she refused to face. He promised, she would think, it couldn't be that again.

She forced her mind away from old memories with a wrench of will. She'd been sent into town, after all, for more important reasons than just hearing her fortune. She bought a chunk of roast pork on a stick and wandered round, nibbling her meal and looking over the other street performers at the fair. The only jugglers she saw were clumsy; there were no slackrope walkers at all. Although she found a band of tumblers, they couldn't compete with the complex routines that the men in her troupe performed. Most

of the solitaires were musicians. Overall, the best show she saw in
that first look round featured trained monkeys and apes.

As she was buying herself a piece of sugared cake, she noticed
a small crowd gathering off to one side in the shade of a big plane
tree. The cake seller gestured with snow-white fingers, all sticky
from her wares.

"If that's the barbarian, you should take a look at him. Puts
on a good show, though I swear the man's demented!"

Marka went over, paying as much attention to the cake as
anything, since it was impossible to eat without getting sugar all
over her chin. She found a spot off to one side, but at first she
could only see scarves flying into the air above the heads of the
crowd and hear the fellow's patter, a running mix of topical jokes
and sheer nonsense, all delivered in a musical voice without any
foreign accent whatsoever. She assumed that his barbarism was
nothing more than a good costume until she wormed her way
closer to the front.

For a moment she could only gawk openmouthed. Never in
her life had she seen anyone so pale, as if he'd been bleached like a
strip of linen soaked in lemon juice and left in the summer sun. His
skin was a light pinky-beige, and his hair, as fine and straight as
silk thread, was the silvery color of moonbeams with just the
barest hint of yellow in it by contrast with his steel-gray eyes. He
was wearing a strange sort of tunic, with long, full sleeves, and
gathered into a yoke at the shoulders and belted over a peculiar
garment that encased his legs in baggy tubes of blue cloth. So he
was indeed one of those fabled barbarians from the savage kingdoms far to the north! It took Marka a few moments to recover
from his appearance before she could appreciate his skill.

And skill he had. In his long, slender hands the silk scarves
seemed to come alive, whisking through the air, floating up only to
plummet down, circling round and round or weaving in and out
while he kept up his stream of jokes and snatches of song. Watching him, she was bitterly aware of what a beginner she was at
juggling and how clumsy she was going to look when her turn
came to perform. When he paused, looking significantly at the
crowd, a rain of coins flew his way. Laughing and bowing, he

flicked the scarves into his sleeves, then hunkered down to pick up the coins, making them fly round his head in a little stream before they all disappeared into his clothes.

"The Great Krysello is pleased!" he announced. "Allow him to delight your noble selves with his humble tricks for a little while longer."

When he bowed again, three eggs seemed to appear out of nowhere and settle into his hands. Before he began this new routine, he happened to glance Marka's way. His eyes widened; he broke into a smile of pure delight; then he wiped the smile away and turned firm attention to his performance. Marka felt utterly flabbergasted. Although she knew that she was a pretty girl, she'd never had a man look at her that way before, as if the very sight of her had made him happy beyond dreaming. Her second thought was that there was powdered sugar all over her face. Blushing furiously, she elbowed her way through the crowd and fled the Great Krysello and his smiles.

She found the public fountain and washed the sugar off, then headed for the city-owned caravanserai at the edge of town. The troupe had four tents and two wagons of its own, set up in a circle under some palm trees at the edge of the campground. It was better to stay away from other travelers, always quick to accuse wandering showmen of being thieves. The five acrobats were practicing their tumbling turns behind the tents, while their leader, Vinto, watched and commented. Out in the middle of the tent circle a big cooking fire was burning. Marka's stepmother, Orima, along with the two other women in the troupe, Delya and Keeta, were stewing spiced vegetables in a hanging pot and slapping rounds of thin bread onto an enormous iron griddle. They fell silent when Marka came up.

"What's wrong, Rimi?"

"Nothing. What makes you say that?"

Marka hesitated on the edge of forcing a confrontation. Orima's dark eyes turned narrow. In the silence Marka could hear the sea booming on the nearby shore and the men chanting out practice cadences.

"Where's Father?"

"Sleeping." She turned away, frowning into the pot. "He's resting before the show tonight."

Before Marka could say anything more, Keeta came up behind her, grabbed her elbow, and steered her away from the campfire. Arguing with enormously tall Keeta, who was as strong as two average men, was a waste of time.

"If you're going to learn how to catch a flaming torch," she said, and firmly, "you've got to start practicing."

They walked to the edge of the sea cliff and stood for a while, looking down at the waves rising higher and higher on the graveled beach. Far off at the horizon the sea made a line like a stretched wire, perfectly flat and landless. Sail far enough to the south, or so Marka had always been told, and you'd come to an enormous waterfall, pouring down into the fiery underworld where the sea boiled off. The water rose again as clouds of steam to make the rain and start the cycle all over again.

"You don't really want to give me a lesson now, do you?" Marka said at last.

"Well, yes, actually I do." Keeta grinned, a flash of white teeth in her dark face. "But I also happen to be sick of hearing you fight with your mother."

"That woman is not my mother, thank you very much."

Keeta sighed sharply.

"Well, how much older than me is she, anyway? Four years, five? How do you expect me to—"

"I don't expect you to do anything." Keeta held one huge hand up for silence. "Except to try not to make things worse. Listen, I know she lords it over you. She lords it over everyone, doesn't she? But we're in a very bad position, stuck here at the edge of nowhere. Your father won't even talk about money. I'm willing to bet that there's not a lot left to talk about."

All at once Marka felt sick to her stomach. She sat down in the scruffy grass and stared fixedly out to sea. After a few minutes Keeta hunkered down next to her with a dramatic sigh.

"You're old enough to know these things now. If the audience gives you special tips, keep them hidden, will you? Don't turn them over to your father. I'm doing the same. We might all need a few extra coins if we're ever going to see Main Island again."

"All right."

"I wonder what's he doing with it?" Keeta got up and stretched. "Spending it all on *her*?"

"Probably." Marka felt the ice-knowledge again, slicing down her spine. You should tell her, she thought, you should tell her the truth right now. Saying the words aloud would mean admitting the truth to herself, as well.

After a long moment Keeta sighed and shook her head.

"Well, let's practice. Some sticks of driftwood are what we want, something unbalanced like the torches."

As Marka followed her down to the beach, she was feeling like the worst coward in the world. But I've got to be sure. I can't tell anyone till I'm sure. That, at least, was her excuse.

A good session's practice with a friend turned Marka as sunny as the day, but when they got back to the campground, she found her father awake, or just barely awake. He came stumbling out of the tent, yawning hugely, rubbing his sticky eyes, and glancing round him with a stupid sort of smile that made him look like a stunned ox. Hamil was as tall as Keeta, and much stockier, a handsome man with his wide black eyes and full mouth, his close-cropped curly hair just touched at the temples with distinguished gray. But just lately he'd been looking old, his eyes often distant or glazed, his speech slow, and he'd been putting on a flabby kind of fat round the middle.

"Marka?" Hamil said. "Did you work over the market?"

"Yes, just about an hour ago. There were only two acts to worry about. One has apes and monkeys, and there's nothing we can do about that. And then there's this juggler, but he's just a single player. I've never seen anybody throw scarves the way he does. He's really fantastic."

"Oh, really?" Orima said with a simper. "Maybe we should prentice you out to him."

Marka opened her mouth for a smart reply, but she noticed Keeta, standing behind her father and stepmother and shaking her head grimly.

"He could teach us all something," Marka said instead. "The best thing is, he's a barbarian. A real northern barbarian."

"A draw in itself." With one last yawn Hamil ambled over to the fire circle and sat down on a low stool near his wife. "Huh. Wonder if he wants to join up with a bigger outfit. We could use a new draw."

"If he's that good, he doesn't need to split his take with anyone." Keeta came forward and joined the circle. "Maybe we should try monkeys."

"Smelly things. And they bite," Orima broke in. "And they leave messes all over. It's all that fruit they eat. I wouldn't want them in my troupe."

"If you ever get your own troupe," Marka snapped. "You can decide then."

"Marka!" Hamil and Keeta snapped in unison. Hamil went on alone. "You apologize to your stepmother."

"For what?"

Hamil got up, raising one broad hand.

"I'm sorry, Rimi."

Orima simpered and sneered; everyone else in the circle looked awkwardly away; Hamil sat down again.

"I'm going to practice some more."

As Marka turned on her heel and strode off, she was wondering if she could murder Orima and get away with it. The thought was so strong that it terrified her.

"It *is* her, O Puissant Princess of Powers Perilous," Salamander said. "Would the Great Krysello be mistaken over a matter of such grave import? Of course not. I saw her, I tell you: my own beloved Alaena, reborn and come back to me."

"I have my doubts," Jill said. "There hasn't really been enough time, you know, since her last life."

Salamander turned sulky and devoted himself to pouring more wine. They were sitting in the best inn chamber that Luvilae had to offer—a palace by Jill's standards though close to a hovel by his—a small room with a chipped tile floor, scattered with cushions for want of furniture. Jill took one of the flat wine cups from him and considered the problem.

"I don't mean to stir up painful memories." She made her voice as gentle as she could. "But how long has Alaena been gone?"

"Thirty years. Well, almost. Well, maybe a score and eight."

"How old is this lass, anyway?"

"Uh, well, sixteen or so."

"That's not much time as the Lords of Wyrd reckon time. It's possible, of course—just not likely."

"I know, I know, but I keep thinking, ye gods, our marriage lasted but such a little while! She would have wanted to come back as soon as she could."

"For your sake I suppose?"

He winced.

"Not for me," he said at last. "But because she loved life so much."

Jill wondered if she could ever be objective in this situation. Since she herself seemed to be destined to lose every man that she allowed herself to love, she refused to let her own bitterness spoil his chance to be happy. He sat frowning into his goblet until the, for him, bizarre silence got on her nerves.

"Does her family live here in town?"

"Um?" He looked up, startled. "My apologies. What did you say?"

"Your heart is really troubled, isn't it?"

"I'll admit to that. I was just remembering when Alaena died."

He got up and paced over to the one small window, leaned against the sill, and stared fixedly out at the courtyard below. Old grief turned his unnaturally handsome face slack. Jill waited for the tale and his usual flood of words. It never came.

"Does her family live here in town?" she repeated.

"It doesn't. I did a bit of asking round in the market before I came back here. She is—of all things—an acrobat. One of a troupe of acrobats just come from Main Island." As he turned back a glossy smile smoothed and masked his face. "Fancy that! I've heard of strange and solemn twists and turns of wild and wandering Wyrd before, but this—"

"Hold your tongue, will you? I suppose there's no harm in

getting to know her a bit. But for the sake of all the gods, will you try to remember this? That even if by some bizarre chance this is the soul you knew as Alaena, she isn't the same person anymore. You have no idea what this child is like. None."

"True enough, much as it aches my eager heart."

There were times when Salamander could irritate Jill beyond belief, and this was one of them. For all that his half-elven blood kept him looking young, he was fifty-some years older than she, but although he'd started studying their mutual craft of the dweomer long before she'd been born, she'd so far overtaken him that she was, in a very real though unspoken way, the master now to his journeyman. Though he acknowledged her authority, which came ultimately from Nevyn himself, it didn't take dweomer to see that he resented it as well.

"You're truly angry with me, aren't you?" Salamander wiped his smile away.

"Ye gods! You promised me you were going to devote yourself to your studies, but you've kept finding one cursed distraction after another. Now this! And there's the lass to consider, too, you know. She's but a child."

"Old enough to have been married for years in Deverry."

"This isn't Deverry."

"I was afraid you were going to say that. Jill, is it me you're angry with, or is it everything? The delay, I mean. We've been wandering round Bardek for months and months, finding but a trace here and there of the things you want to know."

Jill took a deep breath and considered.

"There's that, indeed. Patience has never been my right-hand weapon, has it?"

"And now glorious Luvilae has been but another dead trail, a road with no ending, a house with no doors, a—"

"One wretched image is enough, please. But there's still that bookseller in Inderat Noa. I have hopes of him."

"I suppose you'll want to head back there straightaway."

"I was thinking of it, truly. Why not? Oh, of course. The lass. I suppose you want to spend a few days sniffing round her."

"How crudely you put things!" He grinned, tucking his

thumbs into his belt and leaning back against the wall. "But I did think I might take a stroll in the marketplace tonight. No doubt her troupe performs in the evening, when it's cooler."

When it came time for the show, it seemed at first that the gods were going to grant them a decent take. In the cool of the evening a big crowd gathered in front of their improvised stage, set up between two trees to support the slack wire. As the men raised the huge standing torches and Marka ran round lighting them, she noticed a number of fairly well-dressed people in the crowd, the kind who looked like they weren't above throwing some small change to a street performer. Best of all, her father was wide-awake and alert, laughing and joking with the troupe as they gathered backstage. The first turns went well, too, her own juggling, the apprentice tumblers, and Keeta's routine with the flaming torches. When the troupe broke to sling the slack wire, coins came in a copper shower, but here and there Marka plucked a silver one.

With great ceremony the flute boy and the drummer sat down cross-legged at the edge of the stage, paused a moment, then began the music for the centerpiece of the show, the slack rope routine. Wiping her face on a scarf, Marka stood off to one side and watched the crowd more than the show. Until Orima came along, the slack rope had been her own turn, one she'd learned as a small child from her mother and at which she was particularly skilled. A cow prancing on a string—that's our Rimi, she thought to herself. Then she saw, standing off toward the back, the barbarian juggler. Her heart thudded, her fingers tightened on the scarf, and she couldn't understand why in the least, except, perhaps, that he was so handsome. All at once he noticed her watching and smiled right at her. Blushing furiously, hating herself for it, she turned away.

Dressed in a brief but flowing silk tunic over a loincloth, Orima was just approaching the wire-wound rope, which hung loosely between the twin wooden towers of the mounting platforms, a good six feet above the stage itself. With a big smile for the crowd she climbed up and did a back flip on the platform. She bowed—several times too many in Marka's estimation—then took the balance pole and leapt to the rope for a graceful half run across, balancing in the middle. When the crowd cheered and clapped, she executed a good turn, and ran back to the platform so lightly and easily that the crowd yelled in delight. Marka could practically taste her own anger, a black bile in her mouth. As Orima mounted the rope again, she hesitated for the barest second, just the split of a moment too long. The rope swung, then snapped back; her lead foot groped and grabbed—too late. With a shriek she fell, landing spraddled on all fours, unhurt but furious as the crowd burst out laughing. Swearing under his breath Hamil rushed to help her up while the tumblers ran back on stage and hurled themselves into an improvised routine. It was no good. Laughing and chuckling, calling out a few insults, the crowd broke up and drifted away, and they didn't bother to throw a single coin behind them, not even for good luck.

In a sullen silence, barely able to look at each other, the troupe doused the torches, stripped the stage, and loaded everything into the wagons while Orima cowered under a nearby palm. Marka was frankly terrified, blaming her ill will for the fall even as she told herself, over and over, that such things were impossible. Much to her relief, no one mentioned the fall until they got back to the campground, where Delya and young Rosso were keeping an eye on the tents. While the men tended the horses and wagons, Hamil and the women drifted miserably over to the fire. Delya took one good look at their faces and said nothing. The silence grew until Orima screwed her face in a pout and pointed one painted fingernail at Marka.

"She hexed me!" Orima screeched. "Your precious little daughter hexed me! She's got the evil eye."

"Oh, don't be ridiculous!" Hamil snapped. "We all fall now and then."

"She's got the evil eye!" Orima stamped one slender foot.

"Will you shut up? If your head wasn't so empty you might have better balance on the rope."

"You pig! You filthy rooting hog!"

Orima and Hamil began sneering and screeching in turns. The rest of the troupe rolled eyes heavenward and trotted off, bursting into chatter as soon as they were well away from the slanging match by the fire. Marka raced off after Keeta. She knew how the fight would end; they would suddenly be all kisses and hugs and creep into their tent . . . she didn't want to think about it. In the moonlight the two women walked along the edge of the cliff and watched the waves foaming below.

"Keeta?" Marka said at last. "You don't think wishing someone ill can work them ill, do you?"

Keeta laughed, her dark rumble of a bellow as reassuring as a motherly hug.

"No, I most certainly don't. Why? Feeling a bite of guilt, hum?"

"Well, it sounds silly now."

"Understandable enough, little one. But don't vex your soul over it. She fell because she hurried her step, that's all." Keeta sighed profoundly. "At least we earned enough to eat for a while."

"But how are we going to get home? This is the only stinking town on this rotten little island, and they aren't going to want to watch the cow capering again."

"Oooh! Nasty little tongue!"

"But I'm right."

Keeta made a sort of grunt.

"Well, aren't I right?"

"About the audience, yes. I wouldn't call Rimi a cow. Your father's right. We all fall now and then."

"I never did! And she hates me for it, too. You know what I'm afraid of? That she'll work on Father, and he'll sell me to a slave trader. That'd buy passage for all of you, wouldn't it? I bet I'd fetch a lot."

"Will you be quiet? That's the most awful thing I've ever heard anyone say! Your father would never do such a thing."

"Maybe not, but she would."

Keeta's silence spoke a scrollful of answers.

In the morning Marka slept late. She shared a tent with Keeta and Delya, but woke to find them long gone, their bedrolls neatly folded and stowed off to one side, the hot sun streaming through the canvas. From outside she could hear voices, laughter and amiable squabbling, snatches of singing and pretend-oaths, all the normal life of the camp. She dressed, found her bone comb, and wandered outside to stand blinking in the sunlight and work at smoothing her tangle of curls. Although everyone else was up and around, there was no sign of her father or Orima. Still in bed, probably. She made a face at the thought.

"There you are!" Keeta called out. "Fresh bread in that basket by the fire pit."

Together they sat down by a pile of firewood while Marka nibbled at her breakfast.

"I was talking to Vinto," Keeta said. "He's worried about money, too. Your father's been making hints about not having enough to give the acrobats their full wages."

Marka felt suddenly sick to her stomach.

"But if he shorts them, they'll leave. They're good enough to travel on their own."

"I know. I thought maybe you might have a word with your father. You've still got a lot of influence with him."

"If I say something, the cow will say the opposite, just to be mooing."

"Marka!" But Keeta hesitated, her mouth twisting in a bitter recognition of the truth. "Maybe I'll talk to him, then. I was stranded once, with another troupe, years ago now, but I remember it awfully well. Too well. I don't—" She hesitated again. "Wait a minute. Isn't that the barbarian?"

His face shaded by a floppy leather hat, the juggler was riding up to the camp on a beautiful—and expensive-looking—gray gelding. He dismounted just outside the circle of tents, stood looking round for a moment, then led his horse over to the fire pit while everyone else in camp strolled over to meet him. Marka felt her heart start pounding when he made them all a lazy bow, just because he was so lithe and graceful.

"Good morning, all," he announced with a grin. "My name's Salamander, and I was wondering if I could have a word with the head of your troupe. I might have a business proposition to lay before him."

"Um, well, he's still in his tent," Keeta said. "Should be up anytime now."

Salamander glanced at the sky as if to check the position of the sun. Vinto and Keeta exchanged significant looks and went on surreptitiously judging the cost of his beautiful clothes and horse gear.

"Well, I'm his daughter," Marka said. "Maybe you could tell me what you want."

"Perhaps you can help me, indeed. I was wondering where you were all heading to next, since it would seem that this town no longer provides a fresh and profitable field for your talents to cultivate."

Again Keeta and Vinto glanced at each other, this time with a hint of agony.

"Er, we haven't exactly decided. Going back to Main Island, maybe, but I'm not sure."

"I see. Well, my companion and I are less than sure of our next destination, too, you see, and I thought that . . ." He let his words trail away.

Hamil was crawling out of his tent, and when he stood up, he lurched and swayed so badly that Marka at first thought he was ill. She bolted and ran to steady him, shocked at the inert force of his weight upon her shoulder as he leaned sideways. Dimly she was aware of the camp breaking out into a buzz of talk.

"Papa, what's wrong?"

For an answer he merely smiled, a slow, secretive smile, and his eyes turned her way slowly, too, all heavy lids and droop. Around him hung a smoky scent, like incense. Marka grunted as the ice-knowledge chilled her to the spine. For a moment she felt the earth turn beneath her.

"It's the white smoke again. Well, isn't it? Oh, Papa, you promised!" With a howl she thrust him away.

"Hey." He staggered and sat down heavily. "Little beast."

"Not again! Why . . . it was her, wasn't it? She's been getting it for you! Curse her guts!"

By then the rest of the troupe was hurrying over. Marka dodged away and ducked into her father's tent. Naked, on her hands and knees, Rimi was desperately scraping earth over a hole in the dirt floor. The stem of a pipe stuck up through it. Marka grabbed her by the hair, pulled her up, and slapped her across the face. She squealed like a pig and slapped back, all feeble and limp-wristed.

"Filth! You piece of gutter filth!" Marka hit her again. "You've been giving my father opium. I should turn you over to the archon. I should kill you."

Squealing and swearing, Rimi tried to writhe away. Marka went for her throat just as Keeta grabbed her from behind. There was no use struggling in those massive hands.

"Delya, get the little whore dressed and out here!" Keeta dragged Marka back. "You, young lady, are coming with me."

Outside, the acrobats were mobbing round Hamil, clamoring questions. Keeta marched Marka over to the fire pit, where Salamander was standing and studying the dead coals as if they interested him very much indeed. One or two at a time, the acrobats gave Hamil up as a bad job and drifted over. Marka began to sob convulsively, whether in rage or grief she didn't quite know. Keeta's icy voice cut through her hysteria.

"He's done this before, has he?"

"Not for years. He promised. Why do you think my mother left him?"

"She left you with him?" Vinto broke in.

"He wouldn't let me go. And he promised to stop. He promised."

She forced back tears and looked up. Keeta had turned away appalled, shaking her head over and over. Vinto ran both hands through his hair and stared at the ground for a long moment.

"Well," he said at last. "I'm sorry, little Marka, but me and the boys are pulling out. We can earn enough on our own to get back to Main Island, anyway, and we'll think of something to do then." He glanced at Keeta. "You and Delya are welcome to come with us."

Keeta sighed sharply, hesitated, then looked at Marka.

"Only if you come, too, little one. I can't just leave you here."

Marka felt as if her tongue had swelled to block her throat. She could only stare numbly at her friend's face.

"You little bitch, you viper!" Rimi marched over, dressed now and wrapped in dignity as well. "You'd better go with them! Do you think I'm going to put up with you after this?"

Marka could find nothing to say to her.

"Shut up," Keeta snapped. "Her father's got something to say about this."

"Father will listen to her." Marka heard her own voice whispering like a stranger's. "If they do the smoke together, he'll listen to her. He lost my mother over it, didn't he?"

She began to cry again, a helpless flutter that she hated for its weakness. Through her tears she saw Rimi leering and gloating, her face swimming like some dark moon. Marka raised her hands and stepped forward; then someone caught her firmly and pulled her back: the barbarian juggler.

"Satisfying though it would be, my turtledove, to rake your nails down her beauty, it would be both unprofitable and a waste of time. The opium itself will claw her for you."

Rimi swore like a sailor, then turned on her heel and marched off. Marka wriggled free of his lax grasp and wiped her face on her sleeve. When she looked round, there was no sign of Hamil, but from the purposeful way that Rimi was marching toward the palm grove at the edge of the caravanserai, Marka could assume that he'd taken refuge there. Vinto, his acrobats, Keeta and Delya, Salamander as well—Marka was suddenly aware of the way they all were looking at her, as if she were an invalid who just might die.

"You can't stay with them," Keeta said at last. "You just can't. I don't know what would happen to you, but—"

"I can guess," Vinto snarled. "She's not a child anymore, Keeta! She can hear the truth. How long will it be before her pig-dog of a father has her and Rimi selling themselves to keep him in smoke?"

Marka felt the earth lurch again, but she knew what she had to do. Salamander laid a gentle hand on her shoulder to steady her. She shook it off.

"We'd better pack our stuff up," Marka snapped. "Vinto, at least one horse and wagon should be yours, anyway, for the wages we owe you." Her voice threatened to break, but she forced it steady. "Maybe if we all pool our coin, we can get a ship back to Main Island today."

Keeta let out her breath in an explosive puff and muttered a thanks to the Star Goddesses.

"If you wouldn't mind me joining you with my act," Salamander said. "We could all travel together, indeed. Shall we repair to the inn where I've been staying and have some wine? There shall we foment plans."

"Glad to," Vinto said. "We can discuss shares later. First let's get out of this stinking camp."

During the slow walk to town, Marka suddenly remembered the fortune-teller. Good luck mixed with disaster, was it? Well, she could see the disaster, all right, but where was the good luck?

At Salamander's inn the portly landlord moaned and wrung his hands over the very thought of having traveling acrobats in his common room, but the juggler talked him into serving wine and little cakes, such good wine that Marka was impressed. As they sat on cushions round a low table and made awkward conversation, she noticed that Vinto was already beginning to defer to him, only in little ways, but she had the feeling that sooner or later, this stranger was going to end up managing the entire troupe. Since they were sitting off to one side, she could whisper to Delya.

"Do you mind everything changing like this?"

"Mind? Oh, if Keeta thinks it's a good idea, I'll go along with it. What do you think of this juggler?"

"I don't know. He's awfully good-looking."

"I suppose so. He's certainly used to taking charge. He said he had a companion, didn't he? I wonder what she's like?"

Marka felt so bitterly disappointed that she nearly wept. She'd forgotten that a man like this would have women following him round wherever he went, that he would most certainly never be interested in a gawky girl like her.

Jill first heard of Salamander's newly acquired troupe of acrobats from the innkeep, who came rushing upstairs to tell her as soon as he had the wine served. All quivering jowls and flapping hands, he bowed repeatedly while he blurted.

"There must be ten of them! They're probably all thieves! I don't have room! I don't know what your—uh—friend was thinking of!"

"Thinking? He probably wasn't, knowing him. All right, I'll go down."

By then several pitchers of wine had gone round, and everyone was giggling and talking a little too loudly as they lounged on cushions round the low table. Jill stood in the doorway for a moment and watched Salamander, beaming at his own generosity, playing host like a Deverry lord. Opposite him sat a pretty young woman who studied him in such a fervent mix of desire and misery that she might well have loved him in her last life.

"Oh, Jill, there you are!" Salamander called out. "Come join us! My friends, this is Gilyan of Brin Toraedic, a wandering scholar, who has honored my humble self by traveling with me as she searches out rare manuscripts. She's on a special commission from the scholar-priests of Wmmglaedd, a mysterious and magical isle in the far-off kingdom."

The troupe greeted this cascade of blather with honest awe, the men rising to bow to her, the women bobbing their heads her way, except for Marka, who merely stared. The gray-haired fellow sitting next to Salamander started to get up and cede her his seat, but Jill waved him back.

"I just need a word with Salamander," she said. "Not that it's possible to have but a single word."

At the jab he winced, but he scrambled up and followed her out to the courtyard where they could talk privately. Jill perched on the edge of a tiled fountain and glared at him.

"I wanted to travel quietly."

"Um, well, yes. I do remember you mentioning something of the sort. But we'll be safer with a large group."

"I wasn't aware we were in any danger."

Salamander sighed and sat down next to her.

"Let's have the truth." Jill changed into Deverrian to doubly insure privacy. "You're doing this to have a chance at the lass, aren't you?"

"Bit more to it than that!"

She raised one eyebrow.

"Jill, they needed my aid! The leader of their band had spent all their coin on the white smoke, and there they were, stranded far from home in a town where they'd never earn another copper."

"Your heart's big enough to embrace the world and your

tongue to cover it, too. I still say it's the lass who inspired this outburst of compassion."

"Imph, well." He held up his hand and flicked drops from his fingertips. "Well. Imph." Then he looked up with one of his sunny grins. "But since you want to talk with that bookseller in Inderat Noa again, we've got to go back to Main Island anyway, and travel across its less-than-glorious reaches, so they might as well travel with us."

"Oh, I suppose so! And the lass will doubtless be better off with you to look after her than she would be on her own."

Salamander grabbed her hand and kissed it.

"My humble thanks, O Princess of Powers Perilous!"

Jill snatched her hand away and stood up, shaking her head more at herself for indulging him than him for wanting to be indulged. Later, though, when she heard Marka's story of traveling with her addicted father and his jealous young wife, she decided that she'd done the right thing. The child was better off with them. Certainly the members of the troupe agreed. Late that evening, after the muttering innkeep had found them all rooms and served a grudged dinner, Jill was walking out in the cooler air of the courtyard when Keeta joined her, carrying a pierced tin candle-lantern.

"I just wanted to thank you for allowing Salamander to take us on like this. If he weren't advancing us the passage home, I don't know what we'd do."

"Well, it was his decision, but you're all welcome enough."

"Oh, please!" Keeta laughed, a pleasant if rather deep chuckle. "It's obvious that you do the deciding around here, no matter how much he talks, and by the Star Goddesses themselves, he does a lot of talking, doesn't he? But I'm glad that we'll be taking Marka away from her father before she gets cold feet and runs back to him."

"Kin ties are hard to break, and she's very young."

"Um." Keeta sat down on the edge of the tiled fountain. Even sitting while Jill stood, she looked Jill straight in the face. "She's a wise child, old beyond her years—well, in most things, that is. When it comes to others . . ."

Jill waited, not quite sure of her drift. Keeta frowned at the dappled lantern light on the water.

"I've seen it happen before," Keeta said at last. "A young girl in the same troupe with some good-looking man. Sometimes there's trouble over it—trouble for her, anyway. I intend to talk some sense into her head. You don't need to worry about her making a fool of herself over your man."

"What?" Jill burst out laughing. "Let me assure you that Salamander's nothing of the sort! He's more like a brother to me than anything."

"Oh! Well, that takes care of half the problem, then."

"And the other half is?"

"I'd hate to see little Marka pregnant and deserted."

"He wouldn't do that. Oddly enough. He looks like the sort of man who'd leave with never a backward glance, but he's not. I'll give him a fair bit of credit—he's got more honor around women than most men do."

"Wouldn't be hard, huh?" Keeta considered for a long moment before she smiled. "Well, that eases my mind, I must say. I didn't want to see the child get free of one mess only to land in another."

Although Keeta took the lantern and went back inside, Jill lingered in the cooler air. By then the moon, just past her full, had sailed over her zenith and was beginning to sink off to the west. The silver light fell dappled through the sparse trees and danced on the moving surface of the fountain. As Jill watched, the light seemed to thicken and take shape like the drift of smoke over a dying campfire. At first she assumed that it was merely some of the Wildfolk, in a semimaterialized form, playing in the water; then she realized that the waft of palpable light was swirling, growing, stretching upward as it spiraled round to make a silver pillar some ten feet high and four across. Inside the pillar, glowing all silver, stood a vaguely elven shape, not as solid as water, yet more so than a beam of light.

Jill raised her hands palm-out and chest-high, then spoke in greeting the magical names of the Lords of Water, for she thought that this being was one of the elemental kings. Yet as the form thickened within the pillar of light, she realized that it belonged to an elven woman, familiar-looking at that, with a long mane of silvery-blond hair and steel-colored eyes.

"Dallandra! How did—" Jill was too surprised to say more.

Dressed in an elven tunic and a pair of leather trousers, Dallandra seemed almost solid as she stood hovering over the water in the basin. Jill had never seen her so clearly before. She could pick out the separate curls and masses of her hair, see the folds of cloth in her tunic, and just make out a pale shard of landscape behind her, a grassy meadow and a single tree. Round her neck Dallandra was wearing on a golden chain a single large amethyst carved into some ornamental shape—or so Jill thought of it. Yet when she spoke, Jill heard her voice only as a thought.

"Jill! What are you doing here?"

"Trying to find out the meaning of the word inside the rose ring. Do you remember it? The one Rhodry Maelwaedd has."

"Of course I do. That's why I've been looking for you." She frowned, staring down at something near her feet that Jill couldn't see. "But I meant, why are you in Bardek?"

"You know where I am? How?"

"I can see your surroundings, and they match what I've been told about the islands. But please, I don't have much time."

"Well, it seems that some of the People may have fled south after the Great Burning, and there might be some still living far to the south of here. I've found a map, you see, that shows islands out beyond Anmurdio, and some histories that indicate there were once elves in Bardek. I've come to look for them."

Dallandra gasped, and the surprise broke her concentration. Her form began to fade as the pillar of light changed to a thick pillar of smoke, swirling silver in the moonlight.

"Dallandra!" Without thinking Jill was on her feet and shouting. "Dalla! Wait! How did you get here?"

With one last swirl the pillar seemed to blow away, smoke on the wind, a thickening of moonlight, then gone.

For a long time Jill sat on the bench and did some hard thinking. Dallandra was a dweomermaster of great power who, some hundreds of years earlier, had linked her Wyrd to that of the strange race of beings known as the Guardians. Jill had last seen her back in the Westlands a thousand miles away and, more significantly, far across the ocean. Working dweomer across any large body of water is impossible, because the exhalations of elemental force and the astral vibrations break up an image as fast as even the greatest dweomermaster can build it. Other dweomermasters had told Jill many a time that Dallandra had long left ordinary physical existence behind, even though none of them knew exactly in what state she did exist. At best she was semicorporeal, a thing of etheric substance only, which would make her even more vulnerable to the water forces than an ordinary magically produced shape or image. Yet here she was, or at the least some clear projection of her, coming through onto the physical plane. It was more of a puzzle than Jill could solve.

When she went back inside, she paused for a moment at the door of the common room and watched Salamander lounging at a table with a half-empty wine cup in his slender hands and smiling as he listened to the talk and jests flying like juggling clubs among the troupe of acrobats. He's probably been lonely, Jill thought. The gods all know that I'm poor enough company when I've got some working at hand. Yet her annoyance lingered, that he'd distract himself from his studies this way. She had, after all, promised Nevyn that she would oversee his dweomer training and do her best to get him to work up to his potential. In her mind, any promise she'd made to Nevyn was a sacred charge.

Dallandra had come to Bardek searching for Jill, or to be precise, she'd been searching for Jill on the inner planes and traced her to a place that had turned out to be Bardek. Judging from the way that Time ran in that world in which she was experiencing Time, it had only been a few weeks since she'd left her dweomermaster of a husband, Aderyn of the Silver Wings, back in the Westlands, although she knew, of course, that it was well over two hundred years as men and elves reckoned the span. Even though she was well aware of the split between the two time flows, it was hard to keep track of small variations. It seemed to her that she'd last seen Jill the day before, when in truth it had been nearly three years. During that last meeting, Jill had asked her about the rose ring's secret, and she'd tried to find the answer for the human dweomerwoman.

"I'd forgotten about the lapse of time," she remarked to Evandar. "She was so surprised that I'd remember."

"Eventually you'll grow used to the ebb and flow, and you'll see why we don't concern ourselves with the affairs of that world of yours. It all speeds by, like light on a running stream."

"So it must. How many of their years is a day here?"

"What? How would I know?"

"Haven't you ever thought to work it out?"

"Whatever for? Besides, it changes, how fast things flow."

"It changes? Well, there's a bother, then. On what principle?"

"On what?"

"Well, I mean, there must be some sort of rule or regular order to the way the changes come and go."

Evandar merely looked at her, slack-mouthed and wondering. Dallandra considered and tried again.

"What about bard lore? Would there be any old sayings about Time among your people?"

"In summer the sun runs fast as a girl through the sky," he said and promptly. "In winter like an old woman she goes halt and slow."

"I've never noticed it being winter here."

"Oh, but it has been. You can tell by the way Time limps. Now in the heat of the summer she moves like a bird on the wing."

"And what about spring and autumn? Are there any sayings about them?

"About spring, no, but there's one day in the fall of the year when our time and their time coincides."

"And that is?"

"In the land of men, it's the day between years."

"A day *between* years? I've never heard of such a thing."

He merely shrugged indifferently. They were sitting that evening—or seemed to be sitting—on a grassy hilltop, looking down into shifting mists that alternately covered, then revealed a plain crisscrossed by rivers and dotted with thickets. Far off on the horizon a moon was rising, bloated and golden.

"I don't understand why you won't tell me what that word inside the ring means."

"I don't understand why myself, but I'm still not going to tell you." He caught her hand and kissed it. "Why do you want to help this human woman, anyway?"

"Because she's going to help us. She promised me that she'd look after the child when it's born, and in return, it's only common courtesy to help her find out what she needs to know."

"But it's a riddle, and one of my best riddles, and I'll not tell her the answer."

For a moment she considered him, this strange creature who was in a stranger way her lover now. Although he looked like an elf in most ways, his hair was the yellow of daffodils, no natural blond, his lips were as red as sour cherries, and his eyes were a startling turquoise-blue, as artificial as one of the colors that elven craftsmen grind to decorate tents.

"This island to the south, now," Evandar said in a moment. "That does interest me. Would you like to help her find it? That I will do for her, in return for her help when the child is birthed."

"Bless you, my love. I would, indeed."

"Splendid! You go tell her while I look for the island."

"I will, but I think I'll find Elessario first and take her along. She should be right nearby."

And so, thanks to the vagaries of Time, it was some weeks in Jill's world before Dallandra appeared to her again.

In the meantime, the troupe of traveling players, with Jill and Salamander tagging along, left Zama Mañae behind. The main island of the Orystinnian archipelago is shaped rather like an animal, with the head pointing due north and the long tail of a peninsula trailing some fifty miles off to the south. Once the troupe reached Arbarat, the city at the tail's tip, they had a long, slow journey north with their tumble-down wagons and elderly horses to the next large city, Inderat Noa on the western coast of the animal's body. Marka was delighted when Salamander insisted that she leave the bumpy wagon and ride on his horse, which he then led, walking nearby in the sunny road. They stopped often, of course, to perform in the smaller towns and marketplaces along the way. In every marketplace Salamander bought something for the troupe, a length of silk for a costume here, or a brand-new set of painted leather clubs for the acrobats there, out of his own always substantial earnings.

"It takes coin to earn coin," he would say. "And between us, Vinto and I are going to make this troupe the most splendid show in all of Orystinna."

Marka would merely smile and think that Salamander could no doubt do anything in the whole world if he set his mind to it.

With Orima left behind and gone, Marka reclaimed the star turn on the slack rope. It was some compensation, she supposed, for losing her father, although, as the days went by, she was startled to find that she missed him very little. While Hamil had never treated her badly, he'd never treated her particularly well, either. What she did miss was the fact of having a father, a family, a place or connection in the world. From now on the troupe—or some troupe much like it—would be the only family she would have, just as their troupes were for so many of the wandering performers of the Bardekian islands. She comforted herself by thinking that at least she had Keeta and Delya, whom she'd known for six whole years, practically a lifetime in the fluid world of traveling shows.

And then, of course, there was Salamander, whom she found more than compensation enough. She would pick out a place at a safe distance to sit and watch him for hours on end, whether he was performing or practicing or merely standing by the campfire and eating his dinner. Most times she was afraid to approach him. Once though, when he was working with the silk scarves, he noticed her watching and called her over.

"Want to learn how to throw these?" he said.

"Yes, I would." She was surprised at herself for speaking so easily. "If you wouldn't mind taking the time to show me how."

"Not in the least, not in the least."

After that, she had a legitimate excuse to spend several hours a day in his company, though every now and then, she would notice Keeta or Jill giving them a less-than-approving look.

After one of their practice sessions, he told her that his real name was Ebañy, but he made her promise to keep it a secret from everyone else—which gave her a moment of cold doubt. Even though she was thoroughly besotted with him, Marka was shrewd enough to realize that he was keeping some rather strange truths to himself. Whenever he spoke of the barbarian kingdom in the north, his stories grew guarded. He never mentioned his family or a home city; he never told anyone why or how he'd become a street performer.

"Do you think he's maybe the outcast son of one of their nobles?" Marka remarked to Keeta one night. "Maybe he's even a prince in disgrace."

Keeta snorted.

"The disgrace I'd believe quick enough."

"Oh, don't be mean! But you know, sometimes I wonder if he's married."

"Marka my dear, you do have a good head on your shoulders, don't you? But no, I asked Jill, and she said he wasn't."

"Oh, I'm so glad! We can trust what Jill says, can't we?"

"There's something about Jill, my dear, that makes me think we could trust her with our lives." Keeta frowned, nipping her lower lip in thought. "I feel like a fool for saying it, but there you are."

Marka barely paid attention to this last remark, but she found the news about Ebañy sweeter than the finest wine or purest honey. For days she savored it, bringing out the thought that no other woman had a claim on him. Yet, he remained distant, brotherly at the most, until she reached the bitter conclusion that he merely felt sorry for her.

The day before they reached Inderat Noa, the troupe came upon a public caravanserai beside the road. Although they could have made a few more miles before dark, and the city lay only about five miles ahead, they decided to camp early rather than risk being shut out of the gates by arriving late. Once the horses were tended and the tents raised, Marka went looking for Ebañy. Off to one side of the campground stood some scruffy holm oaks round a spring and a series of stone fountains, provided for travelers by the archons of Inderat Noa. As she walked up, Marka saw him sitting with Jill, and something about the tense set of their shoulders made her hesitate. When Ebañy saw her, he gave such a guilty start and smiled in such a nervous way that she realized they'd been talking about her. All at once she felt about eight years old; she was blushing—she was sure of it. Without a word she turned and ran for the camp, dodged into her tent, and threw herself down onto her blankets for a good cry.

"Whatever happened to the girl's mother, anyway?" Jill said.

"To tell you the truth, I don't know," Keeta said. "She was long gone when I joined Hamil's troupe. It was quite a large show in those days."

They were sitting on a stone bench under some trees in Inderat Noa's marketplace, a big and elegant open square with fountains and little cobbled walkways between the groups of stalls and booths. Afternoon heat danced and shimmered over the paving like the water mist over the fountains. Not too far away Salamander and Vinto were haggling with a pair of archon's men about a performance permit.

"I did hear that Marka's mother went back to Mangortinna," Keeta went on. "I think she was born there."

"I see. I don't understand why she didn't take her daughter with her."

"How could she? She and Hamil were legally married and all."

"Well, what—"

"Oh, wait! You speak so well that I keep forgetting you're a foreigner. Under our laws a child's her father's property. The mother has no say in anything, really, unless he gives her one." Keeta frowned briefly. "One reason why I made my mind up never to marry."

"I can understand that. Mangortinna, huh? Well, if she went back home, we'd probably never find her, even if we did try."

"What do you want to find her for?"

"Oh, it's probably just sentimentality on my part, but I feel like I should . . . well, consult her, I suppose. You see, Salamander wants to marry Marka."

"Marry her? Actually legally marry her?"

"Yes, just that."

"Well, that's wonderful! He's the kind of man who could take good care of her, and she certainly wants to marry him."

Jill laughed.

"You were just telling me how awful marriage is."

"For me, it would be, but I know that the way I've chosen to live my life isn't right for every woman. I was really afraid that Marka was going to end up unmarried and pregnant, no matter what you said about his morals."

"So far he hasn't laid a hand on her."

"So far. She's a pretty little thing, after all."

"True, and even more to the point with our Salamander, she worships him."

"Imph. What's wrong with them getting married?"

"Well, he's a good bit older than her, more so than you'd ever think to look at him. And then, well . . ." She hesitated, unsure of how to explain, of how much she could explain.

Someone called their names. Waving the permit, Salamander came strolling over to them, and Jill let the subject drop. Vinto looked extremely pleased about something, himself.

"We shall be setting up our fabulous cavalcade of wonders on the East Square," Salamander said. "Not only is said square paved and thus quite level, but it's in the more prosperous quarter of town. We had best return to camp and tell the others of our good fortune. And I want to see how Delya and Marka are getting on with finishing those new costumes."

"I'm going to stay in town," Jill broke in. "I want to go see the bookseller, and then I'm supposed to consult with the priests of Dalae-oh-contremo again."

Although Inderat Noa sported several grand public squares, most of the streets twisted like tunnels under arcades of houses and shops, built right out over them for the shade. As Jill made her way through this dim warren she attracted a crowd of Wildfolk, the big purple-striped gnomes peculiar to Bardek, scurrying along after her on their fat little legs. Although her usual gray fellow did materialize, he took a smaller form than usual, so that he could ride upon her shoulder and look down upon the purple gnomes with a lordly disdain. None of the other people in the crowded street could see her companions, of course, although every now and then some passerby suddenly looked down and frowned at what seemed empty air as a gnome bumped into him or brushed rudely past.

The bookseller, however, could see them quite well, because he'd studied the dweomer lore for some thirty years. Daeno's little shop was wedged in between a fruit seller's and a basket weaver's down on a dead-end alley perfumed with lemons and drying grass. When Jill and her crew crowded through the door into the blessedly cool shop, the old man came shuffling forward to greet them all, waggling a finger at the gnomes and warning them to keep their little clawed paws off the rare scrolls and codices stacked up high all round.

"I've found the map," he announced. "My boy just got back with it. Its owner let it go cheap, by the way. It's not much of a collector's item."

The piece of pounded bark paper was about two feet long by a foot and a half wide, all torn and filthy round the edges, and flecked with what looked like ancient wine drops overall. At the very top of the map lay the faded outline of Main Island's tail and the tiny islands just to the south; off to the left lay the Anmurdian archipelago in somewhat darker ink.

"Now, Anmurdio is much farther off than this map makes it look," Daeno remarked. "So who knows how far away these are."

He laid one bony finger on the "these" in question, a group of four islands, drawn entirely too circular to be accurate, floating far to the south of Anmurdio. Out in the middle of the ocean in between, the scribe had drawn a sea serpent and a fat monster with big fangs. Daeno picked up the map and flipped it over to reveal several lines of tiny, spiky writing, faded to a pale brown, on the back.

"Varro the merchant made this map by the grace of the Star Goddesses in the reign of Archon Trono. That was in 977 by Deverry reckoning, Jill, well, give or take a year, anyway."

"You have my sincere thanks for going to all this trouble."

"You're most welcome. I'm afraid it's not much of a map."

"It's better than no map at all, and it'll be something to show round once we get to Anmurdio."

"You know, there are supposed to be cannibals in the smaller islands."

"Just like there's supposed to be sea serpents out in the southern ocean?"

Daeno laughed, nodding his head in agreement while he rolled up the map.

"The thing is," Jill went on. "I'm never going to get a merchant here on Main Island to risk his ship and his fortune on some daft scheme of sailing to the far south. Or well, there was one, but he has a wife and three children, and I couldn't let him. I just couldn't."

"Of course not." Daeno paused to swat at the gnomes, who were scurrying this way and that on the counter. "I'm surprised you found anyone at all. Who was it, by the bye? A local man?"

"No, a merchant up in Orysat, Kladyo by name."

"Elaeno's boy?"

"The very one! Do you know—oh, of course you'd know Elaeno!"

"Well, not intimately or anything, but we've met in the flesh and then, of course, out on the etheric we run into one another from time to time. Hum, am I right in this? I heard that his master in the dweomer was a Deverry man."

"That's true, and it was the same person who taught me. Nevyn, his name was."

Daeno whistled under his breath. The gnomes all went dead-still to listen.

"Not *the* Nevyn?" the old man said. "Oh, listen to me! There could only be one!"

"You've heard of him, then?"

"What?" Daeno laughed aloud. "Every dweomerworker in these parts has heard of Nevyn! He spent years and years in the islands, you know, over the last two hundred years or so. He'd turn up for twenty, thirty years at a time, then disappear again for even longer. Probably sailed back home to your kingdom. You must know all about it."

In fact, Jill didn't, and she was rather surprised to find it out now. Daeno went blithely on.

"But to get back to the problem in hand, if you want to sail south, I suppose that Anmurdio's the best place to look for a ship."

When Jill arrived back at the caravanserai, she found the troupe hard at work, readying costumes and props for the evening show. Salamander himself was sitting on the bed of a wagon with his feet dangling over the edge like a farm boy and whittling like one as well. On a piece of driftwood shaped much like a bird, he was carving details.

"It'll be a fine thing to juggle with." In illustration he tossed it spinning and caught it again in the same hand. "And I know what you're thinking, O Mistress of Magicks Marvelous, that if only I spent this much time and ingenuity, to say naught of cleverness, craft, wit, and willingness upon the dweomer, I should soon match you."

"Surpass me, more like. You've got the fluid natural talent that I never had."

"Oh, please, tease me not and mock me neither."

"Naught of the sort. I've had to work blasted hard for everything I've accomplished, while it comes easy to you. I suppose—no, I know—that's why I get so sour with you."

"Oh." He considered the wooden bird with a frown. "Well, that does put a different complexion on things, truly. Jill, you have my apologies. I try to control my frivolous nature, but it's just somewhat I was born with, I fear me."

"It's somewhat that could be overcome."

He shrugged and went back to refining a small burl that resembled a wing.

"Ebañy, I just don't understand you."

"I don't understand myself."

"Would you please not put me off?"

He looked up, abruptly solemn, yet she couldn't tell if he were sincere or merely arranging the expression she wanted to see.

"Dweomer means everything to you, doesn't it?" he said.

"It does. More than meat and drink, more than life."

"More than love."

"Unquestionably, considering."

"Alas, my poor brother! I don't suppose he'll ever understand why you chose the dweomer over him. No more do I suppose that you particularly care if he does or not."

"That's not fair."

He winced at the bite in her voice.

"Look." Jill tried another tack. "I know the basic exercises and suchlike can be tedious. Why, when I was learning all the proper calls and salutes for the elemental kings and lords, I thought I'd go out of my mind from sheer boredom. But it's been more than worth it. Now I can travel where I will in their worlds and see the marvels there. But you know about that. You've had a taste of it yourself. I simply can't understand how you wouldn't want more."

"I don't have your devotion to the art."

"Oh, horseshit!"

"Ah, the silver dagger's daughter still!" He looked up from his work with a grin, then let it fade. "But horseshit it's not, my friend, my dear and treasured companion. Jill, when you want somewhat, you're so single-minded that it takes my breath away. The rest of the world's not like that."

"I'm not talking about the rest of the world."

"Oh, very well, then. I'm not like that."

Jill hesitated, struggling to understand.

"Well," he went on. "You had your own doubts about taking up the art, didn't you?"

"True spoken. But that's when I didn't know what it offered. You do know. I honestly don't see how you could get so far and then give it up."

"Ah. It's because you do the work out of love, while I have only duty and grim obligation as my whip and spur."

"You honestly and truly don't love the dweomer work?"

"I should have thought that such would be obvious after all these years."

She knew him well enough to know that he was skirting the edge of a lie.

"Well here, consider this." Salamander spoke quickly, before she could pin him down. "Wasn't your father the greatest swordsman in all Deverry? Didn't he gain great glory for himself wherever he rode—the silver dagger, the lowly outcast of a silver dagger, who put the best fighting men in the kingdom to shame? But did he relish that life? Did he revel in his glory and his position? Far from it!"

"Well, true spoken. What are you driving at?"

"Only that a man may have great skill and talent and not give a pig's fart about the life they lead him to."

"And do you feel that way about the dweomer?"

"Not exactly, literally, precisely, or even in substance. A mere example only."

But at that exact moment his thumb slipped on the knife, and he sliced his hand. With a yelp he tossed both bird and blade onto the wagon bed and started cursing himself and his clumsiness. Blood welled and ran.

"You'd better let me bind that for you," Jill said. "I hope that wretched knife was clean."

"Doesn't matter. The cut's deep enough to wash itself out."

It was, too, though mercifully not deep enough to cause permanent harm. Later Jill was to remember that accident and its unconscious confession only to curse herself for not seeing the meaning at the time.

Among the Host, Evandar's people, Dallandra searched on a sunny day through a meadow, bright with flowers of red and gold. In their bright clothes and golden jewelry, the Host too bloomed like flowers amid the tall green grass, and as always, their exact numbers eluded her. Even in the sunlight of a summer noon, shadow wrapped them round, blurring the boundaries that define a person for us in our world. Out of the corner of her eye she would see a pair of young girls, sitting gossiping on the grass, turn to look and find a bevy giggling together, then rising to run away like a flock of birds taking flight. Or it would seem that under the shade of an enormous tree a band of minstrels played, their conjoint music so sweet that it pierced her heart, yet she would find but one man with a single lute. Like flames in a fire or ripples in a stream, they became distinct and separate only to fall back again and meld.

Some of the Host, though, remained discrete, with minds and personalities of their own. Evandar himself, of course, and his daughter, Elessario, were the two she knew best, but there were others, men and women both, who wore names and faces like a mark of honor. In the dancing sunlight they waved in greeting or called out some pleasant remark as she made her way across.

"Have you seen Elessario?" she would ask, but always the answer was no.

By the meadow's edge a river flowed, and at that moment it flowed broad and smooth. At other times she had seen it narrow and churning with white water or come upon it to find a swamp and nothing more, but at the moment the broad water sparkled in the sun, and green rushes stood at the bank like sword blades stuck into a treaty ground. Out among them on one leg stood a white heron.

"Elessario!"

The heron turned its head to consider her with one yellow eye, then rippled like the water and became a young woman with impossibly yellow hair, wading naked to the bank. Dallandra offered a hand and helped her clamber out. Elessario picked up a tunic from the grassy bank and pulled it over her head. Although at first glance she seemed beautiful, with human ears but elven eyes, at second glance one noticed that the eyes were as yellow as her hair, cat-slit with emerald-green, and that her smile revealed sharp-pointed teeth.

"Did you need me for something, Dalla?"

"I did. Come see something with me."

Hand in hand like mother and child they wandered downriver, looking for Bardek. Here in the world of the Guardians, as the elves named Evandar's people, images could become real rather easily, that is, for those with minds trained to build them. First Dallandra created an image of Jill in her mind, as clear and as detailed as possible; then she moved this image out through her eyes onto the landscape—a mental trick, that, and not true dweomer, strange though it sounds to those who don't know how to do it. These mental images were lifeless things, even in this world, and broke up fast like a picture imagined in a cloud or a fire. Every now and then, though, one image would linger for a while longer or seem brighter and more solid. With a fascinated Elessario trailing after, Dallandra would walk to that spot and cast another round of images. Every time, one of the new crop would become solid and endure long enough to point out the next step of their journey.

As they followed these clues, the landscape changed round them. The river narrowed, ran shallow; the lush grass withered till brown and dry. They passed big boulders, pushing up through thin earth, and eventually found a graveled road, leading forward into mist. All at once, twilight turned the world an opalescent gray, shot with lavender.

"Here we are," Dallandra said. "Come look at a city of men."

In the mist they seemed to float, like birds hovering on the wind, then spiraled down and down in ever-twisting arcs till at last the mist vanished in a starry sky. Below lay a white city, shimmering in the heat of a Bardek evening. Here and there in the dark streets a gold point of light bobbed along, a lantern carried in someone's hand. Down in the center of town a vast sea of lamps flickered among the brightly colored banners and booths of the public market. Around this small geometry of streets and light stretched the dark and arid plain out to a horizon glowing faint green with the last of sunset. With a little gasp of delight Elessario began gliding down, following the drift of music that came to them, but Dallandra caught her arm.

"Not now, I'm afraid. It is lovely, isn't it?"

"Shall I see marvels like this once I've been born, Dalla?"

"Well, yes." Dallandra hesitated, caught between truth and sadness. "But you know, they probably won't seem so marvelous. You'll take them for granted, then, like we all do."

One last image of Jill pointed their way to a caravanserai out on the edge of town. Among a scatter of palm trees horses and mules drowsed at tether, and human beings wandered back and forth. Fires bloomed here and there, but far off to one side a silver-blue pillar of water force, glowing like a beacon to guide them down, rose from a fountain. Beside it, sitting with her feet tucked under her on a little bench, was Jill. To Dallandra it seemed that they walked up to her in the usual manner, but judging from the way Jill yelped in surprise, she must have seen them appear all at once.

"Jill, I've brought Elessario. She's the one who'll lead her people into our world."

"You're very brave, then, Elessario." Jill got up to greet them. "I salute you."

The child stared back, all solemn eyes and sudden shyness.

"Does she truly understand what all this means, Dalla?" Jill went on.

"I hope so."

"You'd best make sure of it. To put this burden on someone without them truly knowing what they're doing is—"

"But, Jill, if they don't come through, her people will die. Fade away. Vanish. And until one makes the journey, none will."

"But still, she needs to know what—"

"I'll do my best to tell her. To make her understand."

"Good."

For a moment they considered each other. Although Dallandra could only wonder what she might look like to Jill, to her the human dweomerwoman seemed made of colored glass, glowing and shimmering as they peered at each other across a gulf of worlds. Such niceties as facial expressions and nuances of voice simply refused to come clear, yet Dallandra could feel Jill's urgency as a barb in an old wound of guilt. As she turned inward to her own thoughts, she began to lose the vision entirely: Jill's image flattened, then dwindled as if it were rapidly flying away.

"Jill!" she called out. "The islands! Evandar will look for them!"

She had no way of knowing if Jill had heard her. All round them in a rushy vortex the worlds spun by, green and gold, white and red, faces and parts of faces, words and names flung into a purple wind, strange beings and glimpses of landscapes, round and round, faster and faster, yet flowing always upward. She clutched Elessario's hand tight in both of hers and swept her along as they tumbled, spun, flew higher, ever higher through a rush of voices and images, until at last, with a crack like the strike of a sword on a wooden shield, they fell into the grass of the river meadow, where the Host was dancing in the summer sun. Elessario rolled over onto her back and began to laugh.

"Oh, that was exciting! It was truly a splendid sort of game! Will being born be like that, Dalla?"

"Yes, but backward. That is, you'll go down and down instead of up."

"And where will I come out, then?" Elessario sat up, wrapping her arms around her knees.

"To a place where it's all warm and dark and safe, where you'll sleep for a long time." Dallandra had told her this story a hundred times before, but the girl loved hearing it. "Then you'll find yourself in a bright place, and someone will hold you, and you'll really, really know what love is. But it won't all be easy, Elli my sweet. It truly won't."

"You told me about the hard bits. Pain and blood and slime." She frowned, looking across the flowered fields. "I don't want to hear about them again now, please."

Dalla felt her heart wrench, wondering for the thousandth time if she were doing the right thing, if indeed she had enough knowledge to do the right thing for this strange race, trapped in a backwash, a killing eddy of the river of Time. Unthinkably long ago, in the morning light of the universe when they were struck, sparks from immortal fire as all souls are, they'd been meant to take up the burden of incarnation, to ride with all other souls the turning wheels of Life and Death, but somehow, in some way that not even they could remember, they had, as they put it, "stayed behind." Without the discipline of the worlds of form, they were doomed, but after so long in the magical lands they'd found—or created, she couldn't be sure which—the stinking, aching, grieving inertia called life seemed hateful to them. One by one, they would wink out and die, sparks flown too far from the fire, unless someone led them down into the world. I'm too ignorant, Dalla thought. I don't know what I'm doing, I don't have enough power, I'm doing this for the wrong reasons, I can't, I'll fail, I'll never be able to save them.

Unfortunately, there was no one but her to so much as try.

• • •

The vendor had spread his wares out in the shade near a public fountain. An old man, with pale brown skin and lank white hair, he sat on his heels behind a small red rug and stared out at the crowd unblinking, unmoving, as if he cared not at all if anyone bought his wares. Neatly arrayed in front of him were three different kinds of fortune-telling sets, ranging from a stack of flimsy beaten bark packets filled with cheap wooden tiles to a single beautifully painted bone set in a carved wooden box with bronze hinges. Marka counted her coins out twice, but still, she didn't have enough money for even the cheapest version. As she reluctantly hid her pouch again inside her tunic, the old man deigned to look her way.

"If you're meant to have them, the coin will come," he remarked. "They have the power to pick out their true owners."

"Really, good sir?"

"Really." He leaned forward and ran a gnarled hand over the lid of the bronze-fitted box. "I've sold these sets for years, traveling round Orystinna, and I've come to know all about them. Now, the cheap things, they have no power whatsoever. A man I know up in Orysat brings them in from Bardektinna by the crateful. They're slave-made, I suppose. And those there in the cloth sacks, well, they're good enough, especially for a beginner. But every now and then a really fine set comes my way, like these. You can just feel, somehow, that they're different."

He picked out a tile and held it faceup in his palm. It was the prince of birds, exquisitely carved with a flare of wing and a long beak; into the graved lines the craftsman had rubbed some sort of blue and green dye, staining the bone beyond the power of fingers to rub it away. As she looked at it, Marka felt a peculiar sensation, that somehow she recognized that tile, that in fact she recognized the whole set and particularly its box.

"There's a wine stain on the bottom," she said, and then was horrified to realize she'd spoken aloud.

"Well, so there is." The vendor made the admission unwillingly. "But it's just a little one, and it's faded, too. It hasn't hurt the tiles any."

In the hot summer day Marka turned icy-cold. She managed

to smile, then stood up. All she could think of was running away from the box of tiles. When someone touched her shoulder from behind, she screamed.

"Well, a thousand apologies!" It was Ebañy, half laughing, half concerned. "I thought you'd seen me come up. Didn't mean to startle you."

"Oh, well, I was just, uh, well, talking with this man. He, uh, has these interesting things for sale."

Ebañy glanced down and went as wide-eyed as a child. When he knelt down for a better look, she wanted to scream at him and beg him to come away. Yet, when he gestured at her to join him, she knelt beside him, as close as she dared. He picked the knave of flowers out of the box and held it up to let the golden blossoms catch the light. With an eye for Ebañy's expensively embroidered shirt of the finest linen, the vendor leaned forward, all smiles.

"The young lady found those most interesting, sir."

"Oh, I'm sure she did." Ebañy was smiling, but his gray eyes were oddly cold and distant, like a flash of steel. "Tell me, where did you buy these?"

"From a merchant up in Delinth, last year it was. He'd won them in a gambling game, he told me, over on Surtinna. He trades there regularly."

"You don't happen to remember what city he got them in, do you?" Ebañy put back the knave and picked up a careless handful of other tiles. Seeing them lying in his long, pale fingers made Marka feel like fainting, but why, she couldn't say.

"Um, well." The vendor thought for a moment. "Wylinth, maybe, but I wouldn't swear to that. I've talked to a lot of people and heard a lot of tales since then."

"Of course. How much do you want for them?"

"Ten zotars."

"Huh, and the moon would cost me only twelve! Two zotars."

"What! The box alone is worth that."

"But it's got that wine stain on the bottom. Three zotars."

As they went on haggling, enjoying themselves thoroughly, Marka could barely listen. Ebañy knew about the stain, too, just as she somehow knew, when neither of them had picked the box up and looked at the bottom. She was sorry she'd ever stopped to chat with the vendor, sorry she'd wanted the set of tiles, even sorrier he was buying them—and then it occurred to her that he was buying them just for her, just because he knew she wanted them. When he happened to glance her way and smile, she felt as if she would die from happiness. At last five zotars changed hands, and Ebañy settled the lid on the box, picked it up, hefted it briefly, and gave it to her. Clutching it to her chest, she leaned over and on a sudden impulse kissed him on the cheek.

"Oh, thank you. They're so lovely."

He merely smiled, so warmly, so softly, that her heart started pounding. He rose, then helped her up, taking the box from her to carry it.

"Let's get back to the camp. Oh, and by the way. This isn't much of a place to ask, but will you marry me? I know that under your laws I should be asking your father, but going back to find that esteemed worthy would be a journey tedious beyond belief, and a reunion oppressive beyond sufferance."

"Marry you? Really actually marry you?"

"Just that."

When he laughed at her surprise, she realized just how ready she'd been to do anything that he might ask of her.

"Shall I take your silence as a yes or a no?"

"A yes, you idiot."

With one convulsive sob, hating herself for doing it, Marka began to cry, and she sniveled inelegantly all the way back to the caravanserai.

"You stupid blithering dolt!" Jill was yelling, but she did remember to use Deverrian. "I could strangle you!"

"Do calm down, will you now?" Salamander stepped back, honestly frightened. "I don't understand why your heart is so troubled, I truly don't."

Jill stopped, the anger ebbing, and considered the question as seriously as it did indeed deserve. She was worried about the girl, she supposed, who thought she was marrying a young traveling player much like herself while the truth was a fair bit stranger.

"Well, my apologies for getting so angry," she said at last. "I suppose it's because she's so young, and you're not, no matter how handsome your elven blood keeps you."

"But that's a reason in itself. Here, consider this. I'm well over a century old, my turtledove, old for a human being, young for a full-blooded man of the People, but I'm neither, am I?" His voice cracked with bitterness, quickly covered. "Who knows how long a half-breed lives? Marka's little more than a child, truly. I keep hoping that this time, we'll have the chance to grow old together. Before, even if she hadn't caught that fever, I would have lived long past her."

"Oh." Jill couldn't find it in her heart to reproach him. "Well. I mean, none of my affair, is it now? Whether the lass marries you or no."

"Mayhap I was a bit sudden about it. It was seeing her with those tiles. Ye gods, how many hours have I watched her, sitting there at that little table, poring over those tiles, and joking with me about what she was seeing, or—"

"Even if they should be incarnations of the same soul, Marka and Alaena are not the same person. No one is, truly, from life to life."

His eyes filled with tears, and he tossed his head, turning half away. Jill let out her breath in a long sigh. They were sitting in their tent, off at the edge of the campground. From outside Jill could hear Marka, babbling in a frenzy of joy, and Keeta's low voice, celebrating with her. It was certainly impossible to make Salamander go back on his offer.

"Well, that's torn it, then," she said. "I'll be going on to Anmurdio alone."

"What? I can't let you do that!"

"And I can't let you drag that child along with us, either."

"Why not? Is it any more dangerous than the life she's used to, wandering the roads and never knowing where her next copper's going to come from? We'll be safe enough. That's why I've been building up the troupe."

"Are you trying to tell me, you stupid chattering elf, that you want to take all these wretched acrobats all the way to Anmurdio with us?"

"Of course I do."

Jill could only stare at him. He smiled, all sunny charm.

"List but a moment, O Princess of Powers Perilous, and all will become as clear as a summer sky. Cast your mind backward to our youth, and our adventures in Slaith. Ah, glorious Slaith! Alas, thanks to my brother and his righteous wrath, no more do its beds of fish entrails scent the warm and tropic air, no more do pirates swagger down its rich and arrogant streets, no more do—"

"Are you going to hold your tongue or am I going to cut it out? Get to the point!"

"Well and good, then, but you do take the bloom off a man's rhetoric, I must say. The point, my turtledove, is this: Slaith was a foul and evil den of pirates, but even there, in that den of the accursed, my humble gerthddyn's calling made us both welcome and immune to infamy. Far more welcome, then, in isolate, nay, even desolate Anmurdio shall be an entire troupe of performers."

"Imph. I hate to admit this, but you're probably right."

"Of course I'm right. I've spent many a long and guileful hour in thought, working this scheme through. We'll probably even turn a profit."

"Oh, very well, then! Since there's naught I can do about it all, anyway, I might as well go along with your daft scheme. Poor little Marka—a fine way to start married life!"

"Aha! You're the one who's making the mistake this time. You're remembering pampered Alaena, the rich widow who lacked for naught. Marka has lived as hard a life as ever you did as a child, following your father round the kingdom."

Jill said something foul beyond repeating, simply because he was right, but he merely laughed at her.

Later that afternoon Jill went looking for Marka and found her sitting in front of the tent she shared with Delya and Keeta. She'd spread out a large mat and arranged the tiles, which might possibly have come back to her from another life, in tidy lines to study them.

"Marka?" Jill said. "I've just come to offer my congratulations."

"Oh, thank you!" She looked up with a smile of such sheer,

innocent joy that it wrung Jill's heart. "You know, I never ever thought I'd be this lucky, not ever."

"Well, I'm glad you're so happy." Jill sat down on the ground across from her. "Keeta tells me that the troupe's going to join together to buy you a wedding dress."

"Yes, and it's so wonderful of them." She hesitated briefly. "You look sad, too, just like Keeta and Delya do. Why?"

"Oh, there's just something about a wedding that takes us old crones this way. Don't let it trouble you."

"But it does trouble me. You're all acting like I'm going to get dragged off to the archon's prison instead of married."

Jill hesitated, but the girl deserved an honest answer.

"Well, I suppose it's because this kind of happiness just can't last, just because of the way life runs, I mean. It's sad, in a way, like seeing a spring flower and knowing it's going to fade when summer comes. I know that sounds awfully harsh, but do you think you'll always be this gloriously happy?"

"Well, I wish I could be, but of course you're right. All right, then, if that's all it is."

It was, of course, a great deal more than that, but this was no moment to turn vulture and dwell upon all those worries that used to trouble older women at a wedding: the slow death of a girl's youth, the quick death of the little freedom allowed her in life between her father's house and her husband's, to say nothing, in those days—hundreds of years before the dweomer taught women to control their pregnancies—of her possible literal death in child-birth or from the simple exhaustion of birthing too many children.

"That's a nice set of fortune tiles," Jill said instead. "Did Sala-mander buy them for you?"

"Yes. Aren't they lovely?" But she frowned, tilting her head a little to one side. "You know, it was the oddest thing. I saw these in the marketplace, just sitting in their box, and I didn't pick them up or anything. I didn't even touch them. But I somehow knew that there was this wine stain on the bottom. And you know what the oddest thing was? Ebañy knew it, too. And he never looked, either."

Jill's doubt that the girl might be Alaena reborn vanished.

"Well, odd things like that do happen." She stood up quickly, before Marka could ask further and touch the edge of secrets. "I think it means you were meant to have them. And meant to have Ebañy, too, most like."

Marka favored her with a smile as brilliant as the moon at her full.

Later that evening, after the show, when the troupe was eating its midnight meal round a leaping fire, there was a celebration. Vinto was a fine musician, playing the wela-wela, a zitherlike instrument; another of the acrobats played the drum; the flute boy outdid himself, especially since there was plenty of background noise to cover his occasional squeak. Everyone was laughing and singing, toasting Salamander and Marka with cups of red wine and taking turns in wishing them happiness, and even some of the merchants who were sharing the public field drifted over, getting into the spirit of things by bringing stuffed dates and nut cakes and the other traditional gifts for this sort of celebration. After about an hour the noise and the crowd began to get on Jill's nerves, and when she drifted away for a quiet walk, Keeta and Delya joined her. They found a bench by the public fountain and sat down to watch the water splashing in the moonlight. Although Delya was smiling, a little flushed from the wine and humming a tune under her breath—in fact, she never did add a word to that entire conversation—Keeta looked downright melancholy.

"Ah, well," she said at last. "At least Salamander looks like he'll make her a better husband than most."

"Oh, he certainly will," Jill said. "I've known him a long time, and I can honestly say that."

"Good. By the way, has he mentioned anything about going to Anmurdio to you?"

"Oh, yes. What do you think of the idea?"

"It's a good one. The towns over there are so starved for a good show that we should do really well."

"Well, that's a relief. I didn't want to drag the rest of you along only to have it turn out to be a disaster."

"What I don't understand, frankly, is how there could be any rare books and things over there for you to find."

Jill fell back onto a version of the truth.

"There may not be any, indeed. But a long time ago there was a horrible war in the country adjoining our kingdom, and a large band of refugees fled south. Now, they didn't settle in Bardek proper nor here in Orystinna. What I'd like to know is where they did end up, and what books they brought with them when they fled."

"I must say that you people seem to have a ghastly lot of wars."

"Well, yes, I'm afraid so."

Keeta glanced at her companion and suddenly smiled.

"Delly, you're just about asleep. Want to go back?"

"Mph?" Delya woke with a start and yawned. "I'm fine."

"I think we'd best get back." Keeta got up and held out a hand. "Come along."

With a nod and apologetic smile in Jill's direction, Delya rose and allowed herself to be led off to camp. Jill considered going, too, then decided to sit in the cool and moon-shot dark for a while. Not only did all the noise and fire's heat seem a burden, but she was hoping that Dallandra would come through into the physical plane again. Ever since Dalla had appeared to her with Elessario along, Jill had been trying to puzzle out her cryptic last words, which she'd heard only as "islands Evandar." Whether "Evandar" was the name of the islands where the refugees had settled or of some person, she simply didn't know. Yet, though she waited there for hours, the elven dweomerwoman never returned.

When Jill got back to the camp, she found it silent, with no one up but Keeta, sitting yawning by a dying fire.

"I moved your gear and blankets and things over to our tent. Better let Salamander and Marka have one to themselves. Thought I'd better wait up and tell you."

"Ah, I see," Jill said. "Thank you."

On the morrow, when the troupe marched off into town to register the wedding officially at the archon's palace, Jill stayed in camp, but she came to greet them when they paraded back again. At the head of the line, sitting sidesaddle on Salamander's dapple-gray horse, rode Marka, flushed and smiling, with her new husband walking beside her. In full costume the acrobats followed, singing, laughing, doing a bit of juggling or a dance here and there. A crowd of children and citizens brought up the rear, treating the acrobats' wedding as just another show, although, in all fairness, Salamander and Marka seemed delighted to provide them with it. When they reached camp, he swept her out of the saddle and kissed her soundly. To the cheering of the crowd they held hands and bowed, while the rest of the troupe scurried round collecting the small coins that rained down upon the pair. Jill could only think that indeed, Salamander had found himself a perfect wife.

Toward evening, however, Jill dragged him away from the dancing and music. In the lengthening shadows they walked together among the palms at the edge of the campground. A sunset wind was springing up, sending drifts of dusts across the dead-flat plains.

"Somewhat I wanted to ask you," Jill said in Deverrian. "When you agreed to come to Bardek with me, was it mostly on the hope of finding Alaena again?"

"I cannot tell a lie. Indeed it was."

Jill snorted profoundly, realizing even as she did it that she sounded just like Nevyn.

"But, Jill, it all worked out for the best, didn't it now? Have I not been your guide, your escort, your loyal companion and faithful dog, even, while at the same time rescuing my beloved from a life of virtual slavery to her bestial father?"

"It was Keeta who did the rescuing. You were just the bait."

"Imph, well, I suppose so, but how crudely you put things sometimes."

"My heart bleeds. On the morrow we're going to find a ship for Anmurdio and get on with our search and that's that."

"I've already found the ship." He favored her with a brilliant grin. "We had to wait a fair bit down at the archon's palace, and there was a ship's captain waiting there as well to register his last cargo, and so lo and behold! A deal was struck."

And that was the worst of Salamander, Jill reflected. Just when you were about to allow yourself the pleasure of berating him, he went and did something right.

•　　•　　•

Evandar lounged upon a hilltop that overlooked the remains of a formal garden, roses gone wild and tangled, hedges sending long green fingers into the air, muddy walks cracking. The plan of squares and half circles stretched out skewed, as well, as if the right half had shrunk and the left grown along the diagonal.

"It looks squashed," he remarked to Dallandra. "As if a giant had fallen against it."

"I see what you mean. Is this the garden you showed me when first I came here?"

"It is, yes, but now it's spoilt. And the house, the splendid rooms I made for you—they've all gone away, too, turned into air and blown far, far away. It always happens. I try to build as once your people built, but never does a stone or stick last me out."

"This world was meant for flux, not forms. If only you'd come be born into my world . . ."

"Shan't!" He tossed his head in irritation. "Don't speak of it."

She knew his moods and let the subject drop.

"I found a marvel, Dalla. The islands of which your friend spoke? They've rebuilt Rinbaladelan there, but it's a poor thing, all small and flimsy, wood where once stood stone."

"You found them? You didn't tell me that!"

He shrugged, then rose, standing for a moment to frown at the ruined garden. Twilight gathered purple in the sky and dropped shadows round him like rain. Wind ruffled his yellow hair with a flash of palpable light. At moments like these Dalla found herself wondering who or what he might be, and where they might be, as well, if perhaps even she'd died and all this bright country was only an illusion of life built of memory and longing. It seemed that her very wondering threatened to destroy the world round her. The hill upon which they stood dissolved and began to float away in tendrils of mist, while the garden below became only a pile of weeds and sticks. Evandar grew as thin as a shadow himself, a colored shadow cast upon empty air. Her heart thudded in her throat.

"Don't go!" The words seemed torn out of her. "I love you."

All at once he stood solidly in front of her, and the hands that caught her shoulders, the mouth that caught her own, were warm and substantial. He kissed her again, his mouth all hunger, his hands pulling her tight against him. Together they sank to their knees, then lay down, clasped in each other's arms. She lost all awareness of her body, if indeed it were anything more than a mere image or form of a body, yet she could feel him, twined round, feel the energy pulsing from him as tangible as flesh, feel the power flowing from her own essence as well to mingle with his, while they shared an ecstasy more intense than any sexual pleasure she'd ever known. On waves of sensation that made them both cry aloud they seemed to soar, a twined, twinned consciousness.

And yet, afterward, as always, she couldn't quite remember what had happened to make her feel that way. They lay on the hillside, clasped in each other's arms like an ordinary pair of lovers, and yet, without her conscious thought, whatever illusions of clothing that they wore had returned. She felt cool, alert, almost preternaturally calm, and he merely smiled at her as if he were surprised at what they'd shared. Yet when he released her, she saw the garden blooming down below, renewed and glorious.

"I love you as well," he said, as if nothing had interrupted their earlier talk. "Dalla, Dalla, I thought I was so clever when I lured you here, but you're the hunter and the snare both. And in the end you'll abandon me, no doubt, like some animal left dead so long in a trap that its fur's all rotted and spoilt."

She pulled away from him and sat up, running her hands through her long tangle of hair. Already her hands and the hair itself felt perfectly normal to her, no different from the flesh she remembered. He lay back on one elbow and watched, his face as stricken as a man who's been told he'll hang on the morrow.

"In the end you'll force me to go," she said at last. "I love you too much to stay and watch you die into nothingness."

"That's a cruel speaking."

"Is it? What would you have me do instead?"

"I don't know." He paused, then shook his head. "By those gods you speak of, I'm weary tonight. I went a long way, seeking out those islands. You should see them for yourself."

"I want to, yes. I wish I could talk with Jill about them."

"Why can't you? Go with my blessing, my love."

"It's not that. I just never have enough time to say much once I find her, before the vision breaks, I mean."

"Well, if you insist on going only in vision."

"And how else am I supposed to go?"

"Are you not here in the world between all worlds? Wait! Forgive me. I forget you don't know. Come with me, my love, and you shall learn to walk the roads." He hesitated, cocking his head to one side like a dog. "Where's Elessario?"

"I don't know."

"Let's just go take a look at her. I have the strangest feeling round my heart."

A feeling that, it turned out, was well justified. Hand in hand they drifted down from the hilltop to find the Host feasting in the meadowlands. It seemed a huge pavilion of cloth-of-gold, hung with blue banners, sheltered rows of long tables, set with candles in silver candelabra, but once inside Dallandra realized that she could look through the roof and see stars, spread in the long drift of the Snowy Road. Music floated over the talk and laughter as they made their way through the tables and asked for his child. None had seen her. All at once the pavilion changed, grew stone inside the cloth, the meadow crisping into straw, the banners transmuting to faded tapestries. Out of the corner of her eye Dallandra thought she saw fire leaping in a huge stone hearth, yet when she looked straight at it, she saw only the moon, rising through a mullioned window.

"Come with me." Evandar tugged her hand so hard that he nearly dragged her away. "I don't like this."

At the back door they found Elessario, dressed in a long tunic of blue, kirtled at the waist with a silver, white, and green plaid. In her hands she carried a loaf of bread, which she offered to an old beggar woman, all gnarled hands and brown rags, leaning on a bit of stick.

"Mother, Mother," the child was saying. "Why won't you come in and feast?"

"No more am I welcome in your father's hall. Child, can't you see that they plot your death? Come away, come with me to safety.

Better the life of a beggar on the roads than this murderous luxury."

"Mother, no, they mean to give us life, true life, the like of which we've never had before."

The old woman spat onto the ground.

"Touching, Alshandra, very touching," Evandar said suddenly. "Truly, you should go be born into Deverry and grow into a bard."

With a howl of rage the beggar woman rose up, shedding her rags like water dripping, dressed now in a deerskin tunic and boots; her stick became a hunting bow, and her hair flowed gold over her shoulders. Dimly, at the margins of her sight, Dallandra realized that the stone broch behind them had disappeared, and that the cloth-of-gold pavilion glimmered in the moonlight in its stead.

"My curse upon you, Evandar!" Alshandra snarled. "A mother's curse upon you and your elven whore both!"

With a gust of wind and a swirl of dry leaves from some distant forest's floor, she disappeared. Evandar rubbed his chin and sighed.

"She always could be a bit tiresome," he remarked. "Elli, come with us. I've a lesson to give Dallandra, and I'm not leaving you here alone."

As Bardekian merchantmen go, the ship was a good one, soundly built and deep, with room enough in the hold for the troupe's gear and room enough on deck twixt single mast and stern for them to camp under improvised tents. The troupe's horses had a comfortable place up on the deck tethered by the bow rather than in the stinking hold. During the crossing Jill spent most of her time in their equine company. Even in normal circumstances the troupe lived in a welter of spats and jests, gossip and sentiment, outright fights and professions of undying loyalty, and now that they were sailing off to unknown country, they were as tightly strung as the wela-wela. Tucked in between the horses and the bow rail, Jill could have privacy for her meditations. Every now and then Keeta joined her, for a bit of a rest, as the juggler put it.

"I don't know how you stand this lot sometimes," Jill remarked to her one morning.

"Neither do I." Keeta flashed a grin. "Oh, they're all good people, really, and the only family I've ever had or am likely to have. But they do carry on so. It's Marka's marriage, you see. She started out as nothing, the apprentice, the waif we all pitied, and now here she is, the leader's wife. Everyone's all stirred up and jockeying for position."

"And Salamander's really become the leader, hasn't he?"

"Oh, yes. No doubt about that, my dear, none at all."

At that moment Jill realized why she'd objected to Salamander's marriage. He'd so loaded himself up with responsibility for other people's lives that she couldn't possibly reproach him for letting his dweomer studies lapse. She said nothing, merely watched him over the next few days as he busied himself with the troupe or sat grinning beside his new wife. *Perhaps he knows best,* she would think. *Perhaps he simply doesn't have the strength of will, perhaps he's too weak, somewhere deep in his heart, to take up his destiny.* Yet, despite this sensible reasoning, she felt that she was mourning a death. For Nevyn's sake, she would do her best to keep him from squandering his talent, but a crowded ship was no place to confront him.

From the moment the troupe landed, Jill hated Anmurdio. While Orystinna was every bit as hot, it was a dry heat there, thanks to the way the mountains channeled and deflected the prevailing winds. Anmurdio, the collective name for a group of volcanic islands, caught the tropic-wet winds full in the face. It seemed that if it wasn't actually raining, then the wind was howling round, or if the air was still for a brief while, then it became so humid that everyone wished it would rain. The towns—random clusters of wooden houses—sagged in the ever-present mud between stretches of primal jungle. The water wasn't safe to drink without a good dollop of wine in it; beef was unknown, and bread rare. Yet all of these aggravations might have been bearable if it weren't for the mosquitoes, drifting in twilight clouds as thick as smoke.

Traveling in heavy wagons would be impossible, but fortunately all the hamlets in the archipelago lay right on the ocean.

Swearing and sweating over the expense, Salamander made a bargain with the owner of a little coaster that would just barely hold the troupe. The wagon horses, which Marka loved like pets, had to be stabled at a further cost in the main town—city being far too dignified a word for Myleton Noa—rather than merely sold and abandoned.

Just when all these expensive arrangements were concluded, it began to rain, a dark sodden pour that went on and on and on for three days and washed away the troupe's remaining coin along with their tempers. In a flood of jokes and compliments Salamander moved from person to person, keeping up morale and stopping fights. As she told him late one night, when they got a moment alone together, Jill had to admire him for it.

"But still," she remarked. "If you'd only put this much hard work into your studies—"

He busied himself with slapping mosquitoes.

"I've been meaning to have a talk with you," she went on, relentless. "No doubt you've lost some ground lately, but now that you're married and settled, there's no reason that you couldn't gain it back."

"No doubt you're correct, O Princess of Powers Perilous, as well as accurate, precise, and just plain right, but the times are a bit troubled, not to say noisy, with all of us packed into this stinking inn together, for concentration. At the moment, the only dweomer I feel like working would be a bit of weather magic, to drive away this wretched storm, but I know that such would offend your fine-tuned sense of ethics."

"Things aren't quite desperate enough for that, yet."

"True. It doubtless will clear soon enough on its own. The innkeep assures me that this much rain is most unseasonable."

Apparently the innkeep knew his weather, because they woke on the morrow to clearing skies. In a much improved mood the troupe set about cleaning and readying their equipment for the coming show.

"I hope to every god that I was right about the profit to be made here," Salamander remarked to Jill. "If I'm not, we are well and truly in the thick of battle without a sword, as the old saying would have it."

She said nothing, by a great effort of will.

"I know what you're thinking," he went on with theatrical gloom. "You might as well berate me and be done with it."

"I was merely wondering why anyone bothered to settle here in the first place, and then, in the second, why they bother to stay."

"Pearls." All at once he grinned. "Pearls both black and white, mother of pearl and fine shells of all sorts, the best and the rarest for the jewelers of Bardek. And they quarry the black obsidian, too, to send home, and catch the parrots and other rare birds to delight the fine ladies of Surtinna. Merchant ships sail back and forth all the time, trading for their wares."

"Nothing but a lot of trinkets, if you ask me."

"Trinkets have made men rich before. Of course, a lot of men have died out here, too. The sea's bounty demands its price."

"If it's that dangerous, maybe you should just take the troupe home now."

"Not until I've put my scheme to the test, O Monarch of Might Mysterious. And tonight, here in the very market square of Myleton Noa, will the test come!"

The market square in question was a big sprawl of mud in the center of town. All round the edge stood such civic buildings as the town could muster: a customs house, an archon's residence, a barracks for the town guard, and a money changer, who supported a small guard of his own, according to the wine seller.

"He's a shrewd one, old Din-var-tano," he remarked to Jill. "And as honest as the sea is deep, too. But a miser? Ye gods! He lives like a slave, and he won't have a wife because of the expense of keeping one, you see. I'll wager we won't see him tonight at this here show. He'd feel obliged to part with one of his precious coppers! But it looks like everyone else in town is here, that's for certain."

Jill and the wine seller were standing on the wooden steps of the archon's palace, a little above the crowd swarming round the muddy square. The old man had set up his little booth on the top step, and as they talked, he was busily chaining wine cups to the rail. In the velvet twilight, the troupe was raising crossed pairs of standing torches round the stage while Salamander himself stood underneath the slack rope and pulled on it to make sure it was secure.

"We've never had a show through here before," the wine seller went on. "I wager I'll do good business after it's over."

"No doubt. I take it things are lonely in Anmurdio."

"As lonely as the sea is deep, that's for certain. Sometimes I'm sorry I came, I tell you, but then, a man can live his life as he likes out here without a lot of city clerks laying down the law and grabbing his coin for taxes."

"Ah. I see. Tell me something. Do you ever hear of ships sailing south?"

"South? What for? Nothing out there but sea and wind."

"You're sure?" She paused to kill a particularly big mosquito that had landed on her wrist. "You've never heard of any islands lying far to the south?"

He sucked his stumps of teeth while he considered.

"Never," he said at last. "But I can tell you who you want to ask about that. See over there, that great big fellow standing in the torchlight? The one with the red tunic—that's right, him. Dekki's his name, and he's quite a sailing man, goes to all sorts of places, and not all of them are on maps, if you take my meaning."

Jill sighed, because she did see. A pirate, most likely, and not her favorite sort of person in the world. Before she could ask the wine seller more, on the stage drums boomed out and flutes sang. In a pleasurable shudder of applause, the crowd surged closer. The show had begun.

From the very first moment, when the youngest and clumsiest acrobat cartwheeled across the stage, Jill could see that Salamander's commercial instincts had delivered triumph. No matter whether a performer pulled off a difficult trick or fell in the middle of an easy one, the crowd clapped and cheered. At the end of each turn coins clinked and slithered on the stage. After all, these colonists were rich by the standards of the cities they'd left behind, but lacked luxuries to spend their wealth upon. When the heart of the show appeared, Keeta and her flaming torches, Marka dancing upon the slack rope, the crowd screamed and stamped their feet. Silver flashed like rain in the torchlight. When Jill turned to speak to the wine seller, she found him utterly entranced, smiling as he stared. Salamander himself performed the greatest trick of all, making the crowd fall silent again to catch his every word. It seemed to Jill that he luxuriated in their attention like a man drowsing in a hot and perfumed bath. She felt as if she should slap him awake before he drowned.

Finally, when the performers were exhausted beyond the power of cheers and coins to revive them, the show wound down. By then the moon was low on the horizon, and the wheel of stars turning toward dawn. In a cooler wind from the sea the crowd lingered, watching the troupe strike its stage or drifting over the various booths and peddlers selling food and drink. When Dekki came strolling up, the crowd round the wine booth parted like the sea beneath a prow to let him through, and the wine seller handed him a cup without waiting to be asked. The pirate paid twice its worth for it, though; Jill supposed that his high standing in the town depended on his generosity just as a Deverry lord's respect among his folk depended on his. The wine seller made him a bob of a bow.

"This lady here would like to speak with you, Dekki." He jerked a thumb in Jill's direction. "She's a scholar and a map-maker."

"Indeed?" His voice was a rumble like distant thunder. "My honor, then. What do you want to know?"

They moved away from the press of thirsty customers and stood by a pair of torches. Jill pulled her map out of her shirt and held it unrolled in the flaring light.

"I got this over in Inderat Noa," she said. "Do you see those islands far to the south? You wouldn't happen to know if they really exist, would you?"

"Well, I wouldn't be surprised if you told me they did. Let's put it this way. There's *something* out there." He took the map and frowned at the dim markings. "Once me and my men, we were blown off course by a storm, and a bad one it was, too. We rode south before it for many a day, and we just barely pulled through, and we found wrack from a ship that wasn't so lucky. We spotted what looked like a figurehead and hauled it on board.

We were thinking, see, that it was an Anmurdio ship, and so we'd take it home for the owners' reward. Huh. Never seen anything like it in my life." He handed back the map. "It was a woman, and she was smiling and had all this long hair, a nice job of carving it was, you would have sworn you could have run your fingers through it. But she had wings, or, I should say, what we found had stumps of wings. They must have folded back along the bow, like. But anyway, there were these letters carved round the belt she was wearing. Never seen anything like them. I call them letters, but they were magic marks for all I know."

"And what happened to this thing?"

"Oh, we tossed it back. Wasn't one of our ships."

"I see. So, then, it must have come from somewhere to the south?"

"Most likely. And then there's the bubbles, too. Down on the southern beaches, sometimes you find these glass bubbles after a storm." He cupped his massive hands. "About so big. Bad luck to break one. The priests say there must be evil spirits trapped inside. But someone must have blown the glass and trapped the spirits."

"I don't suppose you'd be interested in sailing south someday, just to find out what lies that way."

"Not on your life!"

"Not even if someone paid you well?"

"Not even then. You can't spend coin down Hades way, can you? That storm took us about as far as a man can sail and still get himself home again, and we all came cursed near to starving to death before we made port."

The way he shook his head, and the edge of fear wedging into his voice, made it plain that not all the persuasion in the world was going to change his mind. Jill stood him to another cup of wine in thanks for the information, then bid him farewell and strolled over to join the troupe. They were laughing, tossing jests back and forth and all round the circle, dancing through their work, so happy—so relieved, really—that she couldn't bear to spoil their celebration. She would wait to talk with Salamander on the morrow, she decided.

"Ebañy?" she called out. "I'm going back to the inn. This trip's wrung me out."

He tossed a length of rope into a wagon and hurried over, peering at her in the flickering torchlight. He himself looked exhausted, streaming with sweat, his eyes pools of dark shadow.

"Jill, are you well? Lately you've looked so pale."

"It's the heat." As she spoke, she realized the grim truth of it. "I'm not used to it, and I'm not as young as I used to be, you know. And it seems to be taking its toll on you, as well."

He nodded his agreement and ran both hands through his sweaty hair to slick it back from his face.

"Don't stay up too late yourself, my friend," Jill said. "As for me, I think I'll go have some of that watered wine or winy water or whatever it is, and then just go to bed."

She was so exhausted that once she lay down in her inn chamber, she fell straight asleep and never even heard the entire troupe clattering in, an hour or so later.

In the middle of the night, though, Jill woke in a puddle of sweat. Since the window was a patch of black only slightly grayer than the room itself, she could assume that the moon had already set but the dawn was still hours away. Swearing under her breath she got up, rubbed herself dry with her dirty shirt, and put on her cleaner one to go outside for a breath of air. The compound was utterly silent, utterly dark except for the faint murmur of water in the fountain and a glimmer of stars far above. She made her careful way across the cracked tiles to the fountain, groped around, and found a safe seat on its edge. Here outside, with a trace of breeze brushing her face and the sound of water splashing nearby, she felt cool enough to think.

Getting an Anmurdio ship for the trip south was out of the question. She decided that straightaway. Even if the crew proved trustworthy, they and their passengers both would still likely die from the bad water and worse food on such a long journey. The more she thought about it, the more she realized that she could never subject the troupe to the journey, not even if they had the best boat in the world to carry them. Not even Marka? She indulged herself with a few choice curses on Salamander's head.

They could neither take the lass along nor leave her behind, not now, unless of course Salamander stayed with her. But go alone? She was willing to admit that the idea of traveling alone across the southern sea frightened her, in spite of all her dweomer, but she also knew that if she had to, she would. When she looked up, the stars hung bright and cold, a vast indifferent sweep dwarfing even a dweomermaster and her concerns in a tide of light and darkness. In the spirit of an invalid demanding a lantern in her nighttime chamber, Jill snapped her fingers and called upon the Wildfolk of Aethyr. They came, clustering round the decayed stone nymph in the center of the fountain and shedding a faint but comforting glow.

The silver light made her think of Dallandra, just idly at first, until an idea struck home like an arrow. Jill pointed at one of the spirits hovering nearby.

"You know the lands of the Guardians. Fetch Dallandra for me."

The spirit winked out of manifestation, but whether it had truly understood the command, Jill couldn't say. She waited for a long time, was, in fact, about to give it up and go back inside when she saw a wisp of silver light gathering above the fountain.

"Dalla?" She breathed out the name.

But it was only an undine, raising itself up, as sleek as a water snake, to stare at her with enormous eyes before vanishing in a swirl of water. Dressed in her elven clothes, though the amethyst jewel no longer hung round her neck, Dallandra herself strolled across the courtyard, as solid as the cobblestones.

"I can't believe I managed it," she remarked, grinning, and she spoke in Elvish. "But it worked, and here I am. Jill, I've got so much to tell you. Evandar's found the islands, first off, and we can take you there."

"Take me there?" Jill felt as muddled as if someone had just struck her on the head. "You've got a ship?"

"No, but we don't need one. It's Evandar's dweomer. But I don't know how many of you we can—"

"I'll be the only person making the trip. I've been dreading taking other people along with me. I can't tell you how grateful I am! For all I knew, we could all drown out there."

"Most likely you would." She paused, glancing over her shoulder at something that only she could see. "I've still got to be quick, even though it's ever so much easier to talk like this. But Evandar said to tell you something else, that these people respect and honor the dweomer more than any other thing under the sun and moon, and so you'll have a welcome there."

"And I can't tell you how glad I am to hear that, too! I'd been rather wondering about it."

"No doubt." She flashed a grin. "When do you want to go? I imagine that you've got farewells to make."

"And some gear to get together. And, well, there's somewhat I've got to do before I leave, not that Salamander's going to thank me for it, I suppose. I don't suppose we can set a time, anyway. If I say a fortnight, how will you know when that comes round?"

"It's difficult, yes. I do have a plan. There's a place that I can wait, one that's next to your world, you see, and so its Time runs a little closer to yours. Get yourself ready, and I'll come to you as soon as I can. Send me one of the Wildfolk for a messenger."

"Splendid. And you have my thanks and a thousand times my thanks."

"Most welcome." She paused again, staring down at the ground and frowning. "The child. She's going to have to be born soon, because there's trouble brewing in our lands. I can't explain. I only half understand it myself. But it's going to have to be soon."

All at once a thought struck Jill. It might well be that Salamander and his new wife would serve the dweomer whether he wanted to or no.

"Tell me something. Could the child be born here? In the islands, I mean?"

"No, not at all. All the omens, and what little logic there is in this thing, for that matter, say she has to be born into the Westlands."

"That's a pity."

"Why?"

"Oh, just that I know a new husband who might make a splendid father for such a child."

"Good, because, you see, there'll be other children born later, lots and lots—at least, if I can carry this thing off. Jill, at times I'm frightened."

"Well, for what my help is worth, you have it."

"It's worth a very great deal."

They clasped hands and shared a smile. Jill was surprised at how warm and solid Dallandra's hand felt; she'd been expecting some cool etheric touch.

"If great things are on the move," Jill said, "I'd best wrap up my affairs here and get on my way back to Deverry."

"When the time draws near, I'll take you back to Deverry, have no fear about that. I've so many marvels to tell you about, to show you, once we've time to talk together for a while, but now—"

"Yes, I understand. You'd best go. It's almost dawn, and if other people find you here, they'll ask questions."

Dallandra walked toward the inn-yard gates, turned once to wave, then vanished in a glimmer of gray dawn light. Marvels, indeed! Jill thought. All at once she laughed aloud, thinking what a wonderful jest it would be on Salamander, if indeed he ended up fathering the body for some dweomer-touched child. Even Nevyn, she supposed, would have been able to see the humor in this, for all that the old man could be downright grim more often than not.

When Dallandra mentioned trouble brewing, she meant nothing more than the ill will that Alshandra bore her, but as things turned out she'd spoken more truly than she knew. After she left Jill at the inn yard, she traveled back through the twisting roads and the mists to Evandar's country. He was waiting for her on the hilltop, standing alone and looking down through the night to the meadow where his people danced by torchlight. The music drifted up to them on the wind, harp and drum and flute.

"You've come back," he said. "My heart ached the whole time you were gone."

"Did you think I'd desert you so soon?"

"I no longer know what to think. I thought I was so clever at jests and riddles, and now you've posed me a riddle that I can't answer." He shook his head and made his yellow hair toss like a horse's mane. "I take it you found Jill?"

"I did, and she'll follow our road with heartfelt thanks. But what do you mean, a riddle you can't answer?"

All at once the life flashed in his turquoise eyes, and he grinned.

"Now that I shan't tell you, because it's a riddle of mine to top the one you posed me. Or perhaps we can say that—" He hesitated, listening.

Dallandra heard it, too, a thin shriek on the rising wind. Together without need for words they turned and hurled themselves into the air, he a hawk, suddenly, a red hawk from Deverry, while she changed to her usual shape of some gray and indeterminate songbird, both of them with wingspreads of fully fifteen feet across. They banked into the rising wind and rode it down, swooping over the grassy hillside to the flowered meadow where now the court screamed and ran about in confusion. In the darkening night torches guttered and sparked.

"Elessario!" The cry drifted up to them. "She's been taken!"

The hawk screamed, a harsh cry, and changed course for the river. Dallandra followed, praying for moonlight, and as if in answer a moon began to appear on the horizon, vast and bloated, casting a sickly yellow light. Far below on the oily river she saw a shape, like a splinter of wood from their height, pushing itself upstream. Evandar stooped and plunged. More slowly in prudent circles Dallandra followed him down and saw a black barge, rowed by slaves, churning against the current. In the prow stood Alshandra, and she seemed that night some ten feet high, a warrior woman dressed in glittering armor, nocking an arrow in her bow. Screaming, the hawk plunged down and upon her before she could aim and loose. His massive claws raked her face and his beak tore at her arms as she fell to the deck, howling in rage, clubbing him with the bow.

Bound round with black chains Elessario crouched, sobbing, some feet away. Dallandra understood enough about this country by then to keep her wits. She landed on the deck and shed her bird-form like a cloak.

"Break the chains!" she snapped. "Just flex your arms, and they'll fall right off."

Elessario followed orders and laughed aloud when the chains turned to water and puddled at her feet. With a howl of rage Alshandra threw the hawk to one side and hauled herself to her knees. Boat, slaves, armor, night—they all vanished as suddenly as the chains. In the golden sun of a late afternoon they stood in elven form on the grassy riverbank while the chattering Host swarmed round.

"Oh, go away, all of you!" Alshandra snarled.

Laughing and calling out to one another they fled. Dallandra put an arm round Elessario's shoulders and drew her close while Alshandra and Evandar faced each other, both dressed in court clothes, now, cloth-of-gold tunics, diadems of gold and jewels, and their cloaks, tipped in fur, seemed made of silver satin. And yet, across her cheek ran the bleeding rake of a hawk's talon, and on his face swelled a purple bruise.

"She's my daughter, and I shall take her wherever I want," Alshandra said.

"Not unless she goes willingly, and the chains show she was less than willing. Where were you going to take her? Farther in?"

"That's no affair of yours." Alshandra turned on Dalla. "You may have my man, because I tired of him long before you came to us, but you shall not have my daughter."

"I don't want her for my sake. I only want her to have the life that should be hers, that should be yours, truly, as well."

With a shimmer of light Alshandra changed her form, becoming old, wrinkled, pathetic in black rags.

"You'll take her far away, far, far away, and never shall I see her again."

"Come with her, then. Follow her, the way all of your people are going to do. Join us all in life." Dallandra glanced Elessario's way. "Do you want to go with your mother?"

"No, I want to stay with you."

Alshandra howled, swelling up tall and strong, dressed like a hunter in her doeskin tunic and boots, the bow clasped in red-veined hands.

"Have it your way, witch! You'll lose this battle in the end. I swear it. I've found some as will help me, back in that ugly little world of yours. I've made friends there, powerful friends. They'll get me my daughter back the moment she tries to leave us. I'll make them promise, and I know they will, because they grovel at my feet, they do."

She was gone, winking out like a blown flame, but all round them the wind seemed cold and the sunlight, shadowed. Shaking and pale, Elessario leaned into Dallandra's clasp.

"Friends? Groveling?" Evandar said. "I wonder what she means by that. I very much do. I'd say it bodes ill, an ill-omened thing all round."

"I'd never argue with you." Dalla felt her voice as very small and weak. "We'd best try to find out what she means by friends."

"Will the finding be a safe thing? I don't know, mind. I'm asking you."

"I don't know, either. Can't we get away from all this music and the noise and all?"

"Of course. Ell, I fear to leave you alone. Come with us."

"I'm so tired, Father. I don't want to."

"Well, I'm not going to leave you sleeping beside the river like a falcon's lure. I—" All at once he smiled. "Very well, my love, my daughter, my darling. Rest you shall have. Dalla, if you'll step here to my side?"

Puzzled, Dallandra did just that. Evandar raised one hand and waved out a circle that seemed to float from his fingers and ring his daughter round. He chanted, too, in some language that Dallandra had never heard before, just softly, briefly while Elessario yawned, reaching up to rub her eyes. It seemed that the wind caught her hair and tossed it, spread it out around her as she reached up higher, grabbed at it, her fingers turning long and slender, growing out, her arms reaching, stretching, stiffening, suddenly, as gray-brown bark wrapped her body round, and her hair, all green and gold, sprouted into leaves. A young oak tree, some seven feet tall and slender, nodded in the evening wind.

"Alshandra the Inelegant will never think to look for her there," Evandar remarked. "She truly can be a bit thick at times."

Dallandra merely stared, gape-mouthed, until he took her hand and led her away.

While Evandar was confronting his wife in his strange homeland, in the world of men Jill was trying to discharge what she saw as her obligation to Salamander before she moved on. After the triumph at Myleton Noa, the troupe set sail, falling into the routine of sailing down the coast some miles, then disembarking at yet another sodden hamlet, where they would be received like kings. Jill had the distinct feeling that Salamander was avoiding her. When everyone was crammed on board the small and smelly coaster, it was of course impossible to get a word alone with him. On land, whenever she went looking for him for their talk about his studies, he always seemed to be negotiating with an innkeep, or teaching a member of the troupe a juggling trick, or solving some problem among the acrobats, or arranging their next show. Finally, though, one evening in a good-sized town called Injaro, he made the mistake of leaving the dinner table early while Marka stayed behind to gossip with her friends. Jill followed him upstairs and cornered him in his inn chamber.

"Uh, I was just going back down," he squeaked. "I have to talk to Vinto and make sure the troupe's ready to take ship. We're leaving on the dawn tide, you know."

"Indeed? Then why have you lit all these lamps?"

"Er, just looking for somewhat. Are you all packed and ready for the journey? Best make sure you are."

"Stop driveling."

With a heavy sigh Salamander sank down onto an enormous purple cushion and gestured at her to find a seat opposite him. Sitting so close, she could smell the scent of sweet wine clinging to him and see the dark circles smudged under his puffy eyes.

"I was only wondering how your studies were going." She made her voice as mild as possible.

"I haven't done one rotten thing, and you know that as well as I do. Jill, I'm so cursed weary!"

"Well, then, when do you plan to take them up again?"

"Never."

The last thing she'd expected was candor. He went so wide-eyed and tense that she knew he'd shocked himself, too, but though she waited, he refused to back down, merely watched the insects swarming round the oil lamps and let the silence grow.

"Do you truly think you can just turn your back and walk away from the dweomer?" she said at last.

"I intend to try." His hands were shaking so hard that he clamped them down on his thighs. "I am sick to my heart of being badgered and prodded."

"What's brought all this on?"

"I should think it would be clear, plain, obvious, and evident. I've found a thing that I want more than dweomer power." He paused for one of his sunny smiles, and never had the gesture seemed less appropriate. "A normal life, Jill, a normal life. Does that have one shred of meaning for the likes of you?"

"What are you talking about? What's so splendid about traveling the roads with a troupe of mangy acrobats and this poor child you've married?"

"Of course it's not splendid. That's the point."

"You're a dolt, Ebañy."

"Oh, I suppose I must look that way to you, truly. I no longer care. I've found the woman I love, and I've found a way to have a family of my own while we travel the roads, just like I've always loved to do, and cursed, plagued, excoriated, blighted, and scourged will I be before I give one whit of it up."

"I'm not asking you to give up one thing, just to develop the talent you were born with."

"Talent? Oh, ye gods!" All at once he exploded, talking much too fast, his voice hissing as he tried to keep from shouting. "I am so sick of that ugly little word. Do you think I ever asked for it? Talent. Oh, certainly, I know I have talent for magic. That's all I've ever heard in my long and cursed life, from the time that my wretched father dragged me to meet Aderyn when I was but a little child. Talent. You have splendid talent for the dweomer. You must study it. It would be a waste to not study it. Your people need you to study it. No one, not one blasted soul, whether elven or human, not one person in the entire world has ever asked me if I wanted to study the blasted dweomer. All they did was push and press and mock and nag until by every god in the sky I'm sick of the very name of dweomer."

"My heart aches for you, but—"

"Don't you be sarcastic with me."

"I wasn't. I'm trying to point out that—"

"I don't want to hear it! By the black hairy ass of the Lord of Hell, Jill, can't you see? I've finally found what I want in life, and I'll have it no matter how many platitudes and how much invective you heap upon my head."

"Whoever said you couldn't have it?"

"The dweomer itself. How can you sit there and tell me that I could have both, you of all people on this blasted earth?"

Jill came perilously close to slapping him. Her rage at having that ancient wound reopened took her so much by surprise that for a long moment she couldn't speak. When he shrank back, suddenly pale, suddenly weak—cringing, or so she thought of it—the rage turned as cold as a steel blade on a winter morning. She got up slowly and stood for a moment, her hands on her hips, looking down as he crouched on the cushion, one hand raised as if to ward off a blow.

"Oho, I think I do see." She could hear her voice crack like a boot breaking ice. "You're a coward."

He was on his feet in a moment, red-faced and shaking with a rage to match hers.

"After all I've risked for you, after all I've done for you—"

"You haven't done one thing for *me*. You've done it for the dweomer and the Light."

"I don't give a—" He caught himself on the edge of blasphemy. "So I did. Wasn't that enough, then, everything I suffered for the Light?"

"You can't measure out service like so many sacks of meal and say 'enough, no more.' But that doesn't matter anyway. My road isn't your road. I couldn't have Rhodry and the dweomer both, but there's no reason on earth you can't raise your family and study as well. If I'd married, my life would have been my husband's. That's a woman's Wyrd, not yours. You can have

Marka's life and yours as well. You're just too cursed lazy to study, aren't you? That's the ugly truth of it. Lazy and a coward."

"Mock and goad me all you want. I've made my decision."

"Well and good, then. Far be it from me to stop you. Not one thing on this earth or over it or under it can force you to take up the birthright you're throwing away. But cursed and twice cursed if I linger to watch you."

She turned on her heel and spun out of the chamber, slamming the door behind her, and strode down the narrow hall that stank of dust and damp in the cloying heat. She meant to go for a walk in the night air and let them both come to their senses, but he was furious enough to follow her.

"I am sick half to death of you lording it over me," he snarled. "Don't you think I know you despise me?"

"Naught of the sort! I'm merely sick at heart to see you pissing your life away into a puddle."

"Oh, am I now? Is that all you think Marka is? A waste of my most exalted and ever so talented self?"

"Of course not! It's got naught to do with the lass."

"It's got everything to do with her. That's what you don't understand. You're just like Nevyn, Jill. As cold and nasty hearted as ever the old man was."

"Don't you say one word against Nevyn."

The snarl in her voice frightened even her. He stopped in midreply and stepped back against the wall as if she were a thief come to murder him.

"You spoiled stinking mincing little fop," she went on. "Have it your way, then. My curse upon you!"

She slammed out of the inn, strode across the courtyard, slammed out of the gates, and stomped off for a long walk round the town. Wildfolk clustered round her like an army, and whether it was her rage or their unseen but bristling presence, she didn't know, but no one, not one single thief or drunkard, so much as came near her all during that long aimless trek. Through the muddy streets of Injaro, out into the surrounding cleared land along a rutted road—only the light from the Wildfolk of Aethyr kept her from breaking her neck and ending that particular incarnation then and there. All at once she realized that she'd gone dangerously far from the town, no matter how much dweomer she had, and turned back. For all that she'd walked herself exhausted, she still was too angry to judge Salamander fairly.

Toward dawn her wandering brought her back to a small rise overlooking the harbor, where she paused among a tangle of huge ferns, as big as trees, to catch her breath. Down below, out at the end of a long jetty, a boat lay at anchor in a pool of torchlight. Like ants the troupe moved back and forth, hauling their personal goods for the sailors to stow below. At the landward end of the jetty, Salamander was supervising while a pair of stevedores unloaded the troupe's props and stage from a wagon. Jill swore aloud. She'd forgotten how early the tide would turn for their journey out. Fortunately there was still plenty of time left. She could trot right down, tell Salamander that she was going back to the inn for her pack and suchlike, then return to the coaster before they sailed.

For a long time she stood there, leaning against one of the tree ferns, and wondered why she wasn't hurrying. Already out to the east the sky was beginning to lighten to the furry gray that meant dawn coming. Her gnome appeared to grab the hem of her shirt and pull on it as if he wanted to lead her to the ship. She picked him up in her arms and made sure she had his attention.

"Go tell Dallandra it's time. Find her among the Guardians. She'll know who sent you."

In a puff of moldy air the gnome vanished. Jill watched the bustle at the pier. It seemed that everyone was on board, but Salamander lingered on land, looking up the road into the town, pacing back and forth, pausing to stare again. When the captain left the ship and walked over to argue with him, Salamander waved his arms in the air and shook his head in a stubborn no. The sky was all silver now, and already the heat of day was building in the humid air. Jill had one last stab of doubt. Was she simply being stubborn? Was she deserting a friend, and him one she'd known for years and years? Yet with the cold intuition of the dweomer she knew that she was doing the right thing, that she could no more force him to take up his Wyrd before he wished than Nevyn had been able to force her, all those years ago.

At last, Salamander flung both hands into the air, shook his head, and followed the captain on board. Just as the ship was pulling away from the jetty, the gray gnome appeared, all grins and bows. Jill picked him up again and held him like a child clutching a doll as she watched the ship sail away, heading south on a rising wind, until it disappeared into the opalescent dawn. In the day's fresh heat, sweat trickled down her back.

"Well, we can hope, at least, that the Elder Brothers found themselves a better island to settle than this one, but somehow or other, I have my doubts."

The gnome mugged a mournful face, then disappeared.

The ship had sailed some miles down the coast before Marka realized that something was wrong with Salamander. She was standing in the stern of the boat, watching the wake and chatting with the helmsman, when a grim Keeta made her way back through the piles of trunks and boxes.

"Marka, you'd best tend to that husband of yours. He's up in front."

When she hurried forward, Keeta followed, but she hovered a respectful distance away, back by the mast. At the prow, Salamander was leaning onto the wale as if he were a lookout, but she could tell that he was staring off toward nothing and seeing nothing as well.

"Ebañy?"

He neither moved nor seemed to hear. For a moment she felt paralyzed by a sudden mad fear, that no words of hers would ever reach him, that if she tried to touch him her hand would pass right through his arm, that never again would he hear when she tried to speak. As if a waking nightmare had dropped over her like a net, the light turned strange, all blue and cold for the briefest of moments. She could not speak, knowing that he would never hear. She caught her breath in a sob, and he spun round, masking his face in a smile.

"Well, we're under way nice and early, aren't we?"

The illusion shattered. Ordinary sunlight danced on the sea and fell warm on her skin and hair. Yet, when he went on smiling, she felt as if he'd slapped her, that he would hide his hurt this way.

"I thought something was wrong."

"Oh, no, no. Just thinking."

In her sudden misery she could only study his face and wonder if he still loved her.

"Salamander?" Keeta strode forward. "Where's Jill?"

"Oh, she's not coming with us. There's really nothing she wants in these stinking islands, so she'll be catching a ship back to Orystinna."

"Really?" Keeta raised one eyebrow.

"Just that." Ebañy smiled again, easily and smoothly. "She's got her work to do, you know, and she could see that she's not going to find any rare books in these rotting little towns."

"Well, that's certainly true enough." Keeta hesitated, on the edge of asking more. "I always wondered why she came out with us in the first place. But do you think she'll be all right?"

"My dear woman!" Ebañy laughed aloud. "I've never known anyone better able to take care of herself than Jill."

Keeta nodded, considering, then smiled herself.

"Well, that's most likely true, too. Just wondering. I'm surprised she didn't say good-bye, but then, she's not the kind of woman who likes a long drawn-out parting. You can see that."

Ebañy kept smiling until she wandered off, picking her way through the deck cargo in search of Delya; then he flung himself round and leaned onto the wale again, staring out as if he were struggling not to cry. Marka could think of nothing to do but lean next to him and wait. Ahead the sea stretched out like a road, green-blue and flecked with brown kelp. Gulls darted and shrieked in the rising sun.

"Ah, well," Ebañy said at last. "Even old friends must part, sooner or later, I suppose."

"Are you going to miss Jill?"

He nodded a yes, staring off to sea.

"Well, darling." Marka felt like sobbing in relief, just from finding something to say. "If the show keeps doing so well, maybe we can go to Deverry someday and see her again. If she's at this Wmmglaedd place, we'll know where to find her."

He turned to look at her, and this time his smile was genuine.

"Maybe so. Somehow I managed to forget that."

"Silly." She laid her hand on his arm. "My beloved idiot."

"You do love me, don't you? Truly, truly love me?"

"What? More than my life."

"Don't say that." He grabbed her by the shoulders so tightly that it hurt. "It's ill-omened."

"I didn't know."

"But do you love me? Oh, by the gods! If you don't love me, I've—" His voice caught in a sob.

"Of course I love you. I love you so much I can't even say."

"I'm sorry." He let her go, caught her again, but gently this time. "Forgive me, my love. I'll admit to having had days when I've been in better humor." He kissed her mouth. "Why don't you leave me to my fit, sulk, temperament, or whatever this may be?"

All morning he stood there alone, brooding over the sea and sky. Marka had a sudden premonition that had nothing to do with dweomer, that even if their marriage lasted for fifty years or more, she would never truly know her husband, realized it then, when by every law in Bardek and Deverry both it was far too late to change her mind. She also remembered the old fortune-teller in Luvilae. The knave of flowers, she thought. That's who it was: Ebañy. I've married the knave of flowers, and I'll never be the princess now.

After she watched the ship sail out of sight, Jill returned to the inn, paid off the bills that the troupe had left behind them, then gathered a pack's worth of possessions: her clothes, the various maps and bits of manuscripts that she'd found in the archipelago, a judicious selection of herbs and oddments, then in a fit of thrift stored the rest with the innkeep, just as if she might come back again someday. Laden like a peddler she strolled out of town by the west gate and followed the road, keeping more on the solid shoulder than the mucky middle, for about a mile. As soon as she turned off into the tangled forest, she saw Dallandra, waiting for her between two trees. In the sunlight the elven woman seemed as insubstantial as a wisp of fog caught in branches.

"You're ready?" Dalla said. "Now remember, Time runs differently, even on our borders. We won't seem to be in the Gatelands very long, but we might come out again years later or suchlike. We have to travel fast."

Together they walked through the dappled shade and between the enormous trees. At first Jill thought that nothing had happened, but then she realized that the thick jungle foliage was so intense a green that it seemed fashioned from emerald. When she took a few steps, she saw ahead of her windblown billows of grass. She spun round and found the jungle gone, swallowed by a mist hanging in the air, opalescent in a delicate flood of grays and lavenders shot through with pinks and blues. As she watched, the mist swelled, surged, and wrapped them round in welcome cold.

"There," Dallandra said. "You're not truly in your body anymore, you see."

Jill felt a weight round her neck and found, hanging from a golden chain, a tiny statuette of herself carved from obsidian. Dallandra laughed.

"Mine's of amethyst. That's rather rude of Evandar, to use blackstone for you. It's so grim."

"Oh, it suits me well enough."

Ahead three roads stretched out pale across the grasslands. One road led to the left and a stand of dark hills, so bleak and glowering that she knew they had no part in any country that Dallandra would call home. One road led to the right and a sudden rise of mountains, pale and gleaming in pure air beyond the mist, their tops shrouded in snow so bright that it seemed as if they were lighted from within. Straight ahead on the misty flat stretched the third. Dressed in elven clothes, a man was walking to meet them down that middle way, whistling as he came, his hair an impossible yellow, bright as daffodils. When he drew close Jill noticed that his eyes were an unnatural sky-blue and his lips red as cherries. She felt magical power streaming from him as palpably as she felt the mist.

"Good morrow, fair lady." He spoke in Deverrian. "My true love tells me that you wish to hurry on your way and not linger here in my beloved land. What a pity, for I've many a marvel to show you."

"No doubt, and truly, I'm honored by your invitation, but

I've another kind of marvel to find. If I remember the tales about you rightly, it's one that I think you'd find interesting yourself, the island refuge of the sea elves."

He grinned, revealing teeth that were more than a little sharp.

"And someday, perhaps, I'll come visit you there." He turned to Dallandra. "I've found the road we want. Shall we travel it?"

For an answer she merely smiled and caught his hand. Jill walked alongside as they sauntered off down the middle road, as casually as a lady and her lover taking a stroll through the park lands of his estate. All round the mist hovered, parting directly ahead in swirls of watery sunlight to reveal dark mounds of trees. Off to her right she could hear a distant ocean crashing big waves onto some unseen shore.

"Those three roads you saw at first? They're the mothers of all roads," Evandar remarked. "Men and elves, every thinking creature under all the suns everywhere—they like to think they're following a road of their own building, don't they? But all those earthly roads are just the daughters of one of these three."

"Indeed?" Jill said. "I won't argue with you when you could well be right, for all I know."

"And since the three are the mothers of all earthly roads, all those earthly roads start and end here. You can move from one to another and come out where you choose, providing, of course, that you know how to get here in the first place."

"I see." Jill allowed herself a smile. "That's the trick, is it?"

"Just so." He smiled in return. "And not so easy a trick to learn."

"I well believe that."

"Now, of course, I could show you that trick, if you'd care to stay and learn it."

Jill felt a pang of temptation as strong as a stab of pain, but she merely laughed and shook her head no.

"I'm grateful for the offer, mind. But I've got a bit of work on my hands just now."

"Your choice, of course." Evandar bowed, a half-mocking sweep of his arm. "Now, it does take a bit of learning to untangle the roads from their mothers. It's rather like a tapestry weaver's remnants, a big basket of yarn of all colors, all tangled up together, and pulling just one strand free without knotting it round the rest isn't such an easy thing to do. Which is why we'd best stop for a moment and let me think."

They had reached a low rise, dropping gently down in front of them to another wide and grassy plain, crisscrossed with tiny streams and dotted with thickets of trees. Off on a far horizon in a gathering mist Jill could just make out a rise of towers, all white stone flecked with the occasional glint of gold, as if some mighty city stood there. Although Evandar had talked of many roads, she could only see one, meandering through the plain like a stream. He seemed to hear her thought.

"It's all in the walking, which road you end up traveling. They all do look alike at first. Come along, we'll just head down past those gray stones, there."

Now that he pointed them out, Jill could indeed see the boulders, shoving themselves clear of the earth about halfway down the rise. As they strolled past, she noticed that the stones seemed worked, shaped into flat slabs with some crude tool, and arranged into a roughly circular ring.

"We turn here, I think," Evandar said.

The sun turned brighter by a sudden streamside, all dappled with coins of gold light and bordered with a spill of yellow wildflowers. Even though it seemed they had traveled a long way, Jill could still hear the mutter of the invisible ocean.

"And what of the sea roads? Do all ships sail on that sea I hear over there somewhere?" She waved vaguely in the direction of the sound. "Is there a harbor where all sailors come to port?"

"There is, truly. Again, if they can find their way to it. If. Your ancestors sailed that sea when Cadwallon the Druid brought them free of slavery and defeat in the land they called Gallia. But, of course, you know that."

"What?" Jill stopped walking and turned to him. "I don't know in the least. What are you saying?"

Evandar tossed his head back and laughed.

"Cadwallon was a splendid man, if a bit dour at times. I knew him well, my lady. Now, if only you'd come take the hospitality of my hall, there's many a tale I could tell you."

When Jill wavered, Dallandra intervened, shooting a scowl in his direction.

"Don't listen to him, Jill. You've not got years and years of idle time to waste over a goblet of mead."

"You are a harsh one, my love." But Evandar was laughing. "Unfortunately, you speak true, and it would be too unscrupulous even for me to tempt our guest further. Look, see where the sun's breaking through? I think me that it shines on the island you're looking for."

The mist ahead opened like a door and let through sunlight in a solid shaft. As they came close Jill felt the steamy heat of a tropical day streaming out to meet them.

"A thousand thanks, Evandar. Dalla, will I see you again?"

"Well, to tell you the truth, I was thinking of coming with you, just for a little while." She glanced at her glowering lover. "To you it'll be but moments."

"So it will, and go with my blessing, as long as you come back."

"Oh, that I will." Dallandra flashed a wicked smile. "This time."

Before he could protest further she dropped his hand and strode forward into the shaft of sun. When Jill hurried after, the light was so strong that it burned her eyes and made them blink and water. Blind and stumbling, she stepped forward and fell to her knees in soft sand.

"Ych, this is awful," Dallandra remarked from nearby. "I feel like I'm made of lead, and I've tripped over some driftwood or somewhat."

Finally, after a lot of swearing and muttering, Jill got her sight back and realized that they were kneeling on a beach under a blazing sun that lay halfway between the zenith and the horizon— whether it was setting or rising, Jill couldn't know. Off to her left the ocean stretched glittering; to her right, cliffs of pale sandstone rose up high; ahead the white sand ran on and on. Wildfolk swarmed round, climbing into their laps, patting their arms with nervous paws. Dallandra rose to her knees and shaded her eyes with one hand to frown up at the clifftops. Her figurine was gone, and when Jill automatically laid a hand at her own throat, she found that hers had vanished as well. She also realized that she could feel her pack on her back again; it had seemed to weigh nothing at all in the misty lands of the Guardians. For a moment Dallandra stood, looking this way and that, chewing on her lower lip in hard thought.

"Wait! I can just see . . . a long ways down the coast there. Look at those black dots wheeling round in the sky."

"I can't make them out at all."

"My apologies; I forget you're not elven. But I can just see what looks like birds, wheeling round and diving and suchlike. I'll wager there's a river mouth, and where there's a river mouth there might be a harbor."

"True spoken. There'll be fresh water at least, and fish and suchlike."

"You'll need food, truly. Are you sure you should do this?"

"I don't have much choice, do I? Don't worry, Dalla. I've spent many a long year alone in wild places, and I have the elementals, too, to help me if need be."

"Well and good, then. And I'll be listening for you. If you call me, I'll come. It may take me a while, but I will."

"You have my thanks, and so does Evandar."

Dallandra smiled, then turned and began walking toward the sea, heading for a place where it seemed the sun laid a road of gold across the water. She waded out into the gentle waves, seemed to step onto the golden road, and disappeared like mist vanishing in the glare of sun. She apparently knew the trick, as Evandar had called it, of traveling to the home of the three mothers of all roads.

Jill allowed herself the luxury of a brief moment of envying her, then made herself concentrate on the job at hand. The Wildfolk were still clustering round, undines thronging all silver in the breaking waves, sylphs and sprites hovering overhead, crystal glimpses in the strong sun. At the head of a pack of warty green and purple gnomes, her faithful gray fellow was wandering around, poking at the sand with a piece of stick. When Jill called him, he trotted over, the others straggling slowly after.

"Now look, I need your help. You know who the Elder Brothers are."

The gray gnome nodded and grinned, revealing a mouthful of needle-sharp teeth. The purple fellows were suddenly all attention.

"Well, somewhere around here they have a city, somewhere away from the shore, most like. I need to know where it is."

With a scatter of sand they all disappeared, leaving her to hope they'd understood her.

Sticking to the hard-packed sand at the water's edge, Jill headed down the beach, keeping the cliffs to her left—going south, she finally decided, once the sun had moved enough for her to judge that it was setting, not rising. It was a long time before she could see the specks wheeling and diving that Dallandra had noticed, and longer still before those specks did indeed resolve themselves into white birds. At that point she realized as well that the land was sloping ever so gently down, and that the cliffs rose lower and lower, finally petering out ahead in a last curve of broken hill. She could also see a brownish surge of water heading out from land and flowing across the ocean. So Dallandra had found her a river, indeed, and Jill was glad of it. In the blazing heat she wanted a swim in fresh water as badly as she was beginning to need the shade of the trees that bordered it.

Unfortunately, when she reached the shallows of the estuary, she found crocodiles, piled on a tumble of gray rocks or flopped onto each other as they lazed on the mud among stands of water reeds. Although Jill started to count them, she gave up after fifty. While the creatures blinked and drowsed in the afternoon sun, little brown birds walked among and over them without the crocodiles even noticing, but Jill had no desire to try the trick herself. She got one of her water bottles out of her pack and had a long swallow—warm, tasting of leather, but at least it was wet. If, as seemed likely, the river got deeper and ran faster upstream, she'd be able to find a safer spot to drink later.

By then the sun was sinking off in the west, and with the

cooler air of evening came swarms of insects, rising like a mist from the riverbanks. Deep in the jungle ahead birds began to call back and forth. With a yawn and a grunt, a few of the crocodiles scrambled out of the pack and flopped into the river. Birds screeched a warning and flew. Jill decided that she'd be better off with a good stretch of dry land between her and them. Rather than face the night jungle she hurried back to the beach and went back the way she'd come for some hundreds of yards. Well above the current waterline she found the bleached-gray trunk of an entire tree, its roots all twisted with dead kelp, and a long scatter of smaller pieces of driftwood, plenty of bone-dry fuel for a fire. Crocodiles, she assumed, would dislike fire as much as other wild animals did. She swung her pack free of her aching shoulders, set it down in the shade of the trunk, and set about making camp.

As she was gathering small chunks and sticks, she discovered her first concrete bit of evidence that Evandar had indeed found her the right island. Lying half-buried in the sand was a broken plank, cut and curved in such a way that it could only have come from a ship. It might, of course, have been nothing more than wrack from some Bardek merchanter, carried hundreds and hundreds of miles by the currents, but she preferred to doubt it. In the last of the day's light she scurried round, searching for more driftwood, scrabbling like a mole in the sand, until at last, just as the twilight was growing thick and gray, she unearthed a flat panel of wood that must have once formed the side of a chest or back of a bench. It seemed to be the splintered half of a big oblong, and it was carved with designs that no Bardekian would have drawn.

Once she got a fire going with less interesting driftwood, Jill studied her discovery by firelight streaked blue from the sea salt impregnating the wood. Although the panel was bleached and blistering, she discovered on one edge two indentations that could only have been made by hinges—so it was part of a chest, indeed. With her fingertip she could trace a long pattern of vines and flowers, looping casually, almost randomly across the entire surface rather than being contained in strict bands, such as a Bardekian craftsman would have chosen, and among the foliage were the little faces of Wildfolk. On the reverse side of the panel she found deep-graved letters, recognizably elven though somewhat different from the profuse syllabary she'd learned.

Enough of the symbols were familiar for her to make a stab at deciphering the words, most of which seemed to have vanished with the missing piece of panel. There was the graceful hook that spelled "ba," and here the slashed cross of "de."

"Tran rinbaladelan linalandal—" she said aloud, and her blood ran cold at the sound of the city name. "Rinbaladelan son of the something? Or wait! The son of Rinbaladelan, not the other way round."

A new city, then, founded by exiles? Quite possibly, if its name had been inscribed on this long-sunk ship to show her home port. She tossed the panel over near her gear, then got up and laid more wood on the fire. In the blue and gold flame the salamanders leapt and sported, rubbing their backs like cats on the burning sea wrack. Jill wandered away from the pool of light so that she could look up at the stars, hanging bright and clear above her, so close, seemingly, that she felt she could stretch up a hand and touch them. She wished she had a navigator's lore, to read the stars and learn how far south she might be, but of course, for all the strange lore she did know, the book of the stars was closed to her. Far down the beach at low tide, the ocean lapped soft waves.

What, then, was the noise? All at once she realized that for some time now she'd been hearing a distant sound that she'd been assuming, only half consciously, was surf, but here in this sheltered bend of coast, and with the tide so far out at that, no waves pounded on the shore. She went cold again, freezing motionless, straining to hear, to place, the soft but rhythmical *boom, boom, boom* floating through the night.

After some long minutes she realized that the sound was growing louder, coming closer, pounding like the footsteps of an enormous animal walking at a stately pace. She hurried back to the fire, wondered if she should keep it or smother it, cursed herself for not traveling armed, decided that one sword wouldn't have been much good, anyway, against a beast as big as this one must be, then laughed aloud at herself. She did, after all, have dweomer to fall back upon. No doubt a blaze of etheric fire would frighten away any animal, gigantic or not, if indeed a beast was what she was hearing. The sound was definitely closer now and definitely coming from the distant river. She walked away from the fire, peered into the dark until her eyes adjusted, then saw pinpoints of light flickering far off in the estuary. The booms grew louder still.

Drums. Drums and torches coming along the riverbank, and she was willing to wager that whoever came marching was pounding those drums to scare the crocodiles off. All at once Wildfolk swarmed into manifestation around her, a whole army of green and purple gnomes, a flock of sprites, jumping or fluttering round in sheer excitement. Her own gray gnome appeared, jigging up and down on top of her pack.

"The Elder Brothers, is it?"

He nodded a yes and grinned, gape-mouthed. In a few minutes she could see the dark shapes of ten men break free of the shadows around the river and turn, torches held high, onto the beach. She could even pick out the drummer, marching at the rear of the line and banging a large, flat drum with some kind of stick. She went back to her fire, threw on more wood to make it blaze in greeting, and waited, arms crossed over her chest, as they drew nearer, stumbling a little on the soft beach sand. With the crocodiles far behind, the drummer fell silent. About ten feet away they stopped, just out of the pool of light, but she could see them clearly enough: elves, all right, with their long, delicate ears and moonbeam-pale hair. They were dressed in full tunics, belted at the waist with a glitter of gold, which came just above their knees, and each man carried a quiver of arrows at his hip and a bow slung over his back. Jill hoped that they spoke the same elven language that she knew.

"I give you my heartfelt greetings," she said, "and hope I might be welcome here."

She could just make out a rustle of surprised whispers. One man stepped from the crowd and walked a few paces in her direction. A dragon's head, worked in gold and as big as the palm of his hand, clasped his belt. When he spoke, she could indeed understand him, but with some difficulty. His dialect was far more different from that of the Westfolk than, say, Eldidd speech is from that of Deverry proper.

"Strangers are always less than welcome. Are you a victim of the sea's rage?"

It took her a moment to realize that he meant a castaway.

"No, good sir. I came here quite deliberately, looking for you and your people, in fact."

Automatically he turned to glance at the cove, turned back to her with a slight frown.

"I see no boat."

"Well, no." There was nothing she could say but the truth. "I traveled by dweomer, and I come to greet you and ask your aid in the name of the Light that shines behind all the gods."

Jill had never seen anyone look so surprised. He turned on one heel, staring at the beach, turned back to her with a shake of his head, his mouth half-open as he fought for words. The men behind him went dead-silent for a moment, then all began talking in a gabble of surprise until their leader shouted at them to be quiet.

"It seems discourteous in the extreme to ask you for some proof, but given the circumstances . . ."

Jill smiled, flung up one hand, and called upon the Spirits of Aethyr. In a blaze and stream of bluish light they flocked to her and made her hand and arm blaze with etheric fire far brighter than a torch. All round them Wildfolk swarmed into manifestation and spread out on the beach like an army.

"Forgive me for doubting you." The elven leader bowed deep. "My name is Elamanderiel, and in the name of the Light, I bid you welcome."

When Dallandra left Jill, she followed the sun road until the gold faded and the dappled tiles gave way to daffodils blooming by a stream. Following the stream uphill led her back past the circle of stones, through the mists, and down the long road by the sea whose waves broke on every shore and none of them. At length she made her way back to the river and found the Host scattered across the meadow and dancing, as if nothing troubling had ever happened in these lands. Under the young oak tree that hid his daughter, Evandar was sitting in the grass and playing sour notes on a bone whistle, about six inches long and bleached dead-white.

"Odd little trinket," he remarked. "I found it lying over there, in among the bushes, as if someone had dropped it by mistake. What do you think it is, my love?"

"Oh, ych! It looks like it was made from an elven finger."

"Doesn't it? What is it? Two joints somehow glued together? No, but it's much too long for a single joint." He held his own hand against it in illustration. "I wondered what it would call up, you see, but so far, naught's appeared in answer to my playing."

"Perhaps it's just as well. It gives me the strangest feeling, seeing it, and a worse one to hear it call. I wish you'd just smash it."

"I would, except it's a riddle, and I think me a good one at that." He tossed it into the air, seemed to catch it, but when he opened his hand it was gone. "Now I know where it lies, but no one else does, and so I've covered a riddle with a riddle."

"I can't imagine any of your people making such a thing."

"Indeed, no, and so I wonder: who dropped it here, and why were they prowling beside my river? I think me we'd best tend to our borders."

All at once they were no longer alone. Like flames leaping out of the ground, soldiers of the Host were gathering round him—how many, she couldn't tell—in a glitter of coppery-colored mail and helmets, each man armed with a long bronze-tipped spear. The music drifted away and stopped as the Host swelled, spreading across the meadow. At some far distance she heard horses neighing.

"While you were gone, Alshandra was seen again," Evandar said to Dallandra. "With some of those from farther in."

"Farther in? I wish you'd explain—"

"There are two hosts, my love, the bright court that I keep, and then the dark who live farther in. And that's all I'll say about it now, for look! our horses!"

A young boy hurried forward, leading two golden horses with

silvery manes and tails. As Dallandra mounted, she saw that the foot soldiers had turned into cavalry as suddenly as changes always came about in this country. In the clatter and jingle of metal-studded tack they followed Evandar as he led the way out with a whoop and a wave of his arm. Dallandra rode up next to him as the road beneath flattened out and broke free into sunlight. Yet always the mist remained, a gray and shifting wall, seeming solid at times, thin and teased to silver at others to reveal glimpses of shining cities or forested mountains. Dallandra noticed that it always hung just at their left hand, as if they were traveling deosil in a vast circle round a grassy plain.

"The riding of the border," Evandar called out.

Behind him the Host roared their approval, and silver horns blew.

On horses that never seemed to tire they rode for hours, till the day faded into a greenish twilight, and a moon hung pink and bloated just above the horizon, never rising, never setting. In that ghastly light they traveled past ruins of cities fallen to some great catastrophe and the black and twisted stumps of dead forests, blanketed with ancient ash stretching as far as Dallandra could see. The horses never stumbled, never paused, ambled on and on and on through death and night, till just as she was ready to scream from the terror of it day broke, blue and clear, to drench them all in golden light. The mist writhed one last time, then blew away on a fresh and rising wind. Just ahead in the flowered meadow stood the pavilion of cloth-of-gold. Dallandra caught her breath in a sob of relief.

"The border lies secure!" Evandar cried out. "Go then to your music and the feast, but come again when I call."

Behind him the host of soldiers blew away, like dead leaves swirling in an autumn wind. He swung down from his horse, helped Dallandra dismount, then turned the reins of their horses over to the same boy, who appeared as silently as before. Dallandra watched him lead them away round the pavilion and wondered aloud if there they would disappear.

"No, they'll return to their pastures, from whence we stole them." He was grinning. "Are you weary, my love? Shall we join the feast?"

"I'd rather you explained a few things to me."

"If a riddle has an answer, it's a riddle no more."

Simply because she was indeed very tired, she dropped the subject and let him lead her into the pavilion. Their seats, couches on which they could semirecline, stood at the head of the hall. She sank gratefully onto the soft cushions and accepted a golden goblet of mead from a page. As always, the mead and the bread seemed real to her fingers and her taste, solid and so delicious that she realized how hungry she was after the long ride. While they ate, various members of the Host would come to Evandar and talk in low voices, reporting things they'd seen, apparently. Harpers played nearby in long, sad harmonies, while young voices sang, until at last, she slept.

2.

The Prince of Swords

The Westlands,
Autumn, 1112

Out on the high plains the elven leader with the most authority—and the largest warband for that matter—was Calonderiel, Banadar of the Eastern Border, and yet, as Deverry men reckoned such things, his claim to power rested on an oddly weak foundation. He was descended from nobody in particular and related to no one much—just the son of a horse herder who was the son of a weaver who was the son of a prosperous farmer back in the old days when the elves lived settled lives in their own kingdom in the far west. No one had ever accused his family of having any connection whatsoever to the noble-born or the renowned. He was, of course, the best archer, the shrewdest tactician, and one of the most respected leaders of men that the high plains had ever seen, and those things, among the People, outweighed any questions of kinship. Despite that, Rhodry ap

Devaberiel was continually amazed that Calonderiel would hold such easy authority without a grumble from anyone. He himself was second in command of the banadar's warband, and since he'd sworn to serve him, he personally would never have argued with a single order or decision his leader made. It was just that, at odd moments, he puzzled about it, or even, Calonderiel being the kind of man he was, felt he could wonder about it aloud.

"And now this Aledeldar shows up for the autumn meeting," Rhodry remarked. "What if he and his son decide to ride with us? Doesn't it trouble you?"

"Why should it?" Calonderiel looked up in surprise. "Something wrong with him?"

"Not as far as I can see. It's just that he's the king, isn't he? Well, the only one you people—we, I mean—have. There's bound to be trouble over it. One wagon but two teamsters makes for a rough journey."

Calonderiel merely laughed. It was late in the evening, and wrapped in woolen cloaks, they were sitting together in front of the banadar's enormous tent. Among the other tents (and there were over two hundred of them), everything was dark and silent, broken only by the occasional bark of a dog or cry of a hungry baby, hushed as fast as the echo died.

"Well, it won't be so funny when he starts countermanding your orders."

"Rhodry, you don't understand us still, do you? How long have you lived with us now? Thirteen, fourteen years? Well, think back over it. You've heard plenty of people mention Del and his son, haven't you? And how? Exactly like they'd mention anyone else they know. You have more real power than he does, as a matter of fact. You're my second, and the men all respect you, and so the People would take your orders long before they'd take his. Nothing can take his position away from Del, mind. He's Halaberiel's son, and Halaberiel was Berenaladar's, and Berenaladar was the son of Ranadar, King of the High Mountain, and that's that. But since the wolves and the owls and the weeds are running his kingdom these days, well, by the Dark Sun herself! He's got no call to be giving himself airs over it."

Baffled, Rhodry shook his head. Calonderiel was right, he supposed. He didn't understand the People, and at times like these, he doubted if he ever would.

On the morrow, with the autumn meeting or alardan as it was called in full swing, his loneliness seemed to double itself. Since it was the last festival before the long trip south to the winter camps, it was a big one. Whenever a new traveling group arrived, some ten families and their horses and sheep, everyone rushed to greet old friends, not seen since the height of summer, and to help them unpack and settle in. Time to visit was short; the herds would crop the available grazing down fast, and the meeting would disperse. Rhodry wandered through the brightly painted tents by himself, saying the occasional hello or exchanging smiles and nods with someone whom he recognized. Wildfolk swarmed everywhere, grinning and gaping, dashing back and forth, pulling dogs' tails and children's hair, then suddenly vanishing only to stream back into manifestation a few feet away. Among the People themselves, everyone was rushing around, getting ready for the enormous feast that evening. Here and there he found groups of musicians, tuning their instruments together and squabbling over what to play; here and there cooks were drawing and dressing slaughtered lambs or pooling precious hoards of Bardek spices. Children ran to and fro, bringing twigs and scraps of bark or baskets of dried dung to the cooking fires that were, as always on the grasslands, short of fuel.

At one of the fires Rhodry found Enabrilia, sitting on a wooden chest, her two grandsons fighting at her feet over a pair of pottery horses. She looked tired, that morning, and scattered through her golden hair shone an obvious sprinkling of gray. When Rhodry hunkered down next to her, she smiled at him, then went back to peeling roots with a small knife.

"The warband's always in the way when there's work to be done," she remarked, but pleasantly. "Hanging round asking when the food's going to be cooked and distracting the girls who are supposed to be working. You're all the same, you know."

"Well, that's true enough. I thought I'd come distract you."

"Oh, get along with you! I'm old enough to be your grandmother—well, three times over, no doubt, and I feel every one of my years this morning, I tell you."

"Is something wrong?"

"Oldana's having one of her bad turns again." She paused with a significant look at the boys, all ears at the mention of their mother, who had been ill for months.

"Ah. I see."

Back in Eldidd, where he'd been a great lord and one of the High King's personal friends, Rhodry would never have given the two children, one barely out of diapers, a thought. Since he was out on the grasslands now, he held out his arms to the younger one, Faren, who toddled over and laid both of his tiny hands into one of Rhodry's callused and weather-beaten palms.

"Let's go for a walk and let your gramma cook in peace. Val, are you going to come with us?"

Val shook his head no and grabbed both horses with a grin of triumph. Carrying Faren, Rhodry went back to his aimless wandering. In the center of camp, near the ritual fire that burned at the heart of every alardan, he found Calonderiel talking with the king and his young son, who at twenty-six was still a child by elven standards. They looked too much alike to be anything but father and son, with raven-dark hair yet pale gray eyes, slit vertically like a cat's to reveal a darker lavender, and they were slender even for men of the People. Rhodry was honestly shocked to see how deferentially the two of them treated the banadar, nodding thoughtfully at his remarks, laughing at his little jokes in exactly the same way as the other men did. When Rhodry joined them, both of them greeted him by holding up their hands, shoulder high and palm outward, in a gesture of profound respect; yet all his instincts were making him want to kneel to their royal blood instead.

"I've wanted to meet you," Aledeldar said. "I have great respect for your father's poems."

"So do I," Rhodry said. "Not that I understand them very well."

Everyone laughed but Faren, who squirmed round in Rhodry's arms and pointed over his shoulder.

"Who's that? She's strange."

"Beautiful, maybe," Calonderiel remarked. "Wouldn't say strange."

When Rhodry turned to look, he saw what seemed to be an ordinary elven woman, with waist-length hair the color of strained honey, bound back in two severe braids, standing among the tents some twenty feet away. She was wearing an ordinary pair of leather trousers and an ordinary linen tunic, and carrying a basket of greens in one hand while she watched the men, but she stood so still, and her stare was so intense, that she did indeed seem strange in some hard-to-place way. Cut off from the bustle around her, perhaps? Rhodry had the peculiar feeling that she wasn't really there, that she stood behind some invisible window and looked into the frantic camp. When Calonderiel gave her a friendly wave, she turned and walked fast away, disappearing into the constant scurry of people among the tents.

"What's her name?" Rhodry asked.

"I don't know," Calonderiel said. "Del, does she ride with your alar?"

"No. Never seen her before. Well, there's a lot of people here. Bound to be a few that we don't know."

Out of curiosity and not much more, Rhodry kept an eye out for the woman all during the rest of that day. Although he described her to a number of friends, no one remembered her or would admit to knowing her, and she should have stood out. Among the People, dark blond hair like hers, with a honey-colored or yellowish tinge, was very rare, enough so that she might have had some human blood in her veins. Once, when he was hauling water for the cooks, he dodged between two tents and saw her, walking away in the opposite direction, but though he called out, she merely glanced over her shoulder and hurried on.

He didn't see her again until late that night, long after the feast was over. On the opposite side of the camp from the herds some of the People had cleared a space for dancing by cutting the long grass down to a reasonably even stubble. By torchlight the musicians gathered off to one side, a rank of harpers backed by drummers and a couple of those elven bundled-reed flutes that produce drones. The People danced in long lines, heads up, backs straight, arms up and rigid while their feet leapt and scissored in intricate steps. Sometimes the lines held their position; at others they snaked fast and furiously around the meadow until everyone collapsed laughing on the cool grass. On and on the dancing went, till the older and less energetic began to drop out, Rhodry among them.

Out of breath and sweating, he flung himself down near a tall standing torch, far enough away from the music to hear himself think, and watched the dance spiral past. A pack of gray gnomes flopped into manifestation around him and lay on their backs, panting in imitation of their elder brothers. When Rhodry laughed, they all sat up and grinned, then began pushing and shoving each other to see who would sit on his lap. All at once one of them drew his lips back from his teeth and pointed at something behind Rhodry; the rest leapt up and snarled; they all disappeared. Rhodry slewed round where he sat to see the honey-haired woman standing behind him. In the torchlight her eyes seemed made of beaten gold.

"And a good eve to you, my lady." He rose to his knees. "Won't you join me?"

She smiled, then knelt down facing him rather than sitting companionably. For a long moment she studied him in a silence as deep and unreadable as the night sky. He was struck all over again by the sense she gave of distance, as if she were a painted image on a temple wall, looking down upon him from a height. In her presence the camp seemed far, far behind him.

"Uh, my name is Rhodry, son of Devaberiel. May I have the honor of knowing yours?"

"You may not, truly." Much to his shock, she spoke in Deverrian. "My name's not for the giving, though I'll trade it for that little ring you have."

Reflexively he looked down at his right hand, where he wore on the third finger a silver band, about a third of an inch wide and graved with roses.

"Well, now, you have my apologies, but I'll not surrender that, not even to please a lady as beautiful as you."

"It's made of dwarven silver, did you know?"

"I do. It's the same metal as this silver dagger I carry."

"So it is, and both were made by a dwarf, too, many a long year ago."

"I know the man who made the dagger, and dwarven he is, but this ring is elven."

"It's not, for all that it has elven writing inside it. It's the work of the Mountain Folk, and not a fit thing for an important man of the People like you, Rhodry Maelwaedd."

"Here! No one's called me by that name for years and years."

She laughed, revealing teeth that seemed oddly sharp and shiny in the flickering light.

"I know many a name, I know all your names, truly, Rhodry, Rhodry, Rhodry." She held out her hand. "Give me that ring."

"I will not! And who are you, anyway?"

"I'll tell you everything if you give me that ring." She smiled, her mouth suddenly soft with a thousand promises. "I'll do more than tell a tale, truly, for that ring you wear. Give me a kiss, Rhodry Maelwaedd, won't you now?"

Rhodry stood up.

"I won't, my thanks. Many a year ago now a dangerous thing happened to me for being too free with my kisses, and I'll not make the same mistake twice."

In cold fury she crouched, staring up at him while he wondered if he were daft for treating one so beautiful so coldly.

"Rhodry! Where are you?" It was Calonderiel's voice, calling out in Elvish with a drunken lilt, coming from a long distance over the music. "Here, harpers! Have you seen Rhodry?"

She flung her head back and howled like a wolf, then as suddenly as one of the Wildfolk she was gone, simply gone, vanished without so much as a puff of dust or a stirring of the torch flame. From right behind him Rhodry heard Calonderiel swear. He spun round.

"There you are!" Calonderiel was half laughing, half afraid. "By the Dark Sun, I've drunk myself half-blind! I didn't see you, and here you were so close by that I nearly tripped over you! Must've drunk too much, that's what it is."

"I've never known you to pass on a skin of mead untasted,

no." Rhodry realized that he was cold-sick and shaking. "Uh, did you see that woman who was here just now?"

"Woman? No, I didn't even see you, much less some female. Who was she?"

"The woman we saw earlier, when we were talking with the king and his son. The one little Faren called strange."

"Oh, her." Calonderiel burped profoundly. "Hope I didn't interrupt anything, er, important."

"Not in the least, my friend, not in the least. Huh, I wonder if Faren has a touch of the second sight or suchlike. We should have Aderyn take a look at the lad the next time we meet up with the old man."

"I thought the Wise One would be here already, as a matter of fact. Um, why are you talking in Deverrian?"

"Am I? Well, I'm sorry." He switched back easily to his adopted tongue. "That woman was speaking it, you see."

"What woman?"

"The one you didn't see. Don't worry about it. Let's get back to camp, shall we?"

When he went to sleep that night, Rhodry was glad that he shared a tent with a warband. Somehow he would have felt in danger if he'd been off by himself.

Close to dawn the entire camp woke in a swirl of yelling and cursing from the herd-guards. Rhodry pulled on his trousers and boots, then dashed outside, slipping on his shirt in the chilly night, to find the rest of the warband running for the herd of horses to the east of the encampment. From the snatches of shouted conversation he could figure out that something had panicked the stock.

By the time they reached the grazing ground, the mounted herders had rounded up most of the runaways. Rhodry found a horse that knew him, swung up bareback, and riding with just a halter joined the hunt for the others. Although he lacked the full night vision of the People, he could see far better than the average human in the dark, and certainly well enough to hunt for horses in moonlight. He found four mares and their half-grown colts, herded them into a little group, and brought them back just as the sky was turning gray in the east with the tardy autumn dawn.

Riding out among the assembled herds were three of the women, counting up the stock with a call or a pat for every animal. Rhodry turned his mares into the milling mass, then found Calonderiel, mounted on his golden stallion off to one side, and rode up beside him.

"What was all this about?"

"Cursed if I know." Calonderiel shrugged eloquently. "One of the boys told me that all of a sudden, the herd just went mad: neighing and rearing, kicking out at something. He said he could just barely see shapes moving, doglike shapes, but then they vanished. Some of the Wildfolk, I suppose, up to their rotten infuriating pranks. They know there's naught we can do to them, blast them, and they probably thought it a fine jest to see us all riding round yelling our heads off."

Rhodry saw no reason to disagree, especially since there was no particular harm done. Once the sun was up and the herds all counted, only three horses were still missing, and their tracks, heading off in three separate directions, were perfectly clear. Rhodry got himself some breakfast, then set off after one of the stragglers.

He tracked the lost horse all that morning, until finally, close to noon, he found the miscreant, a blood-bay gelding with a black mane and tail, peacefully grazing beside a narrow river. Clucking under his breath, holding out a nose bag of oats, Rhodry circled round to approach him from the front. The gelding rolled a wary eye, then spotted the nose bag and trotted over, shoving his nose right in and allowing Rhodry to attach a lead rope to his halter with no trouble at all.

"Well, at least you decided to wait for me, eh? I think I'll have a bit of a meal of my own, and then we'll go home."

Rhodry unsaddled the horse he'd brought with him, let him roll, and tethered him out to rest while he ate griddle bread and cheese from his saddlebags and watched the river flow through its grassy banks. He'd just finished eating when he happened to glance upstream and saw something that brought him to his feet with an oath. About a quarter of a mile away stood a thicket of hazels: absolutely nothing unusual in that, no, except that he'd seen no such thing when he first rode up. For a moment he debated the question, but in the end, he was sure as sure that he'd looked that way and seen nothing but the long green swell of grass stretching out to the horizon. Again, he debated; then curiosity got the better of him, and he strode off for a look.

When he got close, the thicket certainly seemed ordinary enough, a wild tangle of stunted trees and shoots, but someone was sitting among them on what seemed to be a rather anomalous oak stump, and while the day was breezy, the hazels stood unmoving. In the warm sun he felt his blood run cold. Hand on the hilt of his silver dagger, he stopped walking and peered in among the shadows. The seated figure rose and hobbled to meet him, an old, old woman, all bent-backed and dressed in drab browns, leaning on a stick, her white hair escaping in wisps from her black head scarf. She paused a few feet away and looked up at him with rheumy eyes.

"Good morrow, silver dagger." She spoke in Deverrian. "You're a long, long way from the lands of men."

"And so are you, good dame."

"I've come looking for my daughter. They've stolen her, you see. I've looked and I've looked, but I can't find her anywhere in my own country. They've stolen her away, my baby, my only daughter, and now they're going to bury her alive. Oh, they're weaving her a winding sheet, they are, and they'll bury her alive."

"What? Who will?"

She merely looked up at him with a little smile, too calculated, somehow, to be daft. The wind lifted his hair; the hazels never shivered nor swayed. With his heart pounding like a wild thing, Rhodry began to back away.

"Where are you going, silver dagger?" Her voice was all soft and wheedling. "I've got a hire for you."

She strode after, suddenly younger, swelling up tall and strong, and now she was wearing a green hunting tunic and a pair of doeskin boots, and her hair was the color of honey, and her eyes like beaten gold. Rhodry yelped, staggering along backward, afraid to turn his back on her to run. Out of sheer warrior's instinct and nothing more he drew his sword. The moment that the bright steel flashed in the sunlight she howled in rage and disappeared, flickering out like a blown candle.

Rhodry broke into a cold sweat. For a moment he merely stood beside the river and shook; then he turned and shamelessly ran for the horses. With clumsy shaking hands he saddled his gray, grabbed the lead rope of the bay gelding, then mounted and rode out at a fast trot. All the long way back to camp he wished for a good road and a gallop. And yet, when he saw the camp and, in particular, the other men in the warband, his fear seemed not only shameful but foolish, and he told no one what had happened. In fact, the more he thought about the incident, the more unreal it seemed, until finally he convinced himself that he'd fallen asleep in the warm sun and dreamt the whole thing.

Two days later, on the last afternoon of the alardan, Oldana died. Rhodry was walking among the tents when he heard Enabrilia start keening. The high-pitched shriek cut through the noise of the camp like a knife and sobbed on and on. One at a time, other voices joined in, wailing and gasping. Rhodry turned and ran for Oldana's tent, shoved his way through the sobbing mob at the door, and ducked inside. Her hair down and disheveled, Enabrilia was clawing at her own face with her nails while two of her women friends grabbed at her hands to make her stop. Oldana lay on a pile of blankets, her arms thrown wide, her unseeing eyes still open. She had been ill so long that her face seemed, at first, no colder, no paler than before, but her mouth hung slack, her lips flaccid. Huddled in the curve of the tent wall little Faren stood staring and silent, watching his elder brother mourn without truly understanding a thing. Rhodry gathered the pair up and led them out of the tent. In a time of mourning, boys belonged with the men while the women cared for the dead.

Outside, other women were assembling at the tent while the men hurried through the camp, extinguishing every fire as they went. They gathered near the horse herd, where Oldana's brother, Wylenteriel, met Rhodry and took his nephews with a murmur of thanks for the banadar's second in command. Rhodry found Calonderiel swearing under his breath with every foul oath he knew.

"She was so wretchedly young to die! I don't understand the gods sometimes, I really don't!"

"Who can?" Rhodry said with a shrug. "I'm heartsick, too, but I'm worried about her sons more. Where's their father?"

"Up north somewhere with his herds, last anyone saw him. The boys will fare better with their uncle anyway, if you ask my opinion and not that anyone did." The banadar looked briefly sour. "With luck we'll run into their father down at the winter camps. The alardan will break up tonight, and we'll be heading east."

"East?"

"To the death ground. That's right, you've never been there before, have you? We're close enough to take her there for the burning, in this cool weather and all."

Rhodry felt oddly troubled. The sacred death ground lay right on the Eldidd border, not more than a hundred miles from Aberwyn, where once he'd ruled as gwerbret, not far at all from the place he'd always considered home.

"What's wrong with you?" Calonderiel said. "You look pale."

"Do I? Ah, well, it's a sad thing, when one of the People dies so young. We'd best call for the ceremony to end the alardan. The sooner we get moving, the better."

The women sprinkled Oldana's corpse with spices and covered it with dried flowers before they wrapped it round with white linen. They cut a white horse out of the herd to drag the travois that would carry her to the resting place of her ancestors, and when the alar left the rest of the gathering behind for their sad journey east, that horse led the line of march, with Rhodry and Calonderiel riding alongside. The boys, as much confused as grief-struck, traveled far back at the rear with their uncle and grandmother. Out of simple decency the king and the young prince came with them, and their alar, of course, as well, to dignify the eventual ceremony with their presence.

It took them two full days and part of a third to reach the Lake of the Leaping Trout. During that time they ate food left from the alardan feasting, and slept cold at night, too, because no one could light a fire until Oldana's soul was safely on its way to the world beyond. Slowly the grasslands began to rise, until by the third dawn they saw ahead of them rolling grassy downs that were almost hills. Finally, just after a noon gray with the promise of winter, they came to the last crest. Far down the green slope lay the silver lake, a long finger of water caught in a narrow valley pointing southeast to northwest. To the north a thick forest spread along the valley floor, the dark pines standing in such orderly rows that obviously they were no natural growth, but all along the north shore lay an open meadow. Calonderiel turned to Rhodry and gestured at the forest with a wide sweep of his arm.

"Well, there it is. The death ground of my ancestors, and of yours as well. Your father's father was set free and his ashes scattered among those trees, though I think your grandmother died too far out on the grass to be brought here."

When they rode down to the lake, Rhodry realized that the meadow area was laid out as a proper campground: there were stone fire pits at regular intervals and small sheds, too, for keeping firewood dry and food safe from prowling animals. The alar rushed to set up their tents against the darkening sky and tether the horses securely as well, just in case there should be thunder in the night. As the early evening was setting in, Calonderiel fetched Rhodry.

"Let's go take a look at the firewood. The women tell me that we'd better do the ceremony tonight."

They crossed the neatly tended boundary of the forest into the dark and spicy-scented corridors of trees. In a clearing, not ten yards in, stood a structure of dry-walled stone and rough-cut timber about thirty feet long. Inside they found it stacked with cut wood, a fortune in fuel out on the grasslands.

"Good," Calonderiel said. "Fetch the others. Let's get this over with before the rain hits."

But as if in sympathy with their loss, the rain held off. The wind rose instead, driving the clouds away and letting the stars shine through. Close to midnight the alar burned Oldana's body to send her soul free to the gods. Rhodry stood well back toward the edge of the weeping crowd. Although he'd traveled with the

Westfolk long enough to witness several cremations, still they disturbed him, used as he was to burying his kin and friends in the hidden dark of the earth with things they'd loved in life tucked round them. He found himself moving slowly backward, almost without thinking, easing himself out of the crowd, taking a step here, allowing someone to stand in front of him there, until at last he stood alone, some distance away.

The night wind lashed at the lake and howled round the trees like another mourner. Rhodry shivered with grief as much as the cold, because she had indeed been so young, and so very beautiful. Although he'd never known her well, he would miss her presence in the alar. Among the Westfolk, that last remnant of a race hovering on the edge of extinction, where the loss of any individual was a tragedy, the death of a woman who might have borne more children was an appalling blow of fate. In the center of the crowd the women howled in a burst of keening that the men answered, half a chant, half a sob. Rhodry turned and ran, plunged into the silent camp, raced through the tents and out the other side, ran and ran along the lakeshore until at last he tripped and went sprawling. For a long time he lay in the tall grass and gasped for breath. When he sat up the fire was far away, a golden flower blooming on the horizon. The wind-struck water lapped and murmured nearby.

"You coward," he said to himself, and in Deverrian. "You'd best get back."

The alar would expect him, the banadar's second in command, to be present at the wake. He got up, pulling down his shirt, automatically running one hand along his belt to make sure that his sword was still there, and of course his silver dagger—which was gone. Rhodry swore and dropped to his knees to hunt for it. It must have slipped out of its sheath, he supposed, when he'd tripped and fallen flat on his face. In the starry dark his half-elven sight could make out little: the blacker shapes of crushed-down grass against the black shadows of grass still standing. On his hands and knees he crisscrossed the area, fumbling through and patting down the grass, pulling it aside, hoping for the gleam of silver, praying that the wretched thing hadn't somehow or other slid into the lake. A gaggle of gnomes appeared to help, though he doubted if they truly understood him when he tried to explain what he was doing. Finally he gave up in disgust and sat back on his heels. In a flurry like a whirlwind the gnomes all disappeared.

"Rhodry, give me the ring, and I'll give the dagger back."

The voice—her voice, all soft and seductive—spoke from behind him. Swearing, he got to his feet and spun around to see her, standing some five feet away. She seemed to stand in a column of moonlight, as if the air around her were a tunnel to some other world where the moon was at her full, and she was wearing elven clothes, the embroidered tunic and leather trousers in which he'd first seen her. Her honey-colored hair, though, hung free, a cascade over her shoulders. In one hand she held his silver dagger, blade up.

"The ring, Rhodry Maelwaedd. Give me the rose ring, and you shall have your dagger back."

"Suppose I just take it from you?"

She laughed and disappeared, suddenly and completely gone. When he swore, he heard her laugh behind him again, and spun around. There she was, and she was still holding the dagger.

"You shan't be able to catch me, of course," she said. "But I always keep my promises. I promise that if you give me the ring, I shall give you your dagger."

"Well, if you want it that cursed badly . . ."

When he started to slip the ring free, she moved forward, gliding over the grass, and it seemed that she was suddenly taller, her eyes flashing gold in the not-real moonlight that clung to her. All at once he was afraid, hesitated, stepped back with the ring still on his finger.

"Just why do you want this bit of silver so badly?"

"That's none of your affair! Give it to me!"

She strode forward, he moved back. She stood huge now, her hair spreading out in some private wind like flames stirring, and she held the dagger up to strike.

"Stop!" It was a man's voice. "You have no right to that ring!"

Rhodry could see no one, but she suddenly shrank down to the form of a normal elven woman, and the dagger hung in a flaccid hand.

"It was his long before I carved the runes upon it. You know it was. Admit it."

All at once a figure appeared to match the voice, a man with impossibly yellow hair and lips as red as cherries. Smiling, but it was more a wolf's smile than a man's, he strolled in between them. The long tunic he wore matched his unnaturally blue eyes. With a sense of utter shock Rhodry realized that he could see him so clearly because dawn was already turning the eastern sky silver, that the entire night had somehow passed during his brief conversation with the woman. She was staring at the grass now, and kicking a tuft of it like a sulky child.

"Hand it over," the man said.

With a shriek of rage she hurled the dagger straight at Rhodry's head. He ducked, twisting out of the way barely in time, then looked up to find them both gone. The dagger, however, lay gleaming in the rising sun. When he picked it up, he found it perfectly solid—and realized with surprise that he'd expected it to be somehow changed. Although he sheathed it, he kept his hand on the hilt as he started back to camp.

"Rhodry?"

The voice made him yelp aloud. The man with the yellow hair gave him an apologetic smile.

"If I were you," the fellow said. "I'd leave the Westlands. She won't follow you into the lands of men."

He disappeared again. Rhodry ran the rest of the way back to the camp.

The wake was long over. Most of the People, in fact, were asleep after the long night of mourning. Only a pack of dogs, a few of the older boys, and Calonderiel were sitting round the newly rekindled fire in front of the banadar's tent.

"Where were you?" Calonderiel said.

"I hardly know." Rhodry sat down next to him on the ground.

Calonderiel considered for a moment, then waved at the boys and dogs impartially.

"Go. I don't care where—to bed, probably. But go."

Once they'd gone, the banadar laid a few chips and twigs onto the fire.

"I hate to let it go out," he remarked. "What do you mean, you hardly know?"

"Just that. I thought I was but a mile from here, down by the lake, but the whole night passed like a bare moment, and I saw a woman who came and went like one of the Wildfolk."

While Rhodry told the story, and he finally admitted the earlier incidents as well, Calonderiel listened without a word, but the banadar grew more and more troubled.

"Guardians," he said at last. "What you saw were two of the Guardians. I don't exactly know what they may be, but they're somehow linked to the People. They're not gods, certainly, nor are they elves like you and me, nor men like your other tribe, either. No more are they Wildfolk, though they seem more like the Wildfolk than like us at times. I've heard a wagonload of old tales about them. Sometimes they harm those that see them, but more often they help, which is why we call them Guardians. The bards say that at the fall of Rinbaladelan, a man of the Guardians fought side by side with the royal archers, but not even his magic could hold the Hordes off in the end."

"Do you think I should take the fellow's advice, then?"

"Most likely. Ye gods, I wish Aderyn were here! We need a dweomerman's counsel, we do."

"I'm still surprised he never came to the alardan. It's not like the old man to miss one."

"Just so." Calonderiel suddenly yawned with a convulsive little shudder. "Well, let's get some sleep. It's been a miserable night, all told. Maybe your dreams will tell you something useful."

That afternoon, though, Rhodry dreamt of the long road, that is, the time when he'd ridden as a silver dagger into political exile. When he woke, he could remember nothing particular about the dream, and it faded fast as dreams will, but the feeling of it lingered round him, a sour sort of omen. He found himself alone in the banadar's huge tent, with the rest of the warband gone, though he did hear whispering voices just outside. When he dressed and went out, he discovered a clot of men, all white-faced and shaking, standing round the young prince, Daralanteriel, who had his hands set on his hips and an angry toss to his head.

"What's all this?" Rhodry was instantly awake.

"My apologies, sir," the prince said. "The men keep talking about ghosts, and I'm trying to force some sense into their heads."

"Good." Rhodry turned to Jennantar, who of all the men in the warband was usually the most hard-headed. "Now, what—"

"Mock all you like, we saw her!" Jennantar said. "Oldana, standing at the edge of camp clear as clear."

The rest nodded in stubborn agreement.

"There's no such thing as ghosts," Daralanteriel snarled. "Only Round-ears believe in trash like that. Well, begging your pardon, sir."

"Tact isn't your strongest point, lad, is it? But apology accepted. Look at it this way: the men saw something, so the real question is, what was it?"

"I'm glad to see that someone believes our sworn word." Jennantar shot Daralanteriel an evil glance.

"Enough of that! It's a prince you're looking daggers at," Rhodry broke in and quickly. "Where did you see this thing?"

With the others trailing after, Jennantar led Rhodry out of the camp on the forest side. He pointed to a spot between two ancient pines.

"Right there. She was standing between those trees, in the shadows, yes, but we still saw her really clearly, all wrapped up in the white linen, and her hair was all white, too."

"When you looked at her, did she seem solid, or could you see things through her, like you can through smoke?"

"Interesting." Jennantar thought for a moment. "In the bard tales, you can always see right through a ghost, but she looked as real as you or me, and it was sunny, of course, which should have made her look even less real, but it didn't."

"What did you do when you saw her?"

"Well, to tell you the truth, we all yelped and jumped. She didn't say anything, just looked at us. And Wye said, 'Look at her hair, it's not yellow anymore, it's turned white.' And she smiled at that, like, and vanished, sudden as sudden."

"And you're sure it was Oldana?"

"Looked exactly like her, except for that white hair."

The other men nodded agreement. Rhodry sighed with a sharp puff of breath. Whoever or whatever that spirit who coveted his ring might be, there was no doubt that she could shape-change to perfection.

As they walked back to camp, three women came running to meet them. They ringed Rhodry round and all began talking at once: they too had seen Oldana, prowling round her family's tent.

"I suppose she wants a look at her children, poor thing," Annaleria said, her voice shaking with tears. "I know I would."

"Ye gods!" Rhodry snarled. "Where are the boys?"

"With their grandmother in her tent."

"Good. Go join her. Fill that tent with women, and for the love of every god, don't let the apparition near those boys. If she gets her claws into one of them, he'll be gone where none of us can get him back."

Except, no doubt, by handing over the ring.

"Let's go. Hurry!"

Rhodry broke into a run and raced for camp, leaving the others startled behind him. Enabrilia's distinctive tent, painted with scenes of deer drinking at a river, stood off to one side, with nothing beyond it but the lakeshore. As Rhodry jogged up, he saw Val heading down to the water's edge with a leather bucket in his hands. Rhodry took off after him, yelling his name. The boy stopped on the pale sand and looked back, smiling. Out on the water something was forming. It seemed a wisp of mist at first, then shimmered and began to grow thicker.

"Run!" Rhodry shrieked. "Come here, Val!"

The boy dropped the bucket and followed orders, racing to Rhodry's open arms just as the shape took form and stepped off the water to the shore. She looked so like Oldana—and her hair was the other's proper color now, too, a pale gold—that Rhodry swore under his breath. Val twisted in his arms.

"Malamala!" he cried out. "Let me go! It's my mother."

Rhodry held him tighter and swore again as the boy burst into tears. Shouting and cursing, Jennantar and half the alar came running to surround them. The apparition shook one fist in Rhodry's direction, then vanished like smoke blowing away under a wind.

"She's gone," Val sobbed. "Why didn't you let me go? Why?"

"Because she would have taken you with her to the Otherlands, and it's not your time to go." Rhodry said the only thing he could think of, looked round, saw Enabrilia shoving her way through the crowd. "Here's your gramma. Go with her. I'll come talk to you later, little one, but I don't know if I can ever explain."

"I wanted to go with Malamala. I hate you! I want my mother."

When Rhodry handed the weeping child over to Enabrilia, the other women formed round her like a guard and swept them away. Rhodry looked round to find Daralanteriel and the other men standing between him and the lake.

"I'm sorry," Dar stammered out. "Jennantar, I never should have doubted your word, and I'm sorry. I—"

"Don't think of it again." Jennantar laid a gentle hand on the prince's shoulder. "It's all unbelievable enough, isn't it? Rhodry, for the love of every god, what was that—that creature?"

"I don't truly know." Rhodry ran both hands through his hair and felt himself shake like a man with a fever. "But she bodes ill, whatever she is. Let's go find the banadar."

Rhodry could be a stubborn man when he wanted, and indeed at times when he didn't, as well. That she would stoop so low to gain her prize made him suddenly determined that she should never have that ring, no matter what the cost to him. Risking the rest of the alar, of course, was different. When they found Calonderiel, Rhodry told him the story, then led him away from the others out to the edge of the forest, where the corridors of trees stood nodding in the rising wind.

"That Guardian I saw spoke true. I've got to leave, for the alar's sake more than my own. I'm minded to ride north and look for Aderyn. No doubt she'll follow me and the ring and leave the rest of you in peace."

"It seems best, doesn't it? But you can't go alone. Too dangerous. I'll come with you, and we'll take part of the warband, too."

"You have my thanks, and from the bottom of my heart." Rhodry caught himself—he was speaking Deverrian again. After so many years of rarely hearing it, he was surprised that he would so instinctively return to it when he was troubled. He made himself speak Elvish. "I wasn't looking forward to being out there alone, but I've got to talk to Aderyn. I don't know whether to placate her or fight her."

"If she's one of the Guardians, normally I'd say you should do what she wants, but I'm beginning to wonder." Calonderiel thought for a moment, frowning out at the horizon. "I've never heard of a Guardian begging and wheedling a mere mortal like this. Maybe she's some kind of evil spirit. You're right. Aderyn's the one who would know."

"I wonder where the old man is?"

"North, probably, coming down to the winter camps. If he'd been south already, he would have come to the alardan."

Calonderiel turned the leadership of his alar over to the king and his son, just until he should return. With some ten men and a couple of packhorses, Rhodry and Calonderiel rode straight north, making a good twelve miles before pitching the night's camp. Since under the starry sky everyone could see well enough, they dispensed with a fire, merely sat close together in a ring, watching the moon rise. No one seemed to have a thing to say. Twice someone started a song; both times the music died away after a few quiet verses.

"Ye gods!" Calonderiel snarled at last. "What's wrong with us all?"

"Well, it's a hard thing," Jennantar said. "Losing first Oldana and now Rhodry."

"Here!" Rhodry snapped. "I'm not dead yet, curse you and your balls both, but you might be if you keep talking that way."

Everyone managed a weak laugh.

"Not talking about you being dead," Jennantar said. "Talking about you riding east."

"Do you think I want to leave the Westlands? Not without a fight, my friends."

At that exact moment they heard the howl, as if she'd waited to pick the perfect time to appear, the long wail of a banshee, echoing through the moonlight. Without thinking Rhodry was on his feet, facing her as she stood just beyond the circle of elves. Although she no longer wore Oldana's face, she was still dressed all in white, like the burning clothes, and her long hair, hanging free, was silver-white as well.

"My daughter." This time she spoke in Elvish. "You don't understand. They'll take her far away from me. I must have that ring."

"How will my having the ring lose you your daughter?"

"I don't know. Evandar won't tell me, but that ring was omened for you, Rhodry Maelwaedd, long, long ago before you were born again onto this earth of yours. Don't you remember? You gave it to him, long years ago, when you wore another face and carried another name."

Rhodry could only stare, gape-mouthed. He heard Calonderiel get to his feet and come to stand beside him.

"Listen, woman," the banadar said. "If that ring was omened for Rhodry, then it's no doing of yours. I'm truly sorry to hear your grief, but none of us know one wretched thing about this daughter of yours. And what's this nonsense about other faces and names? I'm beginning to think you've gotten Rhodry confused with some other man."

She shrieked once, then disappeared. Rhodry felt sweat run down his back in a cold trickle.

Although they kept a watch that night, and rode on guard from then on as well, they never saw the strange being again. After some days of searching, they found a fresh trail—horses and travois—that eventually led them to another alar, camped in the bend of a stream. As they rode up, a pair of young men came out to hail them and welcome them into the camp. Everyone dismounted and began leading their horses toward the distant circle of tents.

"A question for you," Calonderiel said to the pair. "Does Aderyn of the Silver Wings ride with this alar?"

The two men winced, looking back and forth between them.

"I take it you haven't heard the news."

"News?" Rhodry turned cold, guessing it just from the grim looks on their faces.

"And foul news at that. Aderyn died some twenty days ago.

He was on his way to a big alardan down south somewhere, but he never reached it."

Rhodry grunted like a man kicked in the stomach. Staring at the ground but unseeing, he dropped his horse's reins and walked a few steps away while the others went on talking to the banadar. He heard himself speak, realized that he was shaking his head in an instinctive denial while he muttered no, no, no, over and over. Oldana's death was very sad, but to have Aderyn gone shook his entire world. The old man had always been there, wise and strong and full of good counsel, ever since those days long ago when Rhodry as a lad of twenty rode to war as cadvridoc for the first time, back in the old days, when he was heir to Aberwyn. Calonderiel caught up with him and grabbed his arm.

"How?" Rhodry said. "Did they say?"

"In his sleep. As peaceful as you'd want, or so they heard. Well, he'd lived a full life, after all, not like poor little Oldana, and no doubt he's gone to join those Great Ones that dweomerfolk speak of."

"True spoken." Without thinking, Rhodry slipped into Deverrian. "But it aches my heart all the same. Will his apprentice succeed him?"

"He will, but he's up north somewhere. Shall we ride after him? The gods only know when we'd catch up with him, and I think you're in too much danger for us to wander aimlessly about, my friend."

"So do I. I think me that I've been given an omen as well as sad news."

"You're going to leave us?"

Rhodry hesitated, staring off at the horizon and the endless sea of green, rippling in a rising wind. For years his entire life had been bounded by grass and grazing, the herds and the seasons of the year, the vast freedom of following the herds and the grass. To go back to the lands of men, to cities and to farms—what would he do there?

"Staying here would put you all in danger," he said aloud. "Evandar—I suppose that's the Guardian who spoke to me that night—Evandar seemed to think that leaving was my only choice.

And without Aderyn . . ." He let his voice trail away. "Well, I sold my sword once before. I can do it again."

"Ye gods! Not that!"

"What choice do I have?"

"I don't know. But let's shelter here tonight anyway. Don't go rushing into some decision you'll regret."

"Good advice. Done, then."

But that evening, as they sat around a fire with their hosts, Rhodry barely listened to the talk and the music round him. As much as he hated to leave the Westlands, he felt Deverry pulling at him, the memories of his native land rising in his mind as easily and as vividly as his native language had come back. All at once he realized that he was thinking of his ride east as "going home." He looked up and found Calonderiel watching him in some concern.

"You look like a man with a bad case of boils," the banadar remarked. "Or are you brooding about that female?"

"Neither. I've made up my mind. It's east that I'll be heading."

Calonderiel sighed in a long puff of breath.

"I'll hate to see you go, but it's probably for the best. I suppose you'll be safe there. At least the spirit won't trouble you, but what about the Round-ears?"

"If I stay out of Eldidd, no one's going to recognize me."

"Even if they did, they'd never believe you were Rhodry Maelwaedd anyway. How strange, they'd say, that silver dagger looks a fair bit like the old gwerbret, the one who drowned so mysterious like all those years ago."

Rhodry smiled, but there was no humor in it.

"No doubt. Will you ride with me to the border?"

"Of course. It's too cursed dangerous to let you go alone. Humph. I've got some Deverry coin with me. The handful I got from those merchants a couple of months ago, remember? You're taking it with you."

"Now here, I don't want—"

"Hold your tongue! It won't do me a cursed bit of good, and it'll keep you warm this winter. You have the worst ill luck of any man I've ever known." Calonderiel sounded personally aggrieved.

"Why couldn't this stupid bitch of a spirit at least wait until spring?"

Rhodry started laughing. It came boiling out of his very heart, shaking him, choking him, but still he laughed on and on, until Calonderiel grabbed him by the shoulders and made him stop.

In the days that followed, as he rode back east to the lands of men with Calonderiel and their escort, he found himself thinking of Aderyn, remembering all the times they'd spent together, all the favors that the old man had done him, though "favors" was much too mild a word. Ye gods, he would think, what's going to happen to the kingdoms now? First Nevyn gone in Deverry, and now Aderyn dead in the Westlands! Although he knew that there were other dweomerworkers in both lands to protect their peoples, still it troubled his heart, this feeling that some great and dreadful thing was coming toward them all on a dark wind. The two deaths— Oldana so young, so unjustly taken; Aderyn no surprise, truly, at his advanced age—mingled together in his mind and tipped some inner balance dangerously low.

They rode into Deverry up Pyrdon way, crossing the border on a day still and cold under a lowering sky. The horses were restless, feeling thunder coming, dancing and snorting as their hooves hit the unfamiliar surface of a log-paved road. By a stone pillar carved with the rearing stallion of the gwerbrets of Pyrdon, Calonderiel called a halt.

"There's no use you coming farther in," Rhodry said.

"True spoken. Bitter partings are best over fast."

Yet they lingered, sitting on horseback together and idly looking at the pillar. Since Rhodry could read, he translated the inscription into Elvish: a claim-stone, mostly, for the gwerbrets, though it did deign to tell them that Drw Loc, chief city of the rhan, lay some forty miles on.

"Two days riding," Calonderiel said. "Will you be safe tonight?"

"There's a town just ten miles down the road, or there was, anyway, last time I rode this way. I'll find lodging there. And if the man named Evandar was telling me the truth, I'll be safe enough with human beings around me."

"If."

The other men exchanged grim glances. The silence hung like the heavy air.

"Do you see that device? the Stallion?" Rhodry found himself talking merely to be talking. "Another branch of this clan holds Cwm Pecl under its sign. My cousin Blaen used to rule there, but he rode to the Otherlands many a long year ago. Huh. He named his eldest son after me. Maybe I should ride east and see if young Rhodry's still upon the earth—listen to me! He's not young anymore, is he? If naught else, I can pour a little milk and honey on Blaen's grave."

"Ye gods, you're in a morbid mood!"

"Well, so I am. It aches my heart to leave you, my friend."

"And it aches mine to lose you. Whether you come back or no, Rhodry, you'll always be my friend."

Rhodry felt a lump forming in his throat and looked away fast.

"Tell my father where I've gotten myself to, won't you?"

"I will. Ye gods, I don't relish the task, I tell you. No doubt he'll revile me for days for letting you go off like this. Devaberiel's the only man I know with a worse temper than mine."

They both smiled, briefly, and sat for another long moment more, studying the horizon where it darkened with storm.

"Ah, well," Calonderiel said at last. "For the love of every god, take care of yourself on the long road."

The silence grew. With a wave of his arm, Calonderiel called out to his men.

"Let's ride! No need to twist the arrow in the wound."

Rhodry steadied his horse and kept him still while they gathered in the road and clopped off. He sat, staring out across the empty meadowlands, until he could no longer hear them riding away. He was a silver dagger again, back on the long road, with no more of a name than Rhodry, not Maelwaedd, not ap Devaberiel—no name, no place, no clan to take him in. He started to laugh, his mad berserker's chortle and howl, and headed off toward the east. It was a long time before he could make himself stop laughing.

Late in the afternoon, when thunderheads were piling and sailing in a crisp sky, Rhodry rode into a village called Tiry, a scatter of some two dozen roundhouses, all nicely whitewashed and newly thatched for the winter and set among now-leafless ash and poplar trees. Down by the banks of a small river stood the local inn and tavern behind a wooden fence. When Rhodry led his horse into the yard, the tavernman bustled out to greet him, a stout fellow with hair as yellow and as messy as the thatch.

"You'll be wanting lodging, no doubt," he announced. "And the gods all know that I wouldn't turn anyone away tonight, not even a silver dagger like you."

"My thanks, I suppose. Tonight? What—"

"Ye gods, man! It's Samaen! Now let's get that horse into the stables."

Rhodry was shocked at how easily he'd lost track of the markings of Time in the world of men. How could he have forgotten Samaen, when the gates of the Otherlands open wide and the unquiet dead come walking through the lands of their kin? Those who lie unburied, those who hold grudges, those who've left a true love behind or a hoard buried—they all come wandering the roads in the company of fiends and spirits on this night that belongs neither to this world nor to the other and thus lies common to both.

Once his horse was fed and stabled, and his gear stowed in a neat pile under a table by the hearth, Rhodry and the innkeep, Merro, sat down to have a tankard of dark apiece in the otherwise empty tavern room.

"You're on the road late, silver dagger."

"I am, at that, and a cursed ugly thing it is, too. I couldn't find a hire for the winter, you see."

"Ah, well." The tavernman considered, sucking his teeth. "Well, now, there were some merchants through here not so long ago, from Dun Trebyc way, they were, and they told me about a feud brewing, down in the southern hills."

"Sounds like work for a silver dagger's sword."

"It does, truly. What you do, see, is ride dead east from here till you reach the lake, then take the south-running road. Keep asking along the way. If there's war brewing, it won't be any secret, will it now? Or if that comes to naught, you might give his grace our gwerbret a try. He's a generous man, just like he should be, and he remembers the old days, too, when you lads put a king on his throne, or so he always says. We remember the old days, here in Pyrdon." Merro paused for a sip of ale. "This village, now? It used to be royal land, you see, when there was a king in Dun Drw instead of a gwerbret. That's why it's got this name. Ty Ric, it was once, the king's house. There was a royal hunting lodge here in those days, you see, right where this inn is now, though of course there's not one stick of wood left from it. That's the way things go, eh?"

"Interesting," Rhodry said to be polite. "But it's a free village now?"

"It is, and on good terms at that, when it comes to the taxes. Lord Varyn, he's our local lord, you see, is an honorable man, but even if he weren't, well, we remember the days when this was the king's land, not his, and we hold to our charter, like, and so does the gwerbret, and that's that." Merro raised his tankard in brief salute, had a sip, and proceeded to lecture Rhodry about local politics in great detail.

When the sun sank so low that the storm clouds blazed red and gold, Merro closed the inn. Rhodry went along with him and his family to join the village in lighting the Bel fire. At the crest of a low hill near town two priests waited, dressed in white tunics, gold torcs round their necks, golden sickles dangling from their belts, with the village blacksmith and his son to help them. One at a time each village or farm family panted up the hill with a burden of wood, added it to the stack, and received the blessings of Great Bel. When everyone who lived under the temple's jurisdiction was assembled and blessed, the priests laid the wood ready for a proper fire and sprinkled it with oil. As if in answer to their chanting, the twilight grew as gray and thick as fur. The blacksmith lit torches and stood prepared.

Then came the waiting. Far away, hundreds of miles away in the High King's city of Dun Deverry, the head priest would light the first fire. The instant that the nearest priests on their hilltops saw the blaze, they would torch their own wood. Those next away would see and kindle theirs—on and on it would go, thin lines of light springing up and spreading out across the kingdom in a dweomer web, until beacon fires burned from the sea coast up to Cerrgonney and all across from Cwm Pecl to here on the Pyrdon border. The younger priest raised a brass horn, long and straight in the ancient style, to his lips and stared off to the east. The villagers huddled close together in the gathering dark. All at once the priest tipped his head back and blew, a rasping, shrieking cry straight from the heart of the Dawntime. Down went the torches. The fire blazed up, crackling with oil, a great leap of gold flame lurching in the night wind. When Rhodry spun around, searching the horizon, he saw the neighboring fires like little stars, resting on the hilltops.

The village cried out, praying wordlessly to the gods to keep them safe through the night ahead. Silhouetted by the dancing bonfire, the priests flung their arms over their heads and began to chant. Rhodry found himself remembering Oldana, and the other fire that had bloomed by the Lake of the Leaping Trout. Doubtless Aderyn's alar had burned the old man's body, too, out on the grasslands where he'd died. For a moment Rhodry felt so odd that he wondered if he'd been taken ill; then he realized that he was crying, aloud and helpless like a child, beyond all power to stop himself. Fortunately, in the chanting, yelling mob no one noticed.

When the chanting died away, the horn shrieked again, over and over, sending the villagers on their way. The children ran for home, the adults walked fast—but not too fast, because it didn't pay to let the spirits know you were afraid of them. Rhodry trailed after the innkeep's family and managed to have his face wiped and respectable by the time they reached the inn. Merro set a couple of bowls of milk and bread out on the doorstep to keep the spirits happy, then ushered everyone inside and barred the door with a profound sigh of relief. While his wife poured ale for the grown-ups, Merro lit the new fire laid ready in the hearth.

"Well, there," he said. "May the gods keep us safe in the coming snows, too."

With a murmured excuse, the wife set the tankards down and left the tavern room, taking the young boy with her. The two older girls crouched down by the fire and stared into the flames, trying to see the faces of the men they'd someday marry. Rhodry and Merro sat at a table and drank in silence. Outside the wind picked up, rustling the thatch on the roof, banging the shutters at the windows. Even though Rhodry kept telling himself that it was only the wind, he heard the dead walking.

Merro was just remarking that he might pour a second round when they heard hoofbeats clattering up to the inn. It could only be a horse from the Otherlands. Merro turned dead-pale, staring at the door while the wind whispered and rattled. Someone—something—knocked so loudly that the two girls shrieked. Rhodry sprang to his feet, his hand on his sword hilt, as the knocking came again.

"Innkeep!" The voice sounded human enough, male and deep at that. "Open up, for the love of the gods!"

Merro sat frozen, his face dead-white.

"It's going to rain!" the voice went on. "Have pity on a traveler, even though he was a dolt, sure enough, to let himself get caught on the roads for Samaen eve."

Merro made a rattling sound deep in his throat.

"Ah, by the black ass of the Lord of Hell!" Rhodry said, and he could feel himself grinning. "Let's let him in, innkeep. If naught else, it'll be a fine tale to tell, about the spirit who was afraid to get wet."

The lasses shrieked again, but halfheartedly, as if they were only doing it to keep up appearances. Rhodry strode over and unbarred the door. The man that stood there in the shadows seemed human enough: tall, broad-shouldered, a little beefy, in fact, with windblown blond hair, but in the uncertain light Rhodry couldn't see his eyes to tell if they were demonic or not. He was holding the reins of a normal-looking horse, too, standing head down and weary, a gray as far as Rhodry could see. Up in the sky the clouds hung black. A few drops of rain spattered, then stopped.

"What do you think, Merro?" Rhodry called out. "He looks like flesh and blood to me."

"Oh, well and good, then." With a sigh the innkeep came over. "But by every god in the sky, traveler, you gave me a fright! Now let's get that poor beast some hay."

By the time that Merro and the stranger got back to the tavern room, the rain was pouring down. Rhodry helped himself to more ale, then put one foot up on a bench and leaned onto his knee to watch as the stranger stripped off his wet cloak and shook his head with a scatter of drops. You never knew about men you met on the long road, though in truth this lad seemed decent enough. In the leaping light he looked young, twenty at the most, and his blue eyes were perfectly human, neither cat-slit like an elf's nor blank and empty as those of demons are reputed to be. He accepted a tankard from the innkeep, started to speak, then leaned across the table. His eyes were narrowing in puzzlement even as he smiled, suddenly pleased, suddenly grinning, in fact, in something close to joy.

"Don't I know you, silver dagger?"

"Not that I recall." Yet even as he spoke Rhodry felt his heart twist.

He did know this lad, didn't he? It seemed that the name hovered on the edge of his mind, just out of reach yet as familiar as his own, and on that same edge an image was trying to rise, a memory trying to bloom like a flower.

"Where are you from?" the lad said.

"Down Eldidd way. You're from Deverry proper, by the sound of your speech."

"I am, and never been west till this summer. But it's odd, I could have sworn . . ." He let his voice trail away.

Rhodry hadn't been in Deverry for close to twenty years, when this fellow would have been a babe in arms.

"And who was your father, then?"

"Now that I can't tell you." The lad hesitated, drawing into himself, turning his face expressionless. "And as for my name, you can call me Yraen."

"Well and good, Yraen it is. My name is Rhodry, and that's all the name I have."

"It's enough for a silver dagger, huh?" Yraen hesitated, cocking his head to one side, looking Rhodry over. "You are a silver dagger, aren't you? I mean, I just assumed . . ."

"I am." Rhodry drew the dagger and flipped it point down and quivering into the table between them. "What's it to you?"

"Naught, naught. Just asking."

Yraen stared at the device graved on the blade, a striking falcon, for a long time.

"Mean anything to you?" Rhodry said.

"Not truly, but it's splendid, the way it's drawn. You'd swear that bird could fly, wouldn't you?"

Rhodry remembered the innkeep, looked up to find Merro shepherding his daughters through the door into the family's rooms.

"I'll just leave you two lads," Merro announced. "Bank the fire before you go to sleep, won't you, silver dagger? Dip yourself more ale if you want it."

"I will, and my thanks, innkeep."

He got himself more ale and came back to the table to find Yraen holding the dagger, angling the blade to catch the firelight. Yraen caught his expression and hurriedly put the dagger down.

"Apologies. I shouldn't have touched it without asking you first."

"You're forgiven. Don't do it again."

Yraen blushed as red as a Bardek roof tile, making Rhodry wonder if he were closer to eighteen than twenty.

"You look like you've been on the long road for years," the lad said finally.

"I have. What's it to you?"

"Naught. I mean. Well, you see, I've been hoping to find a silver dagger. Think your band would take me on?"

"Oho. You've got a reason to be traveling the kingdom, have you?"

Yraen stared down at the table, began rubbing the palm of one hand back and forth along the edge of the grease-polished wood.

"You don't have to tell me what got you dishonored," Rhodry said. "None of my wretched business, truly, as long as you can fight and keep your word."

"Oh, I can fight well enough. I got my training . . . well, uh, in a great lord's household, you see. But . . ."

Rhodry waited, sipping his ale. He could tell that Yraen was hovering on the edge of some much-needed confession. All at once the lad looked up.

"They say that every silver dagger's got some great shame in his past."

"True enough. Not our place to judge another man."

"But, you see, I haven't done anything. I just want to be a silver dagger. I always have, from the day I heard about them. I don't know why. I don't want to sit moldering in my, uh, er, my lord's dun down in Deverry. I've talked to every silver dagger who rode our way, and I know in my very soul that I was meant to ride the long road."

"You must be daft!"

"That's what everyone says." All at once he grinned. "And so, think I, well, maybe being daft is dishonor enough."

"Not likely. Listen, once you take this blasted dagger, you're marked for life. You're a shamed man, and you only deepen your shame every time you take coin from a lord for fighting his battles instead of serving him out of fealty. Ye gods, why do you want to throw your young life away? Can't you see that—"

"I know my own mind." There was a growl in his voice. "That's what they all say, you know. You'll only regret it when it's too late, and you've dishonored yourself in the eyes of the entire kingdom, and no one will take you in, then, because you'll just be a cursed silver dagger. Well, I don't care." He stiffened, half rising from his seat. "You asked me if I could keep my word. Well, I could have made up some lie, said I caused trouble in the warband or suchlike, but I didn't. I told you the truth, and now you're mocking me for it."

"I'm not mocking you, lad. Believe me, that's the farthest thing from my mind."

Yraen sat back down. Rhodry considered the empty bottom of his tankard and felt himself yawning. The events of the day, of the past few weeks, truly, all seemed to rush in upon him. He was tired, and he'd drunk more than a fair bit—those were the reasons, he supposed, that his mind kept circling round the peculiar idea. Against his will he found himself remembering the evil spirit, nattering about times when he'd worn another face and another name. And things Aderyn had said, years ago. And a strange woman of the Wildfolk, who had known him when he should never have recognized her—though he did. And Evandar, saying that he'd owned the rose ring long before the Guardian had put runes upon it, when Rhodry had never seen the thing without its inscription. And then Yraen, this familiar stranger. When a man's dead, he's gone, he told himself. The doors to the Otherlands only swing one way. All at once he realized that Yraen was still talking.

"Were you listening to me?" Yraen snapped.

"I wasn't, at that. What were you saying?"

Faced with his direct stare the lad blushed again.

"You're noble-born, aren't you?" Rhodry said.

"How did you know?"

Yraen looked so honestly surprised that Rhodry nearly laughed aloud, but he caught himself in time.

"Go back to your father's dun, lad. Don't throw your life away for the silver dagger. Now look, if you rode here from Deverry, you must have met other silver daggers along the way. None of them would pledge you to the band, either, would they?"

Yraen scowled and went back to rubbing his hand on the edge of the table.

"I thought not," Rhodry said. "We have a bit of honor left, most of us, anyway."

"But I want it!" He hesitated, reining in his temper. "What if I beg you, Rhodry? Please, will you take me on? Please?"

It cost him dear to humble himself that way, and for a moment Rhodry wavered.

"I won't," he said at last. "Because it would be a rotten thing to do to a man who's never wronged me."

Yraen tossed his head and muttered something foul.

"There's naught out to the west of us, so there's no use in you riding that way," Rhodry went on. "On the morrow you'd best head back east to your father. Winter's coming on fast."

As if to underscore his point, a blast of wind hit the tavern. Thatch rustled, shutters breathed and banged, the fire smoked. Rhodry started to get up, but Yraen forestalled him, swinging himself clear of the bench and hurrying to the fire.

"I'll tend it," he said. "I'll make you a bargain. I'll be your page, and we'll travel together for a while. I'll wait on you like I waited on the lord who trained me, when I was a page in his dun, I mean, and then you can see if I'm good enough to carry the dagger."

"You young dolt, it's not a question of you proving yourself."

Yraen ignored him and began to mess about with the fire. Sparks scattered, logs dropped and smothered coals, sticks of glowing charcoal rolled into corners to die.

"I think you'd best let me do that."

"Well, maybe so. My apologies, but the servants always did the fires at home, not the pages."

"No doubt."

"But is this your bedroll? I'll spread it out for you."

Before Rhodry could stop him, he did just that, in the best spot nearest the fire in the cleanest straw, and he insisted on straightening out all of Rhodry's gear, getting his razor out ready for the morning. He would have pulled Rhodry's boots off for him, too, if Rhodry hadn't snarled at him. Whoever had trained him as a boy had taught him a few things, at least, about waiting on a lord on campaign.

Rhodry woke early the next morning. Since the tavern room was cold, and the innkeep and his family not yet up, he lay awake thinking, watching the cracks round the shutters turn gray with dawn and listening to Yraen snore by the other side of the fire. A lad who actually wanted to be a silver dagger! A lad whom, he was sure, he remembered. From somewhere. From some time. From some other . . . his mind shied away from the idea like a horse from a snake in the road. Someone he had known, a long, long time ago and then again, not so long ago at all.

With a shake of his head Rhodry got up, moving as quietly as he could, pulled on his boots and grabbed his cloak, then slipped outside to use the privy round by the stables. As he was coming back, he lingered for a while in the inn yard. It had stopped raining, though the sky still hung close and gray, and he leaned onto the low wooden fence and looked idly down the north-running road, leading toward Dun Drw. The rhan's chief city, it was, the capital of the gwerbrets who once had been kings. We remember the old days, here in Pyrdon, or so Merro had said. Maybe, Rhodry told himself, just maybe I do, too. Then he shook the thought away and hurried inside.

Back in the tavern he found Yraen up and busy. The fire was burning again, the lumps of sod neatly stacked to one side of the hearth; both bedrolls were lashed up and laid ready with the other gear by the door; Yraen himself was badgering the yawning innkeep about heating water for shaving. In the morning light Rhodry could see that the lad did indeed need to shave and revised his estimate of Yraen's age upward again.

"Morrow, my lord," Yraen said. "There's naught for breakfast, our innkeep tells me, but bread and dried apples."

"It'll do, and don't call me your lord."

Yraen merely grinned. Over breakfast Rhodry tried arguing with him, snarling at him, and downright ordering him to go home, but when they rode out, Yraen rode alongside him. The lad had a beautiful horse, a dapple-gray gelding standing close to seventeen hands, with a delicate head but a barrel chest. When Rhodry glanced at its flank, he found the king's own brand.

"A gift to my father from his highness," Yraen said. "And my father gave him to me."

"You don't expect me to believe that you left with your father's blessing, do you?"

"I don't. I snuck out in the night like a thief, and that's the one thing that troubles my heart. But I'm one of four brothers, so he's got plenty of heirs."

"I see, and you had no prospects at home, anyway."

"None to speak of." Yraen flashed him a sour sort of grin. "Unless you count riding in a brother's warband as a prospect in life."

Since Rhodry had once been in the same position, he could sympathize, though not to the point of weakening.

"It's a better prospect than you'll have on the long road. At least if you die riding for your brother, someone will give you a proper grave. A muddy ditch on the battlefield's the best a silver dagger can hope for."

Yraen merely shrugged. Whether eighteen or twenty, Rhodry supposed, he was too young to believe that he would ever die.

"Now look, I'm not going to stand you to the dagger and that's that. You're wasting your time and your breath, following me and begging."

Yraen smiled and said nothing.

"Ye gods, you stubborn young cub!"

"Rhodry, please." Yraen turned in the saddle so that he could see his unwilling mentor's face. "I'll tell you somewhat that I've never told anyone before. Will you listen?"

"Oh, very well."

"When I was about fourteen, just home from serving as a page, my mother gave a fête. And one of her serving women has the second sight, I mean, everyone says she does, and she's usually right if she outright predicts something. So she dressed up like an old hag and did fortunes, looking into a silver bowl of water by candlelight. Mostly she talked about marriages and silly things like that, you see, but when she came to do mine, she cried out and wouldn't say anything at all. Mother made me leave, so the fête wouldn't be spoiled or suchlike, but later I made the woman tell me what she'd seen. And she said she saw me riding as a silver dagger, somewhere far, far away in a wild part of the kingdom, and that when she saw it, she just somehow knew that it was my Wyrd, sent by the gods. And then she started crying, and I had to believe her."

Rhodry gave him a sharp and searching look, but he'd never seen anyone so sincere. In fact, the lad blushed, and that very embarrassment stood as witness to the truth of his tale.

"I'll wager you think it's daft or womanish or both."

"Not in the least. Well, ride with me a while, then, and we'll see what the long road brings us. I'm not promising anything, mind. I'm just not sending you away. There's a difference."

"There is, at that, but you have my thanks, anyway."

As he thought about the story, with its talk of serving women and fêtes, Rhodry realized why Yraen looked like a man of twenty but at times acted like a boy. He must have been raised in a very wealthy clan indeed, sheltered down in Deverry by their power and position from the hard times that aged a man fast on the border. Grudgingly he admitted that he rather admired the boy for wanting to leave all that comfort behind and ride looking for adventure. He'll learn soon enough, he thought. One good rough time of it, and I'll wager I can send him home—if he lives through whatever the gods choose to send us.

At the moment it seemed that the gods were planning on sending them a storm. Slate-gray swirled with black, the sky hung low in the cold morning, though the rain held off for a few miles. They rode through farmland at first; then a twist in the road brought them to a thin stand of pines and an overlook, where they halted their horses. Some thirty feet below them lay Loc Drw, dark and wrinkled in the wind, stretching off to the north where, in a haze of distance, they could just pick out the stone towers of the gwerbret's dun.

"I've heard that it stands on a little island," Rhodry remarked. "You reach it by a long causeway. A splendid defensive position."

"Ah. Well, maybe if this feud in the hills has come to naught, we can find shelter there."

Rhodry merely nodded. Seeing the lake was affecting him in a way that he couldn't understand. Although he'd never been in Pyrdon, not once in his life, the long sweep of water looked so achingly familiar that he wasn't even surprised to hear someone calling his name.

"Rhodry! Hold a moment!"

When Rhodry turned in the saddle, he saw Evandar riding up on a milk-white horse with rusty-red ears. The Guardian was wrapped in a pale gray cloak with the hood shoved back to reveal his daffodil-yellow hair.

"You took my advice, did you?" He smiled in a way meant to be pleasant, but Rhodry noticed his teeth, as sharp and pointed as a cat's. "Good, good."

"I had little choice in the matter, but truly, good advice it seems to be. She hasn't followed me here."

"I doubt me if she will." Evandar paused, rummaging in a little leather bag he wore at his belt. "A question for you. Have you ever seen a thing like this before?"

"A whistle, is it?" Rhodry automatically held out his hand and caught it when Evandar tossed it over. "Ych! It looks like it's made of human bone!"

"Or elven, truly, except it's too long. I thought at first that two finger joints had somehow been joined into one, but look at it, close like."

Rhodry did so, holding it up and twisting it this way and that. All at once he remembered Yraen. The lad was clutching his saddle peak with both hands, leaning forward and staring, his mouth slacked open like a half-wit's.

"I told you that you should ride back to your father's dun," Rhodry said, grinning. "It's not too late."

Yraen shook his head in a stubborn no. Evandar looked him over with a thoughtful tilt of his head.

"And you are?"

"My name's Yraen," he snapped. "What's it to you?"

"Yraen? Now there's a well-omened name!" Evandar laughed aloud. "Oh, splendid! You've found a fine companion, Rhodry, and I for one am glad of it. Good morrow, lads. A good morrow to you both."

With a friendly wave he turned his horse and trotted off along the lakeshore, yet, before he'd gone more than a hundred yards, both he and his horse seemed to waver, to dissolve, to change into mist, a puff of it, blowing across the water and then gone.

"Ye gods," Yraen whispered. "Oh, ye gods."

"Go home, then, where spirits fear to ride."

"Shan't. That's what we get, riding on Samaen day, and cursed and twice cursed if I'll run from some rotten ghost."

"No such thing as ghosts. Our Evandar's a good bit stranger than that, and by the hells, he's gone and left me with the wretched whistle." Rhodry breathed a few quiet notes into it. "It makes a nasty sound, it does."

"Then maybe you'd best just throw it into the lake. Last thing we need is a pack of spirits, coming at your call."

"Well, I don't know about that, lad. There are spirits and spirits, and some can be useful, in their way." He grinned and leaned forward to unlace the flap of his saddlebag. "It's too strange to throw away. Looks like it's been made from the bone of a bird's wing, but one fine big bird it must have been, an eagle or suchlike. Want a look at it?"

"I don't." Yraen cleared his throat to cover the squeak in his voice. "We'd best get riding. Going to rain soon."

"So it is. Well, south and east, our Merro said, and we'll see if this feud has a hire for the likes of us."

At about the time that Rhodry and Yraen were riding away from the lake, Dallandra woke, after what seemed an ordinary night's sleep to her. The cloth-of-gold pavilion was empty except for the sunlight, streaming through the fabric so brightly that it seemed she lay in the middle of a candle flame. Yawning, rubbing her eyes, she got up and stumbled outside, where she stood for a long moment, getting her bearings in the warm day. The dancing was over; the meadow, empty, except for Evandar, sitting under the oak tree. When he saw her coming, he rose and hailed her.

"There you are, my love. Refreshed?"

"Oh, yes, but how long have I slept?"

"Just the night." He was grinning in his sly way. "And you needed a bit of a rest."

"Just the night here, yes. How long?"

"Oh, some years, I suppose, as Time runs back in your country. It was winter there, when I left Rhodry on the road."

"When you what? Ye gods! Will you tell me what you've been doing?"

"I will, but there's not much to tell. I just wanted to see if he was safe and well."

"Let me think. He's the one with the ring, isn't he? You know, I do wish you'd tell me about that ring."

"There's naught to tell. The ring is just a perfectly ordinary bit of jewelry."

"Aha! Then Jill's right. It *is* the word inside that's so important!"

"You're too clever for me, my love. So it is, and I wonder if Jill's found the secret yet. No doubt she will, because she's as clever as you are, in her way. And so, why should I waste my breath, telling secrets that you'll only unravel between you?"

When Dallandra made a mock swing his way, he laughed, ducking back.

"Are you hungry, my love? Should I call a servant to bring you food?"

"No, thank you. There's naught I need but answers."

Grinning, he ignored her hint.

"Help me look for something, will you?" he said. "That wretched whistle. I had it this morning, and now I've lost the thing."

"It's just as well. It was ill-omened, I swear it. Why don't you let it go?"

"Because its owner might come looking for it, and if I had it, I could make a bargain." He paused, frowning at the water reeds. "I was walking over there when I came back. Maybe I dropped it in the river. By those hells men swear by, I hope not."

"Why not scry for it?"

"Of course!" He grinned in a sly sort of way. "Here's a trick you might not have seen before. Watch."

When he knelt beside the river, she joined him and did just that while he described a circle in the air with a flick of one hand. The motion-trace glowed, became solid, then settled upon the flowing water like a circle of rope, but unlike the rope, it remained in the same spot instead of floating downstream. Within the circle pictures appeared, all hazy and strange at first, then forming into clear images: a muddy road, a rainy sky, a vast lake, rippled and dark. Two riders appeared, one dark-haired, one light.

"Rhodry," Evandar remarked. "And the yellow-haired fellow's Yraen. Now here I am, riding up to them."

Riding up, talking, and handing Rhodry the whistle—the memory vision broke when Evandar swore under his breath.

"I forgot to take it back from him. Well, it's gone, then. No use in worrying over it."

"Now just wait! We can't leave him with that ill-omened thing without even a warning. It's as you said: what if its owner comes looking for it?"

Evandar shrugged, turning half away to stare at the swift water, flowing between the sword-sharp rushes. All at once he seemed old, his face fine-drawn and far too pale. The sun darkened, as if it had gone behind a cloud, and the wind, too, blew suddenly cold.

"What's so wrong?" she said, and sharply.

"I forgot, that's what. I simply forgot that I'd handed him the whistle, forgot that I left it back in the lands of men."

"Well, everyone forgets something every now and then."

He shook his head in a stubborn no.

"You don't understand," he snapped. "This is a serious matter. I grow weary, my love, more weary every day, and now, it seems, feeble-minded as well. How long will I be able to keep our lands safe and blooming?" He paused, rubbing his eyes with both hands, digging the palms hard into his cheekbones. "It's true. You've got to take my people away with you, and soon."

She started to make her ritual protest, to beg him to come himself, but an idea struck her, and she said nothing. He dropped his hands and looked at her with a flash of anger in his turquoise eyes.

"Well," she said carelessly. "If you've made your mind up to stay behind, who am I to argue with you?"

"I'm no man to argue with, no." But for the first time, she heard doubt in his voice.

She merely nodded her agreement and looked away.

"Well, someone had best go after Rhodry," she said. "Will you?"

"I can't. One of us has to stay here, on guard. It was foolish of me to leave while you slept, truly."

"But I've never seen him in the flesh. Sharing your memory won't help me scry him out."

"True." He hesitated, thinking. "I know. Scry for the whistle. You've handled it, even."

"True enough. All right, let me see if I can, before I actually go anywhere."

Sure enough, picturing the image of the bone whistle led her in vision straight to Rhodry. Yet, when she found him, she was glad she'd been so prudent and not gone haring off to Deverry in search of him without a look first. The vision showed her a stone dun, far east of the elven border, where a cold and sleeting rain turned the outer wards to mud. Inside, the great hall swarmed with human men, most armed. Off in the curve of the wall the whistle appeared in sharp focus, held in Rhodry's hands, although Rhodry himself was hard to see clearly, simply because she'd never actually met him on the physical plane, merely seen him in several states of vision over the years. As far as she could tell, he was showing the whistle to some lord's bard, who merely shook his head over it and shrugged to show his ignorance of the subject.

Since she saw no elves in the hall, and no one with the golden aura of a dweomermaster, either, Dallandra focused the vision down a level, till it seemed to her that she stood in the great hall at Rhodry's side. From this stance she could see him a good bit more clearly and pick out his companion as well, the young blond fellow that Evandar had called "Yraen," the Deverrian word for iron and thus doubtless only a nickname. The bard, an elderly fellow, set his harp down on the floor and took the whistle, turning it this way and that to study it.

As she hovered there, looking round within the room of her vision, a flash of blue etheric light caught her eye. Over by the hearth something man-shaped and man-sized appeared, swinging its head this way and that, but judging from the shape of that head, flat and snouted like a badger's, and its skin, covered with short blue-gray fur, there was nothing human in its nature. It was dressed in human clothes, but of a peculiar cut: brown wool brigga that came only to its knees, a linen shirt as full as those Deverry men wore, but lacking sleeves and collar. Round its neck it wore a gold torc. Slowly it stood and began ambling over to Rhodry's side, but no one in the room seemed to see it at all. At times, in fact, one of the men might have walked right into it if the creature hadn't jumped out of their way.

All at once Rhodry spun round and yelped aloud, pointing straight at the snouted beast. Dallandra had forgotten that he was half-elven, with that race's inherent ability to see etheric forms, so long, that is, as the forms are imposed into the physical plane. It seemed that the creature hadn't known it, either. It shrieked and disappeared, leaving behind a puff of evil-looking etheric substance like black smoke. Apparently the shriek was a thing of thought only, because none of the men, not even Rhodry, reacted to it. What did happen was that a cluster of men formed round the silver dagger, all of them looking puzzled and asking questions. Talking a flood of explanations, Yraen grabbed the bone whistle with one hand and Rhodry's arm with the other and dragged him out of the hall.

Dallandra followed, hovering round them until she was sure that the badger-thing was gone for good, then broke the vision cold and flew up the planes. She found Evandar waiting where she'd left him on the riverbank. When she told him the story, his mood turned as dark as a summer storm.

"Then it's as I thought, my love," he snarled. "Curse them all! Sniffing and snouting round my country, threatening harm to a man under my protection!"

"Who?"

"The dark court. Those who dwell farther in." He rose, snapping his fingers and snatching from midair a silver horn. "This could well mean war."

"Now wait! If I simply go and fetch the whistle back—"

"That won't matter. This is a question of boundaries, and those are the most important questions of all."

With a toss of his head he raised the horn and blew, a long note that was both sweet and terrifying. In a clang of bronze and silver and a storm of shouting, the Host came rushing to ring him round.

"Our borders! They've breached our borders!" Evandar called out. "To horse!"

With a roar of approval the Host raised their spears and yelled for horses. Servants swarmed out of nowhere to bring them, and these steeds were every one white with rusty-red ears. Evandar helped Dallandra mount, then swung up onto his own horse, gathered the reins in one hand, and rode up beside her.

"If things go against us, my love, flee for your life back to the Westlands, but I'd beg you to remember me for a little while."

"Never could I forget you." She felt cold horror choking her throat. "But what do you think might happen?"

"I don't know." He laughed, suddenly as gleeful as a child. "I don't have the least idea."

The Host howled laughter with him. Holding the silver horn above his head in one hand, Evandar led them out at a jog upstream along the riverbank. Over the mutter of water and the jingling of armor and tack Dallandra found it impossible to ask him questions—not, she supposed, that he would have answered them. There was nothing for her to do but ride and picture horrible imaginings of war.

Once, hundreds of years past as men and elves reckoned time, though it seemed but a few years ago to her, she'd done what she could with herbs and bandages after a battle, when wounded man after wounded man was dragged to her and dumped bleeding or dying onto the wagon bed she was using for a surgery. Hour after hour it went on, till she was so exhausted that she could barely stand, though no more could she bear to stop tending such need. It seemed to her that she could smell all over again the lumps and streaks of gore clotting black on her hands and arms. With a moan of real pain she tossed her head and forced the memories away. Evandar, riding a bit ahead of her, never heard.

By then the river had sunk and dwindled to a white-water stream, cutting a canyon some twenty feet below and to the left of the road. The sun hung red and swollen off to their right, as if they saw it through the smoke of some enormous fire. Ahead lay plains, as flat and seemingly infinite as those in the Westlands, stretching on and on to a horizon where clouds—or was it smoke—billowed like a frozen wave, all bloody red from the bloated sun. Ahead out in the grasslands this hideous light winked and gleamed on spears and armor. Evandar blew three sharp notes on the silver horn. The Host behind him howled, and a dusty wind blew back in answer the sound of another horn and the shouting of the enemy.

"Peel off!" Evandar yelled at Dallandra. "Stay in safety and prepare to flee!"

Sick-cold and shaking, she followed his orders, turning her horse out of line and heading off to the right, where she could lag behind the warband. Yet both her caution and her fear went for naught that day. As they rode closer to the assembled army, waiting out in the plain, a herald broke ranks and came trotting out, carrying a staff wound with colored ribands in the Deverry manner. When Evandar began screaming orders, the Host clattered to a stop behind him and reined their horses up into a rough semicircle, spread out by the river. Clad in glittering black helms and mail, their opponents wheeled round to face them, but they kept their distance. In a muddle of curiosity and fear for her lover's life, Dallandra kicked her horse to a trot and rejoined Evandar as he jogged out to meet the herald. As if in answer to her gesture, one of the enemy warriors broke ranks and trailed after the herald, but he tucked his helm under one arm and held his spear loosely couched and pointed at the ground.

When out between the armies the two sides met, Dallandra nearly lost all her courtesy; with great difficulty she stifled a noise that would have been partly an oath, partly a scream. Although both the herald and the warrior facing them were shaped like men, and both were wearing human-style clothes and armor, their faces were grotesquely distorted, the herald all swollen and pouched, his skin hanging in great folds of warty flesh round his neck, while the warrior was more than a little vulpine, with pointed ears tufted with red fur and a roach of red hair running from his forehead over his skull and down to the back of his neck, while his beady black eyes glittered above a long, sharp nose. The herald was bald and hunchbacked as well, though he did speak perfect Elvish with a musical voice.

"What brings you to the battle plain, Evandar? My lord has committed no fault against you or yours."

"A fault he has done, good herald, against a man marked as mine, and all for the sake of a trinket dropped in my country and thus mine by treaty."

When the herald swung his head round in appeal to the warrior behind him, the swags and wattles of skin grated with a sound like dry twigs scraping over one another. The warrior acknowledged his gesture with a nod, then spurred his horse to the herald's side. For a moment he and Evandar considered each other in silence, while the herald turned dead-pale and began to edge his mount backward. Dallandra noticed then that the ancient creature's eyes were pink and rheumy.

"Not one word of what you say makes the least sense," the leader of the Dark Host said at last. "What trinket?"

"A whistle made of some kind of bone," Evandar said. "And dropped by one of your spies, I'll wager. I gave it to a human man named Rhodry, and now one of your folk's come sniffing round him to fetch it back."

"I know naught of what you say. Never have I owned or seen a bone whistle."

Evandar studied him with narrowed eyes while the herald fidgeted in his saddle.

"Tell me this," Evandar said at last. "Have ever you seen or accepted service from a man with a head and snout as flat and blunt as a badger's, and him all hairy with grey fur, who dresses as the Deverry men dressed when first they came into their new country?"

"And what name does he answer to?"

"I don't know, but he wears a twisted rod of gold round his neck."

"Then I know him, yes, but he's no longer one of mine. Some of my people have broken from my rule and command, Evandar, just as, or so I hear, some have from yours." All at once he grinned, pulling dark lips back from sharp white teeth. "Even your wife, or so the rumors say."

"My liege!" With a little shriek the herald rode in between them. "If we're here to prevent a battle, perhaps the harsh ways of speaking had best be laid aside."

"Go away, old man," the fox warrior snarled. "My brother and I will solve this thing between us."

Dallandra caught her breath in a little gasp. Was this then her lover's true kin and his true form? Sitting easily on his horse Evandar merely smiled at his rival, and he looked so truly elven at that moment, except perhaps for his impossibly yellow hair, that she found it hard—no, she refused—to think of him as anything but a man of her own people. Whimpering, the herald pulled back.

"Women tire of men all the time," Evandar remarked, still smiling. "Tend to your rebels, and I'll tend to mine. Are you telling me that you hold no command over our snouted friend?"

"I am. Just that. Some few have left my host, claiming they've found more powerful protectors elsewhere. At first I thought they'd gone over to you."

"No such thing, not in the least. The woman you spoke of told me about new and powerful friends as well."

For a long moment they stared at each other, each man, if such you could call them, leaning a bit forward over his horse's neck, their eyes locked as if they could read truth from each other in some secret way. Then the fox warrior grunted under his breath and sat back, shifting his weight and bringing up his spear to the vertical.

"This is no time for feuding between us. I'll give you a weapon against this rebel of mine."

"And I'll offer you my thanks in return, but give it to this woman who rides with me, for she's the one who'll need it."

The warrior turned, pausing to look Dallandra over as if he'd just noticed her presence, then with another grunt tossed her the spear. She caught it in one hand, surprised at the length and the heft of it: good oak with a leaf-shaped bronze head, set by its tang into the wood and bound round with bronze bands.

"Make that as short or as long as you please," he remarked, then turned back to his brother. "Farewell, Evandar, and let there be peace between us until we settle this other matter."

"Farewell, brother, but I'd wish for peace between us always and forever."

The fox warrior merely sneered. With a wave of one hand, each finger tipped with a black claw instead of a nail, he wheeled his horse and headed back toward his army. With a roar like a flood racing down a dry ditch they all swung round and galloped off, raising a cloud of dust, shouting, screaming over the clatter of horse gear, till silence fell so hard that it rang louder than the shouts, and the dust settled to reveal an empty field, though the grass lay trampled and torn. Behind Evandar the bright host gathered, muttering their disappointment.

"We ride for home," he announced. "Dalla, that spear's too large for you to carry into the lands of men."

He flicked his hand in its direction, then wheeled his horse round to lead his army away. Dallandra felt the spear quiver in her hand like a live thing. It shrank so fast that she nearly dropped it. She twisted it round and laid it across her saddle in the little space behind the peak, then fought to hold it down as it writhed and shriveled till at last she held a dagger and naught more. A strange thing it was, too, with a leaf-shaped blade of bronze stuck into a crude wood hilt. As she studied it she saw that the bronze band clasping the wood closed round the tang sported a graved line of tiny dragons.

"Dalla, come along!" Evandar called out. "It's too dangerous to linger here."

She slipped the dagger into her belt, then turned her horse and followed, galloping to catch up, dropping to a jog as they led their troops home to the meadowlands. All the way she rode just a little behind Evandar, and she found herself studying his slender back, his yellow mop of hair, all, in fact, of his so accurately portrayed elven form, and wondering just what he really did look like when no glamours lay upon him.

"Tell me somewhat honestly, young Yraen," Lord Erddyr said. "Is Rhodry daft?"

"I wouldn't say that, my lord, but then, I've known him less than a year, now."

"Well, I keep thinking about the way he sees things. Things that aren't really there. I mean, I suppose they aren't really there." Erddyr let his words trail away and began chewing on his thick gray mustaches.

As Time runs in our world, the winter solstice lay months in the past, though it was still some weeks till the spring equinox. Bundled in heavy cloaks against the cold, the lord and his not-quite-a-silver-dagger were walking out in the ward of Dun Gamullyn, where Yraen and Rhodry had spent the winter past as part of the lord's warband. Although the sun had barely risen, servants were already up and at their work, bringing firewood and food into the kitchen hut or hurrying to the stables to tend the horses.

Yawning and shivering, the night watch was just climbing down from the ramparts.

"Ah, well, when the fighting starts, won't matter if he's daft or not," Erddyr said at last. "And I'm willing to wager it's going to start soon. Snow's been gone for what? a fortnight now? And down in the valleys the grass is breaking through. Soon, lad, soon. We'll see if you two can earn your winter's keep."

"I swear to you, my lord, that we'll do our best to repay your generosity, even though it be with our heart's blood."

"Well-spoken lad, aren't you? Especially for an apprentice silver dagger or whatever it is you are."

Erddyr was smiling, but his dark eyes seemed to be taking Yraen's measure, and a little too shrewdly for Yraen's comfort. All winter he'd done his best to avoid the lord's company, an easy enough thing to do, but every now and then he'd noticed Erddyr looking him and Rhodry both over with just this kind of thoughtful calculation.

"Apprenticeship is a good word for it, my lord. Well, I'd best be on my way and not distract my lord from his affairs any longer."

Erddyr laughed.

"Very well spoken, indeed! That's a nice fancy way of saying you want to make your retreat before I ask you any awkward questions. Don't worry, lad. Out here in the west you silver daggers are valuable men, and we've all learned not to go meddling with your private affairs."

"Well, my thanks, my lord."

"Though, well . . ." Erddyr hesitated a minute. "You don't have to answer this, mind, but you and Rhodry are both noble-born, aren't you?"

Yraen felt his face burning with a blush. Here was someone else who'd seen right through his secret, even though he'd been trying to act like an ordinary fellow.

"I can't answer for Rhodry, my lord," he stammered.

"Don't need to." Erddyr gave him a friendly slap on the shoulder. "Well, I'll let you down from the rack, lad. Go get your breakfast."

That afternoon, while Yraen and Rhodry were sitting together over on the warband's side of the great hall, a weary messenger, his clothes all splashed with mud from the spring roads, came rushing in to kneel before Lord Erddyr. The entire warband fell silent to watch while the lord summoned his scribe to read the proffered letter, but they couldn't quite hear the old man's voice over the general noise of the dun. At length, however, the warband's captain, Renydd, was summoned to his lordship's side, and he brought the news back.

"Our lord and his allies have had a bit of luck, lads. Oldadd took Tewdyr's son and half his warband on the road, just by blind chance and naught more." He paused for a grin. "Our lords are going to get themselves a nice bit of coin out of this, I tell you."

The warband broke out laughing and began heaping insults on the name and lineage both of Lord Tewdyr, a famous local miser. As all blood feuds were, the situation was complex. Along with several other noble clans, Lord Erddyr, Rhodry and Yraen's employer, and his young ally, Lord Oldadd, owed various bonds of family and fealty to one Lord Comerr, who was feuding with a certain Lord Adry for many and various reasons, most of which went back several generations. Adry had allies of his own, the chief one being the aforementioned miser, Tewdyr, who was now going to have to ransom back his oldest son and some twenty of their men.

Lord Erddyr spent the afternoon sending messages to all and sundry, and toward sunset Lord Oldadd and his warband of forty escorted their prize into the lord's dun. Since the nights were warming up, the horses were turned out of their stables, which became a temporary prison for the hostages, except of course for the son himself, Lord Dwyn, who upon an honor pledge became Erddyr's guest more than his prisoner. During the dinner that evening, Yraen watched the noble-born at their table across the great hall. Erddyr and Oldadd laughed and joked; Dwyn stared at his plate and shoveled food.

"He might as well eat all he can stuff in," Renydd said with a grin. "His father sets a poor enough table."

When the warband roared with laughter, Dwyn looked up and glared their way. Although he was too far away to have overheard Renydd's remark, he could no doubt guess that he was being mocked. Yraen started to join the general good time, then noticed Rhodry, sitting in the straw by the door and staring at nothing again. His eyes moved as if he watched some creature about the size of a cat; every now and then his mouth twitched as if he were suppressing a smile. Yraen got up and walked over, half thinking of telling him to stop. He was both embarrassed for the man he'd come to consider a friend and afraid that this daft behavior would get them both thrown out of the warband before the war even started. Eventually, whatever Rhodry thought he was watching seemed to take itself off, and the silver dagger turned his attention back to the men around him. When he caught Yraen standing nearby and staring at him, he grinned.

"Beyond this world lies another world, invisible to the eyes of men but not of elves," Rhodry said. "That's a quote from a book, by the way."

"Of course it is: Mael the Seer. His *Ethics,* isn't it?"

"Just that. You've read it?"

"I have. Oh. Curse it!"

"What's so wrong?"

"I just remembered a thing that Lord Erddyr said to me this morning. He asked me if I—we, I mean, you and I—asked me if we were noble-born, and I wondered how he knew, but I suppose I've been acting like a courtly man. I shouldn't even admit I can read, should I?"

"Depends. Out here very few noble-born men can read, so I suppose it'd mark you as son of a scribe or suchlike."

"And what about you? You can quote from the Seer's books, but I can't believe that you were raised in a scriptorium."

"I wasn't, at that." Rhodry flashed him a grin. "But as to where I spent my tender years, I . . . oh, by the gods!"

All at once he sprang to his feet and spun round, peering out the door, and his hand drifted of its own accord to his sword hilt. Yraen glanced back to find that, much to his relief, no one else had noticed. When Rhodry slipped outside, he followed, wondering if he was going daft himself for suddenly and somehow believing that Rhodry was in danger.

Outside, the ward was dark, silent except for the noise spilling through the windows of the dun. Once Yraen's eyes adjusted to the dim light from a starry sky and a sliver of moon, he saw Rhodry standing some five feet away. Otherwise nothing or no one moved, but he couldn't shake the feeling that they were being watched.

"Rhodry?" Yraen whispered it, even as he wondered why he was keeping his voice down. "What's so wrong?"

"Shush! Come here."

As quietly as he could Yraen stepped up beside him.

"There," Rhodry hissed. "By the cart. Can you see him?"

Yraen obligingly looked. Some ten feet ahead of them stood a slab-sided wooden cart, tipped forward with the wagon tree resting on the cobbles. Its whitewashed side caught a square of light from one of the dun windows; Yraen could pick out the blurry shadow thrown by a tankard that someone had set on the windowsill. In the reflected light, he should have been able to see whatever it was that Rhodry saw . . . if indeed it was actually there.

"I can't see a cursed thing." Yet still, he whispered. "Much less anything I could call a 'him.' What do you—"

He stopped, feeling cold fear run down his spine. Although he saw nothing solid twixt the window and the cart, a shadow suddenly fell, a distinct silhouette, on the white square. It looked like a shadow thrown by a man standing sideways, except for the head, which was blunt and snouted. In one clawed paw it carried a dagger, raised and ready. In dead silence Rhodry drew his sword and flashed the blade in the light. The shadow wavered and distorted like an image seen on a still pond will bend and billow when someone throws a rock into the water. Yraen could have sworn he heard a faint and animal squeal; then the shadow disappeared. Chortling under his breath, Rhodry sheathed the sword.

"Still think I'm daft?"

Much to his surprise, Yraen found that he couldn't talk. He shrugged and flapped one hand in a helpless sort of way.

"I've no doubt that every man in this dun thinks I am," Rhodry went on. "And you know, I wish I was. Things would be so much simpler that way."

Yraen nodded with a little gargling sound deep in his throat.

"It's spring. The roads are passable and all that. Why don't you just ride home, lad?"

"Shan't." Yraen found his voice at last. "I want the silver dagger, and I don't give up on things I want so easily."

"As stubborn as a lord should be, huh? Well, as our Seer says, in the book called *On Nobility*, it does not become a noble-born man to quail at the thought of invisible things or to run from what he cannot see merely because he cannot see it."

"I'm not in the mood for great thoughts from great minds just now, my thanks. I—here, hold a moment! What was that bit you recited earlier? Not to the eyes of elves, he said. I always thought elves were some sort of a daft jest or bard's fancy, but . . ."

"But what?" Rhodry was grinning at him.

"Oh, hold your tongue, you rotten horse apple!"

Yraen spun on his heel and strode back into the light and noise of the great hall. For the first time in all the long months since he'd left Dun Deverry and his father's court, he was beginning to consider riding home.

Over the next few days Yraen kept a jittery watch, but never did he see more evidences of hidden things or presences. Mostly he and Rhodry had little to do but sit in the great hall and dice for coppers with the rest of the warband while the negotiations went back and forth between Tewdyr and Erddyr in a regular spate of heralds. The gossip said that Tewdyr was trying to bargain for a lower rate of exchange.

"What a niggardly old bastard he is," Renydd said one morning.

"Just that and twice over," Rhodry said. "But in a way, he's got a point. With a war on, coin's as precious as men."

"It must look that way to a silver dagger."

There was such cold contempt in his voice that Yraen felt like jumping up and challenging him, but Rhodry merely shrugged the insult away. Later, he remarked to Yraen, casually, that causing trouble in the warband was a good way for a silver dagger to lose a hire.

Soon enough, though, the men as well as the lords realized that Tewdyr was holding out for a very good reason. Late the next day a rider came galloping in with the news that Erddyr's allies had marched and were holding Lord Adry under siege. Since Erddyr was required to join them at once, he was forced to lower his demands, at which Tewdyr finally capitulated and arranged the exchange. Early in the morning, Lords Erddyr and Oldadd took their full warbands and escorted the prisoners back to neutral ground, an old stone bridge over a deep-running stream.

On the other side of the bridge, Tewdyr, all red beard and scowls, waited with the remaining men of his warband and another noble lord with twenty-five men of his own. The two heralds walked their horses onto the middle of the bridge and conferred with a flurry of bows. A sack of coin changed hands; Erddyr's herald counted it carefully, then brought it back to his lord. With a grin, Erddyr slipped it inside his shirt and yelled at his men to let the prisoners through. Head held high, Lord Dwyn led his twenty men across to his father's side.

"Good," Renydd said. "Now we can get on with the real sport."

Back at the dun, the wooden carts were drawn up in the ward. Like ants bringing crumbs to a nest, a line of servants hurried back and forth to pile them up with grain and supplies. On the morrow, the warbands would be riding to help hold the siege at Lord Adry's dun.

"This Comerr's got a couple of hundred men at the siege," Rhodry told Yraen. "And we'll be bringing him eighty more. They tell me that Adry's got about ninety men shut in with him, so it all depends on how many Tewdyr and his other allies can raise. Huh —I'll wager Tewdyr's going to put up a good fight now. The old miser's got a thorn up his ass good and proper."

"Did you see how the herald counted that coin? I'll wager Erddyr ordered him to do it."

"So do I. Most heralds have more courtesy than that."

Although Rhodry chattered on, Yraen barely heard the rest of it. Now that the war was finally upon them, he felt his own secret rising in his mind to turn him cold. Even though he'd won many a tournament down in Dun Deverry, even though the royal weaponmasters all proclaimed him one of the finest students they'd ever had, he'd never ridden to a real battle, not once in his young life. Considering the peaceful state of the kingdom's heartland, it was unlikely that he ever would have done so, either, if he'd rested content with his position in life as a pampered minor prince of the blood royal. The very safety and luxury of his life had always seemed shameful to him, a goad that had driven him out, seeking the long road and battle glory. Never once, until this icy moment in Lord Erddyr's great hall, had he considered that he might be frightened when the chance for that glory finally presented itself.

Yet, that evening it seemed his Wyrd was mocking him. Erddyr, of course, had to leave a fort guard behind him. He chose a few of the oldest and less fit men in the warband, then told his men to dice and let the gods decide the rest of the roster. Yraen lost. When his dice came up low, he stared at them for a long while in stunned disbelief, then cursed with every foul oath he could remember. What was this? Was he doomed to spend his entire life safe behind walls no matter how hard he tried to break out? All at once he realized that Erddyr and Renydd were both laughing at him.

"No one can say you lack mettle, silver dagger," Erddyr said. "But if I make an exception for you, I'll have to make exceptions for others, and then what's the wretched use of dicing at all? Fort guard it is for you!"

"As his lordship commands," Yraen said. "But I just can't believe my rotten luck."

Down in southern Pyrdon, the crop of winter wheat had already sprouted. A feathery green dusted the fields bordering the river that Dallandra found when she appeared in the world of men. Judging from the direction of the sun as well as her scant knowledge of the country, the river seemed to lead northeast into the hills. She was well prepared for her journey, with Deverry clothes, a fine horse, and every piece of gear she might need—all stolen, a bit here and there from this town or that, by Evandar's folk. Her only salve for her raw conscience was Evandar's promise that they'd give it all back again when she was done with it. At her suggestion, they'd outfitted her as if she were Jill, the only model she had for a woman alone on the Deverry roads.

Leading a pack mule, laden with herbs and medicines, she rode past tidy farmsteads where aspens and poplars quivered with their first green buds. Behind the earthen walls, skinny white cattle with rusty-red ears chewed sour hay while they longed for meadows. In a lazy curve of the river, she found a town, some fifty round wooden houses scattered around an open square and set off from one another by greening poplar trees, where a gaggle of women in long blue dresses leaned onto their water buckets and gossiped at the stone well. Before they noticed her, she dismounted, gathering her nerve and wondering if Evandar's magic would truly hold against human eyes. When she looked at her own hands or her reflection in water, she saw her usual elven self, but he had assured her that others would see an old, white-haired human woman and nothing more.

Clucking to her horse and mule, she gathered her courage and walked over.

"Good morrow," she said. "Is there a tavern in this town?"

"There is, good dame. Right over there." A young woman smiled at her. "I don't mean to be rude, but how are you faring, traveling the roads all alone, and at your age, too?"

"Oh, I'm like an old hen, too tough even for soup."

The women all laughed pleasantly and nodded to themselves, as if wishing for a life as long for themselves. Feeling a good bit more sanguine about her ruse, Dallandra led her stock across the village square to the tavern. In a muddy side yard she found the tie rail, then went in. The small, well-scrubbed tavern room was empty except for the tavernman himself, a young, dark-haired fellow with a big linen apron wrapped around his shirt and brigga.

"Good morrow, good herbwoman," he said. "Can I fetch you a tankard?"

"Of dark, and draw one for yourself and join me."

They carried their ale to a table by an open window to sit in the pale afternoon sun.

"I was thinking of riding up into the hills to gather fresh medicines," Dallandra said. "But a peddler I met on the road warned me about a blood feud brewing."

"Indeed?" The tavernman had a sip of ale and considered the problem. "Now, a fortnight past, we had a merchant come in with fresh-sheared fleece for the local weaver. He was from the hills to the east of here, and he was fair troubled, he was, about a feud in his lord's lands. Lord Adry, the name was. The wool merchant was telling me that the whole countryside could go up in a war just like tinder, he says, just like dry tinder in a hearth."

"Sounds bad, truly. But I've been looking for someone, and a feud would draw him the way mead draws flies. He's a silver dagger, an Eldidd man, dark hair with a streak of gray in it, blue eyes, the Eldidd way of speaking. Seen anyone like that through here?"

"I haven't, no, but if he's ridden this way, Lord Adry's feud is where you'll find him."

The trouble was, of course, that Dallandra had no idea exactly which way Rhodry had ridden. As far as Evandar had been able to tell from his scrying, the silver dagger was somewhere in this part of Pyrdon, but her main focus was the bone whistle, which spent most of its time in the dark of Rhodry's saddlebags. She was reduced, therefore, to asking round for information like any ordinary soul.

When she left the village, Dallandra crossed the river on a rickety wooden bridge and headed east for the hills and Lord Adry's dangerous feud. She camped that night in a greening meadow by a small stream, where she could water her horse and mule and tether them out to graze. From a nearby farmhouse she bought half a loaf of bread and an armful of wood for a campfire. Once it was dark, she built a fire without bothering to use kindling, called on the Wildfolk of Fire, and lit the logs with a wave of her hand.

Dallandra called up a memory image of the bone whistle, focused it sharply, and let her mind range over the Inner Lands to pick up its trail. She was in luck. All at once, in a swirl of flames, she saw not a memory, but a vision of the thing, lying in Rhodry's hands. He was showing it round to a circle of men standing near a campfire. When she expanded the vision, using Rhodry's eyes as her own, she saw that the campfire was only one of many, spread out in a meadow crowded with soldiers and horses, arranged in a wide arc of a circle. In the center of that circle she could just make

out the dark rise of a towered dun. So Rhodry had found himself a
hire, indeed, and seemed to be in the midst of a siege army as well.
Unfortunately, Dallandra had no idea of where he might be, other
than in a meadow in what seemed like hill country—a description
that could apply to hundreds of miles of territory.

Irritably she broke the vision and got up to pace back and
forth in front of the dying fire. So far, the tavernman's vague report of Lord Adry's feud was the only clue she had, but if all the
lords in this part of the province were about to be drawn into it,
Rhodry could be riding for any one of ten different men. At least a
siege will keep him put in one place, she thought, and by the gods
of both my people and of men, everyone for miles around will be
talking about the thing!

After Lord Erddyr led his men out, his wife took over the command of the dun and the fort guard. Lady Melynda, a stout
woman, was as gray as her husband, with quick-humored blue
eyes. Whenever she smiled, she kept her lips tight together, a gesture that made her seem supercilious. When Yraen got to know the
lady better, he realized that Melynda was simply missing the teeth
in the front of her mouth and hated to show it. During the evening,
the lady sat at the head of the table of honor, with her two serving
women to either side of her. Across the great hall, the fort guard
ate quietly, minding their manners in deference to the lady. The
days passed as slowly and silently as water running in a full
stream, while the fort guard divided their time between keeping
watch on the walls and exercising their horses, riding round and
round the dun. Every now and then they would go perhaps a
quarter of a mile down the main road, then gallop back fast for a
bit of excitement.

After three days, the first messenger rode in, told Lady
Melynda that the siege was going quietly, then rode out that same
night on a fresh horse. The lady began an elaborate piece of needlework—a set of bed hangings, covered with interlaced tendrils
and the red rose blazon of her husband's clan. Up at the honor
table, she and her serving women marked out the vast stretches of
linen in silence and sewed on them grimly and steadily for hours at

a time. Yraen found himself thinking about his mother, even though he was ashamed of himself for doing it, and her own needlework projects, so like the Lady Melynda's, that helped her put griefs and disappointments aside. Most likely she'd started some new bed hangings or suchlike when the chamberlain had reported him gone.

On the fifth day, Rhodry rode back to the dun as Erddyr's messenger. He was so clean and well-shaven that Yraen and everyone else could figure out that the siege was dragging on without incident. While he ate a hasty meal at one of the riders' tables, the fort guard clustered round him and asked for news: There was none.

"Sieges are always tedious," Rhodry said. "I wonder what's happened to old Tewdyr and his lads?"

"Gathering allies, most like." Yraen hoped that he was saying something knowledgeable. "Doesn't Erddyr have any spies?"

"Probably, but no one tells me that sort of thing."

The fort guard all sighed in agreement.

When he was done eating, Yraen walked him down to the gate and saw him off, just for something to do. Rhodry started to mount up, then hesitated, running one hand over his saddlebags.

"I'm thinking of leaving these here with you," Rhodry said.

"Hum? Won't you need— Oh, ye gods, the whistle."

"Just that. It's getting to be a nuisance, having to stay on watch every moment for thieves, and there we are, packed cheek by jowl into the camp, where everyone can hear every word I say, so I can't even swear at the evil beast when I see him prowling round. But I don't want to hand you a curse to guard for me."

"How will these, uh, creatures know I've got the rotten thing?"

"Just so, but still, I hate to put you at risk."

"I doubt me that I'll be at one, and if I'm your apprentice, then it's part of my labor to guard your possessions."

"Well and good, then." Rhodry began unlacing them from the saddle peak. "If you're certain?"

"I am."

Rhodry handed over the saddlebags, then mounted and rode

out the gates. Yraen climbed the wall and watched him riding off into the twilight. Curse my luck! he thought again. If there is a battle, I'll miss it. The worst thing of all was wondering if deep in his heart, he was glad. He'd taken the whistle off Rhodry's hands, he supposed, just in order to share, at least in some small way, his danger.

"Oh, the situation's truly vexed, good Dallandra," said Timryc the chirurgeon. "It seems that every hill lord is up in arms, and so you're going to have a fine job finding your silver dagger."

"So it seems. On the other hand, no doubt I'll find plenty of work for my herbs."

A tiny, wrinkled man with a face as brown as a walnut, Timryc nodded in sad agreement. Drwmyc, Gwerbret Dun Trebyc and master of the Pyrdon hills by the power of the king and the council of electors, was the lord he served as head chirurgeon, a position that kept him current on everything worth knowing about the affairs of the gwerbretrhyn. The exotic medicines from Bardek that Dallandra was carrying (stolen from some priests who were rich enough to spare them, or so Evandar had assured her) had gotten her ushered right in to the presence and the favor of this important man. After buying as much of her stock as she could spare, the chirurgeon had invited her to dine with him, out of sympathy, no doubt, for her supposed advanced age.

"The war started over some cattle rights," Timryc went on. "But now there's a bit more at stake than that. You see, His Grace Drwmyc is going to create a tierynrhyn up in the hill country soon. I'll wager the various lords are sorting themselves out to see who'll receive the honor."

"Ah. And so his grace doubtless won't intervene right away."

"Not unless he receives a direct appeal, which is unlikely. After all, he'll want to appoint a tieryn who has the respect of his vassals." Timryc idly picked up a bone-handled scalpel from the table in front of him and considered the fine steel blade. "Of course, if things get out of hand, and too many of the freemen and their farms are threatened, the gwerbret will intervene. No doubt the feuding lords know that, too."

"Let's hope. A formal little war, then?"

"It should be." Timryc laid the scalpel back down. "It had better be, or his grace will end it. But I'm glad to have that opium and suchlike you've sold me."

Dallandra looked absently round Timryc's comfortable chamber. In the midst of oak paneling and fine tapestries, it was hard to think about warfare, particularly a noble-born squabble, fought by rules as clear as a tournament, with the one difference that death was an allowable part of the sport.

"The latest news is that Lord Adry's dun is under siege," Timryc went on. "A certain Lord Erddyr is leading the faction that's trying to keep Adry's allies from lifting the siege. If you insist on riding up there, be very careful. There'll be skirmishing along the roads."

"Where is this dun, anyway? I'm truly grateful to you for all this information."

"Oh, it's naught, naught. I'll offer you somewhat more valuable—a letter of safe conduct. Even the most ignorant rider can recognize the gwerbret's seal."

Later that evening, with the letter tucked safely inside her tunic and a map of the road to Lord Adry's dun as well, Dallandra returned to her chamber in the inn where she was staying. Since the night was too warm for a fire, she used the dancing reflections of candle flame in a bucket of water for her scrying, but she saw nothing but a stubborn darkness, telling her that the bone whistle was tucked away in Rhodry's gear. In a way, she was relieved to fail and have done with it, because her day's traveling had left her exhausted. Every muscle in her legs and back burned from riding, and she felt as if the rest of her were made of lead. It had been a long time since she'd lived in her physical body. That night she dreamt that she lounged in the sunny grass with Evandar, in the land where life meant ease and dweomer, only to wake in tears at the sight of the dingy chamber walls.

Rhodry rode for most of the night, stopping at the dun of Lord Degedd, one of Erddyr's allies, to get a few hours sleep and a meal, and to pick up his own horse, which he'd changed there for a fresh one on his journey out. About an hour after dawn, he left for the last leg of the journey. As a simple precaution, he rode fully armed and mailed, with his shield ready at his left arm. Once he left the cultivated land behind, he was utterly alone, riding through low brushy hills where every tiny valley could mean an ambush. After so many years of peace out on the grasslands, he found the feeling of danger sweetly troubling, like seeing a pretty woman walk by.

Toward noon, he reached the first plowed fields of Adry's demesne, where frightened farmers leaned onto their hoes to stare at him as he rode past. Rhodry was thinking of very little besides getting something to eat when he rode up the last hill and heard the sound. From his distance, it sounded like a stormy wind in the trees, but his horse tossed up its head and snorted.

"Oh, here, my friend," Rhodry said. "Do you think Lord Tewdyr's here to meet us?"

Chuckling under his breath, Rhodry drew a javelin and trotted up to the hill crest. The sound grew louder and louder, resolving itself into the clang of sword on shield and the whinnies of frightened horses. At the crest, Rhodry paused and looked down into the flat valley below, where the battle raged round Lord Adry's dun, a swirling, screaming mass of men and horses. Off to the left stood the white tents of the besiegers, but as Rhodry watched, fire sprang out among them. Black plumes of smoke welled up and mingled with the dust.

Howling a war cry, Rhodry kicked his horse to a gallop and raced downhill. Round the edge of the fighting, where there was room to maneuver, the mob spread out into little clots of single combats. Rhodry hurled one of his javelins at an unfamiliar back, pulled and threw the other, then rode on, circling the field and drawing his sword. It was hard to tell friend from foe as the smoke spread over the field. At last he saw two men mobbing a third, riding a gray. As Rhodry rode over, he heard the single rider shouting Erddyr's name. He spurred his horse and slammed into the melee. He slashed at an opponent's back, yelled Erddyr's name to warn the man he was trying to rescue that he was an ally, then stabbed at an enemy horse. Screaming, the horse reared, and

Rhodry had a clear strike at the rider as it came down. He flung up his shield to parry, then spurred his quivering horse forward and stabbed with his whole weight behind the sword. The blade shattered the enemy's mail and killed him clean as the horse stumbled to its knees.

With a wrench of his whole body, Rhodry pulled the sword free and swung his horse round, but the second enemy was already down, huddled on the ground as his horse raced away. With a friendly shout the rider on the gray rode up beside him—Renydd, panting for breath and choking on the smoke in the air.

"Back just in time, silver dagger. My thanks."

"Stick with me, will you? I don't know one bastard from another in this lot."

Renydd nodded and gulped for breath. His horse was sweating with acrid gray foam running in gobbets down its neck.

"I owe you an apology, silver dagger," Renydd said. "I haven't treated you too well."

"Don't let it trouble your heart. We've not got time for fine points of courtesy just now."

Out on the field three men broke free and headed straight for them. When Rhodry called out Erddyr's name, the three howled back their answer: for Lord Adry! The name rang with ill omen. If the men from the dun had managed to fight their way out to the edge, the besiegers were losing the battle. With a whoop of laughter, Rhodry flung up his shield and charged to meet them. His thigh slashed open to the bone, one of the three was turning away. Rhodry swerved around him and headed for a man on a black. The enemy wheeled faultlessly to face him and slashed in from the side. Rhodry caught the sword on his shield and leaned, pulling him to one side and opening his guard. When he stabbed in, his enemy twisted back, but blood flowed from his side. Rhodry heard himself laughing his cold berserker's howl. The enemy broke free of his shield and swung; sword clashed on sword as Rhodry parried barely in time. He could barely see his enemy's smoke-stained face, his blue eyes narrowed in pain as he slashed at Rhodry's horse.

The horse dodged too late, and the blow caught it on the side of the head. Staggering, it tried to rear, then stumbled, plowing into the enemy black and throwing Rhodry forward almost into his enemy's lap. Rhodry flung up his shield and thrust as he felt the horse going down under him. With a shriek the enemy reeled back from a lucky gouge of the shield boss across his face, the blood running like a curtain from his eyes. When Rhodry stabbed at him, he missed and hit the black hard. In panic the black bucked up once and writhed, dumping his blinded rider, then pulled free to run away. Deprived of its support, Rhodry's horse buckled to its knees. Rhodry threw his shield to avoid breaking his arm and rolled, falling across his struggling enemy. He heard hoofbeats and flung his arms over his head just as a horse leapt over the pair of them. Rhodry staggered to his feet and grabbed the wounded man by the shoulder.

"You've got to get up," Rhodry yelled.

His former enemy clung to him like a child. His sword in one hand, the other around the man's waist, Rhodry staggered toward the open ground beyond the fighting. He had no idea why he was saving the man he'd just tried to kill, but he knew the reason somehow lay in their both being unhorsed, as vulnerable as weeds in a field. At last they reached a stand of trees. Rhodry shoved the blinded man down and told him to stay there, then ran back toward the battle. He had to find another horse. Suddenly he heard silver horns, cutting through the shouting—someone was calling a retreat. He didn't know who. Sword in hand, Rhodry gasped for breath and tried to see through the smoke. A rider on a gray galloped straight for him: Renydd.

"We're done for!" Renydd yelled. "Get up behind me."

When Rhodry swung up behind him, Renydd spurred the gray hard, but all it could manage was a clumsy trot, sweating and foaming as it stumbled across the open ground. The horns sang through the smoke like ravens shrieking. When Rhodry choked on a sudden taste of smoke, he twisted round and saw fire creeping through the grass round the tents and heading their way. Off to their right, a poplar blazed like a sudden torch.

"Oh, by the hells," Renydd snarled. "I hope it reaches the bastard's dun and burns it for him!"

As they trotted for the road, three of Comerr's men joined

them on weary horses. Cursing, slapping the horses with the flats of their blades, the men rode on while the smoke spread out behind them as if it were sending claws to catch them. Ahead they saw a mob of men milling in confusion around a lord with a gold-trimmed shield.

"Erddyr, thank the gods," Renydd said. "My lord! My Lord Erddyr!"

"Get over here, lad," Erddyr yelled. "We've got a horse for that man behind you."

Rhodry mounted a chestnut with a bleeding scratch down its neck and joined the pack, about fifty men, some of them wounded. As they made their slow retreat back to the dun of another ally, Degedd, Lord Comerr joined them with close to a hundred. A few at a time, stragglers caught up and joined their disorganized remnant of an army. At the top of a hill, the lords called a halt to let the horses rest—it was that or lose them. When Rhodry looked back, he saw no sign of pursuit. In the distance, the smoke pall slowly faded.

Just at sunset, they reached Degedd's dun and mobbed into the ward, bleeding horses, bleeding men, all of them stinking of sweat and smoke and aching with shame. Yelling orders, Lord Degedd worked his way through the mob while he cradled a broken left wrist in his right hand. Rhodry and Renydd pulled a wounded man down from his saddle before he fainted and split his head on the cobbles. They carried him into the great hall, where Degedd's lady and her women were already frantically at work, tending the wounded. The hall swarmed with so many men and servants that it was hard to find a place to lay their burden down.

"Over by the hearth," Renydd said.

Rhodry cursed and shoved their way through until at last they could lay him down flat on the floor in a line of other wounded men, then started back outside to fetch anyone else who needed to be carried. Once the wounded were all brought in, they had the horses to tend.

Degedd's small dun was crammed from wall to wall with the remnants of his allies' army, so crowded that Rhodry felt a surge of hope. Although they'd fled the battle, the war wasn't over yet. By the time Rhodry and Renydd returned to the great hall,

Rhodry's head was swimming. They got a couple of chunks of bread and some cold meat from a servant, then sat on the floor and gobbled it silently.

Up by the hearth of honor, the womenfolk were still working. His wrist bound and splinted, Lord Degedd sat on the floor with the other noble lords—Erddyr, Oldadd, and Comerr—and talked urgently. Although the hall was filled with men, it was oddly silent in a wordless chill of defeat. When Renydd finished eating, he leaned back against the curve of the wall and fell asleep. Many of the men did the same, slumping against the wall, lying down on the floor, but the noble lords leaned close together and went on talking. Rhodry thought he was going to ache too badly from his fall to sleep straightaway, but he was too exhausted to stay on his feet. He'd been awake and riding for the entire cycle of a day.

When he sat down next to Renydd, the captain stirred, looked at him blearily, then leaned against his shoulder. Rhodry put his arm around him just for the simple human comfort of it. All at once his weariness caught up with him. His last conscious thought was that they were all shamed men tonight, not just him.

Rhodry woke suddenly to Lord Erddyr's voice. With a grunt, Renydd sat up straight next to him. Erddyr was on his feet in the middle of the hall and yelling at the men to wake up and listen to him. Sighing, cursing, the drowsy warband roused itself and turned toward their lords.

"Now here, lads," Erddyr said. "I'm going to ask you a hard thing, but it has to be done. We can't stay here tonight and get pinned like rats in a trap. We're leaving the wounded behind and riding back to my dun."

A soft exhausted sigh breathed through the hall.

"I know how you feel," Erddyr went on. "By the Lord of Hell's warty balls, don't you think I'd rather be in my blankets than on the back of a horse? But if we stay, those horseshit bastards have us where they want us. Degedd can't provision a siege. We've got to have time to collect our men on fort guard, and then we can make another strike on the bastards. Do you all understand? If we stay here, we lose the war and every scrap of honor we ever had. So, are you riding with me or not?"

Cheering as loudly as they could manage, the men began to get up, collecting shields and gear from the floor.

"Save your breath," Erddyr called out. "And let's ride!"

A few hours before dawn, Yraen went out for his turn on watch. Yawning and cursing, just on general principles, he climbed up to the catwalk and took his place next to Gedryc, the nominal captain of the fort guard, who acknowledged him with a nod. Together they leaned onto the rampart and looked over the hills, dark and shadowed in the moonlight, to watch the road. In about an hour, just as the moon was setting, Yraen saw a somewhat darker shape moving on the dark countryside, and a certain fuzziness in the air over it—probably dust.

"Who's that?" Gedryc snapped. "Don't tell me it's our lord! Oh, ye gods!"

In a few minutes more the moving shape resolved itself into a long line of men on horseback, and something about the slumped way they sat, and the slow way that the horses limped and staggered along, told the tale.

"A defeat," Gedryc said. "Run and wake the dun, lad."

As Yraen climbed down the ladder, he felt a sudden sick wondering if Rhodry was still alive. Somehow, before this moment, it hadn't really occurred to him that a friend of his might die in this war. He raced to the barracks over the stables, woke up the rest of the fort guard, then ran into the great hall and the kitchen hut to rouse the servants. He came back out in time to hear the men on the walls calling to one another.

"It's Erddyr, all right! Open those gates!"

The servants came pouring into the ward to help the night watch pull open the heavy iron-bound gates. Torchlight flared in the ward as the army filed in, the horses stumbling blindly toward shelter. Wrapped in a cloak over her night dress, Lady Melynda rushed out of the broch just as Lord Erddyr dismounted and threw his reins to a groom.

"Your husband's come home defeated and dishonored," Erddyr said. "But the war's not over yet."

"Well and good, my lord," Melynda said calmly. "Where are the wounded?"

"Back in Degedd's dun, but get the servants to feeding these men, will you?"

Yraen found Rhodry down at the gates. He'd dismounted to lead his horse inside and spare it his weight for the last few yards. When Yraen caught his arm, all the silver dagger could do was turn toward him with a blind, almost drunken smile.

"I'll tend that horse," Yraen said. "Go get something to eat."

When he finished with the horse, Yraen went back into the great hall, filled with men—some still eating, most asleep. At the table of honor the noble lords ate silently while Lady Melynda watched them with frightened eyes. Yraen picked his way through and joined Rhodry, sitting on the floor in the curve of the wall with Renydd, who was slowly eating a piece of bread as if the effort were too much for him.

"Why did you lose?" Yraen said to Rhodry.

"What a comfort my friend is," Rhodry said. "From his mouth no excuses or blustering to lift a man's shame, only the nastiest of truths." He paused to yawn. "We lost because there were more of them than us, that's all."

"Well and good, then. I'm cursed glad to see you alive, you bastard."

Rhodry grinned and leaned back against the wall.

"We comported ourselves brilliantly on the field," Rhodry said. "Renydd and me slew seventy men each, but there were thousands ranged against us."

"Horseshit," Renydd said with his mouth full.

"It's not horseshit." Rhodry yawned violently. "There were rivers of blood on the field, and corpses piled up like mountains. Never will that grass grow green again, but it'll come up scarlet, all for grief at that slaughter."

Yraen leaned forward and grabbed his arm: he was beginning to realize what it meant when Rhodry babbled this way.

"And the clash and clang was like thunder," Rhodry went on. "We swept in like ravens and none could stand before us. We trampled them like grass—"

"That's enough!" Yraen gave his arm a hard shake. "Rhodry, hold your tongue! You're half-mad with the defeat."

Rhodry stared at him, his eyes half-filled with tears.

"My apologies," Rhodry said. "You're right enough."

He curled up on the straw like a dog and fell asleep straight-away, without even another yawn.

All that day, the army slept wherever it could find room, scat-tered through the dun. Before he went to his bed, Erddyr sent men from the fort guard out with messages to the duns of the various allies, warning their fort guards to be ready to join their lords. Other men rode out to scout and keep a watch for Adry's army on the road. The servants went through the stored supplies. The army had lost all its carts, blankets, provisions, and, worst of all, its extra weapons. Not all the scrounging in the world could produce more than twenty javelins for the entire army. Yraen, of course, still had a pair, those he'd brought with him when he'd left home, but he gave one to Rhodry and hoarded the other.

"Here's your saddlebags, too," Yraen said. "I had no trouble with them."

"Good. Huh. I'd say our enemy can't track the whistle by dweomer then, but if that's true, how by the hells did he know I had the ugly thing in the first place?"

"Well, was there someone else who could have told him?"

Rhodry swore under his breath.

"There was, at that, and I'll wager it was our lovely Alshan-dra, all right."

Yraen would have asked him more about this mysterious be-ing, but a couple of other men joined them with rumors to share.

In the afternoon, Yraen had a word alone with Lady Melynda, who bravely smiled her tight-lipped smile and talked of her husband's eventual victory. It seemed that Comerr alone had thirty fresh men in his dun, to say nothing of the men they could muster from other allies.

"If they can assemble them all, my lord swears they'll out-number the enemy. He tells me that Adry and Tewdyr already had every man they could muster at the siege." Her bright smile faded abruptly. "I wonder if that's true, or if he's trying to spare my feelings?"

"It's probably true, my lady, because he's already let the worst

news slip. What matters is whether they can assemble them in
time, and Rhodry says that's a hard thing to do."

"Just so." Melynda was silent for a long time. "I'm going to
try to prevail upon my lord to send to the gwerbret for his judgment on this matter."

"Do you think he will?"

Melynda shook her head in a no and stared at the floor.

"Not with this defeat aching his heart. He'd feel too shamed."

When he left the lady, Yraen climbed up to the walls and
looked out at the silent hills. Somewhere out there was the enemy
army, perhaps riding for them, perhaps off licking its own wounds.
He wondered if Erddyr would stand a siege or sally out right away
should Adry appear at his gates, but in the end, the lords decided
to leave the dun as soon as possible and ride round the countryside
to collect their allies, rather than risk getting trapped in a siege.
Although a dun with an army inside was a prize worth having, it
was unlikely that Tewdyr and Adry would try to take an empty
one, simply because they'd be too vulnerable to attack themselves.
There came a point in any war where it was best to settle the
matter in open country rather than trusting in stone walls, or so
Rhodry always said.

Late that afternoon, one of the scouts returned, rushing into
the great hall and blurting out his urgent message: Adry and his
allies were riding their way and had made camp not fifteen miles
off.

"There's close to two hundred of them, my lord," the scout
finished up. "Fully provisioned."

"Only two hundred?" Erddyr said, grinning. "Well, then, we
left a few scars on them before we called the retreat."

"Maybe so," Comerr said. "But we'd best get out of here
before they pin us at your gates."

The dun turned into an orderly madhouse. The warband ran
to fetch their gear and horses. Servants frantically loaded the last
pair of carts left in the dun and commandeered extra horses for
pack animals to carry what supplies they'd been able to scrape
together. Yraen collected his horse, donned his armor, and realized
that everything he'd wanted was about to come to him. Soon he

would test himself and all the weaponcraft he'd learned; soon he would discover for himself what battle and battle-glory had to teach a man. Now that the time was upon him, he felt preternaturally calm and oddly light, as if he floated through the crowded ward to Rhodry's side. Only his heart refused to quiet itself; he could feel it knocking in his throat, or so it seemed, like some wild creature in a trap.

"We'll be at the rear, no doubt," Rhodry said. "Silver daggers always eat the whole cursed army's dust."

Yraen merely nodded. Rhodry gave him a look as sharp as a knife blade.

"Tell me somewhat, lad. Have you ever fought before?"

The time was past for bluster. Yraen shook his head in a no. Rhodry swore under his breath and seemed to be about to say more, but at the head of the line the horns sang out the order to mount and ride. As the men swung into their saddles and started moving, trying to sort themselves into warbands in the too-small space, Yraen ended up separated from Rhodry, and there was no time to find him again as the riders began filing out the gates. When they first reached the road, Yraen made a futile try at spotting him, then fell back with the squad assigned to guard the supplies.

Once the moon rose, bright and swollen just a night off her full, the lords led their men off the road and began circling to the north through the hills and ravines, good hiding from their enemies. Thanks to the carts and the pack train, they moved slowly, the carters cursing as the carts banged through the rocks and brush. Riding at the very rear, Yraen was the only one who realized that someone was following them.

As they started down the side of a hill, Yraen saw movement out of the corner of his eye, turned to look, and caught the unmistakable shape of a man on foot slinking through the tall grass behind them. He must have left his horse somewhere behind—a mistake that cost him his life. With a shout of warning, Yraen turned his horse out of line and drew his javelin in the same smooth motion. The enemy scout turned and raced downhill, but Yraen galloped after, plunging through the grass and praying that his horse wouldn't stumble and go down. Twisting in a desperate zigzag, his prey ran for the trees at the bottom of the valley, but Yraen gained on him and rose in the stirrups to throw. The point gleamed in the moonlight as it sped to the mark and caught the scout full in the back. With an ugly shriek he went down headlong into the grass. Yraen trotted over and dismounted, but he was already dead. A couple of men from his warband rode up and circled round them.

"Good job, lad," one of them shouted. "We're cursed lucky you've got good eyes."

Yraen shrugged in pretended modesty and pulled the javelin free with a welling up of the enemy's blood. In the moonlight it seemed like dark water, some strange and dreamlike substance. Yraen wondered how it could be possible that he'd killed a man and yet felt nothing, not grief nor gloating.

"Just let him lie," the rider went on. "We've got to get back to the warband, but in the morning, I'll make sure Lord Oldadd knows what you've done."

But apparently the noble-born already realized what had happened. When Yraen returned to the warband, the lords halted the march and had a hasty horseback conference up at the head of the line. Yraen strained to hear as Erddyr leaned over in his saddle to make his points with the wave of a gauntlet. All at once Lord Comerr laughed and gave Erddyr a friendly cuff on the shoulder. Erddyr turned his horse and trotted over to bellow at the warband.

"With their scout dead, we've got a chance to wreak a little havoc, lads," Erddyr called out. "I want fifty men to risk their cursed necks. I'll be leading you in a raid on Adry's camp, just to stick a thorn up the bastard's ass."

Yraen turned his horse out of line to volunteer. As a squad assembled round Erddyr, he kept watch for Rhodry and finally saw him on the other side of the group, or saw, rather, his silver dagger, catching the moonlight with an unmistakable glitter. Although he waved, he had no idea if Rhodry had seen him or not.

Leaning forward in his saddle, Erddyr explained the situation. Comerr and the pack train were going to head for his dun in hopes of meeting the reinforcements on the road, while Erddyr and the squad tried to slow their enemies. It was going to be a quick raid—

Erddyr emphasized that repeatedly—one fast sweep down, then an equally fast retreat.

"The whole point, lads, is to panic their horses, not to make kills. Go for the herd and try to scatter it. If anyone gets in your way, kill him, but leave the real slaughter for later. All we want to do is keep them busy chasing their worm-gut stock instead of chasing us."

Erddyr sent Rhodry and some man Yraen didn't know out in front as scouts, then led his squad back the way they'd come until the scouts rejoined them. At that point they left the road to dodge through the brush and down a narrow valley. On the far side they climbed a hill and found the camp down below, the rough circles of sleeping men and the bulky dark shapes of the supply wagons. Off to one side drowsed the horse herd. At the edge of the camp, guards walked in a circling patrol. Erddyr whispered something to Rhodry, who whispered it to the man behind him. The order made its way back: charge through the guards for the horses, then circle and wheel for the retreat before the men grab their weapons and join the fight.

Steel flashed in the moonlight as the squad drew their swords. Yraen settled his own and felt his heart pounding in his throat again, but he was beginning to wonder if he'd ever see a real battle, the sort he'd heard bards sing about, with proper armies and strategies and all that sort of thing. They walked their horses over the crest of the hill, paused for a moment like a wave about to break, then started down with the jingle of tack and the clank of armor. In the camp, the guards looked up and screamed the alarm.

"Now!" Erddyr yelled.

In a welter of war cries and curses, the squad spurred their horses and galloped full-tilt downhill. When they reached the valley, they spread out in a ragged line and swept toward the horse herd. Although the guards raced over to make a futile stand against them, the line ignored them and charged past. As he galloped past a guard, Yraen swung wildly at him, but he missed by yards. When the squad screamed and plunged into the herd, the horses panicked, rearing up and stretching their tether ropes so tight that it was easy to snap them with one swing of a blade.

Yraen cursed and shrieked and made every ungodly noise he could think of as he sliced ropes and set horse after horse racing away from the attack. At last his wild ride brought him to the edge of the valley. As he turned his horse, he saw men pouring toward the raiders with their swords and shields at the ready. It was time to run.

Yraen kicked his horse and galloped back across the valley with the rest of the squad. Here and there, a panicked horse still at tether bucked and kicked. Yraen cut one last rope, then turned his attention to the men racing to stop them. All at once, one of the panicked horses slammed into the rider ahead of him. That horse reared; the rider went down, with the flash of a gold-trimmed shield that said Lord Erddyr. Yraen pulled his horse up just in time to avoid running right over him. The armed and furious enemy was charging straight for them. Yraen swung down and grabbed Erddyr's arm.

"Take my horse, my lord," he yelled. "I'll guard your mount."

"By the hells, we ride together or die together! Here they come, lad."

Yraen set his back to Erddyr's and dropped to a fighting crouch as the first enemies reached them. Four of them, and in the gauzy moonlight, it was hard to see their swings, impossible to detect all those subtle movements that reveal an enemy's next thrust. Yraen could only hack and swing blindly as he desperately parried their equally blind strikes. His shield cracked and groaned; Erddyr was screaming his war cry at the top of his lungs; but Yraen fought silently, coldly, dodging forward to make a slash across an enemy's arm, then dodging back, slamming into Erddyr's back as the melee thickened. Screaming Erddyr's name, the mounted squad was cutting and trampling through the mob on the ground.

In front of him an enemy feinted in close. Yraen lunged fast and got him, almost without realizing it in the bad light. He felt rather than saw his sword bite deep into something soft and stick. When he yanked it free, a man fell forward at his feet. He flung up his shield to parry a blow from the side, slashed at another man, missed, and saw him fall, cut down by a thrust from a mounted man. Erddyr was laughing aloud as riders swirled round them in a kicking, bucking confusion.

"Mount behind me, lad!" a man yelled.

Yraen sheathed his sword still bloody and swung up behind him, scrambling awkwardly onto his bedroll. The rider turned his horse and spurred it on, slashing down at an enemy in their way. Yraen leaned forward and got a cut on the same man as the horse carried them past at a clumsy gallop.

"Ride!" Erddyr screamed. "Retreat!"

Shouting, swinging, the mounted squad cut its way across the valley and headed for the hills. Yraen saw a couple of Erddyr's men driving what was left of the enemy horses straight for the camp. Howling in rage, half the enemy line peeled out of the battle and ran for the camp to save their gear from being trampled. The squad cut grimly on. Yraen leaned and swung randomly at un-horsed men who had little appetite for a fight. At last they gained the hillside, and the horse stumbled wearily up toward the crest. There Rhodry rode to meet them, leading a riderless bay.

"Transfer him over," Rhodry yelled. "We've got to make speed."

As Yraen mounted the fresh horse, he could tell from the gear that it had once been Lord Erddyr's, who, of course, still rode his own gray. Ahead, the squad was already crashing its way through the underbrush and heading downhill. As he followed, Yraen saw Lord Erddyr, rising frantically in the stirrups as he tried to count his men. They trotted across the next valley and finally assembled in a laughing, shoving mob at the crest of the farther hill.

"Where's that lad whose horse I'm riding?" Erddyr called out. "Come ride next to me, lad, and then we'd best get our asses out of here."

Yraen guided his horse through the warband, which showered him with good-natured insults to show their respect for the way he'd saved their lord. Erddyr waved the line forward. Carefully they picked their way along the dark valleys until they reached the place where they'd left the main column. No one ever tried to follow them. Doubtless Adry and his men were chasing horses and swearing all over the hills round their camp.

"Well played," Erddyr called out as the warband gathered around him. "It's a pity your lord here almost ruined the whole maneuver, but we're born to our place, not picked by wits."

The men laughed and cheered him.

"It's a cursed good thing I hired this silver dagger's apprentice," Erddyr went on. "But we're a bit short on time to have the bard make you a song, lad. Let's get on our way."

When the warband rode out, Yraen and Rhodry rode together. By then the sky was beginning to pale into gray, and in the growing light Yraen could look round and see that their squad had suffered no losses. He remembered then the man who'd fallen at his feet when he'd been defending Lord Erddyr. I must have killed him, he thought—he lay so still. He shook his head hard, wondering why nothing seemed real or even important, then looked up to find Rhodry watching him.

"Not bad," Rhodry said. "You've got sharp eyes, and a cursed good thing, too."

"The scout, you mean?"

"That, too, but I was thinking about Lord Erddyr. Well done."

Yraen felt himself blushing like the rising sun. The fulsome praise heaped upon his princely self by his father's weaponmasters had lost all its meaning, compared to those two words.

"That's true, good herbwoman," Lady Melynda said. "My husband did indeed hire a silver dagger named Rhodry, and young Yraen, too. Of course, you've arrived a bit late to speak with them. The army rode out in the middle of the night, you see."

For a moment the lady's careful calm nearly deserted her. With shaking hands she wiped tears from her eyes, then composed herself with a long sigh that came close to being a gasp. Dallandra looked round the great hall, empty and echoing with silence. Aside from a handful of male servants, the only guards the lady had were three wounded men.

"Well, my lady, before I ride on, I'll see what I can do for these men here."

"My thanks, but I'd be most grateful if you did catch up with the army. You see, my husband doesn't have a proper chirurgeon with his warband, so your aid would be most welcome."

"In the morning, then, I'll be on my way. No doubt they've left an easy trail to follow."

Since it had been some years since Dallandra had tended wounds, she was dreading the job, but once she got the clumsy bandages off her first patient's injuries, her old professional detachment set in. The man's gashed and bloody flesh became merely a problem for her to solve with the medicinals and other means she had at hand, rather than an object of disgust, and his gratitude made the effort well worth it. By the time she finished with the wounded, it was late in the day. She washed up, then joined the lady and her serving women at the table of honor. As they tried to make conversation about something other than the war and the lady's fears for her husband, Dallandra found herself oppressed by a sense of dread so sharp and miserable that she knew it must be a dweomer-warning of sorts. Of what, she couldn't say.

Just at sunset, the answer came in a shout of alarm from the servants who were watching the gates. Dallandra ran after Melynda when the lady rushed outside and saw the stableboys and the aged chamberlain swinging the gates shut. The two women scrambled up the ladder to the ramparts and leaned over. Down below on the dusty road, Lord Tewdyr was leading forty armed men up to the walls.

"And what do you want with me and my maidservants?" Melynda called down. "My husband and his men are long gone."

"I'm well aware of that, my lady," Tewdyr shouted back. "And I swear to every god and goddess as well that no harm will come to you and your women while you're under my protection."

"His lordship is most honorable, but we aren't under his protection, and I see no reason to ask for it."

"Indeed?" Tewdyr gave her a thin-lipped smile. "I fear me it's yours whether you want it or not, because I'm going to take you back to my dun with me and hold you there until your husband quits the war and ransoms you back."

"Oh, indeed?" Melynda tossed her head. "I should have known that spending all that coin would ache your heart, but never did I think it would drive you to dishonor, just to get it back."

"There is no need for my lady to be insulting, especially when she can't have more than a handful of men in her dun."

Melynda bit her lip sharply and went a bit pale. Dallandra stepped forward and leaned over the rampart.

"The lady has all the men she needs," Dallandra called. "This is an impious, dishonorable, and wretched move you're making, my lord. Every bard in Deverry will satirize your name for it down the long years."

"Oh, will they now?" Tewdyr laughed. "And do you claim to be a bard, old woman?"

His voice dripped cold contempt for all things old and female both. In an icy rage Dallandra swept up her hands and invoked elemental spirits, the Wildfolk of Air and Fire. In a swarming, glittering mob they answered her call and rushed among the men and horses in a surge of raw life. Although the men couldn't see them, they could feel them indirectly, just as when a cloud darkens the sun outside and the light in a chamber dims. The riders shifted uneasily in their saddles; the horses danced and snorted; Tewdyr looked wildly around him.

"We have no need of armed men," Dallandra said. "Are you stupid enough to match steel against the laws of honor and the gods?"

The Wildfolk chattered among the men and pinched the horses, pulled at the men's clothes, and rattled their swords in their scabbards until the entire warband shook in fear. Turning this way and that, they cursed and swatted at enemies they couldn't see. Dallandra held up her right hand and called forth blue fire—a perfectly harmless etheric light, but it looked like it would burn hot. She fashioned the fire into a long streaming torch and made it blaze brightly in the fading sunlight. Tewdyr yelped and began edging his horse backward.

"Begone!" Dallandra called out.

With a wave of her hand, she sent the bolt of light down like a javelin. When it struck the ground in front of Tewdyr's horse, it shattered into a hundred darts and sparks of illusionary fire. Dallandra hurled bolt after bolt, smashing them into the ground among the warband while the Wildfolk pinched the horses viciously and clawed the men. Screaming, cursing, the warband broke and galloped shamelessly down the hill. Tewdyr spurred his horse as hard as any of them and never even tried to stop the retreat.

Dallandra sent the Wildfolk chasing them, then allowed herself a good laugh, but a pale and feverishly shaking Lady Melynda knelt at her feet. Behind her the servants huddled together as if they feared Dallandra would attack them simply for the fun of it. Only then did Dallandra remember that she was among human beings, not the People, who took dweomer and its powers as a given thing.

"Now, now, my lady, do get up," Dallandra said. "The honor is mine to be allowed to be of service to you. It was naught but a few cheap tricks, but I doubt me very much that they'll return to trouble you."

"Most likely not, but I can't call them cowards for it."

All that evening the lady and her women waited upon Dallandra as if she were the queen herself, but none of them presumed to make conversation with her. As soon as she could, Dallandra went up to the chamber that they'd readied for her. Although she tried to scry, the whistle stayed hidden and Rhodry with it, giving her a few bitter thoughts on the limits of the dweomer that had so impressed the lady and her household.

In the meadows behind Lord Comerr's dun, the allies had camped their hastily pulled together army of two hundred thirty-six men. For that first day after Erddyr's dawn arrival, the men rested while the lords conferred over the various scraps of news that scouts and messengers brought them. Rhodry spent the day in rueful amusement, mocking himself for how badly he wanted to be included in those conferences. He was used to command, and even more, he knew that he was good at it, better, certainly, than the overly cautious Comerr and the entirely too daring Erddyr. Yet there was nothing for him to do but sit around and remind himself that he was a silver dagger and nothing more. He was also more than a little worried about Yraen, who'd made his first kills by blind luck. The lad himself seemed dazed, saying little to anyone. Finally, when they received their scant rations for the evening meal, Rhodry led him away from the other men for a talk.

"Now listen, you know enough about war to know that you're not ready to lead charges or suchlike. Every rider goes through a time when he's just learning how to handle himself, like, and there's no shame in an untried man staying on the edge of things. Everyone seems to have figured out that this is your first ride."

"Oh, true spoken," Yraen said. "But is there going to be any edge to stay on? It sounds cursed desperate to me. That last scout said that Adry's scraped up almost three hundred men."

"You've got a point. Unfortunately. Well, there's still one thing you can do, and that's think before you go charging right into the thick of things. More men have been saved by a good look round them than by the best sword work in the world."

On the morrow, when the army saddled up and rode out, Lord Erddyr told Yraen to ride just behind the noble-born as a way of honoring the lad for saving his life and allowed Rhodry to join him there. They were heading back east in the hopes of making their stand on ground of their own choosing. Logic foretold that Adry would be riding for Comerr's dun, but the scouts who circled ahead of the main body brought back no news of him. Finally, toward noon, scouts came back to report that they'd found Adry's camp of the night before, but that the tracks of his army led south, away from Comerr's dun and toward Tewdyr's. The noble lords held a quick conference surrounded by their anxious warbands.

"Now why by the hells would he circle when he's got the numbers on his side?" Erddyr said.

"A couple of reasons," Comerr said. "Maybe to draw us into a trap for one. But I wonder—he's heading back to Tewdyr's dun, is he? Here, you don't suppose Tewdyr rode away from the war, and Adry's after him?"

"He'd never withdraw now. He's too cursed furious with me for that. He—oh, by the black hairy ass of the Lord of Hell! What if the old miser's making a strike on my dun?"

"I wouldn't put it past the bastard," Comerr snarled. "I say we ride back for a look."

When the warband rode on, they left the wagon train behind to follow as best it could at its own slow pace. Lord Erddyr rode in a cold grim silence that told everyone he feared for his lady's life. For two hours they kept up a cavalry pace, walking and trotting with the emphasis on the trot, and they left the road and went as straight as an arrow, plowing through field and meadow, climbing up the wild brushy hills. Finally a scout galloped back, grinning like a child with a copper to spend at the market fair.

"My lords!" the scout yelled. "Tewdyr's not far ahead, and the stupid bastard's only got forty men with him!"

Both lords and riders cheered.

It was less than an hour later when the warband trotted down a little valley to see Tewdyr and his men, drawn up in battle order and waiting for them. Apparently Tewdyr had scouts of his own out and had realized that he was pretty well trapped. When Lord Erddyr yelled out orders to his men to surround the enemy, the warband broke up into a ragged line and trotted fast to encircle the waiting warband. Rhodry drew a javelin, yelled at Yraen to follow him, and circled with the others. When he glanced back, Yraen was right behind him.

Sullen and disgruntled, the enemy moved into a tight bunch behind Tewdyr and his son. Tewdyr sat straight in his saddle, a javelin in his hand.

"Tewdyr!" Comerr called out. "Surrender! We've got the whole cursed army surrounding you."

"I can see well enough," Tewdyr snarled.

With a laugh, Comerr made the lord a mocking bow from the saddle.

"Doubtless the thought of paying more ransom aches your noble heart, but fear not—your withdrawal from the war will be sufficient. We all know that dishonor will be less painful to you than losing more coin."

With a howl of rage, Tewdyr spurred his horse forward and threw the javelin straight at Comerr, who flung up his shield barely in time. The javelin cracked it through and stuck there dangling. Shouting, the entire warband sprang forward to Comerr's side as he flung his useless shield away and grabbed for his sword. Tewdyr's men had no choice but to charge to meet them. Yelling, shouting, Erddyr tried to stop the unequal slaughter, but the field turned into a brawl. Like too many flies crawling on a piece of meat, the warband mobbed Tewdyr's men with their swords flashing up red in the sunlight. Rhodry yelled at Yraen to get back, then trotted over to Erddyr, who was sitting on his horse and watching, his mouth slack in disbelief.

"At least the two of you followed my orders, eh?" the lord shouted. "Ah, by the black hairy ass of the Lord of Hell!"

They sat there like spectators at a tournament as the dust plumed up thick over the battle, and this was no mock combat with blunted and gilded weapons down in the Deverry court. Horses reared up, blood running down their necks; Tewdyr's men fell bleeding with barely a chance to defend themselves. Four and five at a time, the warband mobbed them, hacking and stabbing, while the fighting was so thick that half the men never got a chance to close. They rode round and round the edge, shrieking war cries over the shouts of pain and the trampling clanging sound of horses shoving against shields. When Rhodry looked at Yraen, he found the lad decidedly pale, but his mouth was set tight and his eyes wide-open, as if he were forcing himself to watch the way an apprentice watches his master's lesson in some craft.

"It's not pretty, is it?" Rhodry said.

Yraen shook his head no and went on watching. The fighting was down to a desperate clot around Tewdyr, bleeding in his saddle but still hacking in savage fury. Suddenly Yraen turned his horse and galloped down the valley. Rhodry started to follow, but he saw him dismount and take a few steps toward the stream, where he stood with his hands pressed over his face, merely stood and shook. He was crying, most like. Rhodry couldn't hold it against the lad. He felt half-sick himself from the savagery of this slaughter. When he looked Erddyr's way, his eyes met the lord's, and he knew Erddyr felt the same.

Suddenly a distant noise broke into Rhodry's mind and pulled him alert. Erddyr threw up his head and screamed out a warning as silver horns rang out on the crest of the hill. Too late for rescue, but in time for revenge, Lord Adry's army galloped down to join the battle. Shrieking orders, Erddyr circled the edge of the mob and managed to get a few men turned round and ready to face this new threat. Rhodry followed, howling with laughter, and spotted a rider who could only be one of the noble-born, a lean man carrying a beautifully worked shield and riding a fine black horse. Howling a challenge he charged straight for him. Only when it was too late to pull back did he remember Yraen, and much later still did he remember that he was a silver dagger again, no longer a noble lord to challenge one of his peers.

After he stopped crying, Yraen knelt by the stream and washed his face, but the shame he felt for what he saw as womanish weakness couldn't be so easily dealt with. For a moment he lingered there alone, wondering if he could face Rhodry again, realizing that he had no choice. He was walking back to his horse when he heard the enemy horns and saw the enemy army pouring over the hill like water. He ran, grabbed the reins just before the animal bolted, and swung himself up into the saddle. None of his fancy lessons in war mattered now; all that counted was getting to the safety of his own pack of men. As he galloped down the valley, he saw the enemy army spreading out, trying to encircle his own. Just barely in time Yraen dodged through their van.

An enemy rider, carrying a shield blazoned with a hawk's head, swung past. Yraen wrenched his horse after and struck at his exposed side. Although he missed the rider, he did nick the horse, which bucked once and staggered. When the enemy wheeled to face him, Yraen caught a glimpse of pouchy eyes and a stubbled face. They swung, parried, circling, trading blow for blow while the enemy howled and Yraen found himself muttering a string of curses under his breath. The Hawksman was good, almost his match—almost. Yraen caught a swing on his shield, heard the wood crack, and slashed in through his enemy's open guard to catch him solidly on the back of his right arm. Blood welled through his mail as the bone snapped. With one last shout, he turned his horse and fled, clinging to its neck to keep his seat.

Yraen let him go and rode on, weaving his way through the combats, looking desperately round for Rhodry. His fear had shrunk to a dryness in his mouth, a little ache around his heart, and nothing more. Under a pall of dust the battle swirled down the valley. Here and there he saw clots of fighting around one lord or another. Dead men lay on the ground and wounded horses struggled to rise. When at last he heard someone calling Erddyr's name and someone laughing, a cold berserker's laugh of desperation, he turned in the saddle to see Rhodry and Renydd, mobbed by six of the enemy. They were fighting nose to tail and parrying more than they dared strike as Adry's men shrieked for vengeance and pressed round them. Yraen spurred his horse and charged straight for the clot.

Yraen slapped his horse with the flat of his blade and forced it to slam into the flank of an enemy horse. Before the enemy could turn, he stabbed him in the back and turned to slash at another. Dimly he was aware of men shouting Erddyr's name riding to his side, but he kept swinging, slashing, hacking his way through the clot, closing briefly with one man who managed to turn his horse to face him. He parried and thrust, never getting a strike on him, until the enemy horse screamed and reared. Renydd had cut it hard from behind, and as it came down, Yraen killed the rider. He was through at last, wrenching his horse round to fight nose to tail with Renydd.

"I saw you coming into the mob," Rhodry yelled out.

Rhodry pulled in beside him to guard his left side. Sweat ran down Yraen's back in trickles, not drops, as he panted for breath in this precious moment of respite. It was only a moment. Five men were riding straight for them. Yraen heard them yelling at one another: there he is, get the cursed silver dagger.

Yraen suddenly remembered that he had javelins again, distributed the night before. Grabbing his sword in his left hand, he pulled one from the sheath, threw it straight for an enemy horse, and grabbed the second all in the same smooth motion. Caught in the chest, the enemy horse went down, dumping its rider under the hooves of his friends charging behind him. Yraen heard Rhodry laughing like a fiend as the clot of enemy riders swirled and stumbled in confusion. Yraen had just enough time to transfer his sword back again before the enemies sorted themselves out and charged.

When the three of them held their ground, the enemies rode round them, circling to strike from the rear. Yraen was forced to wheel his horse out of line or get stabbed in the back. Riding with his knees, he ducked and dodged and slashed back at the man attacking him, who suddenly wheeled his horse and rode back toward the main fight. When Yraen followed, for a brief moment he could watch Rhodry fight, and even in the midst of danger the silver dagger's skill was breathtaking as he twisted and ducked, slashing with a cold precision. Rhodry's enemy lunged, missed, and pulled back clumsily as Rhodry got a strike across his shoulder. The Hawksman wanted to kill him—Yraen could see it—this was not the impersonal death-dealing of armies but sheer blazing hatred.

"Silver dagger!" he hissed. "Cursed bastard of a silver dagger!"

When he lunged again, Rhodry caught his blow with his sword. For a moment they struggled, locked together, but Yraen never saw how they broke free. All at once his back burned like fire as someone got a glancing strike on him from behind. Barely in time Yraen wheeled his horse away, swung his head round, and made him dance in a circle till they could face the Hawksman swinging at them. Yraen stabbed, and his greater speed won. Before the enemy could bring his shield around to parry, Yraen thrust the sword point into his right eye. With an animal shriek he reeled back in the saddle, dropped his sword, and clawed in vain at the blade as Yraen pulled it free. Yraen swung and hit him with the flat, knocking him off his horse. In a flail of arms, he rolled under the hooves of a horse just behind. When that horse reared and flung itself backward, the mob of enemies pressing for them fell back, cursing and screaming for vengeance.

Horns rang out over the battlefield. The mob ahead hesitated, turning toward the insistent shriek. Yraen started to edge his horse toward them, but Rhodry's voice broke through his battle-fever.

"Let them go!" Rhodry yelled. "It's the enemy calling for retreat this time."

The field was clearing as Adry's men and allies galloped for their lives. Yraen saw Lord Erddyr charging round the field and screaming at his men to hold their places and let them go. Panting, sweating, shoving back their mail hoods, Yraen, Rhodry, and Renydd brought their horses up close and stared at each other.

"Look at them run," Yraen said. "Did we fight as well as all that?"

"We didn't," Renydd panted. "They've got naught left to fight for. Rhodry killed Lord Adry in that first charge."

Rhodry bowed to him, his eyes bright and merry, as if he'd just told a good jest and was enjoying his listener's amusement.

"I shamed myself before the battle," Yraen said to him. "Will you forgive me?"

"What are you talking about, lad? You did naught of the sort."

But no matter how much he wanted to, Yraen couldn't believe him. He knew that the feel of tears on his face would haunt him his whole life long.

Picking their way through the dead and the wounded, what was left of the warband began to gather around them. No boasting, no battle-joy like in a bard song—they merely sat on their horses and waited till Erddyr rode up, his face red, his beard ratty with sweat.

"Get off those horses, you bastards," Erddyr bellowed. "We've got wounded out there!" He waved his sword at the clot of men that included Yraen. "Go round up stock. They're all over this cursed valley."

Gladly Yraen turned his horse out of line and trotted off. Down by the stream the horses that had fled after losing their riders waited huddled together, blindly trusting in the human beings who had led them into this slaughter. When the men grabbed the reins of a few, the rest followed docilely along. Yraen rode farther downstream, ostensibly to see if any horses were in the stand of hazels near the water, but in truth, simply to be alone. All at once, he wanted to cry again, to sit on the ground and sob like a child. His shame ate at him—what was wrong with him that he'd feel this way in the moment of victory?

Yraen found one bay gelding on the far side of the copse. He dismounted and slacked the bits of both horses to let them drink, then fell to his knees and scooped up water in both hands. No fine mead had ever tasted as good. When he looked at the bright water, rippling over the graveled streambed, he thought of all those bards who sang that men's lives run away as fast as water. It was true enough. The evidence was lying a few hundred yards behind him on the field. He got up and tried to summon the will to go back and help with the wounded. All he wanted to do was stand there and look at the green grass, soft in the sun, stand there and feel that he was alive.

Far down the little valley, he saw a single rider, trotting fast, and leading what seemed to be a pack mule. Mounting his own horse, he jogged down to meet her, for indeed, the rider turned out to be a woman, and an old white-haired crone at that. Her voice came as a shock, as young and strong as a lass's.

"Yraen, Yraen," she called out. "Where's Rhodry? Has he lived through this horrible thing?"

Yraen goggled, nodding his head in a stunned yes. She laughed at his surprise.

"I'll explain later. Now we'd best hurry. I fear me there's men who need my aid."

Side by side they jogged down the valley as fast as the pack mule could go. Out on the field, dismounted men hurried back and forth, pulling wounded men free, putting injured horses out of their misery. Near the horse herd, Lord Erddyr knelt next to a wounded man. When Yraen led Dallandra over, Erddyr jumped to his feet.

"A herbwoman!" he bellowed. "Thank every god! Here, Comerr's bleeding to death."

Yraen turned his horses into the herd and left Dallandra to her work. He forced himself to walk across the battlefield, to pick his way among the dead and dying, simply to prove to himself that he could look upon death without being sickened, just as a real man was supposed to do, but he found it hard going. At last he found Rhodry, kneeling by Lord Adry's corpse and methodically going through his pockets, looting like the silver dagger he was.

"A herbwoman's here," Yraen said. "She just rode out of nowhere."

"The gods must have sent her. Did you hear about Comerr? Tewdyr got in a blow or two before he died. Tewdyr's son is dead, too."

"I figured that."

Rhodry slipped a pouch of coin into his shirt under his mail and stood up, running his hands through his sweaty hair.

"Sure you don't want to go back to your father's dun?"

"Ah, hold your tongue! And know in my heart for the rest of my life that I'm a coward and not fit to live?"

"Yraen, you pigheaded butt end of a mule! Do I have to tell you all over again that you're not the first lad to break down after his first battle? I—"

"I don't care what you say. I shamed myself and I'll feel shamed till I have a chance to redeem myself."

"Have it your way, then." With a hideously sunny grin playing about his mouth, Rhodry looked down at the corpse. "Well, what man can turn aside even his own Wyrd? I'd be a fool to think I could spare you yours."

In that moment Yraen suddenly saw that Rhodry was a true berserker, so in love with his own death that he could deal it to others with barely a qualm. The intervals of peace, when he was joking or courtly, were only intervals, to him, things to pass the time until his next chance at blood. And I'm not like that, Yraen thought. Oh, by the gods, I thought I was, but I'm not. When Rhodry caught his elbow to steady him, Yraen felt as if one of the gods of war had laid hands upon him.

"What's so wrong?" Rhodry said. "You've gone as white as milk."

"Just tired. I mean, I . . ."

"Come along, lad. Let's find a spot where you can sit down and think about things. I'll admit to being weary myself."

The army made a rough camp down by the streamside. One squad rode out to fetch the carts and the packhorses; another circled on guard in case Adry's men returned. Since the shovels were all with the pack train, the remaining men couldn't bury the dead. Although they lined the corpses up and covered them with blankets, still the birds came, drawn as if by dweomer to the battlefield, a flapping circle of ravens that cawed and screamed in sheer indignation, that men should drive them away from so much good meat. With the work done, the men stripped off mail and padding, then found places to sit on the ground, too weary to talk, too weary to light fires, merely sat and thought about dead friends. It was close to twilight before Yraen remembered the herbwoman.

"Here's an odd thing. She knew our names, Rhodry. The old herbwoman, I mean. She asked if you were still alive."

Rhodry flung his head up like a startled horse and swore.

"Oh, did she now? What does she look like?"

"I don't know. I mean, she's just this old woman, all white and wrinkled."

Rhodry scrambled up, gesturing for him to follow.

"Let's go find her, lad. I've got my reasons."

Eventually, just as the falling night forced the exhausted men to their feet to tend to fires and suchlike, they found the herbwoman at the edge of the camp. By then the carts had come in, and she was using one of them as a table for her work while servants rushed around, fetching her water and handing her bandages and suchlike. As bloody as a warrior, she was bending over a prone man and binding his wounds by firelight. Yraen and Rhodry watched while she stitched up a couple of superficial cuts for one of Adry's riders, then turned the prisoner back over to his guard.

"*Old* woman?" Rhodry said. "Have you taken leave of your senses?"

"I've not. Have you? I mean, what are you talking about? She looks old to me."

"Does she now?" All at once Rhodry laughed. "Very well. I'll take your word for it."

"Rhodry! What by the hells are you talking about?"

"Naught, naught. Here, I thought for a while there that it might be someone I know, you see, but it's not. Let's go pay our respects anyway."

Wearing only a singlet with her brigga, Dallandra was washing in a big kettle of warm water while a servant carried off her red and spattered shirt. To Yraen she looked even older with her flabby, wrinkled arms and prominent clavicle exposed, but Rhodry was staring at her as if he found her a marvel.

"Well met, Rhodry," she said, glancing up. "I'm glad I didn't find you under my needle and thread."

"And so am I, good herbwoman. Have you ridden here from the Westlands to find me?"

"Not precisely." She shot a warning glance in the servants' direction. "I've too much work to do to talk now, but I'll explain later."

"One last question, if you would." Rhodry made her a bow. "How fares Lord Comerr?"

"I had to take his left arm off at the shoulder. Maybe he'll live, maybe not." Dallandra looked doubtfully up at the hills. "The gods will do what they will, and there's naught any of us can do about it."

Yraen and Rhodry made a fire of their own, then ate stale flatbread and jerky out of their saddlebags, the noon provisions they'd never had time to eat before the battle. Yraen found himself gobbling shamelessly, even as he wondered how he could be hungry after the things he'd seen and done that day.

"Well, my friend," Rhodry said. "You've made a splendid beginning, but don't think you know everything you need to know about warfare."

"I'd never be such a dolt. Don't trouble your heart."

"Is it what you'd been expecting?"

"Not in the least."

Yet he was snared by a strange dreamlike feeling, that indeed it was all familiar—too familiar. His very exhaustion opened a door in his mind to reveal something long buried, not a memory, nothing so clear, but a recognition, a sense of familiarity as he looked at the camp and his own bloodstained clothes, as he felt every muscle in his body aching from the battle behind them. Even the horror, the sheer disgust of it—somehow he should have known, somehow he'd always known that glory demanded this particular price. For a moment he felt like weeping so strongly that only Rhodry's appraising stare kept him from tears.

"Why don't you just ride home?" Rhodry said.

He shook his head no and forced himself to go on eating.

"Why not?"

He could only shrug for his answer. Rhodry sighed, staring into the fire.

"I suppose you'll feel like a coward or suchlike, running for home?"

"That's close enough." Yraen managed to find a few words at last. "I hate it, but it draws me all the same. War, I mean. I don't understand."

"No doubt, oh, no doubt."

Rhodry seemed to be about to say more, but Dallandra came walking out of the shadows. She was wearing a clean shirt, much too big for her, and eating a chunk of cheese that she held in one hand like a peasant. Yraen was suddenly struck by the strong, purposeful way she strode along; if she were as old as she looked, she should have been all bent and hobbling, from the strain of her day's work if nothing more. Without waiting to be asked she sat down next to Rhodry on the ground.

"Yraen here tells me you know our names," Rhodry remarked, without so much as a good evening. "How?"

"I'm a friend of Evandar's."

Rhodry swore in a string of truly appalling oaths, but she merely laughed at him and had another bite of her cheese.

"Who's that?" Yraen said. "Or wait! Not that odd fellow who gave you the whistle!"

"The very one." Rhodry glanced at the herbwoman again. "May I ask you what you want with me?"

"Well, only the whistle your young friend mentioned. It's a truly ill-omened thing, Rhodry, and it's dangerous for you to be carrying it about with you."

"Ah. I'd rather thought so myself. The strangest people—well, I suppose that people isn't the best word—the strangest creatures keep showing up, trying to steal it from me."

At that Yraen remembered the peculiar shadow that he'd seen out in Lord Erddyr's ward.

"You really would be better off without it," Dallandra said. "And Evandar never even meant to leave it with you. He's been much distracted of late."

Rhodry made a sour sort of face and glanced round, finding his saddlebags a few feet away and leaning back to grab them and haul them over. He rummaged for a few moments, then pulled out the whistle, angling it to catch the firelight.

"Answer me somewhat," he said. "What is it?"

"I have no idea, except it feels evil to me."

When she reached for it, he grinned and snatched it away, slipping it back into the saddlebag.

"Tell Evandar he can come fetch it himself."

"Rhodry, this is no time to be stubborn."

"I've a question or two to ask him. Tell him to come himself."

Dallandra made some exasperated remark in a language that Yraen had never heard before. Rhodry merely laughed.

"Well, I don't want to see you dead over this wretched thing," the herbwoman went on. "So I'll give you somewhat for protection." She fumbled at her belt, where something heavy hung in a triangular leather sheath. "Here."

When Rhodry took the sheath, Yraen could see a wooden handle—you couldn't really call it a hilt—sticking out of the stained and crumbling leather. Rhodry slid the sheath off to reveal a leaf-bladed bronze knife, all scraped and pitted as if it had been hammered flat, then sharpened with a file like a farmer's hoe.

"Ye gods, old woman!" Yraen said. "That wouldn't protect anyone against anything!"

"Hold your tongue!" Rhodry snarled. "Better yet, apologize to the lady."

When Yraen stared in disbelief, Rhodry caught his gaze and held it with all his berserker force.

"You have my humble apologies, good herbwoman," Yraen stammered. "I abase myself at your feet in my shame."

"You're forgiven, lad." She smiled briefly. "And I know it looks peculiar, but then, Rhodry's enemies are a bit on the peculiar side themselves, aren't they?"

"Well, the one I saw was. I mean, I didn't actually see it, just its shadow, but peculiar's a good enough word."

Rhodry nodded his agreement; he was busily attaching the sheath to his belt at the right side to balance the dagger at the left. With a shake of her head the old woman got up, stretching her back and yawning.

"Ych, I'm exhausted," she remarked. "Well, have it your way, Rhodry ap Devaberiel. But I've got obligations here and now, at least till we get these wounded men to a chirurgeon, and it may be a longer time than you think before I can tell Evandar to come fetch it back. Until then, you'll be in danger, no matter how many knives I give you."

"I'll take my chances, then. I want some answers from your friend, good herbwoman."

"So do I." She laughed, as musically and lightly as a young girl. "But I've never gotten any from him myself, and so I doubt very much if you will either."

She turned on her heel and walked off into the darkness, leaving Yraen staring after her. Smiling to himself, Rhodry laced the saddlebag up again, then laid it aside right close at hand.

"Why didn't you give her the blasted thing?" Yraen said.

"I don't know, truly. She's probably right enough about Evandar not answering my questions."

"Who or what is this Evandar, anyway?"

"I don't know. That's one of the questions I want to ask him."

"Oh. Well, he and this strange hag seem to know you well enough. Here, wait a minute. She called you Rhodry ap Deva-something. What kind of a name is that? Your father's, I mean."

Rhodry looked at him for a long, mild moment.

"Elven," he said at last, and then he tossed back his head and howled with laughter, his icy berserker's shriek.

Demanding an explanation from him in that mood was the furthest thing from Yraen's mind.

"I'll just go get some more firewood." He got to his feet. "Fire's getting low, and I wouldn't mind some light."

As he hurried off to the area where the provisions were stacked, Yraen was remembering all the old children's tales he'd ever heard about the people called the Elcyion Lacar or elves. If any such race did exist, he decided, Rhodry was the best candidate ever he'd found to be one of them, simply because he seemed so alien at his very heart.

·   ·   ·

When he went to sleep that night, Rhodry tucked the bone whistle into his shirt. Although he doubted very much if Dallandra would stoop to stealing it, he was expecting one of the strange creatures to take advantage of his weariness, and he put the bronze knife right beside his blankets, as well. Sure enough, he woke suddenly in the middle of the night at the sound of someone or something dumping out his saddlebags. When he sat up, grabbing the knife, whatever it was fled. He could see nothing but his strewn gear, and the whistle was still safely in his shirt. Moving quietly he got up, knelt and put the gear away again, then pulled on his boots for a look round and a word with the night watch. Although the camp was ringed by sentries, none of them had seen anything moving, either in the camp or out in the silent valley.

About halfway between two sentries, Rhodry paused, rubbing his face and yawning while he considered offering to stand someone's watch for them. From where he stood he could see the bleak lines of dead men, waiting under their blankets for their burying on the morrow. With a sharp sigh he turned away, only to find Dallandra walking toward him. In the moonlight he could see her quite clearly as a young and beautiful elven woman. With her long silvery-blond hair carelessly pulled back with a thong, she seemed no more than a lass, in fact, but he'd heard enough tales to know who she was.

"Good evening," he said in Elvish. "Looking for me?"

"No, I just couldn't sleep." She answered in the same. "Ych, this slaughter! I feel like crying, but if I let myself start, I'd weep for hours."

"It takes some people that way, truly."

"Not you?"

"It did at first. I grew past it, as, or so I hope, our young Yraen will. If he insists on riding with me, he'll see plenty of this sort of thing."

She merely nodded, staring out over the field with her steel-gray eyes.

"Tell me something," Rhodry said. "You have dweomer, don't you? Every other man in this camp thinks you're an ugly old crone."

"That's Evandar's dweomer, not mine. I should have known

that a man of the People would see through it. You've met me before, Rhodry, in a rather odd way. I think you might have seen me, anyway, even though I wasn't truly on the physical plane. It was a long time ago, when Jill and Aderyn pulled you free of that trouble you'd got yourself into."

Rhodry winced. Silver dagger or no, there were a few shameful things in his life that he didn't care to remember.

"I wasn't truly aware of much, then," he said at last. All at once a thought struck him. "Oh, here, I've sad news for you. Or did you know about Aderyn?"

"Is he dead then?"

"He is, of old age and nothing more."

Her eyes spilled tears, and she spun round, hiding her face in the crook of an elbow. When Rhodry laid a hesitant hand on her shoulder to comfort her, she turned to him blindly and sobbed against his chest.

"That hurts," she choked out. "I'm surprised at how much."

"Then forgive me for being the bearer of the news."

She nodded, pulling away, wiping her face vigorously on the hem of her shirt.

"I'll talk to you later," she said, her voice still thick. "I need a moment or two alone."

She strode off, walking so fast and surely, even in her grief, that he wondered at the blindness of men for believing in the dweomer cloak that Evandar had fashioned for her.

On a bed of blankets, Lord Comerr lay beside Lord Erddyr's fire. His face was dead-pale, his breathing shallow, and his skin cool to the touch—a trio of omens that troubled Dallandra deeply. While she changed the bandages on his wounds, Erddyr knelt beside her and did his best to help, handing over things as she asked for them. Comerr stirred once or twice at the pain, but he never spoke.

"Tell me honestly," Erddyr said. "Will he live?"

"Maybe. He's a hard man, and there's hope, but he's lost a terrible lot of blood."

With a grunt, Erddyr sat back on his heels and studied Comerr's face.

"Let me ask you a presumptuous question, my lord," Dallandra went on. "Have you ever thought of asking the gwerbret for his intervention? Lord Adry is dead, and Comerr close enough to it. Fighting over which of them will be tieryn someday seems a bit superfluous, shall we say?"

"True spoken. And they aren't the only noble lords fallen in this scrap. I've been thinking very hard about sending that message."

"That gladdens my heart. Do you think the other side will submit?"

"They'll have cursed little choice if the gwerbret takes the matter under his jurisdiction. Besides, Nomyr's the only lord left on their side, and he's in this only out of duty."

"Didn't Adry have a son?"

"He does, but the lad's only seven years old."

Dallandra muttered an oath under her breath. Erddyr studied his mercifully unconscious ally.

"Ah, by the fart-freezing hells, it aches my heart to see him maimed like this."

"Better than dead. The arm wasn't worth saving, and I never could have stopped the bleeding in time."

"Oh, I'm not questioning your decision." Erddyr shuddered like a wet dog. "I think I'll take my chance to get him out of this while he can't speak for himself. I'll send messengers tomorrow."

"The gods will honor you for it. You know, my lord, I happen to have a letter of safe conduct with the gwerbret's seal upon it. You'd be most welcome to make use of it."

"My thanks a hundredfold. I will."

"I wonder if his lordship would do me a favor. I'd just as soon have my friend Rhodry out of this. Could you send your pair of silver daggers as the messengers?"

"Oh, I'd grant your favor gladly, but they'd be in worse danger there than here. You're forgetting that Rhodry is the man who killed Lord Adry. If any of Adry's men catch Rhodry on the road, they'll cut him down even if he's carrying letters from the Lord of Hell himself."

"I hadn't realized that, my lord."

Erddyr rubbed his beard and looked at Comerr, who tossed

his head in his sleep and grunted in pain. Suddenly too weary to stand, Dallandra sat down right on the ground and cradled her head in both hands.

"A thousand apologies, good herbwoman," Erddyr said. "I never should have kept you here like this. You need your sleep at your age and all."

"So I do. Since my lordship excuses me?"

Yet, once she was lying down in her blankets, she found herself thinking about Aderyn instead of falling asleep. The surprise of her grief troubled her more than the grief itself, until she realized that she was mourning not so much the man himself, as what their love might have been if only Evandar and his doomed people hadn't claimed her instead. Another painful thing was Rhodry's news that he'd died of simple old age. Even though she'd spent a few months with him when he was already old as men reckon age, in her mind and heart she always saw him as her young lover with his ready smile and earnest eyes. Once more she wept, crying herself asleep, alone at the edge of the armed camp.

It took two days for the army to return to Comerr's dun, simply because the lord's life hung by a thread. Being jolted in a cart tired him so badly that every now and then the line of march was forced to stop and let him rest. At last, close to sunset on the second day, they rode into the great iron-bound gates, where Comerr's young wife waited weeping to receive her husband. Dallandra helped the lady settle Comerr in his own bed and tend his wounds, then went down to the great hall for a meal. Crowded into one side of the great hall, the men were sitting on the floor or standing as they ate. At the table of honor, Lord Erddyr dined alone. When Dallandra went for a word with him, the lord insisted that she join him.

"What do you think of Comerr's chances now?" Erddyr said.

"They're good. He's lived through the worst, and there's no sign of either gangrene or lockjaw."

With a sigh of relief, Erddyr handed Dallandra a slice of bread and poured her alc with his own hands. Sharing a wooden trencher, they ate roast pork and bread in silence. Finally the lord leaned back in his chair.

"Well, naught for it but to wait for the gwerbret's answer to that message of mine. I wonder if Nomyr sent a request for intervention himself?" He held up a greasy hand and ticked the names off on his fingers. "Adry's dead, Tewdyr and his heir are dead, Oldadd's dead, Paedyn's dead, and Degedd's dead. Ah horseshit, I'm not sure I give a pig's fart about this war anymore, but I'll beg you, good herbwoman, don't tell another man I ever said such a dishonorable thing."

In two days the messengers returned with the news that the gwerbret was riding to settle the matter with his entire warband of five hundred men. Erddyr was to select twenty-five men for an honor guard and ride to neutral ground; Nomyr would do the same or be declared a traitor. Although Dallandra would have liked to have ridden to hear the settlement, her first obligation was to the wounded. Although a good half of the casualties had died during the long journey back to the dun, she still had some twenty men who needed more care than the servants could give them. Late that evening, when she was tending them in the barracks, the messenger sought her out; he'd been given a note for her at the gwerbret's dun.

"Can you read, good dame, or should I fetch the scribe?"

"I can read a bit. Let me try."

Although written Deverrian was difficult for her, the note was brief.

"Ah, it's from Timryc the chirurgeon! He's riding our way as fast as ever he can, and he's bringing supplies with him."

She was so relieved that she wept, just a brief scatter of tears while the messenger nodded in sympathy, glancing round at the men whose luck had been worse than his own. She could never tell him or any other human being that her heart was troubled more by revulsion than sympathy for all this gouged and shattered flesh, cut meat exposing splintered bone.

Close to midnight, Dallandra went for a walk out in the ward. By then the gibbous moon was already slouching past zenith. Most of the men were asleep, but she could see through the windows a few servants still working in the firelit great hall. Although she'd come out for a breath of air, the ward stank of dungheaps and stable sweepings, a pigsty and a henhouse. Mud from the spring thaw lay everywhere, slimy and half-alive with sprouting weeds and fungi.

For a moment she wanted to scream and run, to find a road back to Evandar's country no matter who might need her here in the world of men, to leave, in fact, the entire physical world far behind her. How could she condemn Elessario or any of the Host to this foul existence? Even the People, for all their long lives, suffered illness and injury and death out on the grasslands; even they, for all their former glory, spent cold wet winters huddled in smelly tents while they rationed out food and fuel. Perhaps Evandar was right. Perhaps it would be better to never be born, to live for a brief while in the shifting astral world like flames in a fire, then fade away in peace, the fire cold and spent.

She looked up to the moon, waning now, only a bulbous wedge of light in the sky and soon to disappear into the darkness. Yet, in turn again, it would shine forth and grow till it rode full and high in the sky—a visible symbol of the waxing and waning of the Light, the sinking and rising of birth and death. Once Dallandra would have found comfort in meditating on such a symbol; that night in the stinking damp ward she was simply too weary, too sick at heart for it to seem anything but a sterile exercise.

"Evandar, I wish you'd come to me."

Although she only breathed a whisper, she'd surprised herself by speaking aloud at all. There were times when she could summon him by trained and concentrated thought, but that night when she tried she could only feel that he was far out of reach, off perhaps on business of his own rather than hovering near her in the country he called the Gatelands. Perhaps his brother had broken their truce? Remembering the fox warrior, wondering if some peculiar combat was being joined, made her shudder with a sick loathing.

"Evandar!"

No thought, no breath of his presence came to her, yet she was sure that she would know if he was dead or somehow being kept from her against his will.

"Evandar!"

She could hear her voice, the wail of a lost child. Yet she felt nothing but a vast lack, an emptiness where his presence might have been. She had no choice, then, but to face her melancholy alone.

In the vain hope of finding cleaner air, she started for the gates, only to find someone there ahead of her, climbing down the ladder from the ramparts. When he turned round, she could see with her elven sight that it was Rhodry, yawning as he came off watch. In the shadow of the dun she paused, hiding out of a weary reluctance to speak with anyone, but being a man of the People as he was, he spotted her and strolled over.

"You're up late," he remarked.

"I just finished with the wounded. By the gods of both our peoples, I hope that chirurgeon gets himself here soon."

"Shouldn't take him long. Shall I escort you to your luxurious chambers? I trust our lord found you a clean place to sleep, anyway."

"He did, though splendid it's not. One of the storage sheds." All at once she yawned. "I'm more tired than I thought."

Silently they walked round the dun and made their way behind the kitchen hut to the ramshackle thatched shed that was serving her as a bedchamber. Since like cats the People can't see in pitch-darkness, she had a tin candle-lantern, perched on an ale barrel far away from the heap of straw where she'd spread her blankets. When she lit the candle with a snap of her fingers, Rhodry flinched.

"You never truly get used to seeing that," he said, but he was grinning at her. "May I talk with you a little while? I'd like to ask you a few questions and all that, but I can see you're weary, so send me right away if you want."

She hesitated, but not only did he deserve answers, she quite simply didn't want to be alone.

"Not that tired. Bar the door, will you?"

She sat down on her blankets amid a scatter of her gear, and watched him as he sat by the barrel a few feet away. In the shadow-dancing candlelight she was struck by how good-looking he was, especially for a man who was half-human; somehow, in all the danger and hard work of the past few days, she simply hadn't noticed. In her dark mood the streak of gray in his hair and the web of lines round his eyes made him seem only more attractive. Here was a man who knew defeat and suffering both.

"Who or what is Evandar?" he said abruptly. "He's not a man of the People, is he?"

"He's not, and no more is he human. He's not truly incarnated or corporeal at all. Do you know what those words mean?"

"Close enough." He shot her a grin. "Not only did I spend a few years in the company of sorcerers, but I was raised a Maelwaedd. I've a bit more learning than most border lords or silver daggers either."

"Well, my apologies—"

"No need, no need. I don't suppose anyone else in this dun would know what you're talking about, except maybe young Yraen, and he wouldn't believe you."

They shared a soft laugh.

"But Evandar's only one of an entire host of beings, some like him—true individuals, I mean. The others are about as conscious as clever animals but no more, and there's even some who seem to have never truly evolved at all into anything you could call a man or woman."

"Indeed? And what about that badger-headed thing that keeps trying to steal this whistle?" Rhodry laid a hand on his shirt, just above his belt. "Is he one of Evandar's people?"

"He's not, but a renegade from another host, headed by Evandar's brother, and a strange thing that is." She shuddered again, remembering the sheer malice in the black and vulpine eyes. "I don't truly understand them myself, Rhodry. I'm not trying to put you off. You're probably thinking of the old stories, of how I left Aderyn hundreds of years ago, but you've got to remember that as Evandar's world reckons Time, I've only been there a month or so."

His lips parted in a soft "oh" of surprise.

"No more do I know what that whistle may be," she went on. "I suspect that it's not magical at all, but just a trinket, like that ring of yours."

"Now wait! If there's no dweomer on this ring, why does that female keep trying to take it back?"

"Alshandra? Evandar told me about your skirmishes with her. She doesn't truly understand what she's doing. I fear me that she's gone mad."

"Oh, splendid!" Rhodry snarled. "Here I am, chased round two kingdoms by a thing from the Otherlands and a mad spirit, and no one even knows why! I just might go daft myself, out of spite if naught more."

"I couldn't hold it to your shame, but it would be a great pity if you did. You're going to need your wits about you."

"No doubt. I always have, for all of my wretched life, except perhaps for those few years out on the grass. That's the only peace I've ever known, Dalla, those years with the People."

All at once he looked so weary, so spent, really, that she leaned forward and laid her hand on his knee.

"It aches my heart to see you so sad, but you've got a tangled Wyrd, sure enough, and there's naught that I or any other dweomerworker can do about that."

He nodded, putting his hand over hers, just a friendly gesture at first, but it seemed to her that a warmth grew and spread between them. His fingers, the rough, callused fingers of a fighting man, tightened on her hand. She hesitated, thinking of Evandar, but when she sent her mind ranging out, she could sense nothing but a vast distance between them. When Rhodry raised her hand and kissed her fingertips, just lightly, she felt the warmth spread as if it were mead, flowing through her blood. He rose to his knees, pulling her up with him. She laid her free hand flat on his chest.

"In a few days I'll have to leave this world and go back to the one I've made my own. If you ride with his lordship to the settlement, I could well be gone by the time you return, and by the time I come back to your world, a hundred years might have passed."

"And would it ache your heart, to ride back and find me gone?"

"It would, but not enough to keep me here. In all fairness, you need to know that."

He smiled, but in the candlelight his eyes seemed wells of sadness.

"A silver dagger's no man to make demands upon a great lady, or to tax her comings and goings."

She would have said something to comfort him, but he kissed her, hesitantly at first, then openmouthed and passionately when she slipped into his arms. At first she was shocked by how strong, how solid he was, real muscle and bone, warm flesh and the smell of flesh and sweat. When he laid her down in the straw, she could feel his weight, and his mouth seemed to burn on hers, and on her face and neck as he kissed her over and over, as if she were feverish and he, the healer. She found herself digging her fingertips into his back just for the sensation of solid flesh beneath her hands and pressing against him as tight as she could just for his warmth—an animal warmth, she realized suddenly, just as somehow she'd forgotten that she too was an animal, no matter how great her dweomer powers, no matter how far above the world of flesh she'd come to dwell. At that moment she was nothing but glad that he was making her remember.

Afterward, she lay panting and sweaty in his arms and listened to his heart pounding close to hers. The candle threw guttering shadows on the wooden walls as outside the wind rose, whispering in the thatch. Rhodry kissed her eyes, her mouth, then loosened his hold upon her and moved a little away. He looked so sad that she laid her hand alongside his face; he turned his head and kissed her fingers, but he said nothing, merely watched the shadows leaping this way and that. She sat up, running both hands through her hair and sweeping it back from her face.

"Do you really have to ride with Erddyr when he goes?" she said.

He grinned at that and looked her way again.

"I already said we would, Yraen and me."

"Is it going to be safe? Erddyr said something about Adry's men wanting to kill you."

"And the laws will make the gwerbret forbid them any such thing, if I appeal in his court. I want it over and settled before we ride on." He sat up, stretching and yawning. "I don't suppose you've got a fancy to travel the roads with a silver dagger? You don't have to answer that, mind, just a wondering. I know you've work at hand, and I—ye gods! What's that?"

She slewed round and saw someone—or something—crouched in the shadows at the curve of the wall. It was too small to be the snouted creature she'd seen before; more doglike, it had tiny red eyes that glowed like coals in a fire and long fangs that glistened wet. When Dallandra flung up one hand and sketched a sigil in the air, it shrieked and disappeared. Rhodry swore under his breath.

"I wish you'd just give me that wretched whistle and be done with it," she said.

"What? And let you face those creatures instead of me?"

"I happen to know how to deal with them."

"True spoken. But if I give it to you, what will you do? Go back to that other country?" All at once he grinned. "I'd rather you tarried here a little while longer."

"Oh, would you now?"

She saw the whistle lying not far away, where it had rolled when he'd taken his shirt off, and made a grab at it. He was too fast, catching her wrists and dragging her back, even though she struggled with him. She found herself laughing, let him pull her close, kissed him until he let her go so they could lie down together again. But before he made love to her, he picked the whistle up and tucked it into the straw under her head, where nothing could steal it away.

This time, when they were finished, he fell asleep, so suddenly, so completely, that it seemed he would sink into the straw and disappear. She slipped free of his arms and stood up. As naked as a country woman worshiping her goddess in the fields, she raised her arms and called down the light. Moving deosil she used her outstretched hand as a weapon to draw a circle of blue light round the hut and seal it at the quarters with the sigils of the kings of the elements. With a flick of her hand she set the circle moving, turning, glowing golden as it formed into a revolving sphere with the sleeping Rhodry safe in its center. No member of any host, whether elemental or astral, could breach this wall.

As silently as she could, she sat down next to him and worked the whistle free from the straw. She could steal it now, slip out into the night, and be gone to Evandar's country before he even woke for an argument. No doubt Timryc would arrive on the morrow to nurse her charges; she could even scry and make sure of that, then leave in perfect conscience. Yet as she watched her human lover sleeping in the light of a guttering candle, she wondered if she wanted to return to Evandar. She felt not the slightest guilt at having betrayed him, if indeed betrayal was even the proper word. The fleshy, sweaty love she'd just shared with Rhodry was so different from anything she'd ever experienced with Evandar that she simply couldn't equate the two. They belong in different worlds, indeed, she thought to herself. And I? I suppose I belong in this one, no matter what I may want or think, no matter how it aches my heart.

Eventually she would return to the world and the Westlands, once her work was done, her service to Evandar's host all paid. Although she would always see life as a burden, no matter what compensations it might offer from now on, she could thank Rhodry for making her remember that she belonged to the life of the world. In the meantime, too much depended upon her, not merely Evandar's happiness but his soul, and that of his daughter and all their kind as well, for her to linger in the lands of men. No matter what doubts she might have, she loved Elessario and Evandar both too well to condemn them.

In his sleep Rhodry stirred, sighing, burrowing his face into the crook of his arm like a child. For a moment she wondered what it would be like to stay with him a little while, riding the Deverry roads, but she knew that he would only come to bore her, and the fine thing they'd shared would grow tarnished. She would leave Rhodry behind, but she refused to be a thief. She tossed the whistle onto his shirt, put the candle out with a snap of her fingers, then lay down to cuddle next to him for their last few hours together.

Some hours after dawn, Dallandra woke to find Rhodry already gone, and the whistle with him. She threw on her clothes and hurried outside to find the ward empty and silent. Inside the great hall, a page informed her that Erddyr and his ritual escort, including Yraen and Rhodry, had already ridden out, heading for the settlement ground just as dawn was breaking.

"Shall I bring you some food, good dame?"

"My thanks, but I'd best tend the wounded first."

"Oh, Timryc the chirurgeon's doing that. He and one of his apprentices rode in just as the men were leaving."

Again she felt her relief as a rush of tears. She wiped her face on her sleeve while the page watched, all solemn-eyed.

"Then I'll have some breakfast, lad, and my thanks for the news."

It took Dallandra a few hours to settle matters at the dun, discussing her patients with Timryc, making her farewells. Just as she was riding out the gates, Lord Comerr's chamberlain came rushing after with a sack of silver coins, which he insisted she take with his thanks before she rode on. By the time she could no longer see the towers from the road, the sun was at its zenith. Out in the middle of pastureland she found a stream, running through the shelter of trees. She set her horse and mule out to graze, then treated herself to a bath elven style, in the fast-running clean water instead of some dirty wooden tub.

Once she was dressed and dry, she sat on the bank, watched the sun dappling the ripples as it broke through the branches of the trees, and thought of Evandar. This time he came. She felt his presence first as a sound, as if someone called her name from a great distance; then she had the same sensation as a person reading in a chamber who feels rather than sees someone step silently through the door. In a rustle of leaves and branches he walked out from between two trees, and no matter what she might have done with Rhodry the night before, she felt herself smiling as if her face would split from it at the sight of him. Laughing, he folded her into his arms and gave her one of his oddly cool kisses. He smelt clean, like the stream water, not like flesh at all.

"You look pale, my love," he remarked in Deverrian. "Is somewhat troubling your heart?"

"I've just spent a ghastly week or two, truly, tending men wounded in battle, and more than a few of them died, no matter how I tried to help them."

"A sad thing, that."

She knew that he felt no honest compassion, but that he would mimic it for her sake was comfort enough.

"Rhodry still has the whistle," she said. "He wouldn't give it up. He says he wants to have a talk with you, and that you'll have to come fetch it back yourself."

Evandar laughed with a flash of his sharp white teeth.

"Then a talk he shall have. I like a man with mettle, I do. Imph, I suppose I'd best stay here in this world. If I go back with you, I might miss him entirely."

"True spoken. Here, where were you? I called for you—well, last night it would have been here, whatever that might have been in your country."

For a moment he looked puzzled.

"Ah! I'd gone to the islands to see how Jill fares. She's been ill, it turns out, but now she's well again and learning much new dweomer lore. She'll be growing wings like one of us next, if she keeps on this way."

"That's a dangerous thing for a human being to try to learn. I wonder how skilled her teachers are, and if they know the differences from soul to soul."

Evandar laughed aloud.

"I'd wager a great deal that they do, my love, but you look like a mother cat chasing her kittens away from danger! Get on your way back, then. I'll take your horse and follow our Rhodry down. I doubt me if I'll tell him what he wants to know, but maybe he'll have a riddle or two to trade."

"Well and good, then." She paused to kiss him on the mouth. "And you promised me you'd return that stolen mule and all its goods, didn't you now?"

"So I did, so I did. I'll summon one of my people straight-away, I promise you."

"My thanks. Meet me by our river."

With him so close beside her, she could use his particular dweomer to breach the planes. She floated onto the surface of the stream and dashed along the rippled road, saw the fog of the Gate-lands opening out, and stepped up and through. She had just time to turn and wave to Evandar, standing on the streamside, before the fog shut her round. At her neck hung again the amethyst figurine. She kept walking through the misty landscape beyond the gate until she could be sure that Evandar and the lands of men lay far behind her. Then she sat down on a cold, damp hillside and wept for Rhodry Maelwaedd, whom most likely she'd never see again.

The neutral ground turned out to be a day and a half's ride from Lord Comerr's and down in the plains on the Deverry side of the Pyrdon hills. Out in front of the walled dun of a certain Tieryn Magryn, whose chief distinction lay in his lack of ties to either Comerr or Adry, the gwerbret's warband had set up camp in a meadow lush with spring grass. As soon as Lord Erddyr and his escort dismounted, a hundred men surrounded them—all in the friendliest possible way, but Yraen knew that they were being taken under arrest to keep them away from Lord Nomyr and his riders. Some of the gwerbret's men took their horses; others escorted them on a strict path through canvas tents. At the far end, a few hundred yards from the hill of the dun, stood a long canvas pavilion, draped with the green and blue banners of the gwerbrets of Dun Trebyc to cover the rips and weather stains. A tall blond man in his thirties, Gwerbret Drwmyc sat in a chair carved with the eagle blazon of his clan. Behind him stood two councillors, and a scribe sat at a tiny table nearby.

Kneeling at the gwerbret's right side, Lord Nomyr was already present; his honor guard sat in orderly rows behind him. With a wave at his men to settle themselves, Erddyr knelt at the gwerbret's left. The gwerbret's men stood round the scene with their hands on their sword hilts, ready for the first sign of trouble.

"It gladdens my heart to see you both arrive so promptly," Drwmyc said. "Now. Lord Erddyr, by whose authority do you come?"

"Comerr's himself, Your Grace. He gave me his seal and swore in front of witnesses to abide by the settlement I make in his name."

"Well and good. Lord Nomyr?"

"By the authority of Lady Talyan, regent for her son, Lord

Gwandyc, Adry's heir. She too has agreed to abide by his grace's arbitration."

"Well and good, then. Lord Erddyr, since you're the one who called upon me, speak first and present your tale of the causes of this war."

Erddyr recited the story of the dispute of the cattle rights and many another cause of bad blood between Adry and Comerr. When he was done, Nomyr had the chance to tell a slightly different version. Back and forth they went, working through the actual events and battles, while their men grew restless. To the riders, this judgment seemed a pitiful way to end the fighting, a coward's out, and tedious. While the two lords wrangled over Tewdyr's raid on Erddyr's dun, the warbands leaned forward, staring at each other narrow-eyed and hostile. Yraen noticed four of Nomyr's guard studying Rhodry in barely concealed fury. He elbowed him and pointed them out.

"Adry's men," Rhodry whispered. "Hawk blazon."

Yraen was profoundly glad that the gwerbret's warband stood on the watch for trouble. While the two lords argued furiously, the hot summer day turned the pavilion stifling, another spur to ill temper. At last the gwerbret cut the argument short with a wave of his hand.

"I've heard enough. I intend to set aside all charges of misconduct during the actual fight, because for every wrong on one side, there was one on the other to countercharge it. Will their lordships agree?"

"On my part, I will." Nomyr bowed to his liege lord.

Erddyr debated for several minutes.

"And I, too, Your Grace," he said at last. "After all, my wife came to no actual harm, and Tewdyr's dead."

"Done, then." Drwmyc motioned at the scribe to record the agreement. "We can turn now to the disputes of cause."

Adry's four men looked at each other and risked a few grim whispers. Nomyr glared and waved at them to be silent.

"What troubles your men, Lord Nomyr?" Drwmyc said.

"They used to ride for Lord Adry, Your Grace, and his lordship's death troubles them."

"By the gods themselves!" Drwmyc lost patience with ritual courtesy. "The death of so many lords troubles us all, but men do die in battle."

"Begging his grace's pardon." A heavyset blond rider rose to his feet and made the gwerbret a bow. "Never did we mean to disturb his grace's proceedings, but we're all shamed men, Your Grace, and that's a hard thing to bear in silence. Our lord was killed by a cursed silver dagger, and Lord Nomyr called the retreat before we could avenge him. How can we live with that?"

With a ripple of trouble coming, the warbands turned toward the speaker.

"You'll have to live with it," Drwmyc answered. "If you retreated on order of your lord's faithful ally, then no man can both hold you shamed and himself just."

"We hold ourselves shamed, Your Grace. It's a bitter thing to choose between disobeying the noble-born and letting your lord lie unavenged. And now here's that silver dagger, sitting in your court with honest men. It gripes our souls, Your Grace."

Yraen grabbed Rhodry's arm and pulled it away from his sword. Nomyr swung round to face the rider.

"Gwar, hold your tongue and sit down," Nomyr snarled. "We're in the gwerbret's presence."

"So we are, my lord. But begging your lordship's pardon, I swore to Lord Adry, not you."

When his three companions rose to join him, everyone around went tense, murmuring among themselves. The gwerbret rose from his chair and drew his sword, holding it point upward, a solid symbol of justice.

"There will be no murder in my court," Drwmyc snarled. "Gwar, if the silver dagger killed your lord in a fair fight, that's the end to it."

The four men tensed, glancing at one another, as if they were debating their choices. Since their honor lay buried in a shallow grave with Lord Adry, they were likely to leave Nomyr's service and hunt Rhodry down on the roads no matter what the cost to themselves. Rhodry pulled away from Yraen's restraining hand and got to his feet.

"Your Grace," Rhodry called out. "I'm the silver dagger they mean, and I'll swear it was a fair fight. I'll beg your grace to settle this here and now under rule of law. I don't care to be hunted on the roads like a fox." He turned to Gwar. "Your lord died by the fortunes of war. What do you have against me?"

"That you killed him for a piece of silver! What do you think? A good man like him, killed for a cursed bit of coin."

"I didn't kill him for the coin. I killed him to save my life, because your lord was a good man with his blade."

"You wouldn't have been on the field if it weren't for the coin." Gwar paused to spit on the ground. "Silver dagger."

Yraen and Renydd exchanged a glance and rose to a kneel, ready to leap up to Rhodry's defense if Gwar and his lads charged. Drwmyc's hand tightened on his sword hilt when he saw them.

"No one move," the gwerbret said. "The first man to draw in my court will be taken alive and hanged like a dog. Do you hear me?"

Everyone sat back down, even Gwar, and promptly.

"Good," Drwmyc continued. "Silver dagger, are you appealing to me?"

"I am, Your Grace, under the laws of men and gods alike, and I swear upon my very life to abide by your decision. Either absolve me of guilt or set me some lwdd to pay for Lord Adry's death."

"Nicely spoken, and so I shall." The gwerbret considered for a moment. "But on the morrow. I have one matter before me in malover already, you know."

"I do, Your Grace, and never would I set my own affairs above those of honorable men."

When Yraen stole a glance at Gwar and his friends, he found them looking as sour as if they'd bitten into a Bardek citron. Apparently the last thing they'd expected from a road-filthy silver dagger was eloquence.

"Until I hold malover upon this matter of the silver dagger and the death of Lord Adry, his life is sacrosanct under all the laws of Great Bel," the gwerbret said. "Gwar, do you and your lads understand that?"

"We do, Your Grace, and never would we break those laws."

"Good." Drwmyc allowed himself a thin smile. "But just in case temptation strikes, like, I'm putting guards on the silver dagger. Captain?" He turned to one of the men standing behind him. "See to it, will you, when we leave the pavilion?"

With the morning the malover reconvened, and the proceedings over the war droned on. Round noon, the gwerbret ruled in Comerr's favor, that his clan should rule the new tierynrhyn. Since Tewdyr was dead without an heir, his grace split his lands twixt Erddyr and Nomyr, as a reward for bringing the matter under the rule of law. Since there was a vast sea of details to sail across, however, it was late in the day before everything was settled. Yraen was half expecting that Rhodry's matter would be postponed yet again, but the gwerbret had forgotten neither it nor his obligation to even the least of the men in his rhan. When the proceedings were finally concluded to the lords' satisfaction, Drwmyc rose, looking over the assembly.

"There you are, silver dagger. Let's settle your matter now, and then we'll have a good dinner to celebrate, like. Maybe I can talk Tieryn Magryn into standing for some mead for all you men. Come forward. We'll hear what you and that other fellow, the spokesman—Gwar, was it?—have to say."

The gwerbret's jovial mood certainly boded well for Rhodry's case, Yraen decided. In answer to the summons, Rhodry went forward, bowed, then handed his sword to a guard and knelt at the gwerbret's feet. Gwar, however, seemed to have disappeared, though his three friends were sitting over at the right side of the pavilion. They got up and began bowing and making apologies, while everyone else started grinning and making jokes about privies. After a few brief moments Gwar did indeed appear, hurrying into the big tent and threading his way down to the front. Yraen was suddenly struck by an oddity; after being so bold the day before, Gwar looked toward the ground as he walked as if he were afraid to meet anyone's gaze.

"Good, good. Hurry up, lad," the gwerbret said. "The rest of you, hold your tongues now! Let's get the judgment under way."

Yraen saw Rhodry studying Gwar as his enemy handed his sword over, and though he couldn't see the silver dagger too clearly from his distance, he would have sworn that Rhodry had gone a little pale. Certainly he half rose from his kneel as if on sudden guard. Gwar walked forward, heading, or so it seemed, for the other side of the gwerbret's chair. All at once he hesitated for a bare flick of an eyelash, then spun round and rushed at Rhodry, who had no time to get to his feet. Yraen saw Gwar throw himself on Rhodry and grab him round the throat, and the bronze knife gleam in Rhodry's hand, before the pavilion erupted into shouting. Men leapt to their feet and swarmed forward. With a yell Yraen jumped up, thanking the gods for making him tall enough to see over this pack.

The gwerbret himself was on his feet, sword in hand and slashing at the man who'd broken order in his malover, but Gwar was already dead, crumpled over Rhodry's shoulder like a sack of meal. As Yraen shoved himself forward through the mob, Rhodry slowly rose, shoving the corpse off, staggering to his feet with the reddened bronze knife in his hand. His neck bled from scratches and punctures, as if he'd been clutched by a gigantic cat.

"Chirurgeon!" the gwerbret yelled. "Get one of the chirurgeons!"

"Your Grace, it's only a scratch." Rhodry's voice was choked and rasping, his face dead-pale. "But ye gods!"

Yraen managed to reach his side just as the captain of the gwerbret's guard knelt and turned the corpse over. For a moment he stared, then he began cursing in a steady foul stream. The gwerbret looked and went pale himself. Lying at Rhodry's feet was a creature in Gwar's clothes, a badger-headed thing with a blunt snout and fangs. Protruding from the sleeves of its shirt were hairy paws with thick black talons. Rhodry held up the bronze knife.

"Told you not to mock the herbwoman," he croaked. "Without this, he'd have strangled me."

All round them men were pushing forward to see, swearing or yelping and passing the news back to those who couldn't get close. Suddenly Yraen thought of the obvious.

"Gwar!" he snapped. "What's happened to him, then?"

While the apprentice chirurgeon washed Rhodry's throat clean and put a few stitches in the worst wounds, his grace's entire warband began searching the area. It wasn't long before they

found Gwar, naked and strangled, round back of the dun. At that
point the assembled warbands, battle-hardened men all of them,
began to break and panic. Even though the gwerbret sent to the
tieryn's town for every priest he could find, morale washed away
like sand under a tide of rumors and speculations. All his grace
could do was to call the various lords to him.

"Get your men on the road," he snapped. "We'll settle any
last things with heralds. Get your men together and riding for
home, and do it now."

The lords were entirely too ready to obey for Yraen's taste,
but he did have to wonder at himself for being one of the calmest
men in the pavilion.

"I guess it's because I saw the shadow-thing, and I was there
when the herbwoman gave you that knife, and all that. Hold a
moment—herbwoman, indeed! Who was she, Rhodry?"

Rhodry merely shrugged for an answer.

"He shouldn't be talking," the chirurgeon snapped.

"One thing, though, lad." Rhodry immediately broke this sensible rule. "Lord Erddyr. Find him and get our hire."

"I can't be asking him for coin now!"

Rhodry looked at him with one raised eyebrow.

"Oh, very well," Yraen sighed. "I'm gone already and running, too."

Yraen found his lordship in his tent, where he stood watching
his body-servant shove his possessions all anyhow into whatever
sack or saddlebag presented itself. The lord was more than a little
pale, and his mouth was slack as he rubbed his mustaches over and
over. When he saw Yraen, however, he made an effort to draw
himself up and salvage dignity.

"I owe your wages, I know," he said. "You're not coming
back with us, are you?"

The question contained an obvious "you're not welcome."

"I don't think Rhodry should ride, my lord." Yraen was more
than willing to play into the courtesy of the thing. "We'll find an
inn or suchlike to rest in, and then be on our way."

Erddyr nodded, concentrating on opening the pouch that
hung at his belt. He poured out a random handful of coin and

shoved it in Yraen's direction. Briefly Yraen thought of counting it, but he wasn't that much of a silver dagger, not yet, at least.

For all that Rhodry kept saying his wounds were mere scratches, his face was so pale by the time the chirurgeon was done tending them that Yraen begged him to go lie down somewhere. The gwerbret, however, had other ideas.

"I think me you'd best ride out, silver dagger. I hate being this inhospitable to a man who's done me no wrong, but once news of this thing gets round . . ."

"I understand, Your Grace," Rhodry croaked.

"Don't try to talk, man." Drwmyc turned to Yraen. "Do you both have decent horses?"

"We do, Your Grace. Rhodry lost his in the war, but Lord Erddyr replaced it."

"Good. Then saddle up and go." He turned, looking down at the corpse. "I'm going to have this thing burned. If the common folk see or hear of it, the gods only know what they'll do, and I doubt me if you two will be safe here."

"Your Grace, that's cursed unjust! Rhodry's the victim, not the criminal."

"Hold your tongue!" Rhodry managed to speak with some force. "Listen to his grace. He's right."

Yraen found their horses, saddled them and loaded up their gear, then brought them round to the rear of the pavilion where Rhodry was waiting for him, still under guard, but this time, Yraen supposed, the men were there to keep him away from others, as if he carried some kind of plague of the supernatural that the populace might catch. Yraen felt the injustice of it eating at him, but since he had no desire to molder in the gwerbret's dungeon keep, he kept his mouth shut.

At least they could travel unmolested; he doubted if Gwar's three friends would bother to follow them, and with old Badger Snout dead, Rhodry was probably safe enough from creatures of that sort, whatever they might be. Yet, as he thought about it, Yraen no longer knew what might or might not be probable. His entire view of the universe had just gotten itself shattered like a clay cup hitting a stone floor. The calm and literate air of his father's court, where bards and philosophers alike were always welcome, seemed farther away and stranger than the Otherlands. As they rode out of the dun, he found he had nothing to say. He could only wonder why he'd ever left the Holy City.

Already the sun hung low, catching a few mares' tails high in the sky and turning them gold, a promise of rain coming in a day or two. A few miles from the dun, they crested a rise and saw down below them an unmarked crossroads, one way heading roughly east and west, the other running off to the north. A rider was waiting in the cross, a tall blond man on a white horse with rusty-red ears.

"Evandar, no doubt," Rhodry whispered. "And me too hoarse to talk!" He tried to laugh, but all that emerged was a rusty cracking sound that made Yraen feel cold all over.

"Just be quiet, then! I'll try to bargain with him."

As they walked their horses down, Evandar waited, sitting easy in his saddle and smiling in greeting, yet as soon as they drew close, his eyes narrowed.

"What happened to your neck?" he snapped at Rhodry.

"This thing tried to strangle him," Yraen broke in. "A fiend from the hells with a badger head, like, and claws. Rhodry killed it with the bronze knife that the old herbwoman gave him."

"Good, good." Evandar was still looking at Rhodry. "It came for that whistle, you know. Why don't you let me have it back? They won't come bothering you anymore."

"Who are you, anyway?" Yraen said with as much authority as he could summon. "We want some answers."

"Do you now?" Evandar paused to smile. "Well, I spoke to Dallandra, and she did mention that, but I've none to give you. That whistle, however, is mine by right of a treaty sealed in my own country, and I do wish to have it back. You wouldn't want me riding to the gwerbret and accusing you of theft, would you now?"

Rhodry made a painful gurgling noise that made Evandar frown.

"You've been hurt badly, haven't you? That aches my heart, that you've taken a wound over a thing of mine. I consider you under my protection, you see." Evandar held out one slender, pale hand. "Rhodry, please?"

Rhodry considered, then shrugged. He wrapped his reins round his saddle peak, then loosened his belt and reached inside his shirt to pull out the whistle. In the graying twilight it glimmered an unnatural white.

"Now here," Yraen snapped. "You can't just give it back after all that's happened. He should at least give us a price for it."

"Well put, lad, and fair enough." Evandar raised one hand, snapped his fingers, and plucked a leather bag out of midair. "Here's a sack of silver, given to Dallandra by that lord, but she has no use or need of it in my country." He tossed it to Yraen. "How's that for a price?"

"Not enough. I'll hand the silver back again in return for some answers."

"Keep the silver, for answers you shall not have until you guess them. I pose riddles, and men must find the answers. I never solve a riddle for free, lad, and it's unwise of you to keep asking."

Maybe it was only the darkening light, or the cool spring wind ruffling his hair, but Yraen abruptly shuddered. When he glanced at Rhodry, he found the silver dagger grinning in his usual daft way, as if leaving this exchange to his apprentice.

"Very well, then," Yraen said. "We'll take the silver."

When Rhodry flipped the whistle over, Evandar caught it in one hand and bowed from the saddle.

"I'll give you somewhat more in return, then, as thanks for your graciousness. Which way are you riding?"

"North, I suppose, to Cerrgonney." Yraen glanced at Rhodry, who nodded agreement. "There's always work for a silver dagger to the north."

"Or east." Rhodry cleared his throat with a rasp. "The Auddglyn, maybe."

"I can't ride through Deverry to get there."

"And Rhodry had best stay clear of Eldidd," Evandar broke in. "Why the Auddglyn, Rhodry?"

"We need a smith, and I used to know one down in Dun Mannannan."

"Otho the dwarf!" Evandar smiled suddenly and bowed again. "Did you know that he made that ring you wear? Ah, I didn't think you did. Well, he's gone from Dun Mannannan, but his apprentice took over his shop, and he's a skilled man, for a human being. Follow me."

When Evandar turned his horse and headed for the east-running road, Rhodry followed automatically. Yraen hesitated, knowing in some wordless way that dweomer hung all around him. At this crossroads he had reached the crux of his entire life. He could sit here and restrain his horse, let them ride off without him, and then return to his safe life in Dun Deverry. His clan would forgive him for their joy in having him back; he would put his one adventure into his memory like a jewel locked in a casket and take up again the ceremonial duties of a minor prince. Ahead neither Rhodry nor Evandar looked back, and as Yraen watched, he saw what seemed to be gray mist rising from the road, billowing up to hide them—or was it to hide him, to rescue him from the foolish choice he'd made when he left home?

"Hold! Rhodry, wait for me!"

Yraen kicked his horse hard and galloped into the mist. Ahead he could see the glimmer of the white horse and hear hooves, clopping on what seemed to be paving stones. All at once sunlight gleamed, and he saw Rhodry on his new chestnut gelding and Evandar on the white nearby. Sunlight? Yraen thought. Sunlight? Oh, ye gods! Yet he jogged on, falling into place beside the silver dagger, who turned in the saddle to grin at him.

"You don't want to lose your way round here, lad."

Rhodry's voice sounded perfectly normal, and when Yraen looked, he saw that his friend's neck bore only a few green and yellow bruises, all faded and old.

"I can see that I don't, truly."

Ahead the mist thinned to a sunny day, and Yraen could hear the sea, muttering on a graveled shore. Evandar paused his horse and waved them on past.

"You're a bit east of Dun Mannannan and the shop of Cardyl the silversmith," he called out. "Farewell, silver daggers, and may your gods give you luck that's good and horses to match it."

The mist sealed him over, then vanished, blowing away in a sunny spring wind, tanged with the smell of the sea. They were riding on a hard-packed dirt road that ran through fields where young grain stood maybe two feet high, nodding pale green in a morning breeze. Far off to their left stood cliffs, dropping to the ocean below. All at once Yraen realized that he was having trouble seeing, that he was shaking and sweating all at once, that his hands simply wouldn't hold his reins. Rhodry leaned over and took them from him, then brought both horses to a halt.

"Go ahead and shudder," Rhodry said. "There's no shame in it."

Yraen nodded, gulping for breath and clutching at the saddle peak. Rhodry looked away, watching the swell and rise of the distant ocean while he spoke.

"I'm glad I thought to mention silversmiths to Evandar. It's time we got you a knife of your own. Still want it?"

Yraen had never thought that he would ever feel such pride, the sort that comes from knowing you've earned a thing yourself, and against all odds.

"Well, call me daft for it, but I do."

"Good. You know, I just realized a thing that I should have seen years ago. Once the wretched dweomer's had its hand on you, there's no going back; there's no use in pretending that things will ever be all quiet and peaceful and as daily as before." He turned, glancing Yraen's way. "You're a silver dagger now, sure enough, as much an outcast as any of us."

Yraen started to make some jest, but all at once he could think of nothing to say, just from hearing the bitter truth in his friend's words.

By the time Dallandra reached Bardek, summer was well along in Deverry, though the journey seemed to take only a day to her. As usual, she started from the Gatelands in Evandar's country, at a spot near the river where white water foamed and churned over black rock. When she thought of Jill, the image that rose, seemingly standing between two trees, seemed so faint and silvery that Dalla was alarmed. She hurried over just as it disappeared, called up another image, followed that, trotting faster and faster until at last the river disappeared far behind her, and she heard the ocean.

In a swirl of mist upon a graveled beach, Jill's image appeared again, a little more solid and bright this time. When she approached it, Dallandra felt the gravel underfoot turning to coarse, stunted grass, rasping round her ankles. The ocean murmur disappeared. She hesitated, looking over a brown and treeless plain, wondering if she'd made a wrong turn, but tracking the images had never failed her before.

As she walked on, she kept expecting to find herself emerging into a jungle, but the air stayed cool and the landscape barren. It seemed that the very sunlight changed, turning pale while she picked her way through huge gray boulders along the crest of a hill. All at once she realized that the amethyst figurine was gone. She was fully back in her body, shivering in cold sunlight, breathing hard in thin air. Below her a cliff dropped down to a long parched valley gashed by a dry riverbed; far across rose mountain peaks, black and forbidding, peaked with snow. A wind blew steadily, whining through the coarse grass. The stunted slant of the few trees she saw told her that the wind rarely stopped.

When she turned round, she saw directly behind her more of the deformed trees, scattered round a spread of low wooden buildings, long oblongs roofed with split shingles. They were covered with carvings, every inch of the walls, every window frame and door lintel, of animals, birds, flowers, words in the Elvish syllabary, all stained in subtle colors, mostly blues and reds, to pick out the designs. From round behind the complex she could hear a faint whinny of horses, and a snatch of song drifted on the swirling dust. Out in front of the nearest building a gray-haired woman sat reading on a wooden bench, a pair of big tan hounds lounging at her feet.

"Jill! By the gods!"

The dogs leapt up and barked, but Jill hushed them, laying a slender scroll down beside her just as Dallandra hurried over. She was much thinner, and her hair was going white round her temples, but when she shook hands, her clasp was firm and strong, and her voice steady.

"It gladdens my heart to see you," Jill said in Deverrian. "What brings you to me?"

"Just concern. Evandar said you'd been ill."

"I have been, truly, and I've been told I still am, though I feel mended. I've had a shaking fever. I picked it up in the jungle. They have a tree there, whose bark has the virtue to cure the symptoms, but they say it gets in your blood and lies quiet for years and years, only to flare up when you get yourself cold or tired or suchlike."

"That's a grave thing, then."

Jill merely shrugged, turning to snap at the dogs bounding round them. With little whines they lay down on the hard-packed reddish ground.

"Where are we?" Dallandra said.

"Outside the guest house of . . . well, the only word I can find for it in my own language is temple, but it's not that. It's a place where a few scholars of the People keep lore alive, and teach it to any who ask."

"I've heard about such places from the days of the Seven Kings. I think the People sent their children to them as a matter of course, but I'm not sure why."

For a moment they both turned, looking at the huddled long-houses, some hardly better than huts, that sheltered what was left of one of the finest university systems the world has ever known, then or now, not that either of them realized what such a word meant, of course. Once Dallandra saw a man of the People, dressed in a long gray tunic gathered at the waist with a rope belt, crossing from one house to another, but he never so much as looked their way.

"It's so lonely up here," Dallandra remarked at last. "Why did they choose this place?"

"See those mountains over there? Well, on the other side and down below them lies the jungle. All the clouds that come from the sea fetch up against those peaks and drop their rain. So up here, the air's dry as a bone, and books and scrolls last a fair bit longer than they would down in the jungles. It was a long hard journey getting here, let me tell you, and of course, I had to go and get sick on the way."

"Oh, come now! Don't blame yourself for that."

"I should have been able to turn it aside." Jill sounded genuinely aggrieved. "Well, but it's too late now to worry about it, I suppose. What's done is done. I must say, I've come to have a lot of respect for the physicking your People know."

"Oh, by the gods! Forgive me, I feel like a dolt, but you know, it's just dawned on me what all of this means." Dallandra waved her hand round at the buildings. "It's true, isn't it? Refugees did reach the islands."

"Quite a few of them, Dalla, quite a few." All at once she grinned, a flash of her old humor. "Here, I've forgotten all my courtesies! Won't you come in?"

Dallandra hesitated, suddenly afraid, wondering why she should be afraid rather than eager to learn this ancient lore of her people.

"I can't stay long. I need to get back to Elessario. She might be in danger."

"Ah. Forgive me. Of course, you've got your own work to do. Don't worry about me. I'm as well as I need to be. And you know where to find me now."

"So I do. I take it you'll be here a long while?"

"Oh, you could spend a life here, if you had one to spare. It's amazing, Dalla, just simply amazing! They've managed to preserve so much, most, I'll wager, of what they brought with them. It's their whole life, up here, copying things. You know, my teacher here, Meranaldan, his name is, told me that men risked their lives —gods! some actually died, saving these books when the city was falling." She shook her head in something like sadness. "The history of your race, their songs and poems, some of their magic, though not as much of that as I'd like to see, and all sorts of odd bits of craft lore and learning—scrolls and codices, heaps of them. A true marvel it is, all of it."

All at once Dalla knew why she was afraid, and that she'd have to face that fear.

"And what of the Guardians? Do they speak of them?"

"They do, but I don't suppose they know much about their true nature. I'd wager that you know more about Evandar's folk than any person alive, man or woman both."

Dallandra smiled, glancing away to hide her stab of relief that no one but her knew just how strange her lover was, and how unnatural a love they shared.

"Well, you know, maybe I should come in and talk awhile. Jill, the time's coming near for the child to be born. I can feel it, deep in my heart. If I'm to succeed, then I've got to make my move soon."

"When you need me, we'll go back to Deverry together." She hesitated, looking across the far valley. "And we'll pray that this rotten fever's gone for good."

Yet even as she spoke, Dallandra saw a shadow cross her face, not some trick of the physical light, but a dweomer warning, as if the dark bird of Death were blessing her with a flick of its wing.

future

How then, you say, will I know when the omens are ful-
filled? When all the twined strands of Time weave their
final knot, you will know. If you do not know, then you
have such a measly knack for magic that you should never
have studied it in the first place.

The Pseudo-Iamblichus Scroll

1.

The Queen of Golds

Arcodd,
Summer 1116

"Those brigga don't fool me none. I know a pretty lass when I see one."

The girl looked up from her bowl of stew to find the man leaning, elbows splayed and his dirty face all drunken smile, onto the table directly across from her. Around them the tavern fell abruptly silent as the customers, all men except for one old woman sucking a pint of bitter in a corner, turned to watch. Most grinned.

"What's your name, wench?" His breath stank of bad teeth.

In the uncertain firelight the tavern room seemed to shrink to a frieze of leering faces and the pounding of her heart.

"I said, what's your name, slut?"

He was leaning closer, red hair and beard, greasy, dabbed with food, the stinking mouth twisting into a grin as he reached for her with broad and dirty fingers. She wanted to scream but her throat had turned stone-dry and solid.

"Er, ah, well, I wouldn't touch her, truly I wouldn't."

The man jerked up and swirled round to face the speaker, who had come up so quietly that no one had noticed. He was old, with a pronounced stoop, his hair whitish though touched with red in places, and he had the most amazing pair of bags she'd ever seen under anyone's eyes, but her would-be molester shrank back from him as though he'd been a young warrior.

"Ah, now, Your Holiness, just a bit of fun."

"Not for her—no fun at all, I'd say. She's quite pale, you see. Er, ah, well, I'd leave if I were you."

At that she noticed the two enormous dogs, half wolf from the look of them, that stood by the priest's side with their lips drawn back over large and perfect fangs. When they growled, the man yelped and ran out the tavern door to the accompaniment of jeers and catcalls. The priest turned to look at the other customers with an infinite sadness in his blue eyes.

"Er, well, you're no better. If I hadn't come in . . ."

The laughter stopped, and the men began to study the ground or the tables or the wall, looking at anything but his sad and patient face. With a sigh the priest sat down, smoothing his long gray tunic under him, the dogs settling at his feet.

"After you finish that stew, lass, you'd best come with me. You've picked the worst tavern in all Arcodd for your dinner."

"So it seems, Your Holiness." She was surprised that she could speak at all. "You have my humble and undying thanks. May I stand you a tankard?"

"Not so early in the afternoon, my thanks. I'll have a drop of ale of an evening, but truly, these days, it doesn't sit so well in my stomach." He sighed again. "Er, well, um, what *is* your name?"

She debated, then decided that lying to a priest and a rescuer was beyond her. Besides, her ruse was torn already.

"Carramaena, but call me Carra. Everyone does—did—people who know me, I mean. I've been trying to pass for a lad and calling myself Gwyl, but it doesn't seem to be working."

"Um, well, it isn't, truly. Gwyl? The dark one?" He smiled in a burst of surprising charm. "Doesn't suit you. With your yellow hair and all. Now my name does suit me. Perryn, it is."

"You don't seem foolish in the least."

"Ah, that's because you don't know me very well. You probably never will, seeing as you must be going somewhere in a great hurry if you'd ride with only a lie for company." He paused, frowning at the far wall. "Have to do somewhat about that, you traveling alone, I mean. Are you going to eat that stew?"

"I'm not. I'm not hungry anymore, and I've already picked one roach out of it. Will the dogs want it?"

"Mayhap, but it'll make them sick. Come with me."

When he got up and headed for the door, Carra grabbed her cloak from the bench and hurried after, her head as high as she could hold it as she passed the men by the fire. Outside, drowsy in the hot spring sun, her horse stood tied to the hitching rail in front of the round tavern. A pure-bred Western Hunter, he was a pale buckskin gelding.

"It was the horse that made me go in," Perryn said. "I wondered who'd have a horse like that, you see. You shouldn't just leave him tied up like that in this part of the world. Um, well, he could get stolen."

"Oh, he'll kick the demons out of anyone but me who comes near him. I'm the only person who could ever touch him, much less ride him. That's why he's mine."

"Ah. Your father give him to you?"

"My elder brother." Try as she might to hide it, bitterness crept into her voice and tightened it down. "He's the head of our clan now."

"Ah. Then you *are* noble-born. I, er, um, rather thought so."

She felt her cheeks burn with a blush.

"Truly, you're not much of a liar, Carra. Well, fetch your horse and come along. Do you like dogs?"

"I do. Why?"

"I've got a pair to give you at home. If they like you, and I truly do think they will, they'll take care of you on the road." He sighed in a profound melancholy. "I've got such a lot of them.

Cats, too. We always had cats, my wife and I. She's dead now, you see. Died over the winter."

"I'm so sorry."

"So am I. Well, I'll be joining her soon, I hope, if Kerun wills it. He should. I really am getting on in years. No use in outstaying your welcome, is there?"

Since Carra was only sixteen, she had no idea of what to say to his melancholy and busied herself with untying her horse. He stood staring blank-eyed up the street, as if he were talking to his god in his mind, while the dogs wagged quietly beside him.

The priest's house lay just beyond the village. He pushed open a gate in an earthen wall and led her into a muddy farmyard, where chickens scratched in front of a big thatched roundhouse. Cats and puppies lolled in every patch of shade: under the pair of apple trees, under a watering trough, under a battered old wagon. With a cheerful halloo a stout, red-faced woman of about forty came out the front door.

"There you are, Da. Brought a visitor? You're just in time for your dinner."

"Good, and my thanks, Braema." The priest glanced at Carra. "My youngest daughter. She's the only . . . well, er, ah, only truly human one of the lot."

At that Braema laughed in gut-shaking amusement. Carra dutifully smiled, suspecting some hoary family joke.

"There's lots of sliced ham and some lovely greens, lass, so come right in. Oh, wait—your horse." She turned in the door and bellowed. "Nedd, come out here, will you? Got a guest, and her horse needs water and some shade."

In a moment or so a young man slipped out of the door behind her and stood blinking in the sun. As slender and lithe as a young cat, he was just about five feet tall, a good head shorter than Carra, with hair as coppery red as a sunset, and a pinched face dominated by two enormous green eyes. When he yawned, his intensely pink tongue curled up like a cat's.

"Braema's lad, my grandson," Perryn said with a long sigh. "And, um, well, fairly typical of the lot. Of my offspring, I mean."

With a duck of his head Nedd glided over and took the buckskin's reins. Carra reached out to stop him, but the gelding low-ered his head and allowed the boy to rub his ears without his usual rolling eye and threat of teeth.

"His name's Gwerlas."

The lad smiled, a flick of narrow lips, and led the gelding away without so much as a glance in her direction. Gwer seemed so glad to go that Carra felt a jealous stab.

"Now come in and eat." Braema waved Carra in. "You look like you've ridden a long way, eh?"

"Long enough, truly. I come from Drwloc."

"All the way down there? Ye gods! And where are you going, or may I ask?"

"I don't know." For a moment Carra nearly wept.

The priest and his daughter sat her down at a long plank table in the sunny kitchen, scattered with drowsy cats, and loaded her up a trencher with ham and greens and fresh-baked bread, the first real meal she'd had in days. After she stuffed herself, she found herself talking, partly because she felt she owed them an explana-tion, partly because it felt so good to talk to someone sympathetic.

"I'm the youngest of six, you see, three sons and three daugh-ters, and my eldest brother's head of the clan now, and he's a miserly rotten beast, too. He gave Maeylla—that's my oldest sister —a decent dowry, but it wasn't anything for a bard to remember, I tell you, and then Raeffa got a scraped-together mingy one. And now it's my turn, and he doesn't want to spend on a dowry at all, so he found this fat old lord with half his teeth gone who'll marry me out of lust and ask for naught more, and I'd rather die than marry him, so I ran away."

"And I should think so," Braema said with a firm nod of her head. "Do you think he's still chasing you?"

"I don't know, but I wager he is. I've made him furious, and he hates it so much when anyone crosses him, so he's probably coming to give me the beating of my life just on the principle of the thing. I've got a good lead on him, though. I worked it out with a friend of mine. I went to visit her and her new husband, but I told my brother that I'd stay a fortnight, while she told her husband I'd leave after an eightnight. And in an eightnight leave I did, but I rode north, not home, and my brother wouldn't even have suspected anything till days and days later. So as long as I keep moving, he can't possibly catch up to me."

"Um, well, I see." Perryn pursed his lips and sucked a thoughtful tooth. "I know how purse-proud noble-born kin can be, truly. Mine always were."

"Ah, I see. I was thinking of going west."

"West?" Braema leaned forward sharply. "There's nothing out there, lass, nothing at all."

"I'm not so sure of that. You hear things down in Drwloc. From merchants, like."

The woman was staring at her in such puzzlement that Carra felt her face burning with a blush.

"You could starve out there!" Braema sounded indignant. "Your fat lord would be better than that!"

"You haven't seen him."

When Braema opened her mouth to go on, her father silenced her with a wave of one hand.

"You're hiding somewhat, lass. You're carrying a child, aren't you?"

"How did you know? I only just realized myself!"

"I can always tell. Sort of an, um, well . . . trick of mine."

"Well, so I am." She felt her eyes well tears. "And he—my lover, I mean—he's, well, he's . . ."

"One of the Westfolk!" Braema's voice was all breathy with shock. "And he deserted you, I suppose."

"Naught of the sort! He said he'd come back for me before the winter rains, but he didn't know I was . . . well, you know. And my brother doesn't know, either, which is why he was trying to marry me off, but I didn't dare tell him."

"He'd have beaten you half to death, I suppose." Braema sighed and shook her head. "Do you truly think you've got a chance of finding this man of yours?"

"I don't know. I hope so. He gave me a token, a pendant." Lightly she touched the cool metal where it hung on its chain under her shirt. "There's a rose on it, and some elven words, and he said that any of his people would know it was his."

"Humph, and I wonder about the truth of that, I do! Easy for the Westfolk to talk, but what they mean by it . . ."

"That's enough, Braema." Perryn cut her off with a small wave of one hand. "Can't meddle in someone else's Wyrd, can you? If she wants to go west, west she'll go. She seems to, er, well, know her own mind. But, um, well, I want to give you those dogs." This to Carra. "Come out to the stable with me, will you?"

The stables were round back and a good bit away from the house. Out in front of the long wooden building Nedd was watching Gwerlas drink from a bucket.

"Your Holiness? Most people think I'm daft because I want to ride after my Daralanteriel."

"Mayhap you are, but what choice do you have?"

"None, truly. Not unless I want to get myself beaten first and married off to Old Dung-heap second."

The dogs turned out to be a pair of males, more than half wolf, maybe, with their long sharp faces and pricked ears, and just about a year old. One was gray and glowering, named Thunder, and the other a pale silver with a black streak down his back who answered to Lightning. When the priest introduced them, they sniffed her outstretched hand with a thoughtful wag of their tails.

"They like you," Perryn announced. "Think they do, Nedd?"

The boy nodded, considering.

"I'm going to give them to Carra. She's riding west, you see, and she'll need them along to protect her."

Nedd nodded again and turned to slip back into the stables. He didn't walk, exactly, so much as glide along from shadow to shadow, there one minute, gone the next.

"Uh, Your Holiness, can he talk?"

"Not very well, truly. Only when he absolutely has to, and then only a word or two. But he understands everything. Um, right, that reminds me. I've taught this pair to work to hand signals, and I'd best show you what they know. They'll come to their names, of course." He squatted down and looked at the dogs, who swiveled their heads to stare into his eyes. "You belong to Carra now. Go with her. Take care of her."

For a long, long moment they kept a silent communion, while

Carra decided that contrary to all common sense, the dogs understood exactly what he meant. Nedd came whistling out of the stable. He was leading a nondescript bay gelding, laden with an old saddle, a bedroll, a woodsman's ax, and a pair of bulging saddlebags. Perryn rose, rubbing his face with one hand.

"What's this? You're going, too?"

Nedd nodded, glancing this way and that around the farmstead.

"You'll have to ask Carra's permission."

The boy swung his head around and looked at her.

"You want to come west with me? Look, if my brother catches us, he'll hurt you. He might even kill you."

Nedd considered, then shrugged, turning to stare significantly at his grandfather.

"No use trying to keep someone who doesn't want to stay, is there?" the priest said. "But you take care of the lady. She's noble-born, you see. Don't cause her a moment's trouble, or Kerun will be livid with you. Understand?"

Nedd nodded a yes.

"Well and good, then. Run up to the house, will you? I'll wager your mam is packing up a bit of that ham and bread for Carra to eat on the road."

Nedd grinned and trotted off. Perryn turned to her with an apologetic smile.

"Hope you don't mind him coming along. He won't trouble you. Might even come in handy, because he likes having someone to do things for. Poor lad, it makes him feel useful, like. And he can show you how to work the dogs."

"All right, but here, won't his mother be furious that he's just . . . well . . . leaving like this?"

"Oh, I doubt that. He's like me and his uncles. We mostly come and go as we please, and there's no use in trying to stop us." He sighed again, deeply. "No use in it at all."

Yet even so, they left by the back gate and circled round to hit the west-running road out of sight of the house. Carra took the lead, with the dogs padding along either just ahead or to one side of her as the whim took them, while Nedd rode a length behind like her servant, which he was now, she supposed, in his way. She only hoped that she could take care of him properly, and the dogs, too, though she suspected that they were feral enough to hunt their own food if need be. She had a handful of coins, copper ones mostly, stolen from her brother in lieu of her rightful dowry, but they weren't going to last forever. On a sudden thought she turned in the saddle and motioned Nedd up beside her.

"You must have heard tales about the Westfolk, too. That they're very odd but kind to strangers?"

The boy nodded, his hair glinting like metal in the strong spring sun.

"Do you think they truly are kind?"

He grinned, shrugging to show his utter ignorance, but excited nonetheless.

"I hope they are, because I don't know how we're going to find Dar without some help. He told me that he wanders all over with his tribe and their horses, you see, but I'm not truly sure just how big this 'all over' is."

"North with the summer. South with the rains."

He spoke so softly, so lightly, that she barely heard him.

"Did someone tell you that?"

He nodded a yes.

"Is that how the Westfolk travel? Well, it makes sense. It's more than I've had to go on before. But maybe we should be riding south, then, to meet them as they come north. Or due west. But they may have already passed us up, like, if they left their winter homes early or suchlike."

Nedd nodded, frowning.

"So let's head north," Carra went on. "That way we'll either meet up with them or be in the right place to wait for them."

For the rest of that day and on into the next one they traveled through farm country, but although they stopped to talk with the locals along the road, everyone heaped scorn on the very idea of going off to look for the Westfolk. Arcodd province is still on the very edge of the kingdom of Deverry, and in those days it was a lonely sort of place, where little pockets of settled country dotted a wilderness of grassland and mixed forests. And more wilderness was all, or so they were told, that could possibly lie to the west—except, of course, for the wandering clans of the Westfolk, who were all thieves and ate snakes and made pacts with demons and never washed and the gods only knew what else. By the third day Carra was disheartened enough to start believing them, but turning back meant her brother, a beating, and the pig-breathed Lord Scraev. At night they camped out in copses near the road, and here Nedd showed just how useful a person he was. Besides insisting on tending the horses, he always found firewood and food as well, hooking fish and snaring rabbits, grubbing around to find sweet herbs and greens to supplement the bread her coin bought them in villages.

In his silent way, he was good company, too, patient as he taught her how to command the dogs with subtle hand gestures and a few spoken words. Sleeping on the ground meant nothing to him; he would roll up in a blanket with Thunder at his back and go out while Carra was still tossing and turning, trying to sleep with a patient Lightning at her feet. Although she was used to riding for long hours at a time, either to visit her friends or to ride with her brother's hunt, sleeping on the hard, damp ground was something new, and she began to ache like fire after a few nights of it, so badly that she began to worry about her unborn child, still a tiny knot deep within her but as real to her as Nedd and the dogs. When, then, on the fourth night they came to a village that had an inn, she was tired enough to consider spending a few coins on lodging.

"And a bath," she said to Nedd. "A proper hot bath with a bit of soap."

He merely shrugged.

From outside the inn didn't look like much: a low round-house, heavily thatched, in the middle of a muddy fenced yard, but when she pushed open the gate and led her horse inside, she could smell roasting chickens. The innkeep, a stout and greasy little man, strolled out and looked her over suspiciously.

"The common room's full," he announced. "Ain't got no private chambers."

"Can we sleep in your stables?" Carra gave up her dream of a hot bath. "Up in the hayloft, say?"

"Long as you don't go bringing no lantern up there. Don't want no fire."

The hayloft turned out to be long and airy and well supplied with loose hay, a better night's lodging, she suspected, than the inn itself. After the horses were taken care of, Carra and Nedd, with the dogs trotting busily behind, headed for the tavern. In the half round of the common room, set off from the innkeep's quarters by a wickerwork partition, were a couple of wobbly tables. At one sat a gaggle of farmers, gossiping over their ale; at the other, two men, both road-stained, both armed. Carra stopped in the shadowy curve of the wall by the door; when she snapped her fingers and pointed down, the dogs sat and Nedd fell back a step or two. In the smoky light of a smoldering fire she could see the pair fairly clearly: warriors, by the easy arrogant way they sat, but their stained linen shirts bore no blazons at the yokes or shoulder. One, blond and burly with a heavy blond mustache, looked young; the other, sitting with his back to her, was more slender, with wavy raven-dark hair. When the passing innkeep threw a couple of handfuls of small sticks onto the fire, it blazed with a flare of light, glinting on the pommel of the knives that the men wore at their belt. Three distinctive little knobs. Silver daggers, little better than criminals if indeed they were better at all, or so she'd always been told. Behind her Nedd growled like one of the dogs.

"True enough," she whispered. "Let's get out of here."

But as she stepped back the burly blond saw her and raised a dented tankard her way with a grin.

"Here, lad, come on in and join us. Plenty of room at the table." His voice sounded oddly decent for a man of his sort.

She was about to make a polite refusal when the dark-haired fellow slewed round on the bench to look her over with enormous cornflower-blue eyes. He was clean-shaven and almost girlishly handsome; in fact, she'd never seen such a good-looking man among her own people. As she thought about it, his chiseled features reminded her of the Westfolk and even, because of his coloring, of her Dar. He rose, swinging clear of the bench with some of Nedd's catlike ease, making her a graceful bow, and the warmth of his smile made her blush.

"Lad, indeed!" His voice was a soft tenor, marked by a lilting accent that reminded her of the Westfolk as well. "Yraen, you're growing old and blind! My lady, if you'd care to join us, I swear on what honor I have left that you're perfectly safe."

The dogs were thumping their tails in greeting. When she glanced at Nedd, she found him staring at the raven-haired stranger.

"He looks decent enough to me," she whispered.

Nedd nodded with one of his eloquent shrugs, registering surprise, perhaps, to find a man like this on the edge of nowhere. Carra gestured the dogs up, and they all went over, but Nedd insisted on sitting on the floor with Thunder and Lightning. She settled herself in solitary comfort on one bench while the raven-haired fellow went round to join his friend on the other.

"My name's Rhodry," he said as he sat down. "And this is Yraen, for all that he's got a nickname for a name."

Yraen smiled in a rusty way.

"My name is Carra, and this is Nedd, who's sort of my servant but not really, and Thunder and Lightning."

The dogs thumped their tails; Nedd bobbed his head. The innkeep came bustling over with a big basket of warm bread for the table and a tankard of ale for her. He also brought news of roast chickens, and while he and Yraen wrangled about how many there'd be and how much they'd cost, Carra had a brief chance to study the silver daggers, though most of her attention went to Rhodry. It wasn't just because of his good looks; she simply couldn't puzzle out how old he was. At times he would grin and look no older than she; at others, melancholy would settle into his eyes and play on his face like a fever, and it would seem that he must be a hundred years old at the least, to have earned such sadness.

"Innkeep?" Rhodry said. "Bring some scraps for the lady's dogs, will you?"

"I will. We butchered a sheep yesterday. Plenty of spleen and suchlike left."

Carra gave the man a copper for his trouble. Yraen drew his dagger and began to cut the bread in rough chunks.

"And where is my lady bound for?" His voice was dark and rough, but reassuringly normal all the same.

"I . . . um, well . . . to the west, actually. To visit kin."

Yraen grinned and raised an eyebrow, but he handed her a chunk of bread without comment. Even though Carra told herself that she was daft to trust these men, she suddenly felt safe, and for the first time in weeks. When Rhodry took some bread, she noticed that he was wearing a ring, a flat silver band graved with roses. She was startled enough to stare.

"It's a nice bit of jewelry, isn't it?" Rhodry said.

"It is, but forgive me if I was rude. I just happen to have some jewelry with roses on it myself. I mean, they're very differently done, and the metal's different, too, but it just seemed odd . . ." She felt suddenly tongue-tied and let her voice trail away.

Rhodry passed Nedd the bread. For a few minutes they all ate in an awkward silence until Carra felt she simply had to say something.

"Where are you two going, if you don't mind me asking, anyway?"

"Up north, Cengarn way," Yraen said. "We've got a hire, you see, though he's barricaded himself in a woodshed for the night. Doesn't trust the innkeep, doesn't trust us, for all that he's hired us as guards. Calls himself a merchant, but I've got my doubts, I have. However he earns his keep, he's a rotten-tempered little bastard, and I'm sick to my heart of his ways."

"Your own temper at the moment lacks a certain sunny sweetness itself." Rhodry was grinning. "Our Otho's carrying gems, and a lot of them, and it's making him wary and even nastier than he usually is, which is saying a great deal. But we took his hire because it may lead to better things. I was thinking that maybe Gwerbret Cadmar up on the border might have need of us. He's got a rough sort of rhan to rule."

"Is that Cadmar of Cengarn?"

"It is. I take it you've heard of him?"

"My . . . well, a friend of mine's mentioned Cengarn once or twice. It's to the west of here, isn't it?"

"More to the north, maybe, but somewhat west. Think your kin might have ridden that way?"

"They might have." She busied herself with brushing imaginary crumbs off her shirt.

"What did this man of yours do?" Rhodry's voice hovered between sympathy and a certain abstract anger. "Get you with child and then leave you?"

"How did you know?" She looked up, blushing hard, feeling tears gathering.

"It's not exactly a new story, lass."

"But he said he'd come back."

"They all do," Yraen murmured to his tankard.

"But he gave me—" She hesitated, her hand half-consciously clutching at her shirt, where the pendant hung hidden. "Well, he gave me a token."

When Rhodry held out his hand, she debated for a long moment.

"We're not thieves, lass," Rhodry said, and so gently that she believed him.

She reached round her neck to unclasp the chain and take the token out. It was an enormous sapphire as blue as the winter sea, set in a pendant of reddish-gold, some three inches across and ornamented with golden roses in bas relief. When they saw it, Rhodry whistled under his breath and Yraen swore aloud. Nedd scooted a little closer to look.

"Ye gods!" Yraen said. "It's a good thing you keep this hidden. It's worth a fortune."

"A king's ransom, and I mean that literally." Rhodry was studying it as closely as he could in the uncertain light, and he muttered a few words in the language of the Westfolk before he went on. "Once this belonged to Ranadar of the High Mountain, the last true king the Westfolk ever had, and it's been passed down through his descendants for over a thousand years. When your Dar's kin find out he's given it to you, lass, they're going to beat him black and blue."

"You know him? You must know him!"

"I do." Rhodry handed the jewel back. "Any man who knows the Westfolk knows Daralanteriel. Did he tell you who he is?"

Busy with clasping the pendant, she shook her head no.

"As much of a Marked Prince as the Westfolk will ever have. The heir to what throne there is, which isn't much, being as his kingdom lies in ruins in the far, far west."

She started to laugh, a nervous giggle of sheer disbelief.

"Kingdom?" Yraen broke in. "I never heard of the Westfolk having any kingdom."

"Of course you haven't." Rhodry suddenly grinned. "And that's because you've never gotten to know the Westfolk or listened to what they've got to say. A typical Round-ear, that's you, Yraen."

"You're having one of your jests on me."

"I'm not." But the way he was smiling made him hard to believe. "It's the solemn truth."

To her horror Carra found that she couldn't stop giggling, that her giggles were rising to an hysterical laugh. The dogs whined, pressing close to her, nudging at her hands while Nedd swung his head Rhodry's way and growled like a wolf. The silver dagger seemed to notice him for the first time.

"Nedd, his name is?" Rhodry spoke to Carra. "I don't suppose he has an uncle or suchlike named Perryn."

"His grandfather, actually." At last she managed to choke her laughter down enough to answer. "A priest of Kerun."

Rhodry sat stock-still, and in the dancing firelight it seemed he'd gone pale.

"And what's so wrong with you?" Yraen poked him on the shoulder.

"Naught." Rhodry turned, waving at the innkeep. "More ale, will you? A man could die of thirst in your wretched tavern."

Not only did the man bring more ale but his wife trotted over with roast fowl and greens and more bread, a feast to Carra after her long weeks on the road, and to the silver daggers as well, judging from the way they fell upon the meal. In the lack of conversation Carra found herself studying Rhodry. His table manners were those of a courtly man, one far more gracious than any lord she'd ever seen at her brother's table. Every now and then she caught him looking her way with an expression that she simply couldn't puzzle out. Sometimes he seemed afraid of her, at others weary—she decided at length that in her exhaustion she was imagining things, because she could think of no reason that a battle-hardened silver dagger would be afraid of one tired lass, and her pregnant at that. Once she'd eaten, though, her exhaustion lifted enough for her to focus at last on one of his earlier comments.

"You know Dar." She said it so abruptly that he looked up, startled. "Where is he? Will you tell me?"

"If I knew for certain, I would, but I haven't seen him in years, and he's off to the north with his alar's herds somewhere, I suppose." Rhodry paused for a sip of ale. "Listen, lass, if you're with child, then you're his wife. Do you realize that? Not some deserted woman, but his wife. The Westfolk see things a good bit differently than Deverry men."

The tears came, spilling down before she could stop them. Whining, the dogs laid their heads in her lap. Without thinking she threw her arms around Thunder and let him lick the tears away while she wept. Dimly she was aware of Yraen talking, and of the sounds of a bench being moved about. When at last she looked up, he was gone and the innkeep with him, but Rhodry still sat across from her, slouching onto one elbow and drinking his ale.

"My apologies," she sniveled. "I've just been so frightened, wondering if he really would ever want to see me again."

"Oh, he will. He's a good lad, for all that he's so young, and I think me you can trust him." Rhodry grinned suddenly. "Well, I'd say he's a cursed sight more trustworthy than I was at his age, but that, truly, wouldn't be saying much. If naught else, Carra, his kin will take you in the moment you find them—ye gods, any alar would! You don't truly realize it yet, do you? That child you're carrying is as royal as any prince up in Dun Deverry. You've got the token to prove it, too. Don't you worry, now. We'll find him."

"We?"

"We. You've just hired yourself a silver dagger to escort you to your new home—well, once we get Otho to Cengarn, but that's on the way and all." He looked away, and he seemed as old as the rocks in the mountains, as weary as the rivers themselves. "Whether Yraen's daft enough to ride with me, I don't know. For his sake, I hope he isn't."

"But I can't pay you."

"Oh, if I needed paying, Dar's alar would see to it. Here, you still look half out of your mind with fear."

"Well, it's just all been so awful." She sniffed hard, choking back tears. "Realizing I was pregnant, and then running away, and wondering if maybe Dar had just up and left me behind like men do. And then I met Nedd's grandfather, and truly, that was strange enough on its own, and then we just stumble in here like this, and here you are, telling me all these strange things, and I've never seen you before or anything. It's so odd, finding someone who knows Dar, out of the blue like this, that I . . ." She paused, blushing on the edge of calling him a liar.

"Odd, truly, but not some bizarre coincidence. It's my Wyrd, Carra, and maybe yours, too, but no man can say what another's Wyrd may be. Wyrd, and the dweomer that Wyrd brings with it—I can smell it all round us."

"You look frightened, too."

"I am. You're carrying my death with you."

Nedd, who'd been close to asleep, snapped up his head to stare. Carra tried to speak but could only stammer. Rhodry laughed, a long berserker's howl, and pledged her with his tankard.

"I don't hold it against you, mind. I've loved many a woman in my day, but none as much as I love my lady Death. I know what you're going to ask, Carra—I'm drunk, sure enough, but not so drunk that I'm talking nonsense. Indulge me, my lady, since I've just pledged my life to you and all that, and let me talk awhile. I've lived a good bit longer than you might think, and every now and then I get to looking back, like old men will, and I can see now that I've never loved anyone as much as her. Once I thought I loved honor, but honor's just another name for my lady Death, because sooner or later, as sure as sure, a man's honor will lead him to her bed." Abruptly he leaned onto the table. "Do you believe in sorcery, Carra? In the dweomer, and those who know its ways?"

"Well, sort of. I mean, I wouldn't *know*, but you hear all those things—"

"Some of them are true. I know it, you see. I know it deep in my heart, and it's a harsh and bitter knowing in its way." He gave her a lopsided grin that made him look like a lad of twenty. "Do you think I'm mad?"

"Not truly, but a bit daft—I can't deny that."

"You're a practical sort of lass, and you'll need to be." He finished the ale in his tankard, then refilled it from the flagon with an unsteady hand. "There's only been one woman in my whole life that I've loved as much as I love the lady Death, but she loved the dweomer more than me. It's enough to drive any man daft, that. Be that as it may, she told me a prophecy once. Run where you will, Rhodry, said she, but the dweomer will catch you in the end. Or somewhat like that. It was years ago now, and I don't quite remember her exact words. But I do remember how I felt while she was speaking, that she was telling me the truth and naught more, and somehow I knew that when the time came and my Wyrd sprang upon me, I'd feel its claws sink deep, and I'd know that my lady Death was getting ready to accept me at last for the true lover I've been, all these long years. And while you were telling me your tale, I felt those claws bite. Soon I'll lie with her at last, though it's a cold and narrow bed we'll share, my lady and me."

Nedd was asleep in the straw with the dogs. In the hearth the fire was dying down, throwing a cloak of shadows over Rhodry's face. With a wrench of will Carra got up and went to the hearth to put on more wood. She felt so cold at heart that she wanted the heat as much as the light. As the fire blazed up, she heard him moving behind her and turned just as he knelt in the straw at her feet.

"Will you take me into your service, my lady?"

"What? Of course I will. I mean, I don't have a lot of choice, do I? Since you know Dar and all."

"A very practical lass." He grinned at her and rose, dusting off the knees of his filthy brigga as if it would make a difference. "Good. Nedd! Wake up! Escort your lady to her elegant chambers, will you? And make sure you stand a good guard tonight, because I feel trouble riding for all of us with an army at its back."

Drunk as he was, he made her a graceful bow, then wove his way out of the tavern room. Nedd got up, signaling to the dogs to join him.

"What do you think of that silver dagger, Nedd? Do you like him?"

Nedd nodded his head yes.

"Even though he's half-mad?"

Nedd pursed his lips and thought. Finally he shrugged the question away and went to open the door for her with a clumsy imitation of Rhodry's bow. As she followed him out to the stables, Carra was both thinking that she'd never wanted to be a queen and wishing that she felt more like one.

Early on the morrow Yraen woke them by the simple expedient of standing under the hayloft and yelling. As they all walked back to the tavern for breakfast, he announced that he was riding north with them.

"Against my better judgment, I might add. First we take on this cursed little silversmith, and now our Rhodry starts babbling about Wyrd and dweomer and prophecies and the gods only know what else! He's mad, if you ask me, as daft as a bard, and he drinks harder than any man I've ever seen, and that's a fair bit, if you take my meaning, not that he shows his drink the way an ordinary man would, but anyway, I know blasted well I should be riding back east and finding some other hire, but when he gets to talking—" He shook his head like a baffled bear. "So I'm coming along, for all that he warned me I'll probably die if I do. I must be as daft as he is."

In the morning light Carra had the chance for a good look at him. He was a handsome man, Yraen, at least in the abstract, with regular features and a mane of thick golden hair to match his mustaches, but his ice-blue eyes were as cold and hard as the iron of the joke that stood him for a name. The dogs and Nedd watched him with a cold suspicion of their own.

"Have you known Rhodry long?" Carra said.

"We've ridden together this four years now."

"You know, neither of you seem like the sort of men who usually turn into silver daggers."

"I suppose you mean that well." Yraen was scowling, but in an oddly abstract way. "Look, my lady, no offense and all that, but asking a silver dagger questions isn't such a pleasant thing—for both sides, if you take my meaning."

Since she did, Carra held her tongue against a rising tide of curiosity. Inside the tavern room Rhodry was sitting cross-legged on the floor under a window, shaving with a long steel razor and a bit of mirror propped against the wall.

"Be done straightaway," Rhodry said. "Yraen, get the lady some bread and milk, will you? The innkeep's drunk in his kitchen again, and she's got to keep up her strength and all that."

With a growl like a dog, however, Nedd insisted on being the one to wait upon his lady.

"I've been thinking," Yraen said abruptly. "If the point of this daft adventure is finding our lady her man, why don't we just ride straight west?"

"You're forgetting Otho."

"True enough, and that's my point. I want to forget Otho. Can't we give him his coin back?"

"We still couldn't just ride west. The grasslands are huge, and there aren't any roads, and we could wander out there for months till we starved to death." Still a bit damp, Rhodry joined them at table just as Nedd and the bleary innkeep appeared with bread and bacon. "Cadmar of Cengarn buys horses from the Westfolk, and so we're bound to find some of the People there—well, they'll show up sooner or later, anyway. And then we can pass the message along, that Dar's wife is waiting for him under the gwerbret's protection."

"Sounds too easy. You're hiding somewhat, Rhodry."

"I'm not. I've got no idea, none at all, of what might happen."

"Then what's all this babbling about Wyrd and dweomer?"

Rhodry shrugged, tearing bread with his long and graceful fingers.

"If I knew more, I'd tell you more." He looked up with a sunny and inappropriate grin hovering round his mouth. "But that's why I warned you earlier. Leave Otho if you want—leave us all. Ride east, and don't give me or mine another thought."

Yraen merely snarled and speared a chunk of bacon with an expensive-looking table dagger. At that point Carra heard someone swearing and cursing at the innkeep. The dogs laid back long ears and swung their heads toward the sound as the voice rose into a veritable litany of oaths, a bard's memory chain of venom, a lexicon of filth. Rhodry jumped up and yelled.

"Hold your tongue! There's a lady present."

Snorting inarticulately under his breath a man came stumping into the room. He was only about five feet tall, but built as thickly and strongly as a miniature blacksmith, though his walk was stiff and slow. Since his hair and long beard were snow-white, it might have been mere age that was stiffening him, but from Rhodry's talk of the night before Carra suspected that his heavy leather jerkin hid sewn jewels. He was also wearing a short sword at one hip and a long knife at the other.

"Don't you yell at me, you misbegotten silver dagger," Otho said, but levelly enough. "The day I take orders from a cursed elf is the day I curl my toes to heaven and gasp my last. I . . ."

He saw Carra and stopped, his mouth slacking, his eyes misting with tears.

"My lady," he whispered. "Oh! My lady."

He knelt before her and grabbed her hand to kiss it like a courtier. Carra sat stunned while Rhodry and Yraen goggled. All at once Otho blushed scarlet, jumped to his feet, and made a noisy show of blowing his nose on a bit of old rag.

"Uh, well now," Otho snapped. "Don't know what came over me, like, lass. My apologies. Thought you were someone else, just for a minute there. Humph. Well. Forgive me, will you? Just going outside."

He rushed out before anyone could say a word, leaving all of them stunned and silent for a good couple of minutes. Finally Yraen sighed with an explosive puff of breath.

"All right, Rhodry lad. Dweomer it is, and Wyrd, too, for all I know about it. I'm not arguing with you anymore."

After Rhodry settled up with the innkeep, they rode out, heading straight north on the hard-packed dirt road that would, or so the villagers promised, eventually lead them to Cengarn and Gwerbret Cadmar. The road here ran through farms, stretching pale gold with the ripening crop of winter wheat, but to the north, like a smudge of storm clouds, hung a dark line of hills and forests. All morning the line swelled, and the land rose steadily toward it, till by the time they stopped to rest the horses and eat their midday meal, they could see waves and billows of land and trees at the horizon.

"How are you faring, lass?" Otho asked as he helped her dismount. "Our Rhodry tells me you're with child."

"Oh, I'm perfectly fine. You don't need to hover over me, you know. I'm not very far along at all."

"If you say so. I just wish we had a woman of the People with us, someone who knew about these female matters."

"I'm doing splendidly."

Yet, when Carra sat down in a soft patch of grass, she was surprised at how good it felt to be out of the saddle and still. She'd learned to ride at three, clinging to her brother's pony, spent half her life riding, but now she found herself tired after a morning in the saddle. She decided that she hated being pregnant, married or not. Thunder and Lightning flopped down on either side of her with vast canine sighs. When Nedd hurried off to fetch her water and food, Otho sat down as if on guard.

"If I'm truly a queen now," she said, "the dogs must be my men at arms, and Nedd my equerry. Do you want to be my high councillor, Otho? I wonder if I'll get any serving women; maybe we should have taken some of his holiness's cats along for that."

Otho frowned in thought, pretending to take the game seriously.

"Well, Your Grace," he said at last. "I'd rather be your chief craftsman, in charge of building your great hall, like."

"Truly, the one we've got now is rather drafty." She waved one arm round at the scenery. "Let me see, who'll be councillor. Well, it can't be Rhodry, because he's daft. I know—I need a sorcerer! An aged sorcerer like in the tales. Aren't there tales like that? About marvelous dweomermasters who turn up just when you need them?"

Otho turned a little pale. She could have sworn that he was terrified, but she couldn't imagine why. Suddenly troubled herself, she looked up at the sky.

"Do you see that bird circling up there?" She pointed to a distant black shape. "Is it a raven?"

"Looks like it. Why?"

"I've been seeing it all morning, that's all. Oh, I'm just being silly. Of course there's lots of ravens . . ." She let her voice trail away, because Otho was staring up, shading his deep-pouched eyes with one hand, and within the welter of dirty beard his mouth was set and grim.

"What's so wrong?" Rhodry strolled over, a chunk of cheese in his hand.

"Maybe naught," Otho said. "But that's one blasted big raven, isn't it?"

Just as he spoke, the bird broke and flew, flapping with a harsh cry off to the west, just as if it knew it had been spotted. Otho tossed his head to shake the sun from his eyes.

"You a good hand with a hunting bow, silver dagger? You're the one who used to ride with the Westfolk."

"True spoken, and my heart yearns for a longbow now."

Suddenly cold, Carra stood up just as Nedd and Yraen hurried over.

"Was there somewhat strange about that raven?" she said.

"Maybe. You've got sharp eyes, lass, and I think me you're going to need them."

"Now, wait." Yraen sounded exasperated. "A bird's a bird, big or not."

"Unless it's a sorcerer." Rhodry grinned at him. "What would you say if I told you that some dweomermen can turn themselves into birds and fly?"

"I'd say that you were even dafter than I thought."

"Then I won't tell you. It's still not too late for you to go back."

"Will you hold your tongue about that?"

"Well and good, then, because you've been warned three times now, and that's all that the laws and the gods can ask of me."

That afternoon, when they rode on north, Carra kept a nervous watch for the raven, but she saw only normal birds of several

kinds, flying about on some avian business. Every time she saw a
raven or a crow, she would tell herself that Rhodry's talk of shape-
changers was his madness speaking at worst or some daft jest at
best.

The land kept rising, and the road turned snaky, winding
through the low places and crossing a couple of small streams. Just
at sunset they topped a low rise and saw, some two or three miles
ahead, a wild forest spreading out across hill and valley. Between
them and the verge, as dark as shadows, stood a village huddling
behind a staked palisade. Yraen muttered something foul under his
breath.

"Don't like the looks of that, Rhodry. That wall's new built."

"So it is. We'd best hurry before they shut us out for the
night."

In spite of the fortifications, the village was hospitable
enough. Although Carra was expecting the farmers to stare at
Otho or at least comment on his small stature, they acted as if he
were nothing out of the ordinary at all. The blacksmith let them
stable their horses in his shed, and a farm wife was glad to feed
them for a few coppers and let them sleep in her hayloft for a
couple more. Half the village crowded into her house to talk to the
strangers, too, and warn them.

"Bandits on the roads," said the blacksmith. "Never had bandits round here before. We sent a lad off to Gwerbret Cadmar to
beg for help, and his grace sent word back that he was trying his
best to wipe the scum out. Told us we'd better put up some kind of
wall until he did."

"Sounds like we might find a hire in Cengarn," Rhodry said.
"He might need extra men."

"Most like." The blacksmith paused, looking Carra over.
"What are you doing on the roads, lass?"

Carra opened her mouth to blurt the truth, but Rhodry got in
first.

"She rides with me," he snarled, and quite believably. "Anything wrong with that?"

"Since I'm not her father, I don't have a word to say about it,
lad. Now let's not have any trouble, like."

"Save it for the bandits, Rhodry," Yraen put in with a sigh. "How wide is the forest, anyway? Traveling from south to north, I mean."

"Oh, let's see." The blacksmith rubbed his chin. "I've never been north, myself. But it stretches a fair ways. Then you come to some more farming country, and then forest again. Cengarn's right up in the hills. Lot of trade comes through Cengarn."

"Trade?" Carra said, startled. "With the Westfolk?"

"Them, too, lass." The blacksmith gave Otho a conspiratorial wink. "I take it she's never ridden our way before. I think the lass is in for a surprise or two."

The hayloft turned out to be quite big enough for all of them, though Nedd insisted on piling up a barrier of hay to give Carra a bit of privacy in one curve of the wall. Before she went to this improvised bower, she asked Rhodry outright why he'd lied to the blacksmith.

"Because the truth could be dangerous, that's why. Bandits have been known to hold important people for ransom."

"Important . . ."

"Carra, believe me. The Westfolk would hand over every fine horse they own to ransom Dar's wife and heir, to say naught of that bit of jewelry you're carrying. From now on, just pretend you ran off with me. It's perfectly believable."

"The vanity of the man!" Otho said. "But women do stupid things sometimes, sure enough."

"And men are the soul of tact?" Carra snapped.

"It's not like you really did run off with Rhodry. This man of yours couldn't be any worse, even if he is an elf."

Lightning picked up her mood and growled. At the sound Thunder swung his head around and bared teeth.

"My apologies," Otho said, and quickly. "No offense meant."

Carra decided that as men at arms went, the dogs had much to recommend them.

In the morning, when they rode out, Rhodry and Yraen held a last conference with the blacksmith, then decided to wear the mail shirts they'd been carrying in their saddlebags. Much to Carra's surprise, Otho produced one as well. As they followed the road into the forest, Nedd put the dogs on alert with a few hand signals; their noses would provide the best warning they could have against possible ambushes. Although she tried to keep her courage up, a few hours of this dangerous riding brought Carra an acute case of nerves. Every flicker of movement in the underbrush, every ripple of wind in the trees, every distant crack of a twig or hammer of a woodpecker, made her flinch.

Rhodry and Yraen rode in silence, as alert as the dogs. When they finally came clear of the forest, just after noon, she offered up a prayer of thanks to the Goddess. Yet, paradoxically enough, it was out in the open farmlands that the reality of their danger struck her like a blow across the face. Thanks to heavy cutting by the locals, the trees ended in a welter of stumps just at the edge of a broad valley. As they jogged their horses out into the open air, the dogs growled and threw up their heads to sniff the sudden gust of burning that greeted them. When Carra looked up, she could see a lazy drift of smoke, yellowing the sky. Circling up high flew the raven. Yraen swore—he'd seen it, too. Rhodry, oddly enough, started singing, just a few lines of some looping melody in the language of the Westfolk.

"Would that I had my good yew bow to speed an arrow to your lying heart," he translated. "So your blood could water the tree of my revenge—but that bit isn't really to the point, being as that cursed bird hasn't done anything to us yet. I suspect it of having plans. What do you think, Otho?"

"I think we should turn back, that's what."

The raven headed off west and disappeared into the bright sun beyond the smoke.

"Normally I'd agree, but there's a farmstead burning over there." Rhodry rose in his stirrups and squinted across the valley. "Somebody might be still alive."

But the gods weren't so kind as that. At a fast jog they cut across the fields, the dogs racing to keep up, and reached the farmstead to find the fire burning itself out in a smolder of smoking thatch and glowing embers. Just at the road lay the corpse of a woman, her head half cut from her shoulders, in a blackening pool of blood. She lay on her back, her arms thrown akimbo, her stomach swollen with a late pregnancy.

"Get back!" Rhodry turned in his saddle and yelled at Carra. "Get back with the dogs!"

She wheeled her horse around, but it was too late. Mixed with the smoke hung a sweet scent, much too much like burnt meat. She pulled Gwerlas up after a few lengths, dismounted as fast as she could, and vomited into the long grass. Sick, cold, and shaking, she wiped her mouth on a pull of grass and got up, staggering back to her horse, just as the two dogs reached her. Whining, they crowded close. She let her hands rest on their necks while she stared at the sky and resolutely tried to put the sight of the murdered woman out of her mind. It was impossible.

"There, there, lass." It was Otho, and his voice was full of soft concern. "You'll come right in a moment."

When she tried to answer the words stuck like lumps of vomit in her throat. Finally she decided that she'd have to face what needed facing and turned to look at the distant village. She could just see Rhodry and Yraen circling round the burning, with Nedd close behind them. She realized suddenly that if there were trapped survivors, the dogs would find them. She snapped her fingers and pointed.

"Nedd. Go to Nedd."

They bounded off.

"Oh, well," Carra went on. "It's still better than marrying Lord Scraev. I'll tell you about him sometime, Otho. You'll laugh and laugh."

Her voice sounded so weak and shaky to her own ears that she nearly wept. Otho laid a surprisingly gentle hand on her shoulder. "Tears help, lass."

"I can't weep. I'm a queen now. Sort of, anyway. The queens in all the old tales face this sort of thing with proud sneers or maybe a supernatural calm. Like what's-her-name, King Maryn's wife, when her enemies were accusing her of adultery and stuff."

Otho's face turned pale and oddly blank.

"Haven't you heard that old story? Bellyra, that was it, and she stared them all down till her witness could get there and keep them from killing her."

"Many a time and from many a bard."

"You know, he was a smith like you, wasn't he? I think that's the way the tale ran. He was her jeweler or suchlike." Carra forced a smile. "And she wasn't killed, and so I'll just take that as a good omen."

"Now listen, lass, things look dark. I won't lie to you. But for all that I love to slang him, Rhodry ap Devaberiel's the best swordsman in this kingdom and points beyond as well, and young Yraen's his match. We'll get you through to Cengarn."

"Shouldn't we turn back?"

"Well, the raiders left plenty of tracks. Didn't seem to see any reason why they should cover them, like, the arrogant bastards. I'd say they're heading south right now. No use in riding after them, is there?"

"Oh, Goddess, I wish Dar were here! I . . . hold a bit. Did you say that Rhodry's father is one of the Westfolk? I mean, with that name—"

"He couldn't be anything but an elf, truly. That's what I said, all right, but I'm not saying another word about it. Rhodry's affair, not mine."

In a few minutes the other men came back, Rhodry and Yraen grim, shaking their heads, Nedd dead-pale and sweating, the dogs slinking, all limp tails and ears. When they reached the body of the dead woman, Rhodry sent the others on ahead, then knelt down beside it. Carra turned her back on him and took a deep gulp of air.

"Are there more people dead?" she said to Yraen.

"There are. Not one thing we can do for the poor bastards. Three dead men, one lad of maybe fifteen. That woman we saw first. And the child she was carrying, of course."

"That's all? I mean, a farm this big—usually there's a couple of families, working it."

"I know." Yraen muttered something foul under his breath before he went on. "I wonder if these bandits maybe took the other women and the children with them."

"We're not close enough to the coast for that." Rhodry joined them. "It doesn't make sense."

"What?" Carra broke in. "What are you talking about?"

"Slaves for the Bardek trade. But the bandits would have to get them all the way down to the sea, avoiding the Westfolk and Deverry men alike on the way. Can't see them bothering."

"Well." Yraen rubbed the side of his face with a gauntleted hand. "They might have wanted the women for—"

"Hold your tongue!" Rhodry hit him on the shoulder. "Look what I found in the dead woman's fingers. She must have grabbed her attacker or suchlike."

He held out a tuft of straw-colored hair, each coarse strand about a foot long.

"Looks like horse hair to me," Yraen said.

Nedd sniffed it, then shook his head in a vigorous no.

"There weren't any hoofprints anywhere near her, but there were boot prints, so I think I'll side with Nedd." Rhodry rubbed the strands between thumb and forefinger. "The fellow might have packed his hair with lime, like the High King does—the old Dawntime way, I mean. It makes your hair turn to straw like this."

"Oh, and I suppose you've been close enough to the king to tell," Yraen muttered.

Rhodry flashed a brief grin, shot through with weariness.

"Let's get out of here." Nedd spoke so rarely that all of them jumped and swirled round to face him. Although he was still pale, his mouth was set in a tight line, and his eyes burned with an expression that Carra could only call fierce. "Tell the gwerbret. We've got to."

"So we should." Rhodry glanced at Otho. "Looks like they headed south, anyway."

"So I told our lady. Can't turn back."

"I'm on for the ride." Carra thought of ancient queens and forced her voice steady. "I say we get to the gwerbret as fast as ever we can."

"Done, then." Rhodry looked up with a toss of his head. "Nedd, can you and Carra each carry one of the dogs? You can sling them over the front of your saddles, if they'll allow it."

Nedd nodded his head to indicate that they would.

"Good. We want to make speed."

That night when they camped, Rhodry and Yraen set a guard with the dogs to help them. It became their pattern: rise early, tend the horses, then ride hard all day, making a late camp and a guarded one, especially once they reached the second stretch of forest, where no one slept much. The dogs were especially nervous, whining and growling, turning their heads this way and that as they rode. When they were allowed down they would trot round and round the horses and look up, every now and then, to growl or bark at the sky. Carra wondered if the raven were following them, somewhere above the sheltering trees. As they traveled steadily north, the land kept rising, and it turned rocky, too, with huge boulders pushing their way through the earth and stunting the black and twisted pines. The muddy track they were following wound and switched back and forth through the jagged hills until Carra wondered if they'd ever reach Cengarn.

Finally, though, on the third day after they'd found the ravaged village, they reached a road, made of felled trees, trimmed into logs and half-buried, side by side in the dirt. At its abrupt beginning stood a stone marker carved with a sunburst and a couple of lines of lettering. Carra was surprised to learn that Rhodry could read.

"Well, we're not far now, twenty miles from Cadmar's city." He laid one finger on the carved sun. "This is his device."

The country here was broken tableland. On the flat the pine forest grew all tangled round with ancient underbrush, like a hedge on either side of the road, only to break suddenly and tumble down a small gulch in a spill of green or reveal huge boulders, heaped and tumbled like a giant's toys. When the sunlight was falling in long and dusty-gold slants through the trees, the road flattened out and straightened. As they traveled along at a steady walk, Carra heard a distant noise ahead of them, went stiff with fear, then realized that it was the sound of a river, racing and tumbling over rock. As the road snaked west, at the end of a leafy tunnel they could see both the river and a blessed token that some kind of human presence lay close at hand. On either side the riverbank had been cleared of trees and underbrush; the rocks out in the water itself had been hauled around and arranged to floor a level if deep-looking ford. But while they were still in the forest's shelter, Rhodry threw up his hand for a halt.

"What's wrong?" Carra said. "Can't we camp here? I'd be so glad to see the sky."

All at once the dogs began growling and squirming so badly that neither Carra nor Nedd could keep them on the saddle. They slithered down and rushed to the head of the line, bristling and snarling on the edge of barks. At their signal Rhodry began yelling at Carra and Nedd to get back into the forest. In a swirl of confusion they did just that, but as Carra looked up reflexively at the sky, she saw the raven flap away. Whistling and yelling, Nedd got the dogs to come to him, but they kept growling. Up ahead Rhodry, Yraen, and Otho peered across the river into the forest on the other side. Nothing moved. It was dead-silent, not the chirp of a bird, not the rustle of a squirrel.

"Ill-omened places, fords," Yraen remarked.

"So they are." Rhodry rose in the stirrups and stared as if he were counting every distant tree. "Think there's someone waiting on the other side?"

"The dogs think there is," Otho put in. "I say we ride upstream."

"Upstream?" Yraen said. "What's upstream?"

"Naught, I suppose. So they won't expect us to go that way."

Rhodry laughed, a little mutter under his breath like a ferret's chortle. Carra went ice-cold. She was going to die. She realized it all at once with a calm clarity: what waited for them across that river was death, and there was no escaping it. They couldn't go back, they couldn't go forward, they might as well cross over to the Otherlands and be done with it. Although she tried to tell the rest of them, when she opened her mouth she simply couldn't speak. Not so much as a gasp came out.

"Well spoken, Otho my old friend," Rhodry said at last. "Let's give it a try. See those boulders up there a ways? Shelter of a sort. But we'd best dismount, I think."

Since the trees thinned out toward the clearing's edge they

could lead their horses, single file, without leaving this imperfect shelter, but they couldn't do it without cracking branches and snapping twigs and setting the underbrush rustling. After some twenty yards the dogs began growling and snarling, anyway, no matter how Nedd tried to hush them.

"They know we're here," Rhodry said to him finally. "Don't trouble yourself about it. But there can't be a lot of them or they'd have rushed us already." He pointed across the river. "Look."

In among the trees at the far side of the clearing on the opposite bank someone or something was moving to follow them, some three or maybe four shapes, roughly man-shaped, that slipped along when they moved and stopped again when they halted.

"Otho," Rhodry said. "You and Nedd take Carra into the trees. We won't fool them, but maybe—"

Carra never learned what he intended. Pressed beyond canine endurance, Thunder suddenly began to bark, then bounded away and raced straight for the river before Nedd could grab him. Just as he burst free of the trees something flashed and hissed in the air: an arrow. Carra flung herself on Lightning to hold him back and screamed as the arrow struck Thunder in the side. Another followed, another, catching him, throwing him to the ground—pinning him to the ground, but still alive he writhed and howled in agony. The horses began to dance and toss their heads in terror. Dead-silent as always Nedd ran.

"Don't!" Rhodry and Yraen screamed it together.

Too late. Nedd reached the dog, flung himself down beside the dying Thunder just as another flight came hissing down, bright death catching the fading sunlight. He never screamed, merely jerked this way and that while the long shafts struck until at last he and Thunder both lay still, the dog cradled in his arms, in the middle of a spreading pool of blood. Carra felt herself sobbing and choking, but in an oddly distant way, as if she stood beside herself and watched this girl named Carra howl and retch until she could barely breathe. Just as distantly she was aware of horses neighing and men cursing and shouting, then the sound of some large animal crashing through the underbrush. All at once Otho grabbed her by the shoulder with one hand and Lightning's collar by the other.

"Move!" he howled. "Run, lass!"

For such a small man he was terrifyingly strong. Half dragged, half stumbling, Carra got herself and the dog into the hollow among the rocks and fell, half spraddled across the whining, growling Lightning. Otho threw himself down beside her. He was cursing a steady stream in some language she'd never heard before.

"Rhodry, Yraen?" she gasped out.

"Right here." Rhodry hunkered down beside her. "Hush, lass. They won't come for us here."

Her tears stopped of their own accord, leaving her face sticky and filthy both. She wiped it best she could on her equally filthy sleeve, then looked around her. In that last panicked dash they had reached the cluster of boulders and what shelter they were going to find. The river ran too deep to cross some yards off to the north; the forest grew thick and tangled to the south; the rocks rose up and melded with a cliff to the west behind them. Ahead and east, they had a clear view of the ford, some distance away, and the dark shape sprawled in the gathering shadows that had once been Nedd and Thunder.

"They can't get round back here without the dog letting us know." It was Yraen, sliding down the rocks behind them. "And they won't get a clear aim to skewer us in here, and we can see them coming if they rush us. Couldn't have been more than ten of them, Rhodry. If they try to squirm in here, on this broken ground, we'll drop them easy."

"True spoken. Think we can hold off a small army? We might have to. I'll wager they're on their way to fetch a few friends."

"Or one or two of them are. I'd say they left a squad behind, some archers, too, in case we take it into our heads, like, to try to cross the river. Huh. Told you there was somewhat wrong with that cursed ford, didn't I?"

"Did I argue with you?"

By then Carra was too spent to be frightened. She leaned back against a rock and looked straight in front of her with eyes that barely saw.

"Is there any water?" she whispered.

"There's not," Otho said. "Nor food, either. The horses bolted."

"Ah, I see. We're still going to die, aren't we?"

No one said a word.

"I only mind because of the baby, really." She needed, suddenly, to make them understand. "It seems so unfair to the poor little thing. It never had a chance to live and now it's going to die. I mean, when it comes to me, I might have died in childbirth anyway, and this is still better than Lord Scraev, but—"

"Hush, my lady!" The words sounded as if someone were tearing them out of Otho under torture. "Ah, ye gods! Forgive me, that ever I should let this happen to you!"

"It's not as if you had any choice in the matter." Carra laid a hand on his arm.

She was shocked to see tears in his eyes. He wiped them vigorously with both hands before he went on.

"As soon as it's dark, I'm going to try creeping through the forest a ways. We can move quiet when we want to, my people. The way those horses were tearing through the brush, a saddlebag or two might have gotten itself pulled free."

"And if there's someone out there?" Yraen said. "Waiting for one of us to try just that?"

Otho merely shrugged. Rhodry was examining the leather pouch he carried at his belt.

"This should hold a little water." He dumped the coins in a long jingle onto the ground. "I think I can reach the river and get back again. I hate to think of our lady going thirsty."

"I'll do it." Otho snatched the pouch from him. "You need to be here. Just in case, like."

In the gathering dusk Otho slipped off, moving silent and surefooted around the rocks. In a few moments, though, they heard him chuckle.

"My lady, come here," he called. "I think you can squeeze through, and there's a nice little stream, there is. Bring the dog, too."

Sure enough, by sliding and cramming herself between two massive boulders, Carra popped out into a flattish opening big enough for her to crouch and Otho to stand upright, where a trickle of water ran down one rock, pooled, then disappeared under an overhang in the general direction of the river. She flung herself down and drank as greedily as the dog beside her, then washed her face. Otho was looking round with a grin of triumph on his face.

"When they come for us, my lady, you can hide in here. We'll draw them off, down toward the ford, say. Once all the shouting's over, you'll have a chance to make your way north to the gwerbret. Not much of a chance, but better than none. If we tie that blasted dog's mouth shut, we can hide him, too, and you'll have company, like, on your journey. I'll die easier, knowing that. Think of the child, my lady. It'll keep you strong."

"I am. It's worth a try, isn't it?"

Yet with the hope fear returned and a grief sharper than any she'd ever known. Otho, Yraen, Rhodry—all dead for her sake? As Nedd already was. Lightning whined, pushing into her lap, reaching up to lick her face and whimper over and over again. She threw her arms around his neck and would have cried, but all her tears were spent.

"Come now, lass, come now." Otho's voice was very soft. "I was only going home to die, anyway, and Rhodry loves death more than he ever loved life, and well, I'm sorry for Yraen, not that you'd best ever tell him that, but then, he made his choice when he took to the long road, and who can argue with Wyrd, anyway, eh? Come now, hush. We'll take them some water and tell them what we've found."

By then a gibbous moon was rising, silvering the river, picking out Nedd's body and the gleam of arrows lying on the grass. Although Carra wished with all her heart that they could bury him and Thunder, too, it seemed too trivial to mention to men who would doubtless lie dead and unburied themselves in the morning. She sat with her back to one of the boulders and stared fixedly in the opposite direction while Otho went back and forth fetching pouches of water for the two silver daggers. All at once she realized that her body had a thing or two that needed attending to, and urgently. Ever since she'd gotten pregnant, it seemed, when she needed to relieve herself there was simply no arguing about it. She got up and slipped away, keeping to the safe shelter of the boulders and broken terrain, to find a private spot.

When she was done she walked a few steps toward the forest and stood looking into the silver-touched shadows. For miles and miles the trees stretched, hiding enemies, maybe, or maybe promising safety. She wondered how far away the rest of the bandits were, and how fast their advance scouts would reach them. They won't attack till dawn, she thought. We've got that long. Out in the shadows something moved. Her heart thudded, stuck cold in her chest; her hands clenched so hard her nails dug into her palms. It seemed that a bird, a strange silvery bird with enormous wings, dropped from the sky and settled deep among the trees.

A trick of moonlight—it had to be a thrown shadow and naught more—but a branch rustled, a tree shivered. Something snapped and stamped. Carra wanted to run, knew she should run, tried to call out, but she was frozen there, ice-cold and stone-still, as something—no, someone—made its way, made his way through the trees—no, her way. A silver-haired woman, wearing men's clothing but too graceful and slender to be a man, stepped out into the clearing. She carried a rough cloth sack in one hand, and at her belt gleamed the pommel of a silver dagger.

"I'm a friend. Where's Rhodry?"

Carra could only raise a hand and gesture mutely toward the boulders. As she led the way back, she could hear the woman following, but she was afraid to turn round and look behind lest the woman disappear. All Rhodry's talk of shape-changers rushed back to her mind and hovered like a bird, half-seen in moonlight.

In among the broken rocks they found the men sitting in a circle, heads together, talking in low voices about the coming battle, if one could call it that. Carra suddenly realized that she could see them clearly, could pick out the expressions on their faces as they looked up startled. Only then did she realize that the woman gave off a faint silver light, hovering round her like scent.

"Jill!" Rhodry leapt to his feet and stepped back as if in fear. "Jill. I—ye gods! Jill!"

"That's the name my father gave me, sure enough. Come along, all of you! We've got to get out of here and right now."

"But those guards, they've got archers . . ." Yraen let his voice trail away.

"Who no longer matter at all." Jill glanced Otho's way. "Hurry! Get up!"

Lightning sprang up at the command and Otho followed more slowly, grumbling to himself.

"Good." Jill glanced her way. "You've got guts, lass. You *are* Carramaena, aren't you?"

"I am. But how did—"

"Someone told me. No time to explain. Let's get out of here. I can't deal with a whole pack of raiders, and they're on their way. Rhodry, get up here with me. Yraen, take the rear guard with Carra. Otho, keep a hand on that dog's collar, will you? I don't want him bolting."

As they picked their way through the broken rocks and headed downstream toward the ford, Jill pulled a little ahead. Carra could see her looking around, frowning every now and then and biting her lower lip as a person will when they're trying to remember something. Daft though this exercise seemed, Carra could pay no attention, because they were walking straight toward the ford where Nedd and Thunder lay. She could hear Lightning whining and Otho's reassuring whisper, and she clung to the sound as if to someone's hand. When they reached the bodies, she turned her head away and stared across the river. Something was moving among the trees. Even in the poor light she—they all—could see the underbrush shaking at the approach of someone or something.

"Keep walking," Jill snapped. "You have to trust me. Keep walking straight ahead."

No one hesitated, everyone moved, striding forward even though Carra suspected that they were all waiting for the hiss of an arrow, flying them their deaths. They walked a few feet, and a few more, and on and on, until Carra suddenly realized that they should have been wading right into the water instead of walking on dry land. All around her trees towered. The men began to swear in a string of foul curses.

"By every god!" Yraen snarled. "How did you manage that?"

"None of your cursed affair, silver dagger," Otho broke in.

"We're across, aren't we? That's all that matters, and I for one am not going to be flapping my lips at a dweomerwoman."

Only then did Carra realize that the river lay behind them—far behind them, out of sight, in fact. All she could hear was the merest rustle and murmur of distant water flowing over rock.

"Our friends can wait in ambuscade all they like," Jill remarked. "And poke around in the rocks as if they were hunting badgers, too, when the dawn rises, but we'd best be on our way."

Carra turned for one last look back.

"Farewell, Nedd, and it aches my heart to lose you. I only wish I could build you a cairn."

"Nicely spoken." Rhodry laid a comforting hand on her shoulder. "But truly, I doubt me if it matters to his soul, and the gods all know that we might be seeing him in the Otherlands soon enough."

With Jill hissing at them to hurry, they headed into the forest, picking their way along a deer track that ran east and downstream. In the middle of the line of march Carra stumbled along, shivering and exhausted, praying to the Goddess every now and then to keep the unborn baby safe, for what seemed like hours, though when they finally stopped she realized that the moon was still riding close to zenith. There in a clearing stood all their horses, their gear still intact, even Nedd's.

"How did you . . ." Rhodry said.

"The Wildfolk collected them," Jill interrupted him with a wave of her hand. "And brought them round by the other ford."

Carra giggled, thinking she was having a jest on them.

"And how did you find us?" Rhodry went on.

"There's no time for talk now. Listen, you're going to have to ride as fast as these poor beasts can carry you. I can't just take you to the city, because of the way time would run all wrong. You need to arrive straightaway, not weeks from now, you see."

Carra didn't see, and she was willing to wager that none of the others did, either, but oddly enough, not one question got itself asked.

"Follow the river back to the road, and then make all the speed you can," Jill went on. "The forest peters out about ten miles north of the river, and then you come to farming country, and finally to the gwerbret's town. I wish to all the gods that you'd been coming from the east. You'd have been safe, then—it's settled country all the way."

"My humble apologies, my fair sorceress." Rhodry made her a mocking sort of bow. "But if you'd been good enough to appear and warn us that we'd be set upon by bandits, I'd have—"

"Not bandits. But there's no time. Get to Gwerbret Cadmar. Tell him you met up with the raiders, and tell him you're a friend of mine."

"Aren't you coming with us?" Otho broke in.

"Not exactly." She allowed herself a brief smile. "But I'll be there soon enough."

Carra remembered the bird, dropping gracefully from the silver sky, and shuddered.

"My lady, you must be half-frozen," Otho said. "Let me get your cloak."

Once she was mounted and wrapped in the heavy wool cloth, Carra turned to say farewell to Jill only to find her already gone, slipped off into the forest, apparently, when none of them were looking. But all during that long and miserable ride down the wooden road, Carra would look up every now and then to see or think she saw a bird-shape sailing in the moonlight, high above them as if it were on guard.

The rest of the ride as well crossed over into that mental land where everything could be either real or dream. At times she drowsed, once so dangerously that Otho woke her with a shout; he grabbed the reins from her and led her horse along after that. At other times she felt that she'd never been so wide-awake in her life. She would see some detail of the forest around them, a spill of moonlight on a branch, say, or a carved stone slab rising out of a clearing, so plainly and precisely that the image seemed burned into her consciousness to last forever. Yet, when she would try to place that image into a context, she would realize that she'd been half-asleep again and for miles.

Toward dawn they stumbled free of the forest to the relative safety of open and cultivated land, a roll of ripening wheat over long downs, striped green with pastures where white cows with rusty-red ears were lurching to their feet in the brightening sun. A few more miles brought them to a spiral of earthwork walls enclosing a round, thatched farmhouse. Much to Yraen's surprise, Otho—Rhodry's coin still lay in the dirt among the boulders— spent some of his precious coin to get a hot meal for them all. The farm wife, a stout woman missing half her teeth, clucked over Carra and brought her a steaming cup of herbed water.

"To warm your innards, like. You look to me like you need to sleep, lass."

"I do, truly, but we've got to get to the gwerbret. On top of everything else, I'm with child, you see."

"Well, may the Goddess bless you!" The woman smiled, all brown stumps but good humor. "Your first, is it?"

"It is. Well, if I don't lose the poor little thing, anyway, or die myself or something."

"Now, now, don't you worry. I've had six myself, lass, and don't you go listening to them ever-so-fine town ladies, moaning and groaning about how much pain they felt and all that. Why, no reason for it to be so bad, say I! My first one, now, he did give me a bit of trouble, but with our last, our Myla that is, I had her in the morning and was out digging turnips that night."

Late that day, when the horses were stumbling weary and Carra herself so tired that she felt like sobbing aloud, they wound their way past one last farm and saw the rough stone walls of Cengarn, Gwerbret Cadmar's city, circling round to enclose three hills. Above the walls, she could see roofs and towers climbing up the slopes; at the rocky crest of the highest hill a tall stone broch rose in a flutter of gold-colored pennants. As they rode up, they found a river flowing out through a stone arch, guarded by a portcullis, in the walls. Although Rhodry and Yraen had been worrying about the sort of reception they'd get, at the city gates the guards hailed them with an urgent friendliness.

"Silver daggers, are you? Is that young woman with you her ladyship Carramaena of the Westlands?"

"Well, I'm Carramaena, sure enough." Carra urged her horse a little forward. "How do you know—"

"Your husband's waiting for you up in the dun, my lady. Come along, if you please. I'll escort you there straightaway."

Although the men dismounted to spare the horses their weight on the steep slopes, Rhodry insisted that Carra ride whether Gwerlas was tired or no, and she was too exhausted, shivering with worry about her unborn child, to argue with him. As the guard led them along, she clung to the saddle peak with both hands and barely noticed the crowds of curious townsfolk who scurried out of their way. Their route took them round and about, looping round half the town it seemed, yet always leading them higher and higher, up to the gwerbret's dun.

Even though it was a rough sort of place at that time, Cengarn was already the strangest city in all Deverry, as much green with trees and gardens as gray with stone. At first glance the round, thatched houses, set randomly on curving streets, seemed ordinary enough, but here and there on the flanks of the steep hillsides little alleys led to huge wooden doors set right into the slopes themselves. Not only did the river, spanned by a dozen wooden bridges, wind through the valley between the hills, but right in the center of town a tiny waterfall cascaded down the steepest slope of all. Their escort pointed it out with a certain pride.

"There's a spring up in the citadel," he remarked. "Cursed handy thing for a siege."

"And more than passing strange," Rhodry said. "A spring at the top of a hill like that, I mean."

The guard merely winked and grinned in a hint of secrets.

The dun itself was all carved stone and slate tiles, set behind a second rise of walls and gates of oak bound with iron. At the entrance to the main tower, Carra allowed Rhodry to help her dismount—in fact, she nearly fell into his arms. As she stood there, trying to collect her energy for the last little walk into the broch, she heard an elven voice yelling her name and looked up to see Dar, racing toward her with an escort of ten men of the Westfolk trailing after. In the sun his dark hair gleamed, flecked with bluish highlights like a raven's wing. *He never goes anywhere alone,* was her muddled thought. *I should have known he was a prince because of that.*

Lightning leapt in between them and growled, tail rigid, ears flat.

"It's all right." Carra caught the dog's attention and signaled him back to her side. "He's a friend."

Dar laughed, striding forward, throwing his arms tight around her, and she could think of nothing but him.

"Oh, my love, oh, my heart!" He was stammering and weeping and laughing in a vast confusion of feeling. "Thank the gods you're safe. Thank the gods and the dweomer both! I've been such a dolt, such an imbecile! Can you ever forgive me?"

"What for?" She looked up, dazed by the flood of words, ensorcelled by warmth and safety.

"I never should have left you for a moment. I'll never forgive myself for making you ride after me like this. I should have known your pig-faced Round-ear of a brother would try to marry you off."

"Well, I didn't let him. Please, Dar, I've got to sit down. Can't I forgive you and all that later?"

He picked her up like a child and carried her toward the door, but she fell asleep in his arms long before he reached it.

As soon as Dar appeared in the doorway to the great hall with Carra in his arms and Lightning trotting faithfully behind, a flurry of womenfolk sprang up like a whirlwind and surrounded them, blew them away in a storm of practical chatter. Rhodry stood at the foot of the spiral staircase and watched Dar carry her up, the elven lad as surefooted as a goat on a sloped stone roof as he navigated the turns. After him went the women, the elderly serving women puffing and talking all in the same breath, the gwerbret's lady giving calm orders.

"Silver dagger?" A page appeared at his elbow. "His grace wants to speak to you."

"What about our horses?"

"Oh, the stable lad's taken them already. Don't worry. They'll get plenty to eat and a good grooming. The gwerbret's a truly generous man."

To prove his point the page led them straight to the table of honor, where a serving lass brought them ale and a big basket of bread. While they were stuffing that in, a platter of cold roast pork appeared to go with it. Yraen and Otho ate steadily and fiercely, like men who wonder if they'll ever eat as well again, but Rhodry, hungry though he was, picked at the food and sipped the ale sparingly. He was preternaturally awake, drawn as fine and sharp as a steel wire from his hunger and the danger of the night just past, and for a little while he wanted to stay that way. He slewed round on the bench and considered the circular great hall, the entire ground floor of the gwerbret's broch. On one side, by a back door, stood enough tables for a warband of well over a hundred men; at the hearth, near the table of honor itself, were five more for guests and servitors. On the floor lay a carpet of fresh braided rushes. The walls and the enormous hearth were made of a pale tan stone, all beautifully worked and carved. Never had Rhodry seen a room with so much fine stonework, in fact: huge panels of interlacement edged the windows and were set into the walls alternately with roundels of spirals and fantastic animals, and an entire stone dragon embraced the hearth, its head resting on its paws, planted on the floor, its winged back forming the mantel, and its long tail curling down the other side.

"Nice bit of work, that," Otho said with his mouth full.

"The dragon? It is. Did one of your people carve it?"

"No doubt." Otho paused for a long swallow of ale. "Think our lady's in safe hands?"

"I do. Jill told us to bring her here, didn't she?"

"True. Huh. I suppose she knows what she's doing."

"Ye gods!" Yraen looked up from his steady feeding. "You *suppose* she knows . . . the woman's a blasted sorcerer, isn't she? Ye gods! Isn't that enough for you?"

"Why should it be? The question is, is she a competent sorcerer?"

"After the way she carried us across the river, I'd say she is."

"Well, maybe. Hum, you've got to realize that I've known her ever since she was a little lass, and it's hard to believe that sweet little child's up and grown into a—"

"Hold your tongues, both of you!" Rhodry broke in. "Here comes his grace."

Even though he limped badly on a twisted right leg, Gwerbret Cadmar was an imposing man, standing well over six feet tall, broad in the shoulders, broad in the hands. His slate-gray hair and mustaches bristled; his face was weather-beaten and dark; his eyes gleamed a startling blue under heavy brows. As he sat down, he looked over Rhodry and Yraen for a moment, then turned to Otho.

"Good morrow, good sir, and welcome to my humble dun. I take it that you're passing through on the way to your homeland."

Yraen choked on his ale and sputtered.

"I am at that, Your Grace," Otho said. "But I'll beg your leave to spend a while in your town. I have to send letters to my kin, because I've been gone for many a long year now, and I've got no idea if I'm welcome or not."

"A family matter, then?"

"It was, truly, and I'd prefer not to speak of it unless your grace requires me to do so."

"Far be it from me to pry into the affairs of another man's clan. But by all means, good sir, make yourself welcome in my town. No doubt you'll find an inn to suit you while you wait."

Yraen recovered himself and stared at Otho in an angry bafflement.

"Now, silver daggers," the gwerbret went on. "I owe you thanks for bringing the lady Carramaena safely here. No doubt the prince will reward you with something a bit more useful than mere thanks."

"Prince?" Yraen snapped. "Your Grace, you mean he really is a prince?"

"Of course he is." Cadmar favored him with a brief smile. "And his good favor's important to all of us here on the border, I might add. I don't have the land to raise horses. No one does in these wretched hills. If the Westfolk didn't come here to trade we'd all be walking to battle soon enough."

"One up for you, Rhodry. I'll admit I didn't believe you when you started talking about elven princes and suchlike."

"Maybe it'll teach you to listen to your betters. Your Grace, I've somewhat to tell you. One of the southern villages was destroyed by raiders, and we were nearly killed on the road here."

All attention, the gwerbret leaned forward to listen as Rhodry told the tale of their ride north and the ambush by the ford. When it came to their escape, though, Rhodry hesitated, wondering how he was going to hide the dweomer in it.

"How did you get out of that little trap, silver dagger?"

"Well, Your Grace, this is the strangest bit of all, and I'll beg your grace to believe me, because truly, if it hadn't happened to me, I wouldn't believe it myself."

"Ah. Jill got you out of it, did she?"

It was Rhodry's turn for the surprise. He stared open-mouthed, searching for words, while Cadmar laughed at him, a grim sort of mutter under his breath.

"She showed up here last fall, just in time to save this leg." The gwerbret laid one hand on his twisted thigh. "The chirurgeon was going to cut it off, but our traveling herbwoman makes him stay his hand and then, by the gods! if she doesn't go and cure the fever in the blood and set the thing in such a way as I can actually walk. Not well, truly, but it's better than stumbling around on a wooden stump. And so needless to say, I was inclined to treat her generously. All she wanted was a little hut out in the wilderness, and I was more than glad to give her that and all the food she could eat and wood for warmth as well. She's done many a fine thing for my folk over the winter. And of course, they all say she's got the dweomer, and truly, I've seen enough now to believe it myself."

"Well, Your Grace, I think she does, because she got us clear of the raiders and got us our horses back as well, and then she told us to come and tell you our tale. And so we have."

Nodding a little, Cadmar leaned back in his chair and looked out over the hall. Off at their side his warband sat drinking in silence, straining to hear the story that these strangers were telling their lord.

"And did she say when she'd return to my dun?"

"She didn't, Your Grace."

"Imph, well." Cadmar thought for a long moment. "Well, silver daggers, we'll wait the day, at least. You need to sleep, and I've got to summon my vassals. Then we're riding out after these bastards. Want a hire?"

"Never have I been so glad of one, Your Grace."

"Me, too," Yraen broke in. "I can still see that village in my mind, like, and that poor woman we found."

"Pregnant, was she?" Cadmar turned to him.

"She was, Your Grace, and murdered."

Cadmar winced.

"They've been doing that, you see. Killing the women with child. It's almost as if . . . well, it sounds ridiculous, but it's almost as if that's why they're here, to kill all the women carrying children. Every now and then one of the survivors heard things, you see. A lad who managed to hide under an overturned wagon told me he heard two of them say somewhat like: time to ride on, we've gotten all the breeding sows in this pen."

Rhodry went sick cold, thinking of Carra.

"And who are they, Your Grace?" Yraen said.

"A band of marauders. Men like you and me, not Westfolk or dwarves. All the survivors have been clear as clear about that. They appeared last summer, started raiding the outlying farms. Bandits, think I, starving and desperate. We tried to track them down. That's where I took this wound." Reflexively he rubbed his thigh. "The bastards got away from us that time, but they didn't come back. I thought I'd scared them off, but with the spring they showed up and worse than ever. I doubt me very much if they're ordinary bandits. They're too cursed clever, for one thing. And they've got good weapons, good armor, and they've been trained to fight as a unit."

"Not bandits at all, then, Your Grace," Rhodry said. "They must have some kind of a leader. I don't suppose any of the survivors got a look at him."

"One or two think they might have. An enormously tall man, they say, all wrapped in a dark blue cloak with the hood well up, giving orders in an odd growl of a voice. All they saw clear like was his hands, huge hands with hair on the backs, and they swear up and down that he only had three fingers on each of them."

Some fragment of lore pricked in Rhodry's mind and made his blood run cold. He was too tired to remember exactly why, but he somehow knew that those missing fingers meant something, meant a great deal, and none of it good.

"You're dropping where you sit, silver daggers," Cadmar said with a grin. He hauled himself to his feet and motioned toward his warband. "Maen, Dwic, get over here. Find these silver daggers bunks and some clean blankets." He turned to Otho. "Good sir, would you care for an escort into town?"

"If you could spare a lad to show me the way to an inn, Your Grace, I'd be grateful."

Yraen stared goggle-eyed as a page appeared to play servant to the dwarf and lead him away. At the door Otho turned and honored them with a cheery wave. It was the first time Rhodry had ever seen him grin.

"Well, I never!" Yraen hissed. "By all the gods and a rat's ass, too!"

"I told you that anyone rich enough to hire us must be some sort of a personage, didn't I now?"

Yraen was in for one more surprise. As they were leaving the hall, they passed the table where Daralanteriel's escort was sitting, though Dar himself seemed to be lingering with his lady upstairs. At the sight of Rhodry all of the men leapt up, yelling his name, mobbing him round, slapping him on his back, and talking as fast as they could and all in Elvish. Rhodry answered in the same; as tired as he was, he was near to tears just from hearing that musical tongue again.

"And Calonderiel," he said at length. "How is he?"

"As mean and stubborn as ever," one of the archers said, grinning. "If he'd known you were on your way here, he'd have ridden east with us, I'm sure."

Rhodry started to make some jest, then saw Yraen, watching all of this with his mouth hanging open. The gwerbret's man seemed more than a little surprised himself.

"I'd best go," Rhodry said to the archers. "I'll come drink with you all later."

When Rhodry extricated himself and rejoined him, Yraen started to speak, then merely shrugged and looked heavenward, as if reproaching the gods.

"Well, come along, then," Rhodry said. "No use in just standing here, is there? Let's go see what our new lord's barracks are like."

Quite decent, as it turned out. Made of good oak and freshly whitewashed, the barracks stood on top of the stables and up against the dun wall in the usual style. The bunks were solid, the mattresses new, and Maen issued them both good quality blankets.

"The gwerbret must be a grand man to ride for," Rhodry said. "If he'll treat a silver dagger this well."

"He is." Maen, a pale slip of a lad, stood for a moment looking them over. "Well, we need every man we can get now."

Yraen growled under his breath, but Rhodry stepped in front of him.

"Thanks for your help. We'll just be getting some sleep."

Maen shrugged and slouched out of the room. Yraen ostentatiously spit onto the straw-strewn floor.

"I always warned you about the long road, didn't I?" Rhodry suddenly yawned and flopped down on the edge of his bunk to pull off his boots. "Ye gods, I just realized somewhat. Otho never paid us."

"Little bastard! Well, we'll have it out of his pockets or his hide. Either one's fine with me. Rhodry, those men. The prince's escort, I mean. Uh, they're not human, are they."

It was not a question.

"They're not, truly. Do you remember years and years ago, when we first met, and we talked one night about seeing things that weren't there?"

"And Mael the Seer's book, and the way he was always mentioning elves. I do. It aches my heart to admit it, but I do."

"Well, then, I don't need to say a cursed lot more, do I now?"

Yraen merely sighed for a no and busied himself with making up his bunk. Rhodry lay down, wrapped himself in his blankets, and fell asleep before he even heard Yraen start snoring.

When he woke, the barracks were pitch-dark and empty, but Jill was sitting on the end of his bunk. Her he could see in the silver cloud clinging to her, an ever-shifting light that hinted of half-seen forms. He stifled a yelp of surprise and sat up.

"My apologies," she said. "I didn't mean to startle you."

"It'd give any man a turn, seeing a woman he once loved and all that glowing like the moon. Ye gods, Jill, are you a ghost or suchlike?"

"Close to it." She paused to smile at him. "But spirits from the Otherlands can't set broken legs and suchlike, so you can lay your troubled heart to rest. I'm real enough. The light's only the Wildfolk of Aethyr. I'm surprised you can't see them. They've taken to following me around, and most times I don't have the heart to shoo them away."

"Well, I can see somewhat moving there, sure enough. It still creeps my flesh."

Here he at last had the leisure to take a good look at her. Her hair, cropped off like a lad's as usual, had gone perfectly white, and her face was thin, too thin, really, as he studied her, so that her eyes seemed enormous, dominating her face the way a child's do. Overall, in fact, she was shockingly thin, and quite pale, yet she hardly seemed weak. It was as if her skin and blood and bone had all been replaced by some finer substance, some magical element halfway between glass and silver, say, or some sort of living silk.

"Have you been ill or suchlike?" Rhodry said.

"Very ill. In the islands it was, what they call the shaking fever. I've had it a number of times, now, and there's no guarantee that I'm rid of it, either. They say that once it gets into your blood, it's yours for life."

"That aches my heart."

"Not half as much as it aches mine." She grinned with a flash of her old good humor. "I must look hideously old, I suppose."

"You don't look truly *here*. It's like you've already left us for the Otherlands or suchlike."

"In a way, perhaps, I have."

"Ah. You know, you look like Nevyn used to. I mean, you'd think he was old, truly, and then he'd speak or do somewhat, and you'd know it no longer mattered in the least how old he was."

She nodded, considering what he'd said.

"But here, where's Yraen? And is the lass safe and well?"

"Safe, she is, and Labanna—that's the gwerbret's lady—tells me she'll be back to her old self in a day or so. I was truly worried about that child she's carrying, but the womenfolk say she's not far enough along to lose it just from being tired and cold and suchlike. As for Yraen, he's eating his dinner in the great hall. I came out to fetch you."

Yawning and stretching, he found his boots and put them on.

"By the way, about Yraen," he said. "Do you know who he really is?"

"Of course. Don't you?"

"Some son of a noble house who went daft and ran off some years back, but I don't know his real name, no."

She laughed with a toss of her head.

"Well, then, maybe it'll come back to you, sooner or later."

"What? Are you telling me that I used to know him or suchlike?"

"Well, not to say 'know' him, not intimately or some such thing. You weren't in any position to make a friend out of him."

"Jill, curse it all! I'm as sick as I can be of dweomer riddles!"

"Indeed? Then what do you want to know?"

"For a start, how did you know where I was?"

"I scried you out, of course. In the fire and water."

Rhodry felt profoundly foolish.

"Ah, curse it! Let's just go to the great hall. I want some ale, I do, and the darker the better."

"What? No more answers?"

She was smiling as if she might be teasing him, daring him, even, to ask her the questions that suddenly frightened him, no matter how badly he'd ached to know them before.

"Just one thing. Our Yraen? Does he have royal blood in his veins?"

"He does, at that, but he's a long, long way from the throne, the youngest son of a youngest son. The kingdom won't miss him. I'm glad you decided to pledge him to the silver dagger and let him follow his Wyrd."

"I decided? Since when have I had one wretched chance at deciding anything, whether for me or some other man?"

"Well, that's a fair complaint." She laid a hand, as light as the touch of a bird's wing, onto his arm. "You've been thrown about like a shipwrecked man at sea, haven't you? But I think me that the land's in sight at last. Let's go join the others." She stood up. "Cadmar's having somewhat of a council of war, and I've told him he should include you in it. And you shouldn't be sleeping out here in the barracks, either."

"Why not? It's good enough."

"That's not the point. I might need you to watch over Carra."

"Oh, here! Dar's with her and twenty fighting men as well."

"But they haven't seen the dweomer workings you have or lived through some of your battles, either. Rhoddo, don't try to tell me that you haven't realized there's dweomer at work here."

"Very well, then, I won't, though I will say that I'd hoped I was wrong. Do you know what these raiders want?"

"I've got an idea, but I'm hoping it's a wrong one. I'd like to think it was only gold and slaves, but I have my doubts."

"They're not trying to kill Carra, are they?"

Jill winced.

"Her child, actually. Someone's threatened to, anyway."

"Who? We should tell the gwerbret, and he can drag the culprit to justice."

"This culprit lives where the gwerbret can't ride, but I doubt if I can explain."

"Ye gods, I'm sick of being treated like a simpleton!"

"My apologies, Rhoddo, but the sad truth of the thing is, I don't understand it all myself. This being lives—well, wait, you've met Dallandra, and so you know a bit of it already. She has an enemy who—"

"Alshandra! Am I right? The Guardian who drove me from the grasslands."

"The very one. She's sworn to kill Carra."

"Crazed, isn't she? Alshandra, I mean. She scared the wits out of me, babbling of her daughter and saying someone was trying to steal her away."

"Oddly enough, she was right. Carra and Dar have done just that, not that they meant to. But I don't know if these raiders are connected with Alshandra, or just some other evil come upon the land. Until I find that out, it's hard to know exactly what to do."

"That makes sense. Can't fight an enemy when you don't know his resources and allegiances."

"Exactly." Jill laid her hand upon his arm. "I'm glad you're here, I truly am. Great things are on the move. Carra's Wyrd, your Wyrd—the Wyrd of the elven folk, too, maybe. I don't know the all of it yet."

"I see." Not, of course, that he did. "Do you want to know another odd thing? That dog of Carra's? Perryn gave him to her."

Jill swore like a silver dagger under her breath.

"You know, that's one of those little things that can mean a great deal, when you're dealing with omens. So Perryn's had a hand in this, has he?"

"Well, he sacrificed more than a dog, truly. That lad lying dead at the ford? That was his grandson. He was more than a bit simple, but it wrung my heart when he died."

"No doubt." Her voice turned sad. "Poor lad! Well, you'll have your chance to avenge him on the morrow. Cadmar's leading his men out with the dawn."

"Good. If we strip the dun of men, will Carra be safe? Well, that's no doubt a stupid question! Here we are, in the middle of a city."

"Not stupid at all. That's what I mean about your instincts, Rhoddo. True, an army couldn't get at her here with the town gates shut, but a traitor might. I'm taking her to stay with Otho till the warband returns. Now, *there* she'll be safe." She hesitated briefly. "I don't suppose you'd stay with her."

"If you order me to, I will, but I want revenge, I do. For Nedd and those villagers both."

She considered, straying to a stop in the dark ward. Ahead the broch loomed against the sky and spilled light out of its windows along with laughter and talk, a familiar scene, a familiar sound, yet with Jill there, Rhodry felt as if he'd walked through an invisible door into another world.

"Well, go with the gwerbret, then," she said at last. "I want someone reliable to keep a watch over Dar, too. He's bound and determined to take his men and ride with the warband, and I don't much care to lose him, either."

"Then I'll keep an eye out for him. I must say I don't mind having archers along. Come in cursed handy, they will, if we can find these swine."

"Oh, I've set the Wildfolk looking for them, and I'll be along, as well. We'll find them. Don't trouble your heart about that."

About an hour before dawn, Carra was sitting on the edge of her bed, wearing a pair of silk dresses that were a gift from the gwerbret's lady, when Jill came to fetch her. Lightning thumped his tail in greeting as the older woman opened the door.

"You're not all silver and glowy," Carra said.

"So I'm not. That was beginning to be a bit of a nuisance, though sometimes it comes in handy, I must admit. How are you feeling?"

"Very well, actually. I'm still tired. I probably could have slept for days if her grace hadn't woken me."

"Most like. Carra, there's somewhat I wanted to ask you, not that you have to answer, mind. How did you meet Dar?"

"At the horse market near my brother's dun, well over a year ago it was now. He and his people rode in to trade, and I happened to be there with my brother. And he made this horrid jest—my brother, I mean, not Dar—he asked one of the Westfolk men if he'd take me in trade for a horse. And when my brother laughed, Dar came striding up and told him that he wouldn't sell him the geldings he wanted. And my brother got mad as mad and swore at him, demanding to know why, like." Carra grinned at the memory. "And Dar said that any man who'd be so cruel to his sister would probably beat his stock half to death. Which wasn't true, mind. My brother's a grand man round his horses. But anyway, later that day, when I was wandering round alone at the fair, Dar came up to me, and we got to talking."

"Ah, I see." Jill smiled briefly. "Love at first sight?"

"Oh, not at all. I was grateful to him, but he had to court me all summer before I fell in love with him. You see, Jill, he's the first man I've ever met who wanted me, not my brother's favor or some alliance. Of course, Lord Scraev was lusting after me, too, but he's so awful, and the way his mouth smells!" She shuddered at the memory. "But even if my brother had found some decent man for my husband, he still would have asked about the dowry. I don't think Dar even knows what a dowry is, and I doubt me if he'd care if he did."

"I agree with you, truly. Trade you for a horse—the stinking gall! Well, now, it's time we got on our way. Get your cloak. Otho should be waiting for us. I sent him a messenger last night."

The great hall was filled with armed men, gobbling bread and downing a last tankard of ale while they stood or sat in quiet packs. Up at the table of honor the gwerbret and two noble lords —vassals, no doubt—were huddled together, squinting at a map by the leaping firelight. Dar detached himself from the group and came over, signaling to ten of his escort to follow. He favored Jill with a respectful bow.

"Good morning, my love," he said to Carra. "I see you've got the dog with you. Good. He'll be the best sentinel you and the dwarves can have."

"I'm sure I'll be fine. Dar, you will be careful, won't you? It'd break my heart to lose you, you know."

He merely laughed, tossing his head, his hair as dark as Loc Drw in winter, and caught her by the shoulders to kiss her.

With Dar and his men for guards, they left the dun and hurried through the twisting streets of Cengarn. Here and there a crack of candlelight gleamed through wooden shutters, or firelight glittered in a hearth, half-seen through an open door, but mostly the town lay wrapped in its last hour of sleep before the gray dawn broke. They trotted downhill for a bit, then cut sideways through an alley between two roundhouses, panted uphill again, turned down and to the left past a little stream in a stone culvert, crossed a bridge and walked across a grassy common, soaked with dew. When Carra glanced uphill, she found the gwerbret's dun much farther away than seemed possible and gave up trying to figure out their route. At last they came to a hillside so steep it was half a cliff. Set right into it, between two stunted little pines, stood a wooden door with big iron hinges. Otho was waiting with a candle-lantern.

"Come in, come in, my lady. It gladdens my heart to see you, and my thanks for taking our humble hospitality. Don't you worry, Jill. No one'll get near the lass with us to guard her."

"I've no doubt of it, and my thanks to you."

Carra gave Dar one last kiss, felt her eyes fill with tears, and clung to him, so reluctant to let him go that her heart sank with dread. All she could think was that the Goddess was giving her an omen of coming disaster.

"Please be careful, my love. Promise me you'll be careful."

"As careful as I can be. I promise." Gently yet firmly he pried himself free of her arms. "Here, I'll have my own men with me, and Rhodry ap Devaberiel as well, and if somewhat happens to me in the middle of all of them, well, then, it's my Wyrd and there's not one blasted thing anyone can do about it."

"I know." She forced the tears back and made herself smile. "Then kill a lot of bandits, will you? I keep thinking about that poor woman."

"I'll promise you twice for that, my love. Farewell, and I'll see you the moment we ride home."

In the brightening dawn he strode off, his men trailing after, while she waved farewell and kept the smile on her face by sheer force of will as long as he might turn back and see. Otho cleared his throat, then blew out the candle in his lantern with a thrifty puff.

"We'd best be getting in. Town's waking up."

"Just so," Jill said. "Very well, and, Carra, try not to worry. I'll be traveling with the warband, you know."

"I didn't, and truly, that does gladden my heart."

Jill strode off uphill, her tattered brown cloak swirling about her, and turned once to wave before she disappeared among the houses. Something drifted free of the cloth, a thing as pale as a moonbeam, and floated up in the rising wind. Without thinking Carra darted forward and snatched it: a silver-gray feather, about a foot long. She gaped at it while Otho muttered under his breath and Lightning whined, as if agreeing with the dwarf.

"My lady, we really must get in off this street."

"Of course, Otho, my apologies. But this feather! It's really true, isn't it? She really can turn herself into a bird."

"Well, so she can. You didn't realize that? Humph, what are they teaching you young folk these days, anyway? Now let's get inside where it's safe."

Carra tucked the feather into her kirtle, then hurried after him through the wooden door.

"Inside" turned out to be a tunnel, made of beautifully worked stone blocks, that led deep into the hill. Here and there on small ledges, about six feet from the ground, heaps of fungus in baskets gave off a bluish glow and lit their way. The air, startlingly cool, blew around them in fresh drafts. After a couple of hundred yards, they came at last to a round chamber, some fifty feet across, scattered with low tables and tiny benches round a central open hearth, where a low fire burned and a huge kettle hung from a pair of andirons and a crossbar. Automatically Carra glanced up and saw the smoke rising to a stone flue set in the ceiling, and there were a number of other vents up there, too, that seemed to be the sources of the fresh air. Three doorways in the walls opened to other tunnels leading deeper into the inn. At one of the tables, two men, a little shorter than Otho but younger, muscle-bound, and heavily armed, sat yawning and nodding over metal cups of some sort of drink.

"Everyone else is abed," Otho said. "But I was tired enough when I finally got here yesterday to sleep the night away."

He turned and spoke to the two men in still another language that Carra had never heard before. Both jumped up and bowed to her, then spoke in turn.

"They're the guards for this watch, my lady. Just finishing their breakfast and all. Now, you have a seat over here by the wall. I'll fetch you somewhat to eat."

Next to a wooden chest, Carra found a wooden chair with a cushioned seat and a proper back, a low piece, but comfortable. With a canine sigh Lightning flopped down at her feet and laid his head on his front paws. Otho bustled at the hearth, came back with a bowl of porridge, laced with butter, and a hunk of bread, then bustled off again to fetch a tankard of milk sweetened with a little honey.

"Jill says you should be having plenty of milk, for the child, you see," he said.

While Carra ate, Otho opened the chest beside her and pawed through it, finally bringing out a miscellaneous clutch of things—two oblong wooden trays, a sack that seemed to be filled with sand, some pointed sticks, a bone object that looked like a small comb—and arranged them on the table. The pale white river sand got itself poured into the trays; he used the comb to smooth it out as flat as parchment. With a stick he drew lines on one surface from corner to corner to divide the tray into four triangles. Then, on the outer edges, that is, the bottom of each triangle, he found the midpoint and connected those, overlaying a diamond on the triangles so that the entire surface divided itself into twelve.

"The lands of the map," he announced. "This is how we dwarves get our omens, my lady, and if ever a man needed an omen or two, it's me. See, each one is the true home of a metal. Number one here is iron, two copper, and so on. The fifth is gold, and that stands for a man's art, whether it's the working of stone or of metals, and nine is tin, for our religion, you see, because like tin the gods are cheap things more often than not."

"Otho! What an awful thing to say!"

"Oh, you people can swear by your gods all you want, but it's little good they do for you, for all your sacrificing and chanting and so on. But each land is the home of a metal but the last, number twelve here, right above one, so it all circles back, like. And that one is the home of salt, not a metal at all. And that land stands for all the hidden things in life, feuds and suchlike, and the dweomer."

"This is fascinating. How do you tell fortunes with it?"

"Watch. I'll show you."

Otho took the second stick, held it over the second tray, then turned his head away and began to poke dots into the sand, as fast as he could. When he was done, he had sixteen lines of dots and spaces to mull over.

"Now, these are the mothers, these lines. You take the first lines of each to form the first daughter, and the second lines for the second, and so on. I won't bother to explain all the rules. It'd take me all day, and you'd find it tedious, no doubt. But here in the land of iron, we'll put the Head of the Dragon, just for starters." Deftly he poked a figure into the waiting sand, two dots close together and below them three dots vertically for the dragon's body. "And humph, I can't resist looking ahead. Oh, splendid! The Little Luck goes in the land of salt. That gladdens my heart, because it means the omens won't be horrible. They might not be good, mind, but they won't be horrible."

Carra leaned on the table to watch while he muttered to himself in a mix of several languages, brooded over the lines of dots, and one at a time poked corresponding figures in the lands of the map. When he was done he stared at the map for a long time, shaking his head.

"Well, come on, Otho, do tell me what it means."

"Not sure. Humph. That's the trouble with wretched nonsense like telling fortunes. When you need it the most it's the least clear. But it looks like everything'll work out right in the end. You see, I just sent off letters to my kin, asking if I could come home again. I got into a spot of trouble in my youth, but that was . . . well, a good long time ago, let's just say, and I've got some nice little gems that should do to pay a fine or two if they want to levy one." He paused, chewing on the ends of his mustache. "Now, it seems like they'll take me back, but this I don't understand." With the stick he pointed at the third land. "Quicksilver with The Road in it. Usually means a long journey and not one you were planning to make, either. It troubles my heart, it does."

Carra leaned forward for a better look, but The Road was a simple line of four dots and not very communicative.

"It wouldn't just mean the journey you already made, would it? To get here, I mean. I—"

A hiss, a spitting sound like water drops on a griddle—Carra jerked her head up and saw one of the young dwarves, his sword drawn, walking slowly and ever so steadily toward the table. Otho suddenly hissed, as well, an intake of breath.

"Don't move, my lady. Still as stone, that's what we want."

Wrapped in such a false calm that Lightning never barked or moved, the dwarf reached the table, slowly raised his sword, hesitated, then smacked it down blade-flat onto the planks not a foot from Carra's elbow. Carra jerked back just as something under the blade crunched—and spurted with a trickle of pale ooze. The second guard came running and swearing; Otho hurried round the end of the table to look as the young man lifted his blade and turned the crumpled, long-legged creature over with the point. All three men muttered for a moment.

"See that brown mark on what's left of its stomach? Looks like a stemmed cup? We call that the goblet of death." Otho turned to her. "This particular creature's a spider—well, it used to be, I should say. Big as your fist. Poisonous as you could want. Or not want."

"Ych! That's disgusting!" She looked up at the ceiling and shuddered, half expecting to see a whole nest of them ready to drop. "How common are they?"

"They're not common, my lady. You almost never find them in civilized tunnels and suchlike. They're shy, like most wild things. Find 'em hiding under rocks in the high mountains, if you find them at all."

"Then how, I mean, why—" She fell silent, seeing their answer in their faces. "Someone brought it here, didn't they?"

"They did." Otho was staring up at the ceiling. "And whoever dropped it down through one of them vents is long gone, I'll wager. There's another floor up there, a gallery, like, so a workman can get up and clean out the air vents. Anyone could climb up there easy. No one would ever see 'em." He turned and snarled something in Dwarvish at one of the young men, who rushed off. "I'm sending him to get the landlord and wake this place up. If we make a big fuss about it, whoever this was won't dare to make more mischief. Don't you worry, my lady. Safety in numbers and all that."

Carra let go of Lightning's collar and sat down, feeling a little sick as she realized the truth. Someone had just tried to kill her, and she didn't even know why.

Thanks to the support of his vassals, Gwerbret Cadmar led out close to two hundred men that morning, far too many to assemble in the ward of his dun. A long swirl of men and horses spread out through the streets of Cengarn, made their way out several different gates, then re-formed into a warband down on the plain at the base of the city's hills. Although Rhodry and Yraen, silver daggers as they were, expected to ride at the very rear and breathe the army's dust, one of the gwerbret's own men sought them out and grudgingly informed them that they were to ride with his grace.

"It's because of the sorceress, you see. She told our lord that you were the only one who could follow her directions. Cursed if I know what she meant by that."

"No more do I," Rhodry said. "Jill has a fine hand with a riddle, I must say, and so blasted early in the morning, too."

Yet soon enough he found the answer. They followed the rider up to the head of the line of march, where the gwerbret and his lords were sitting on horseback and conferring in low voices. Although Cadmar acknowledged them with a smile and a nod of his head, the two lords, Matyc and Gwinardd, merely looked sour. While they waited for the gwerbret to have time to speak to them, Rhodry glanced idly around, sizing up the men in the warbands. They all had good horses, good weapons, and here and there he spotted men with the confident air of veterans. Off to one side, waiting on horseback for the gwerbret's orders, sat Dar and his archers, each man with his unstrung longbow tucked under his right leg like a javelin and his short, curved hunting bow close at hand on his saddle peak. Rhodry waved to Dar, happened to glance at the sky, and swore aloud. Hovering above was an enormous bird with the silhouette of a hawk but, as far as he could tell by squinting into a bright morning, of a pale silvery color. It also seemed to be carrying something in its talons, a sack, perhaps, of some sort. As he watched it circled and began to drift off toward the west. With a cold certainty he knew that Jill had mastered elven dweomer as well as the lore proper to humankind.

"Your Grace? Your pardon for this interruption, but we're to ride west. Our guide's just arrived."

"Um, indeed?" Cadmar looked up automatically and saw the bird, hovering on the wind some distance off, too far for his human vision to judge its size. "What's that? A trained falcon or suchlike?"

"Just so, Your Grace. Jill always did have a way with animals. No doubt she's riding off somewhere with its lure. Or somewhat like that, anyway."

"Whatever she thinks fit. Well, then, let's ride. My lords, to the west!"

All that morning the hawk led them onward. At times she circled directly overhead, but only for brief moments, as if Jill were ensuring that she had Rhodry's attention. Most of the time it kept so far off that only elven eyes could spot it, but always, in loops and lazy wind drifts, it moved steadily west and down, as the hills round Cengarn fell toward the high plains. Gradually the terrain opened up to rolling hills, scattered with trees at the crests and thick with underbrush in the shallow valleys between. It was good country for bandits, Rhodry thought. They could hide their camps and their loot in among the scrubby brush, keep guards posted on the open crests, and send scouts along them, too, when they wanted to make a raid. He was blasted glad, he decided, that the gwerbret and his men had dweomer on their side in this little game of hide and seek.

As they rode, he had a chance to study the two lords riding just ahead with the gwerbret. Gwinardd of Brin Coc was no more than nineteen, come to the lordship just last year, or so the dun gossip said, on the death of his father from a fever. Brown-haired and bland, he seemed neither bright nor stupid, an ordinary sort of fellow who was obviously devoted to the gwerbret. Matyc of Dun Mawrvelin was another sort entirely. There might well have been some elven blood in his clan's veins, because his hair was a moonlight-pale blond, and his eyes a steel-gray, but he had none of that race's openness or humor. His face, in fact, reminded Rhodry of a mask carved from wood. All day long, he rarely frowned and never smiled, merely seemed to watch and listen to everything around him from some great distance away. Even when the gwerbret spoke directly to him, he answered briefly—always polite, to be sure—merely thrifty to a fault with his words.

Once, when the lords had drifted a fair bit ahead, Rhodry had a chance at a word with Yraen.

"What do you think of Matyc?"

"Not much."

"Keep your eye on him, will you? There's just somewhat about him that makes me wonder."

"Wonder what?"

"Just how loyal he is to our grace."

Yraen's eyes widened with questions, but since the lords ahead had paused to let their men catch up with them, he couldn't ask them.

There were still some four hours left in the day when the warbands reached the crest of a hill fringed with tall beeches. Rhodry saw the hawk circle round once, then dip lazily down to disappear into a scrubby stand of hazels in the valley below.

"My lord?" he called out. "Jill seems to want us to stop here. There's water for a camp. Shall I ride on down and see if she's there?"

"Do that, silver dagger. We'll wait here for your signal."

Rhodry dismounted, tossed his reins up to Yraen, then strode on downhill on foot. Sure enough, he found Jill, in human form, kneeling by the streamside and drinking out of cupped hands. Though she was barefoot, she was wearing a thin tunic in the Bardek style over a pair of brigga. An empty sack lay beside her on the ground. It seemed to him that she was as light and fragile as the linen cloth.

"Aren't you cold?"

"I'm not." Shaking her hands dry she stood up. "But I'll beg a blanket from you for tonight, truly. The falcon can't carry much, you see."

"No doubt." In spite of all the years that he'd lived around dweomer, Rhodry shuddered, just at how casually she took her transformations. "Ah, well, I take it we're following the right road and all."

"Just so. The raiders aren't all that far. I thought the army could camp along this stream and rest their horses, then mount a raid. They've got guards on watch, of course, but no doubt you could send some of Dar's men to silence them."

"No doubt." Rhodry smiled briefly. "Let me bring the others down, and then we'll have a little chat with the gwerbret."

"Very well. Oh, and tell Cadmar to forbid any fires. I don't want smoke giving our prey the alarm. I'll wait until you've made camp, and then I'll fetch you and his grace."

She gave him a friendly pat on the arm and headed off downstream, disappearing into the trees and brush beyond the power of even his elven eyes to pick her out. Dweomer, he supposed. Swearing under his breath, Rhodry hurried back to the gwerbret and the waiting army.

It turned out that the raiders were camped not five miles away. When Jill reappeared, about an hour before sunset, she led Rhodry and the gwerbret downstream for a ways, to the place where the water tipped itself over the crest of the hill in a gurgle and splash to rush down into a river far below. By peering through the trees, they could see the river twisting, as gray and shiny as a silver riband in the twilight, across a grassy plain. Far to the west, a mist hung pink in the setting sun.

"There!" Rhodry said, pointing. "Smoke from campfires! Right by that big bend in the river off to the west, Your Grace."

"Don't tell me there's elven blood in your veins, silver dagger!" Cadmar was shading his eyes with one hand. "I can't see anything of the sort. Well, I'll take your word for it."

"I've scouted them out, Your Grace," Jill said. "About fifty men, all settled in by the river, as bold as brass, in a proper camp with tents and everything. They've even got a couple of wagons with them. For loot, I suppose."

Cadmar swore under his breath.

"Well, we'll cut them down to size soon enough. What about the prisoners?"

"They seem to be tied and chained off by themselves, between the camp proper and the wagons."

"I say we ride before dawn. Won't be easy, riding at night, but if we fall on them with the sun, we can wipe them out like the vermin they are."

Although Jill took the blanket and the food that Rhodry had brought her, she refused to come back to camp with them. Rhodry escorted the gwerbret back to Lord Gwinardd's side, then went looking for Yraen. He found him with Lord Matyc, near the edge of the camp. Since his lordship was telling Yraen a long involved story about the bloodlines of some horses, Rhodry merely waited off to one side. It seemed obvious that Matyc would have preferred to cut the matter short, but Yraen kept asking such civil questions, so very much to the point, that Matyc was forced to answer. Finally, and by then the twilight had replaced the sunset, Yraen thanked his lordship in a flood of courtesies and let him make his escape. Rhodry waited while Matyc picked his way through the camp, until he was well out of earshot.

"What was all that about?" Rhodry said.

"Maybe naught, but you told me to keep an eye on him. So after I spread our bedrolls out and suchlike, I went looking for his lordship. He was just leaving camp, you see, over behind those trees there, and I would have thought he needed to make water or suchlike, except that he had his dagger out."

"He what?"

"He was holding it in one hand, but up, like he was studying the blade. He'd turn it, too, with a flick of his wrist, like, and every time he did, it flashed with light."

"Ye gods! You could signal a man that way, someone who was off to the west when the sun was setting."

"Exactly what I thought, too." Yraen's smile was grim. "We couldn't prove a thing, of course, and it could well be that I'm dead wrong, and it was just some nervous twitch like men will get, to fiddle with his dagger that way."

"It could be, truly."

"But I thought, well, if it's nerves and naught more, he'll feel better, won't he now, for a bit of talk. So I kept him there, chatting about this and that, till the sun went down in the mists."

"If I were a great lord, I'd have the best slice of roast pig brought to your plate at the honor table tonight."

"But things being what they are, let's go have some flatbread and cheese. I'm hungry enough to eat a wolf, pelt and all."

Later that evening Rhodry finally had a chance to speak with Dar alone. Dar may have been a prince, but he was also one of the Westfolk, and he went out to check on his horses himself rather than leaving the task to one of his men. Rhodry saw him go and followed him out to the herd, tethered down the valley.

"It's good to see you again," Dar spoke in Elvish. "We've all missed you, in the years since you left us."

"And I've missed the People as well. Are things well with your father?"

"Oh, yes, very well indeed. He's still traveling with Calonderiel's alar, but I left it a while back. I can't say why. I just wanted to ride on my own for a while, I suppose, and go from alar to alar, but Cal insisted on giving me this escort."

"Did he say why? It's not like the People, to give someone an honor guard just as—well, just as an honor."

In the dim starlight he could see the prince grinning.

"That's what I thought, too. But Cal said a dweomerwoman had come to him in a dream and told him to do it, so he did."

"Dallandra?"

"That was her name, all right."

Rhodry shuddered like a wet dog. *Great things are moving, indeed!* he thought to himself. Dar looked away, a different kind of smile hovering round his mouth.

"What do you think of my Carramaena?"

"Oh, she's lovely, and a good sensible lass."

Dar's grin deepened. He looked down and began scuffing the grass with the toe of his boot.

"But well, I hate to say this," Rhodry went on. "But haven't you let yourself and her in for grief? I mean, you're young as the People reckon age, and you'll live ten times her years."

"I don't want to hear it!" Dar looked up with a snarl. "Everyone says that, and I don't care! We'll have what joy we can, then, and that's all there is to that!"

"My apologies for—"

"Oh, you're right, I suppose. But ye gods, from the moment I saw her—she was so lovely, standing there in the market, and she needed me so badly, with that wretched brother of hers, and I just, well, I tried to talk myself out of it, but I just kept riding back to see how she fared, to see if she was well, and—" He shrugged profoundly. "And you know what, Rhodry? She's the first grown lass I've ever met who was younger than me. There was just something fascinating about that."

Rhodry swore under his breath, but not for Dar's love affair. The young prince had spoken the truth, that out among the elves, young people were becoming the rarity. How long would it be, he wondered, before the People were gone, and forever?

"Well, you two will have a fine daughter, anyway," Rhodry said at last.

"A daughter? How by the Dark Sun do you know?"

"Call it the second sight, lad, and let it go at that. We'd best get back."

Some hours before dawn the gwerbret's captain moved through the camp, waking the men with whispers. In the fumbling dark they armed themselves and saddled their horses, then rode out while it was still too dark to move at more than a slow walk. Not more than a few hundred yards from camp, Rhodry saw Jill, standing by the side of the road and waiting for them. He pulled out of line and went over to her, with Yraen tagging behind.

"That horse can carry both of us, can't he?" she said. "It's not like I'm wearing mail or suchlike."

"Ye gods, you don't weigh much more than a child these days, or so it seems. Are you coming with us?"

"As a guide. Let me mount, and then let's go ride with the noble-born."

Rhodry got down, settled her in the saddle proper, then swung up behind her. As they were catching up to the army, he reminded Yraen to watch Lord Matyc in the coming battle—if they were all going to be riding together when the charge came, it might be just possible for Yraen to keep him in sight. Jill led them downhill and across the grassy plain by a roundabout way, keeping to what cover there was.

Whether it was dweomer or only shrewd tracking, Rhodry

would never know, but it seemed to him that they reached the bandit camp remarkably soon and ended up in a remarkably good position, too, on a wooded rise behind the enemy's position just out of earshot. From there, Dar sent four of his men ahead on foot to take out the enemy guards. Just as the dawn was lightening the sky, the four returned, grinning at how easy a job they'd had. Jill swung herself down from the saddle and let Rhodry regain his place.

"Your Grace?" she whispered to the gwerbret. "May the gods ride with you. I'll see you after the battle."

Although she turned and jogged off back the way they'd come, Rhodry had no time to watch where she might be going. It would be impossible to keep surprise on their side for more than a few moments. When the gwerbret drew a javelin from the sheath beneath his right leg, every man of the army did the same—with a horrendous jingling of tack.

"Let's go!" Cadmar yelled.

The men kicked their horses to a trot and swept up the side of the rise just as a ragged scream of panic burst out down in thep camp. The warband crested the rise like a wave and charged, screaming war cries. They could see the enemy rushing round, rolling free of blankets, grabbing for weapons. Behind the camp ran the river, cutting off retreat. Off to the left, some hundred yards away from the main camp, roped-together prisoners jumped to their feet and started cheering and sobbing out the gwerbret's name. To the right, at about the same distance, panicked horses began to neigh and rear.

"Throw!" Cadmar yelled.

A shower of steel-tipped javelins flashed ahead of the charge and swooped down among the scurrying bandits. With a rush and whisper elven hunting arrows rained down from the side. Rhodry saw a few hits, but what he was hoping for was panic, and panic was what he got. Screaming, shoving one another, the bandits milled around and grabbed at weapons. Dashing among them, wrapped in a cloak, was an impossibly tall man, waving a sword and howling orders. No one listened. The bandits broke and ran as the warband swept down upon them with drawn swords. Leaning, slashing, the riders raced through the camp, pulled up, and parted like water round a rock to turn at the riverbank and gallop back again. Here and there a few desperate men were making a stand, but most were running. Some, swords drawn and ready, were heading for the prisoners.

"Cut them off!" Rhodry howled it out, then gave his voice over to his bubbling berserk laugh.

With a squad behind him he raced at an angle toward the would-be murderers, and now he was riding to dodge anything in his way. Swords flashed to meet him; he swung down as he passed. Ahead, the little pack of bandits heard hooves and turned to make their stand. The squad hit them in full slaughter. Rhodry's horse suddenly screamed and reared. He brought it down, rolled off as it fell to its knees, and struck up, killing the man who was swinging down at him. Somewhere Yraen was yelling at him, but Rhodry could only laugh. He grabbed another man's shield from the ground and slashed another bandit across the knees. When the man fell, screaming, Rhodry scrambled to his feet and killed him, stabbing him through the throat.

Yraen's words finally forced their way through to his mind.

"We've got this lot! The leader's trying to escape."

Yraen was waving his sword, red and blooded, in the general direction of the wagons, which were standing behind the prisoners. With the squad following him like a captain, Rhodry raced off, dodging round the sobbing women and children, seeing his enemy's cloak flash and flutter just ahead as he dodged through the carts and leaning wagon trees. Although there were a couple of horses tethered beyond, the leader would never reach them in time. Huge as he was, he was clumsy on the ground, so bowlegged that he was waddling more than running.

The leader swirled to face them, and as he turned, he tore off his cloak and whipped it round and round one massive forearm, an improvised shield. The men behind Rhodry howled, half a shriek, half a war cry, and even Rhodry himself hesitated for the trace of a moment, just long enough for their enemy to get his back against a wagon. This was no human being that they were facing. By some visual trick, without the enveloping cloak he seemed even larger, well over six feet tall, perhaps even a bit over seven, his height crowned by a huge mane of hair as stiff as any Dawntime hero's—indeed, it seemed to have been bleached out with lime in just that way, so that it rose stiff and dead-pale straight from his black eyebrows and poured up and over his back like a waterfall. His face might have been any color naturally, because blue, purple, and green tattoos covered it so thickly you couldn't see a trace of skin. His massive hands bore red and purple tattoos like gloves. He drew back thin lips from white teeth, fanged like a wolf's mouth, and snarled.

Rhodry started to laugh.

"Get back!" he choked out between howls of demon-mirth. "Get back and leave him to me!"

He might have been only a silver dagger, but every man behind him followed his order gladly. His opponent laughed as well, a rumble under his breath. He jumped to the wagon bed and dropped to a fighting crouch.

"Shield you got, man. But I got taller."

"And a fair fight it is, then."

Even though he was chortling like a mad ferret, Rhodry's mind was icy calm, telling him that the victory in this scrap depended on the strength of his left arm. He was going to have to hold his shield up high, like one of those sunshades the fine court ladies in Dun Deverry sported, and pray it held against the other's blows. With the shield low he feinted in, slowly it seemed to him, oh, so slowly moving cross the uneven ground, saw a glint of steel moving, swung up the shield and caught the huge blade full on the boss. The brass plate sliced like butter; the blade stuck, just for the briefest of moments, but Rhodry got a hard stab on his enemy's upper arm. Blood spurted thick and flowed slowly, oh, so slowly, down the sleeve.

Rhodry danced back just in time as the leader sliced backhanded in a blow that would have gutted him had it landed. For a moment they panted for breath, glaring at each other; then Rhodry began sidling toward his opponent's left. Caught as he was against the wagon protecting his back, the other was forced to turn slightly—then all at once lunged. Just in time Rhodry flung up his shield, heard the wood crack in half, and stabbed as fast and as hard as he could. Later he would realize that this stab had been his last and only chance, but as the pieces of shield fell away from the handle he knew only laughter, welling out of him like a tide of fire as he thrust with every bit of strength and skill he possessed. The enormous sword swung up over his head, hovered there, trembled down, then fell from a dying hand as his opponent grunted once and crumpled over Rhodry's sword, buried in his guts. When Rhodry pulled it free, he realized that blind instinct had made him angle the blade. Dark heart's blood gushed out with the steel.

As the berserk mist cleared, Rhodry staggered back, gulping for breath, sweating rivers down his back, half-dizzy, half-dazed, unsure for that moment exactly where he was or what fight he'd just won. All round him he heard cheers and shouting, managed to recognize Cadmar's bellow as the gwerbret shoved his way through what proved to be a crowd.

"Oh, may Great Bel preserve us," the gwerbret whispered. "What is that?"

"I wouldn't know, Your Grace."

For a moment, while he got his breath back, Rhodry studied his dead enemy's face and got his second shock of the day. The tattoo designs were all elven. He'd seen many like them on horse gear and painted tents out in the Westlands: animal forms, floral vines, and even, here and there, a letter or two from the Elvish syllabary.

"Let Jill through," Cadmar was yelling. "Ye gods, someone get our Rhodry some water."

Jill, it turned out, was carrying a skin of just that. She handed it over, then stood for a long time staring down at the corpse. In the bright sun Rhodry was struck again by how thin her face was, all pale stretched skin and fine bone, as delicate as a bird's wing. He gulped water down while she went on with her study of the dead man.

"I was afraid of this," she said at last. "He's exactly what I thought he'd be."

"Indeed?" Cadmar said. "And would you mind telling us what that is?"

"Not at all, Your Grace." She reached into her shirt and took out a stained and faded silk pouch, opened that, and handed over a thin bone plaque, a square about three inches on a side.

Rhodry stepped round to peer over the gwerbret's shoulder. The plaque sported a picture, graved into the yellowed bone and stained with traces of color. Once, he supposed, the portrait had been as vivid as a flower garden, but even his utterly untrained eye perceived it as ancient, older than anything he'd ever seen, older, perhaps, than the kingdom itself. In such a skilled drawing that every hair, every fold of cloth, seemed real and tangible, the picture displayed the head and shoulders of a being much like the one that lay dead at their feet: the same mane of hair, the same ridged face and heavy jaw, but while indeed this face was tattooed, the marks were only rough lines and dots. Cadmar swore under his breath.

"Jill, where did you get this? What are these creatures?"

"I got it far south of Bardek, Your Grace, on an island where some of the Westfolk live. As for what, well, the elves call them Meradan, demons, but their own name for themselves is Gel da'Thae: the Horsekin."

All the old stories he'd been trying to remember rose to the surface of Rhodry's mind.

"The Hordes!"

"Just that, silver dagger." Jill smiled, a brief twitch of her mouth. "His grace doubtless remembers those old tales about the cities of the Westfolk, the ones destroyed back in the Dawntime by demons? Well, destroyed they were, but by real flesh and blood." She nudged the corpse with her foot. "This flesh and blood, Your Grace. Huh, they don't seemed to have changed a great deal, have they? They've learned a good bit about tattooing, that's all. They're still as bloodthirsty."

Cadmar nodded, his mouth grim, and handed back the bit of bone.

"And they've come east," Rhodry put in. "That bodes ill."

"You always had a gift for understatement, didn't you?" Jill was putting the plaque away.

"But what do they want?" Cadmar said.

"I wouldn't know for certain, but I'll wager it's the same things they've always wanted: land, slaves, jewelry and other such trinkets." Jill looked up at last. "Look at his hands, Your Grace. See how some of his fingers have been cut off? Their warriors do that to themselves, you see, so they'll be fit for no craft but war."

Cadmar shuddered.

"And how do you know all this?"

"I read it in an elven book, written by one of the survivors of the Great Burning. That's what they call the fall of the cities. It was over a thousand years ago now, but the elves remember it, clear as clear. I wish I could have brought you this book, for your scribe to read aloud in your hall. You and your men need to know what we're facing."

Cadmar threw up his head like a startled stag. Rhodry laughed aloud.

"Oh, my lady Death's in for a fine time of it now. Her dun will fill with her guests, her tables feast thousands. That's what you're saying, isn't it, Jill?"

"I am. Your Grace, I pray to every god in the sky and under the earth that I'm wrong, but in my heart I know that the worst war that ever the Westlands have seen lies ahead of us."

"And soon?" the gwerbret said.

"It will be, Your Grace. Very soon."

Rhodry threw back his head and howled with laughter, choking and bubbling out of his very soul. All through the shattered camp the warband fell dead-silent to listen, and not a man there felt his blood run anything but cold.

With all the prisoners and suchlike, it took the warband two full days to ride home. With Otho and a squad of dwarven axmen standing around her, Carra was waiting at the gates of Cadmar's dun when they walked their horses up the hill. At first, in the dust and confusion, she found it impossible to tell one man from another, and her heart began pounding in dread, but Dar broke free of the pack at last and ran to her.

"Thank every god in the sky!" She flung herself into his arms. While she sniveled into his filthy shirt, he stroked her hair.

"Here, here, my love! I'm home safe again, just like I promised you."

Otho snorted profoundly.

"Egotistical young dolt," he remarked in a conversational tone of voice. "Wasn't you we were worried about."

"What?" Dar let her go and turned to confront the dwarf. "What are you saying, old man?"

"I'm saying what I said, you stupid elven fop. Someone tried to kill your wife while you were running around the countryside playing warrior."

Dar went dead-still.

"Well, but they didn't," Carra said. "I mean, that sounds stupid, but Otho and his men have kept me safe, really they have."

"And for that they'll have my undying thanks."

She had never heard Dar speak like that, so low, so still, each word careful and distinct, and now he was trembling in rage.

"Where's the man who tried to harm her?"

"Don't know, Your Highness." Otho's manner changed abruptly. "He did it by stealth, and we couldn't catch him."

"When we do, I'll kill him with my own hands." He threw one arm around Carra's shoulders and pulled her close. "Name your reward."

Otho thought for a good long minute, then sighed.

"None needed, Your Highness. We were glad to serve your lady. But someday, mayhap, we'll remember this, and call in a favor done."

All around them men were dismounting in a welter of confusion. Pages and stableboys came running to take horses and unload gear, warriors strode by, heading for the great hall and ale. Dar's archers gathered round like a dun wall to shut their little group off from the potentially dangerous commotion.

"Is Jill with you?" Carra said.

"The Wise One?" Dar said. "She's not. She left us before we reached the city. There's Rhodry, though. Look, right behind him, see that horse Yraen's leading? We captured him from the raiders. He belonged to their leader."

Carra looked, then caught her breath in a little gasp. Never had she seen such an enormous animal, fully eighteen hands high and broad, too, with a deep chest and huge arch of neck. A blood bay with white mane and tail, he walked solemnly, gravely, planting each big foot down as if he knew that everyone watched him. Rhodry turned his own horse over to a page, then worked his way free of the mob to join them.

"Otho," Rhodry said. "I've a bone to pick with you."

"You remembered, did you?" Otho looked sour. "Well, I owe you your hire, I suppose, though with all the trouble you got me into, that ambush at the ford and all, I don't see why I should pay you one blasted coin."

"Because if you'd ridden north without me and Yraen, you'd have been dead long before you reached the cursed ford."

"That has a certain logic to it, truly. Well, I've got the coin back at my inn."

"Good. Make sure you fetch it, then."

And Carra was honestly shocked that a man like Rhodry, whom she was starting to consider as fine and noble as any man in the kingdom, would worry about a handful of coin.

That night in the great hall the gwerbret held a feast for their victory, and his lady made sure that it also served to solemnize Carra's wedding in the human way. Before the bard sang his praise-song for the raid and the true drinking began, the gwerbret himself made a fine flowery speech and toasted the young couple with a goblet of mead. The bard performed a solemn declamation, cobbled together from other occasions, perhaps, but elegant all the same. Their arms twined round each other, Carra and Dar took turns drinking mead from a real glass goblet, traded all the way north from Bardek through Aberwyn. Although custom demanded that they smash the thing, it was far too valuable, and besides, as Carra pointed out to her new husband, she certainly wasn't a virgin anymore anyway. With a laugh Dar agreed and handed the goblet back unharmed to the hovering seneschal.

Later, after the bardsong and the assigning of praise, after the mead and the feasting, the gwerbret called for music, and there was dancing, the circle dances of the border, half-elven, half-human, stepped out to harp and drum. For the ritual of the thing, Carra danced one with Dar, then sat down again beside the gwerbret's wife, who caught her hand and squeezed it.

"You have my thanks, my lady," Carra said. "For honoring me this way."

"Well, you're most welcome, and truly, I thought we'd best take our merriment while we can." Labanna's dark eyes turned haunted. "The omens are poor, and the news worse."

Carra nodded, moving instinctively a little closer to her. Out in the center of the great hall, the music pounded on, and the dancers moved gravely, circling round and round. In her grim mood it seemed that they were weaving an immense and ancient spell rather than celebrating an event as common as a wedding. Yet, even over the music, when Carra turned toward the window she heard or thought she heard the harsh cry of a hawk, as if some huge bird drifted overhead on the rising night wind.

Characters' Various Incarnations
in This and Other Books, Some Yet to Come

835	Branoic	Maddyn	Caradoc	Maryn	Aethan	Bellyra	Tibryn	Elyssa	Merodda
1063	Jill	Rhodry	Blaen	. . . . .	Gwin	. . . . .	Sarcyn	Alaena	Mallona
1116	Jill	Rhodry	. . . . .	Yraen	Blaedd	Carra	Verrarc	Marka	Naena

Author's Note

Many readers and reviewers have assumed that the Deverry books take place in some sort of alternate Britain or that the people of Deverry came originally from Britain. In fact, they emigrated from northern Gaul, as a couple of obscure clues in the text tell the compulsively careful reader who also knows an awful lot about Celtic history. Since only a few people fall into that rather strange category, myself being one of them, allow me to explain further. For one thing, the great heroes often mentioned, Vercingetorix and Vindex, are real, historical Gauls. For another, those "vergobretes" who became in Deverry "gwerbrets" are mentioned in Julius Caesar's *Gallic Wars* as magistrates among the Gauls, though, he says, the Britons have no such kind of leader, relying instead upon "kings." The Gaulish king, it seems, was more what we'd term a "warleader," the "cadvridoc" of Deverry, than the ruler of an organized state. Even in Britain, however, the Celts elected their kings more often than they accepted them by inheritance, a pan-Celtic political tradition that lies behind the instability of the Deverry kingship.

The language of Deverry also derives from that of Gaul, but Gaulish was not, as far as scholars can tell, very much different from the Old British that evolved into the language we know today as Cymraeg or Welsh. Thus the Deverrian language looks and sounds much like Welsh, but anyone who knows this modern language will see immediately that it differs in a great many respects. Now, not a lot of Gaulish survives. The Gauls had never been big on writing things down, and when the "cursed Rhwmanes" conquered the place and imposed Latin as the official language, the native speech and oral literature died out. Fortunately a good many personal and place names survive among the remnants—the very thing a fantasy author needs!

As for the Deverrian forms of these names, remember that not only do all languages change over time, but each family of languages changes according to its own rules. In our own family, Indo-European, which includes among others the Germanic, Persian, Hindi, and Slavic groups as well as the Celtic languages, these changes have been studied and codified by linguists. For instance, any "g" sound caught between two vowels tends to first soften, then drop away; "-nt" or "-nd" at the end of a syllable changes to a simple "n," the old Indo-European sound "wh" or digamma either hardens or disappears, and so on and so forth.

What I've done, then, is taken old Gaulish names and subjected them to these rules of change to produce the Deverrian names you find in the books. Consider the ancient word *isarnos,* iron, which has become in Deverrian *yraen.* Although the spelling seems similar to our word, we actually pronounce iron *eye-urn,* in defiance of the order of its consonants, a pronunciation similar to the Welsh *haearn.* Both are different from the Deverrian *ee-rain,* the nickname of one of my characters in this volume. As well, I've cribbed a few of my favorite names from Welsh history, for instance Rhodry (spelled Rhodri in Welsh orthography). That some of the others have ended up sounding like actual Welsh names goes to show just how much alike Old British and Gaulish were. Most Deverrian names, though, such as Gwersyn, the remnant of Vercingetorix itself, were never found in Welsh, or at least not as far as I know.

To consider some history, the people of Bel, that is, those tribes who chose the god Belinos to be their special patron deity from all the wide and rather randomly organized Celtic pantheon of gods, lived in a vaguely defined area of Gaul known as Devetia Riga. While the precise location has been lost, we may surmise that it was somewhere on the Atlantic coast, and more north than south. The Devetii, as they would have been known to the Romans, first came in contact with the classical Mediterranean cultures around 200 B.C. or so when Greek traders came their way, bringing wine, the art of writing, and other such luxuries. Civilization had little effect on them, however, until they were conquered by Julius Caesar just as so many other Gaulish tribes were. Although the great hero Vercingetorix made a gallant last stand at Alesia, in the end Roman organization and Roman stubbornness wore him down the way they wore down the heroes of so many other peoples of the ancient world.

With a great deal of grumbling, the people of Bel accepted to some extent the Roman yoke. They learned some Latin, adopted a few Roman customs, and studied the Hellenistic system of herbal medicine. They also sent a few of their druids to Rome as ambassadors, where, as so many other Gaulish ambassadors did, they met Cicero before his untimely end and purchased, upon the ex-consul's recommendation, learned books to bring back to the tribe. Yet unlike so many other Gauls, the people of Bel always remembered their days of freedom.

When in A.D. 69 Julius Vindex, a Gaul who had risen high in the Roman government, led his rebellion against the corrupt emperor Nero, the men of Devetia were among the first to support him. When his rebellion failed, they would have followed him to the Otherlands by honorable suicide, as well, if it weren't for the counsel of that rather mysterious figure, Cadwallon the Druid. It was Cadwallon who, along with the cadvridoc, Bran, led the Devetians on the Great Migration by means that could only have been magical. (The readers of this volume, in fact, are now in a position to know exactly how this journey was accomplished.) In the end, this migration took them to the shores of the continent that would be home to the new kingdom, Devetia Riga reborn, though over the years its name wore down to Deverry.

Glossary

ABER (Deverrian) A river mouth, an estuary.

ALAR (Elvish) A group of elves, who may or may not be bloodkin, who choose to travel together for some indefinite period of time.

ALARDAN (Elv.) The meeting of several alarli, usually the occasion for a drunken party.

ANGWIDD (Dev.) Unexplored, unknown.

ARCHON (translation of the Bardekian *atzenarlen*) The elected head of a city-state (Bardekian *at*).

ASTRAL The plane of existence directly "above" or "within" the etheric (q.v.). In other systems of magic, often referred to as the Akashic Record or the Treasure House of Images.

AURA The field of electromagnetic energy that permeates and emanates from every living being.

AVER (Dev.) A river.

BARA (Elv.) An enclitic that indicates that the preceding adjective in an Elvish agglutinated word is the name of the element following the enclitic, as can + bara + melim = Rough River. (rough + name marker + river.)

BEL (Dev.) The chief god of the Deverry pantheon.

BEL (Elv.) An enclitic, similar in function to bara, except that it indicates that a preceding verb is the name of the following element in the agglutinated term, as in Darabeldal, Flowing Lake.

BLUE LIGHT Another name for the etheric plane (q.v.).

BODY OF LIGHT An artificial thought-form (q.v.) constructed by a dweomermaster to allow him or her to travel through the inner planes of existence.

BRIGGA (Dev.) Loose wool trousers worn by men and boys.

BROCH (Dev.) A squat tower in which people live. Originally, in the Homeland, these towers had one big fireplace in the center of the ground floor and a number of booths or tiny roomlets up the sides, but by the time of our narrative, this ancient style has given way to regular floor with hearths and chimneys on either side of the structure.

CADVRIDOC (Dev.) A warleader. Not a general in the modern sense, the cadvridoc is supposed to take the advice and counsel of the noble-born lords under him, but his is the right of final decision.

CAPTAIN (trans. of the Dev. *pendaely*) The second in command, after the lord himself, of a noble's warband. An interesting point is that the word *taely* (the root or unmutated form of *-daely*) can mean either a warband or a family depending on context.

CONABER (Elv.) A musical instrument similar to the panpipe but of even more limited range.

CWM (Dev.) A valley.

DAL (Elv.) A lake.

DUN (Dev.) A fort.

DWEOMER (trans. of the Dev. *dwunddaevad*) In its strict sense, a system of magic aimed at personal enlightenment through harmony with the natural universe in all its planes and manifestations; in the popular sense, magic, sorcery.

ELCYION LACAR (Dev.) The elves; literally, the "bright spirits," or "Bright Fey."

ENGLYN (Welsh, pl. englynion.) A metrical form, consisting of a three-line stanza, each stanza having seven syllables, though an extra syllable can be added to any given line. All lines have end rhyme as well. In Deverry at the time of which we write, this form was so much the rule that its name would translate merely as "short poem," hence my use of the corresponding Welsh term to give it some definition.

ENSORCEL To produce an effect similar to hypnosis by direct manipulation of a person's aura. (Ordinary hypnosis manipulates the victim's consciousness only and thus is more easily resisted.)

ETHERIC The plane of existence directly "above" the physical. With its magnetic substance and currents, it holds physical matter in an invisible matrix and is the true source of what we call "life."

ETHERIC DOUBLE The true being of a person, the electromagnetic structure that holds the body together and that is the actual seat of consciousness.

FOLA (Elv.) An enclitic that shows the noun preceding it in an agglutinated Elvish word is the name of the element following the enclitic, as in Corafolamelim, Owl River.

GEIS A taboo, usually a prohibition against doing something. Breaking geis results in ritual pollution and the disfavor if not active enmity of the gods. In societies that truly believe in geis, a person who breaks it usually dies fairly quickly, either of morbid depression or some unconsciously self-inflicted "accident," unless he or she makes ritual amends.

GERTHDDYN (Dev.) Literally, a "music man," a wandering minstrel and entertainer of much lower status than a true bard.

GORCHAN (Welsh, trans. of the Dev. *gwerganu.*) Literally, a "supreme" or last song, an elegy or death-poem.

GREAT ONES Spirits, once human but now disincarnate, who exist on an unknowably high plane of existence and who have dedicated themselves to the eventual enlightenment of all sentient beings. They are also known to the Buddhists, as Bodhisattvas.

GWERBRET (Dev. The name derives from the Gaulish *vergobretes.*) The highest rank of nobility below the royal family itself. Gwerbrets (Dev. *gwerbretion*) function as the chief magistrates of their regions, and even kings hesitate to override their decisions because of their many ancient prerogatives.

HIRAEDD (Dev.) A peculiarly Celtic form of depression, marked by a deep, tormented longing for some unobtainable thing; also and in particular, homesickness to the third power.

JAVELIN (trans. of the Dev. *picecl*) Since the weapon in question is only about three feet long, another possible translation would be "war dart." The reader should not think of it as a proper spear or as one of those enormous javelins used in the modern Olympic Games.

LWDD (Dev.) A blood-price; differs from wergild in that the amount of lwdd is negotiable in some circumstances, rather than being irrevocably set by law.

MALOVER (Dev.) A full, formal court of law with both a priest of Bel and either a gwerbret or a tieryn in attendance.

MELIM (Elv.) A river.

MOR (Dev.) A sea, ocean.

PAN (Elv.) An enclitic, similar to fola, defined earlier, except that it indicates that the preceding noun is plural as well as the name of the following word, as in Corapanmelim, River of the Many Owls. Remember that Elvish always indicates pluralization by adding a semi-independent morpheme, and that this semi-independence is reflected in the various syntax-bearing enclitics.

PECL (Dev.) Far, distant.

RHAN (Dev.) A political unit of land; thus, gwerbretrhyn, tierynrhyn, the area under the control of a given gwerbret or tieryn. The size of the various rhans (Dev. *rhannau*) varies widely, depending on the vagaries of inheritance and the fortunes of war rather than some legal definition.

SCRYING The art of seeing distant people and places by magic.

SIGIL An abstract magical figure, usually representing either a particular spirit or a particular kind of energy or power. These figures, which look a lot like geometrical scribbles, are derived by various rules from secret magical diagrams.

TAER (Dev.) Land, country.

THOUGHT-FORM An image or three-dimensional form that has been fashioned out of either etheric or astral substance, usually by the action of a trained mind. If enough trained minds work together to build the same thought-form, it will exist independently for a period of time based on the amount of energy put into it. (Putting energy into such a form is known as *ensouling* the thought-form.) Manifestations of gods or saints are usually thought-forms picked up by the highly intuitive, such as children, or those with a touch of second sight. It is also possible for many untrained minds acting together to make fuzzy, ill-defined thought-forms that can be picked up the same way, such as UFOs and sightings of the Devil.

TIERYN (Dev.) An intermediate rank of the noble-born, below a gwerbret but above an ordinary lord (Dev. *arcloedd*).

WYRD (trans. of the Dev. *tingedd*) Fate, destiny; the inescapable problems carried over from a sentient being's last incarnation.

YNIS (Dev.) An island.